VOLUME
TWO

Sa

IMAGE COMICS, INC.

Robert Kirkman
CHIEF OPERATING OFFICER

Erik Larsen
CHIEF FINANCIAL OFFICER

Todd McFarlane
PRESIDENT

Marc Silvestri
CHIEF EXECUTIVE OFFICER

Jim Valentino
VICE-PRESIDENT

Eric Stephenson
PUBLISHER

Ron Richards
DIRECTOR OF BUSINESS DEVELOPMENT

Jennifer de Guzman
PR & MARKETING DIRECTOR

Branwyn Bigglestone
ACCOUNTS MANAGER

Emily Miller
ADMINISTRATIVE ASSISTANT

Jamie Parreno
MARKETING ASSISTANT

Kevin Yuen
DIGITAL RIGHTS COORDINATOR

Jonathan Chan
PRODUCTION MANAGER

Drew Gill
ART DIRECTOR

Tyler Shainline
PRINT MANAGER

Monica Garcia
PRODUCTION ARTIST

Vincent Kukua
PRODUCTION ARTIST

Jana Cook
PRODUCTION ARTIST

www.imagecomics.com

ISBN 978-1-60706-692-7

ga™

BRIAN K. VAUGHAN
WRITER

FIONA STAPLES
ARTIST

FONOGRAFIKS
LETTERING+DESIGN

ERIC STEPHENSON
COORDINATOR

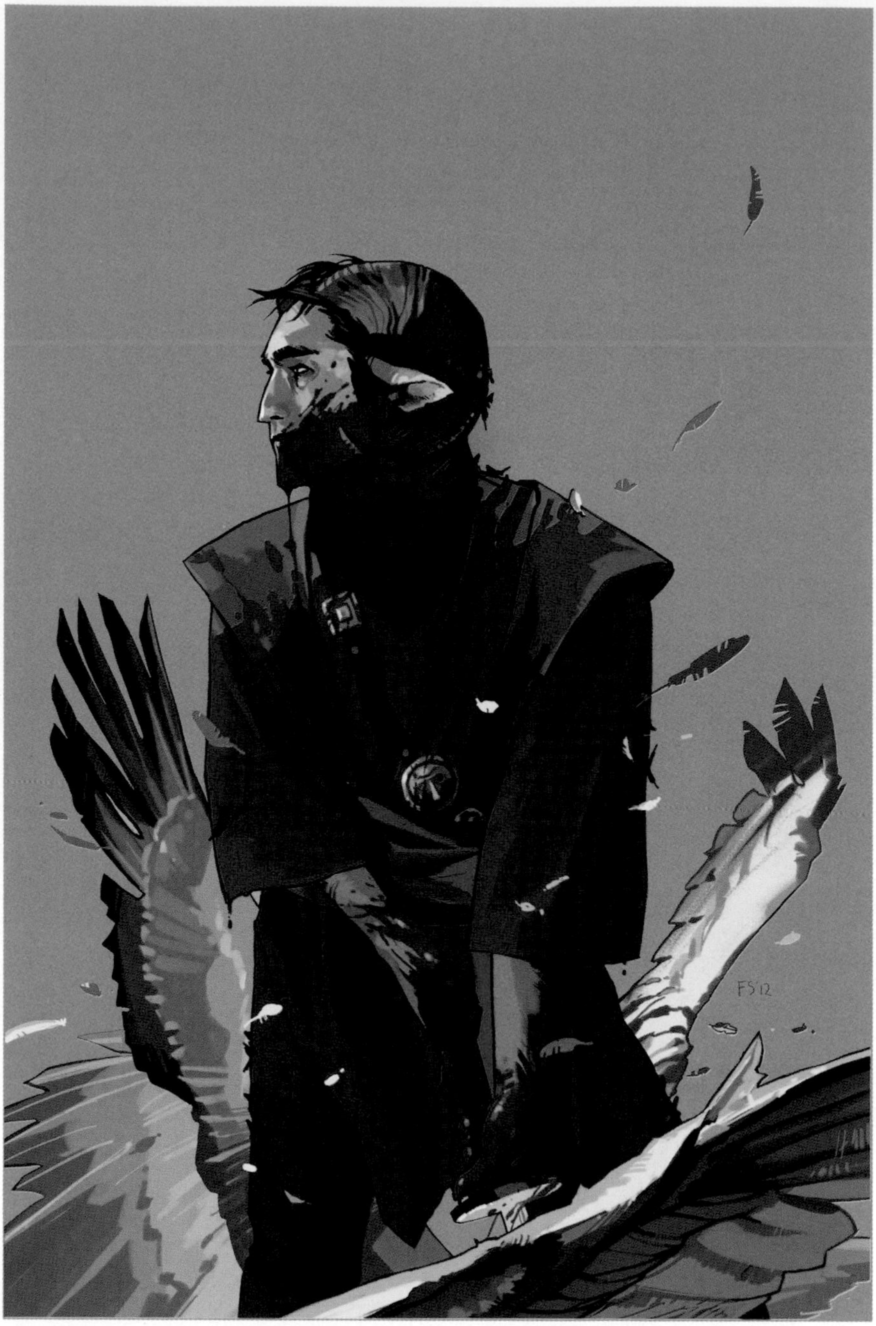
FS'12

CHAPTER SEVEN

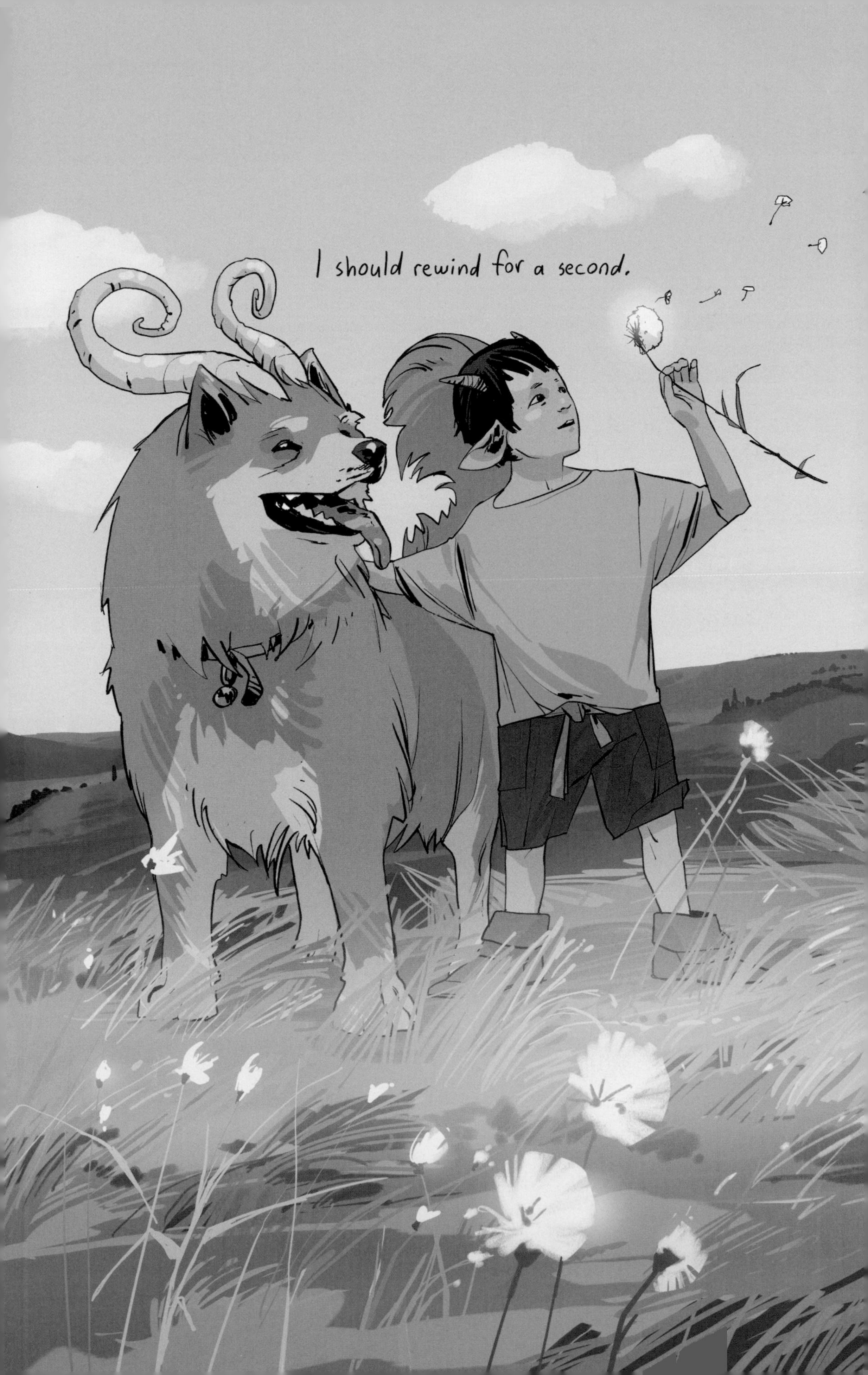
I should rewind for a second.

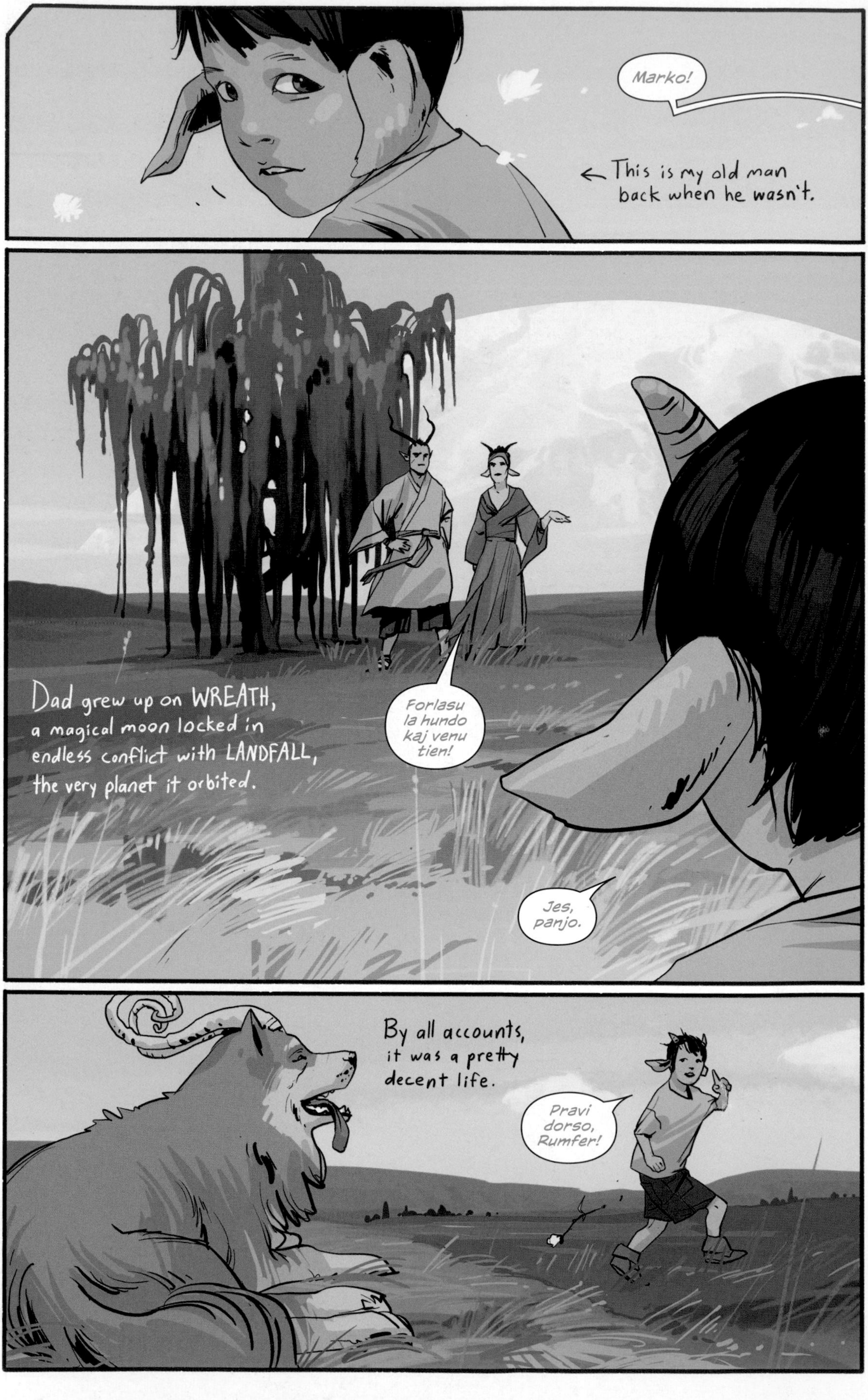
Marko!
← This is my old man back when he wasn't.
Dad grew up on WREATH, a magical moon locked in endless conflict with LANDFALL, the very planet it orbited.
Forlasu la hundo kaj venu tien!
Jes, panjo.
By all accounts, it was a pretty decent life.
Pravi dorso, Rumfer!

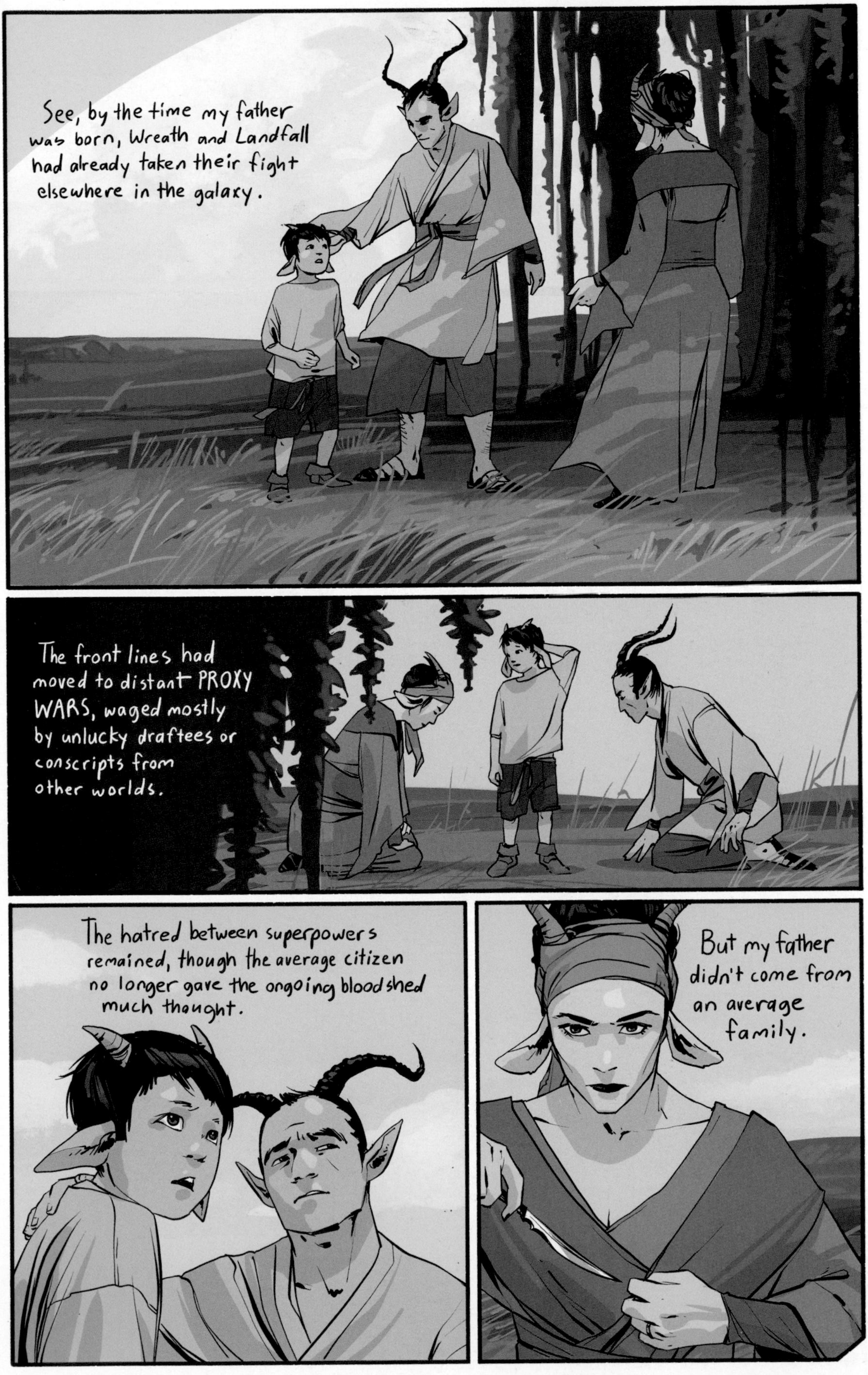
See, by the time my father was born, Wreath and Landfall had already taken their fight elsewhere in the galaxy.
The front lines had moved to distant PROXY WARS, waged mostly by unlucky draftees or conscripts from other worlds.
The hatred between superpowers remained, though the average citizen no longer gave the ongoing bloodshed much thought.
But my father didn't come from an average family.

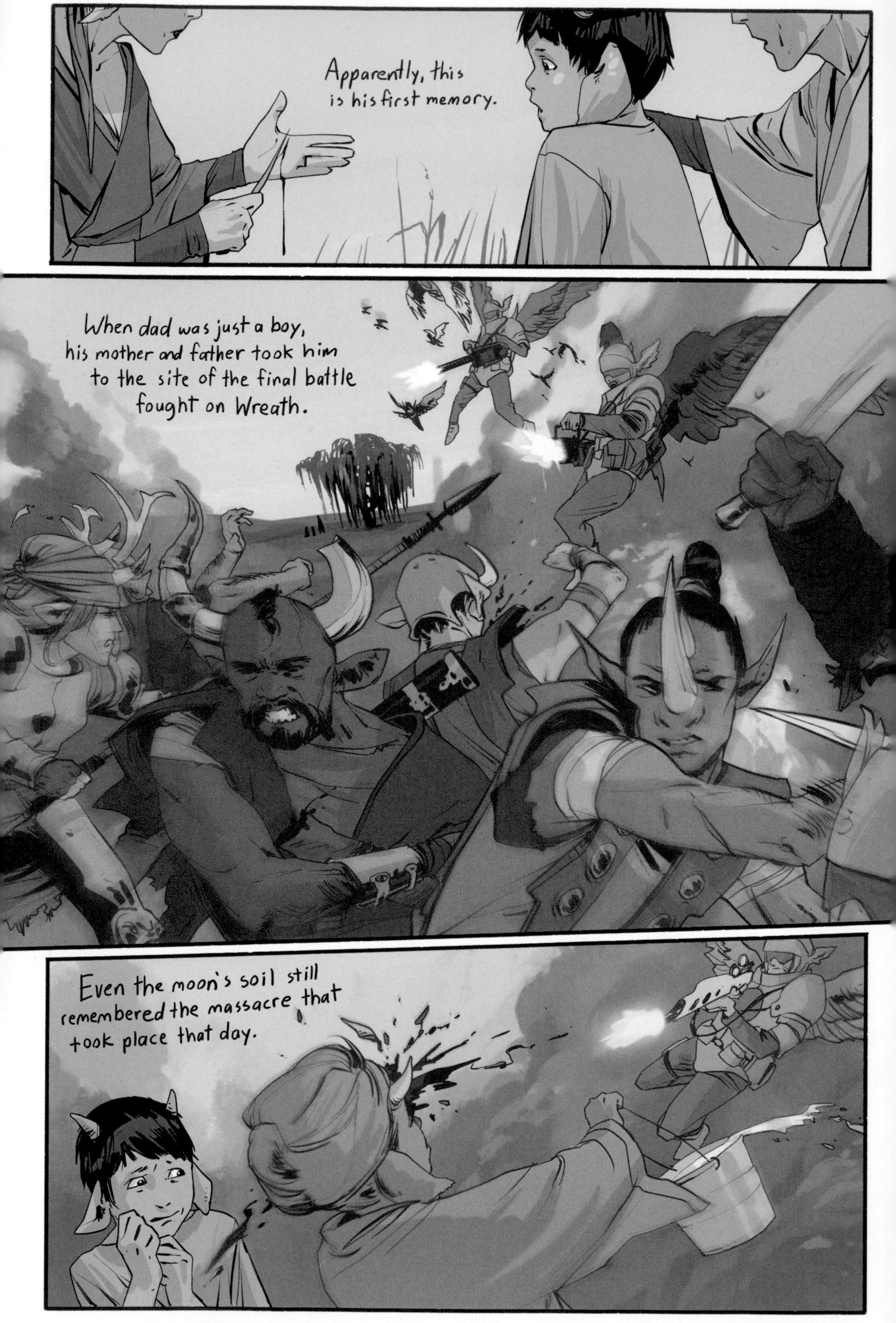
Apparently, this is his first memory.
When dad was just a boy, his mother and father took him to the site of the final battle fought on Wreath.
Even the moon's soil still remembered the massacre that took place that day.

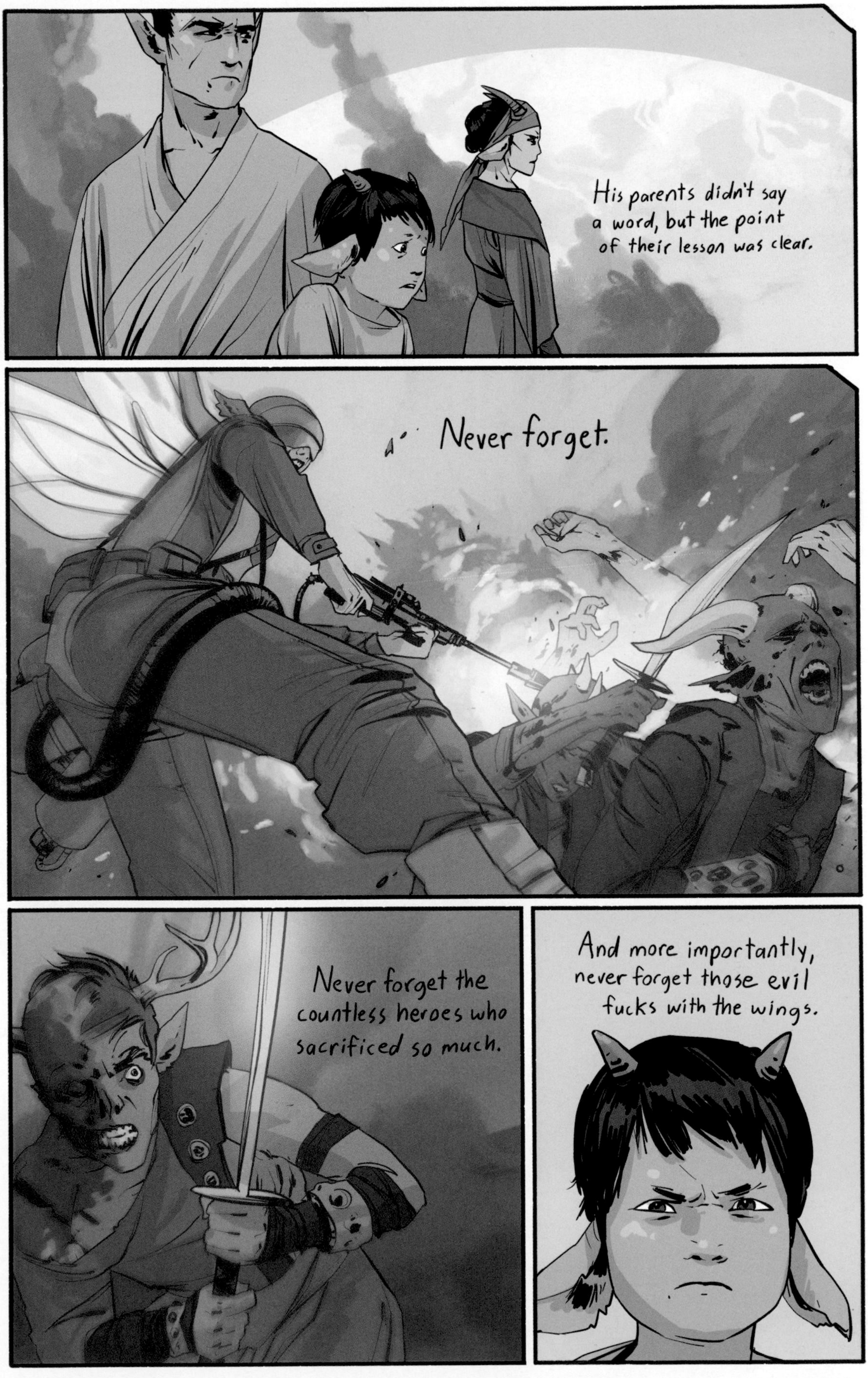
His parents didn't say a word, but the point of their lesson was clear.
Never forget.
Never forget the countless heroes who sacrificed so much.
And more importantly, never forget those evil fucks with the wings.

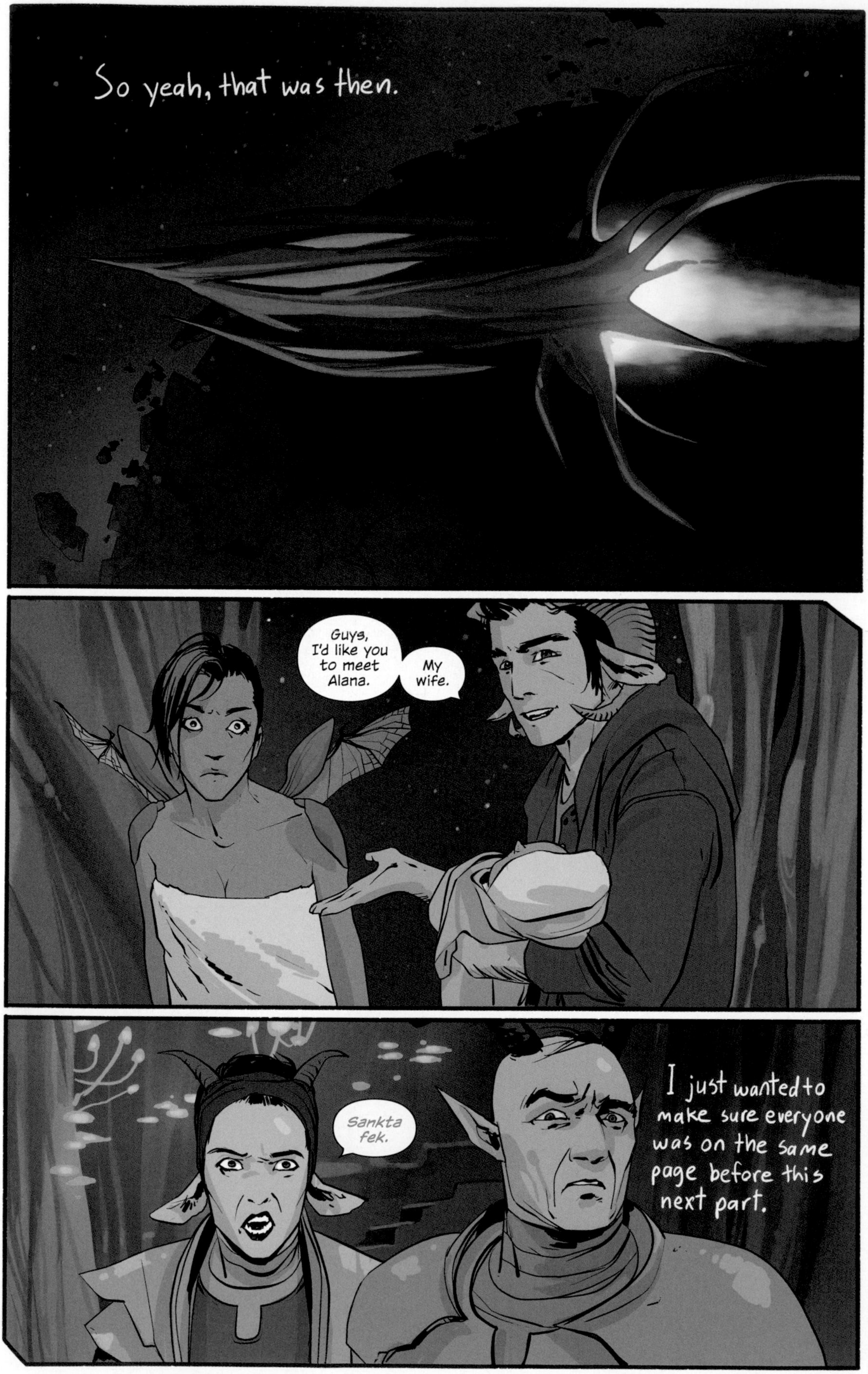
So yeah, that was then.
Guys, I'd like you to meet Alana.
My wife.
Sankta fek.
I just wanted to make sure everyone was on the same page before this next part.

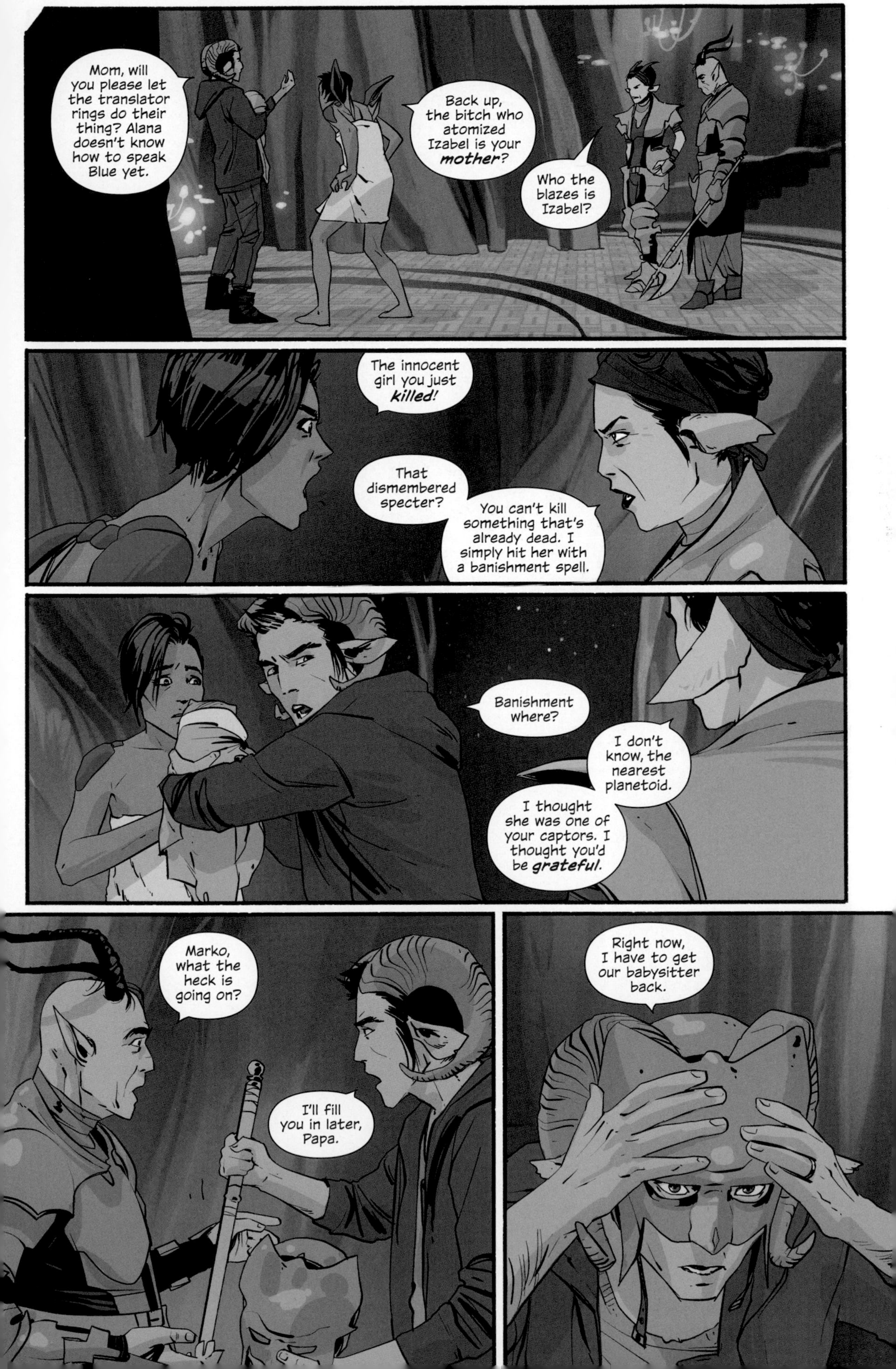
Mom, will you please let the translator rings do their thing? Alana doesn't know how to speak Blue yet.
Back up, the bitch who atomized Izabel is your *mother*?
Who the blazes is Izabel?
The innocent girl you just *killed!*
That dismembered specter?
You can't kill something that's already dead. I simply hit her with a banishment spell.
Banishment where?
I don't know, the nearest planetoid.
I thought she was one of your captors. I thought you'd be *grateful*.
Marko, what the heck is going on?
I'll fill you in later, Papa.
Right now, I have to get our babysitter back.

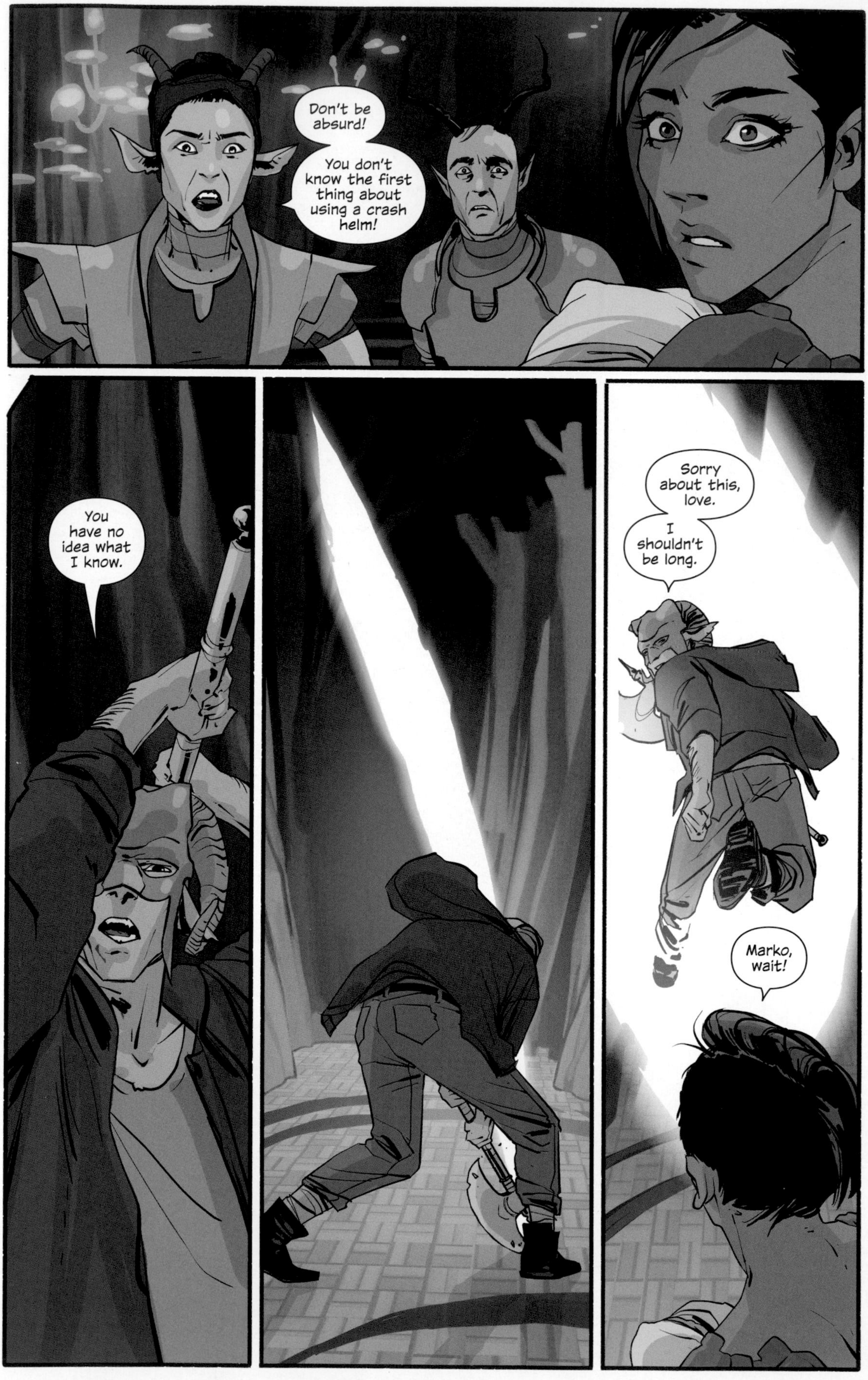
Don't be absurd!
You don't know the first thing about using a crash helm!
You have no idea what I know.
Sorry about this, love.
I shouldn't be long.
Marko, wait!

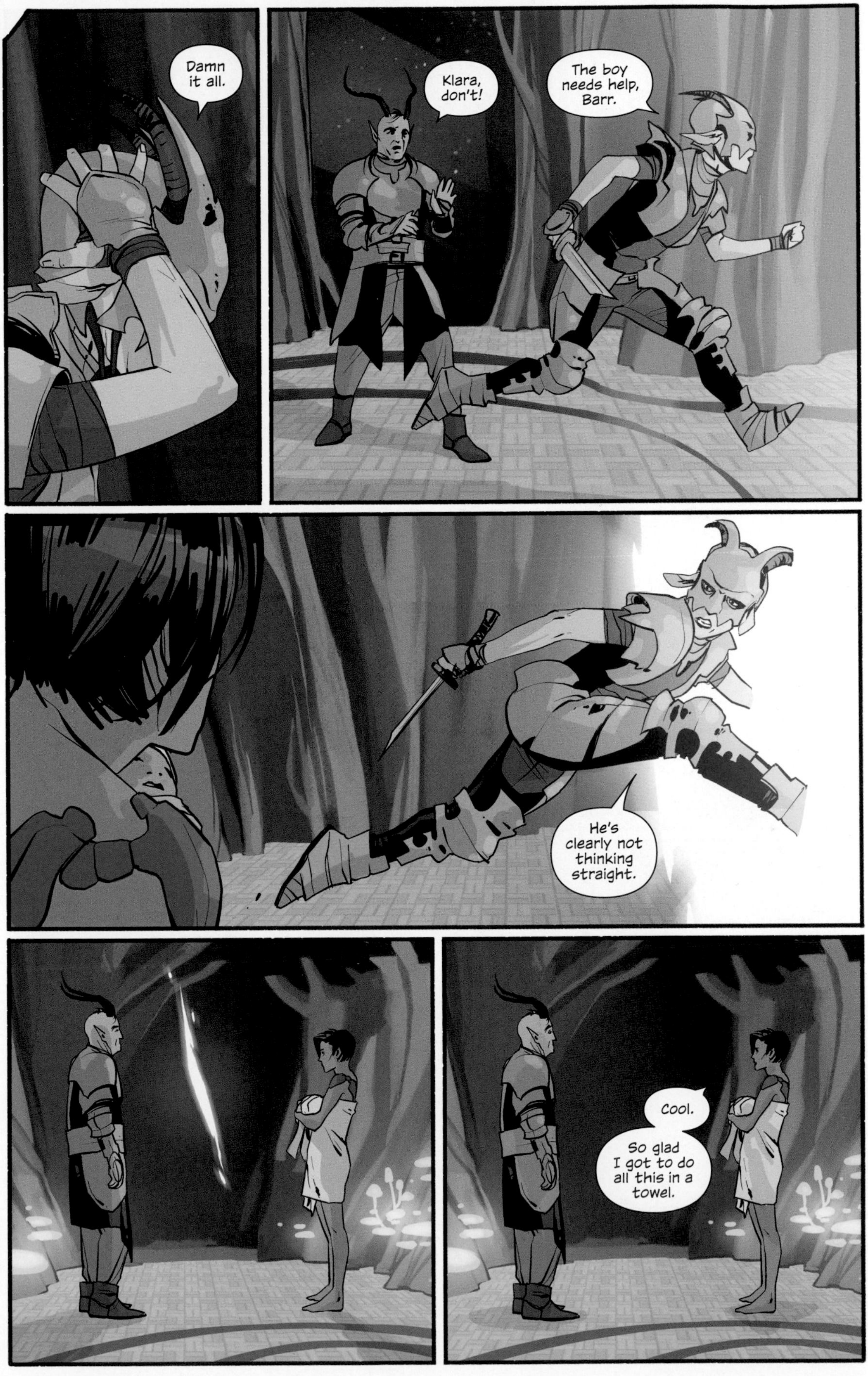

Damn it all.
Klara, don't!
The boy needs help, Barr.
He's clearly not thinking straight.
Cool.
So glad I got to do all this in a towel.

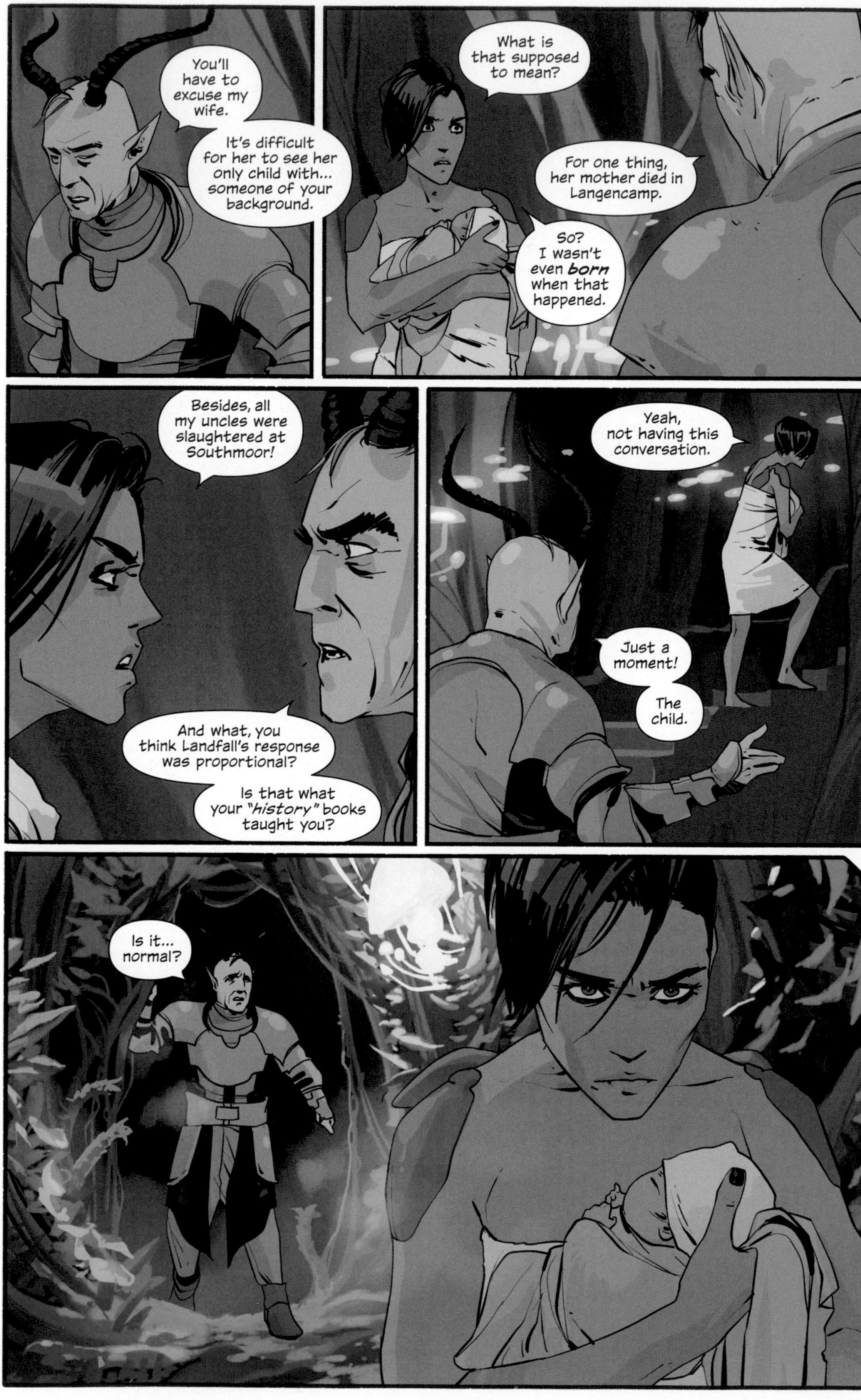
You'll have to excuse my wife.
It's difficult for her to see her only child with... someone of your background.
What is that supposed to mean?
For one thing, her mother died in Langencamp.
So? I wasn't even born when that happened.
Besides, all my uncles were slaughtered at Southmoor!
And what, you think Landfall's response was proportional?
Is that what your "history" books taught you?
Yeah, not having this conversation.
Just a moment!
The child.
Is it... normal?

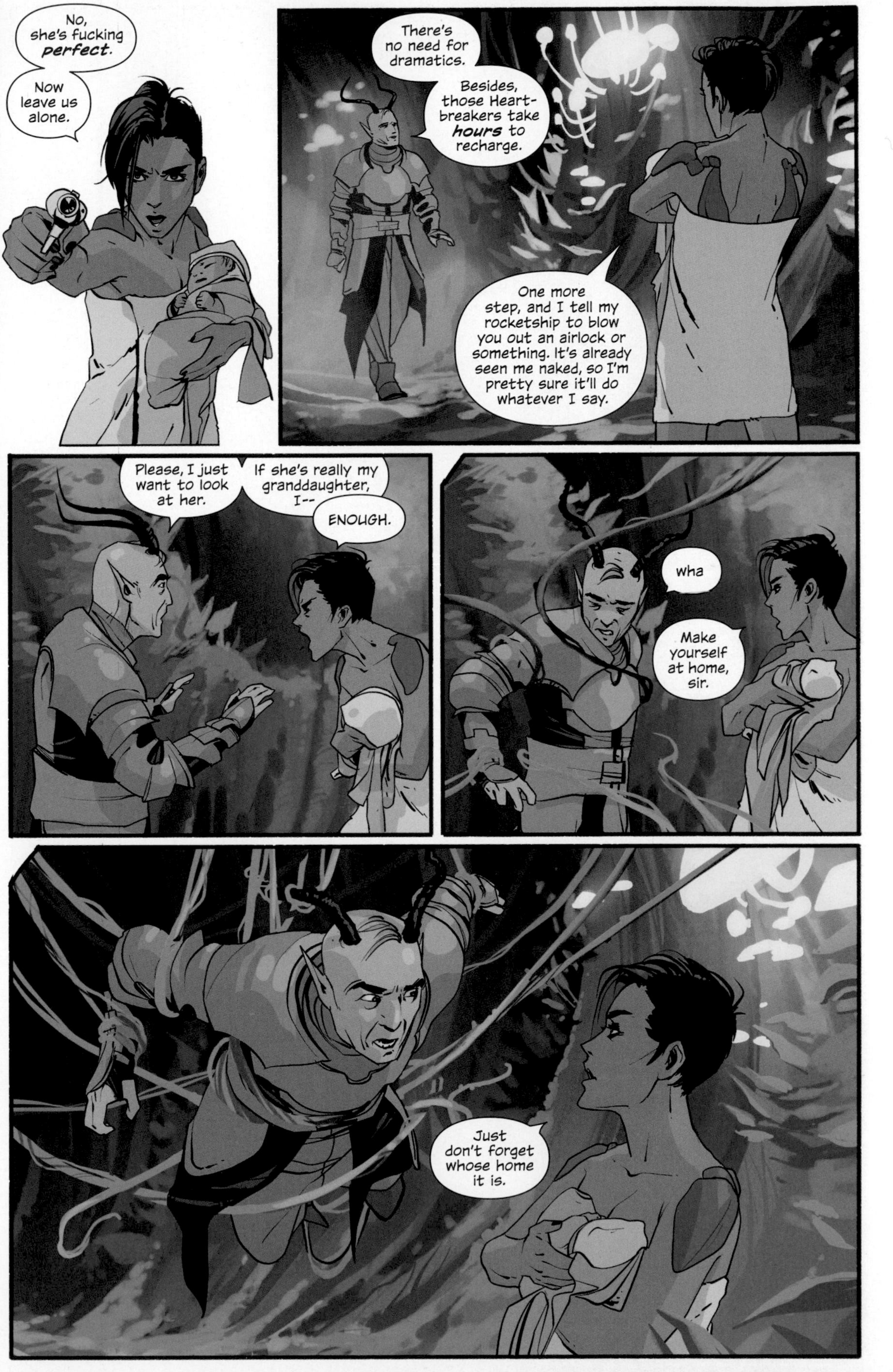
No, she's fucking ***perfect***.
Now leave us alone.
There's no need for dramatics.
Besides, those Heart-breakers take ***hours*** to recharge.
One more step, and I tell my rocketship to blow you out an airlock or something. It's already seen me naked, so I'm pretty sure it'll do whatever I say.
Please, I just want to look at her.
If she's really my granddaughter, I--
ENOUGH.
wha
Make yourself at home, sir.
Just don't forget whose home it is.

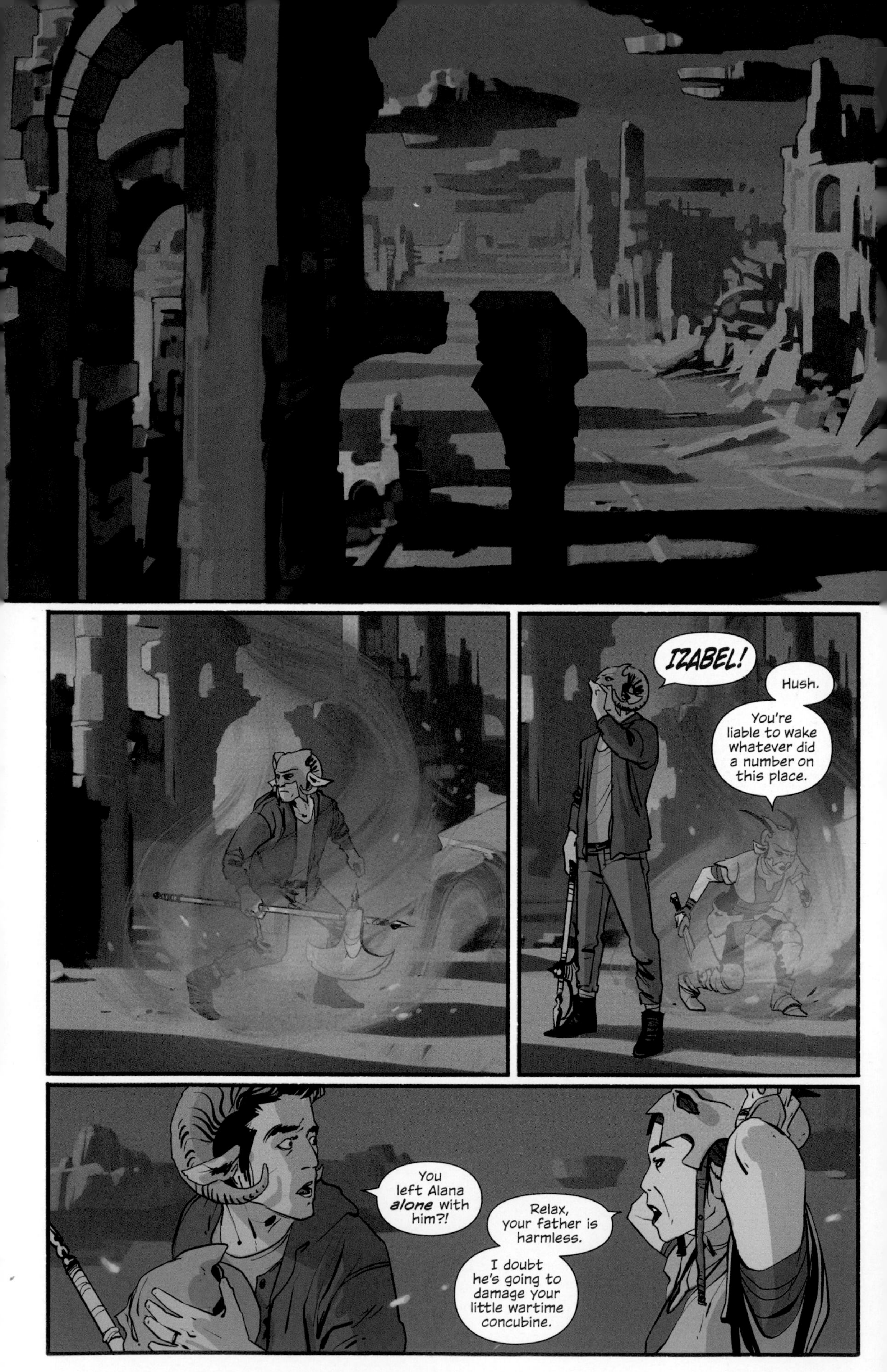
IZABEL!
Hush.
You're liable to wake whatever did a number on this place.
You left Alana alone with him?!
Relax, your father is harmless.
I doubt he's going to damage your little wartime concubine.

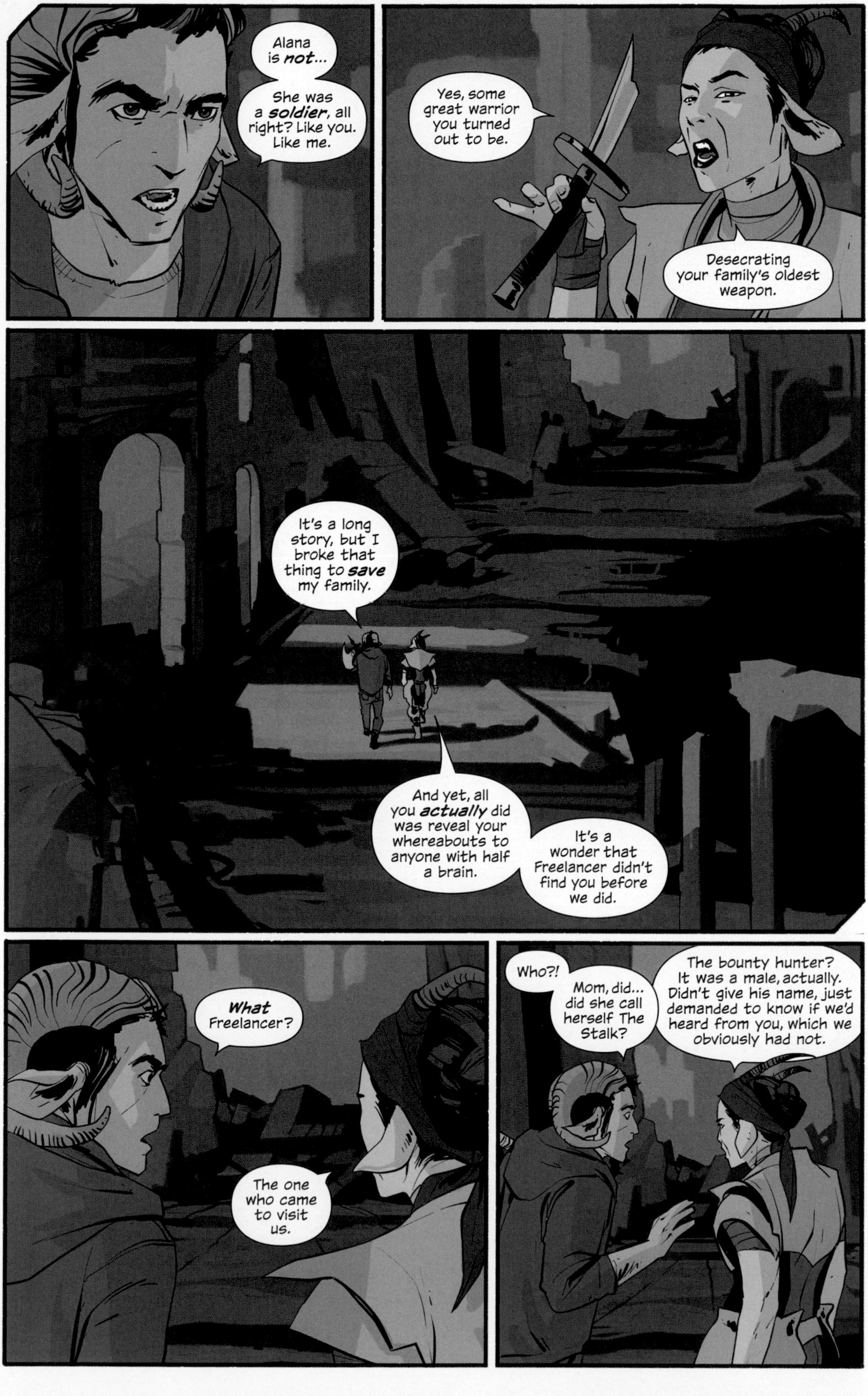
Alana is **not**...
She was a **soldier**, all right? Like you. Like me.
Yes, some great warrior you turned out to be.
Desecrating your family's oldest weapon.
It's a long story, but I broke that thing to **save** my family.
And yet, all you **actually** did was reveal your whereabouts to anyone with half a brain.
It's a wonder that Freelancer didn't find you before we did.
What Freelancer?
The one who came to visit us.
Who?!
Mom, did... did she call herself The Stalk?
The bounty hunter? It was a male, actually. Didn't give his name, just demanded to know if we'd heard from you, which we obviously had not.

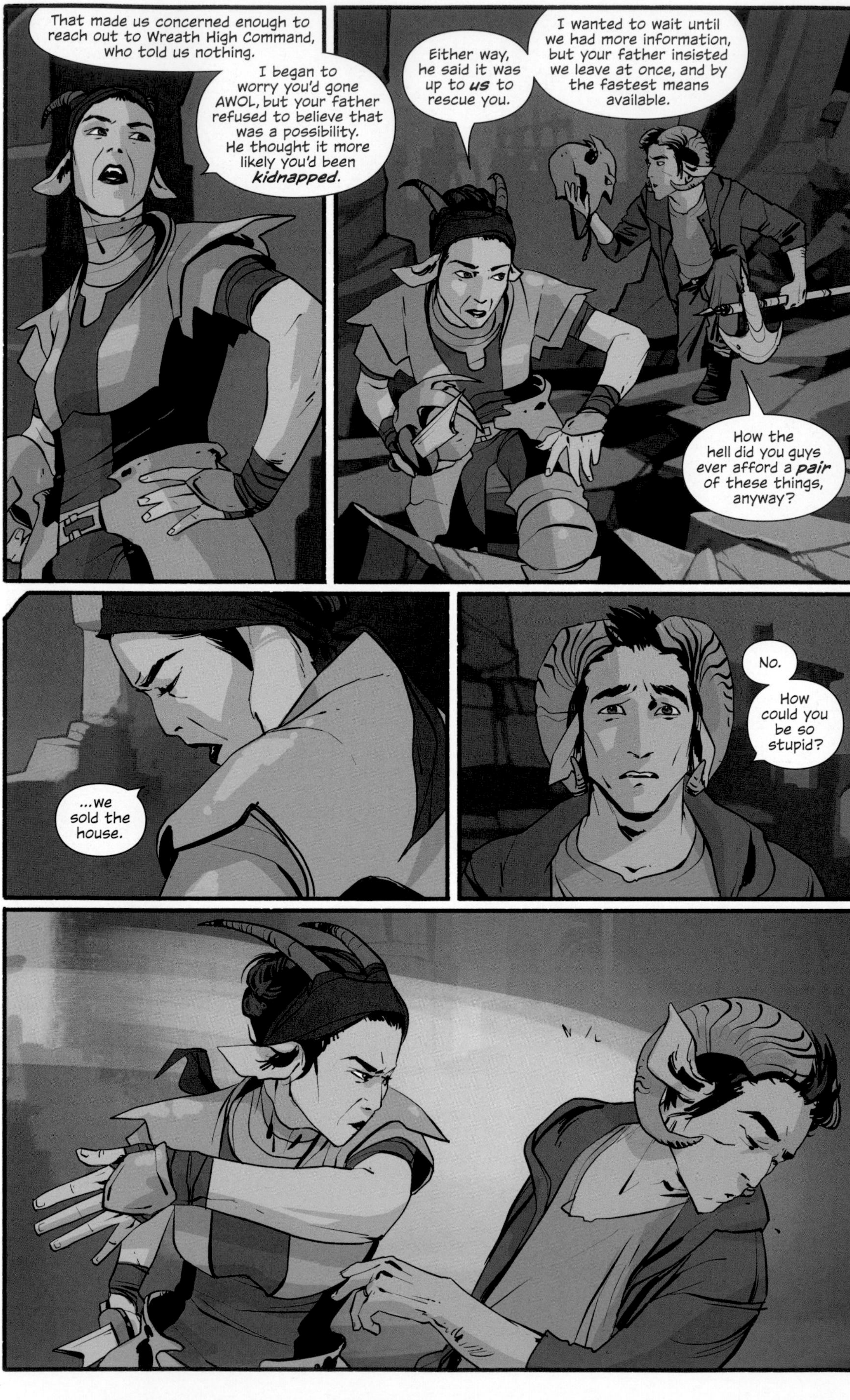
That made us concerned enough to reach out to Wreath High Command, who told us nothing.
I began to worry you'd gone AWOL, but your father refused to believe that was a possibility. He thought it more likely you'd been **kidnapped**.
Either way, he said it was up to **us** to rescue you.
I wanted to wait until we had more information, but your father insisted we leave at once, and by the fastest means available.
How the hell did you guys ever afford a **pair** of these things, anyway?
...we sold the house.
No.
How could you be so stupid?

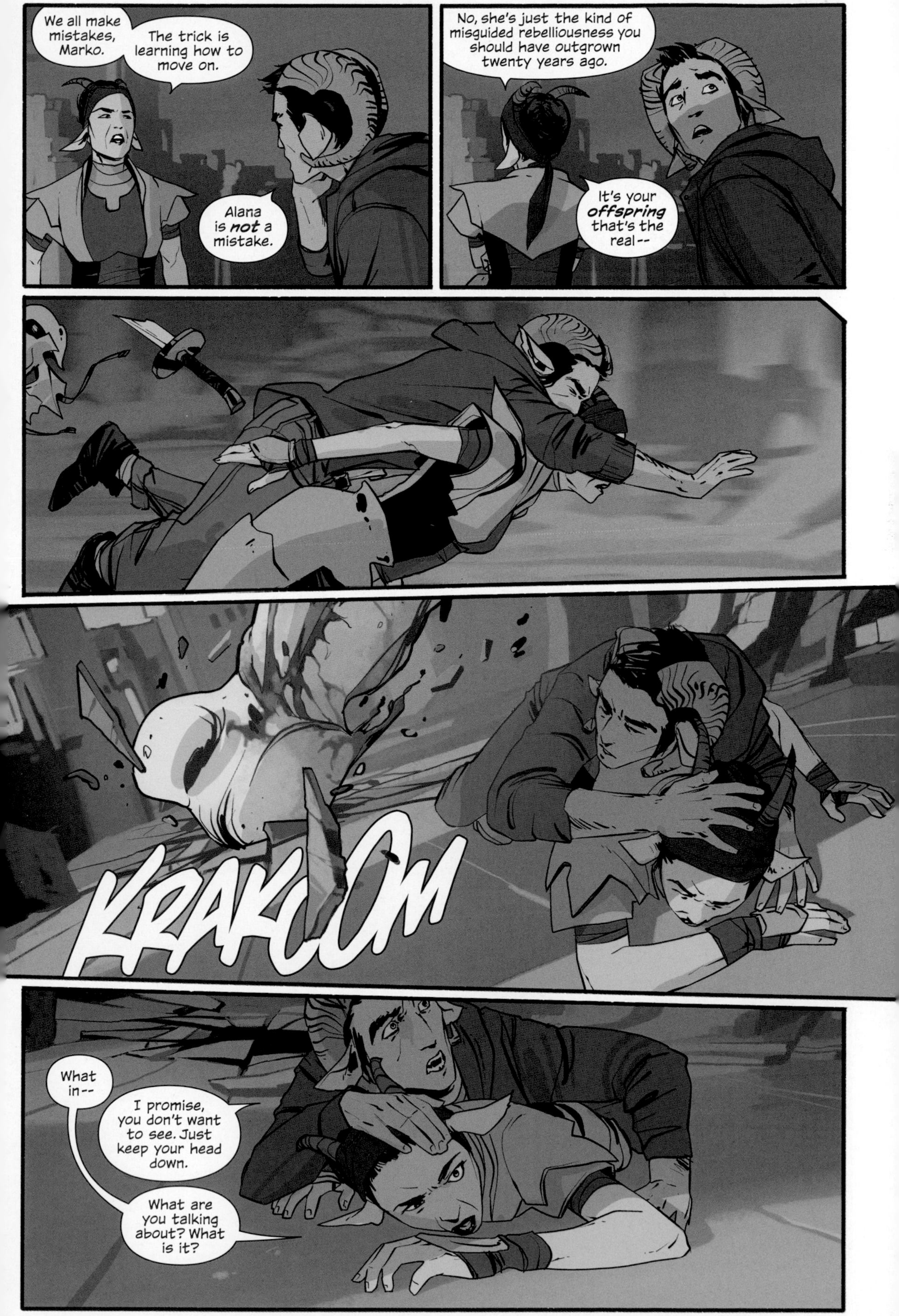
We all make mistakes, Marko.
The trick is learning how to move on.
Alana is *not* a mistake.
No, she's just the kind of misguided rebelliousness you should have outgrown twenty years ago.
It's your *offspring* that's the real--
KRAKOOM
What in--
I promise, you don't want to see. Just keep your head down.
What are you talking about? What is it?

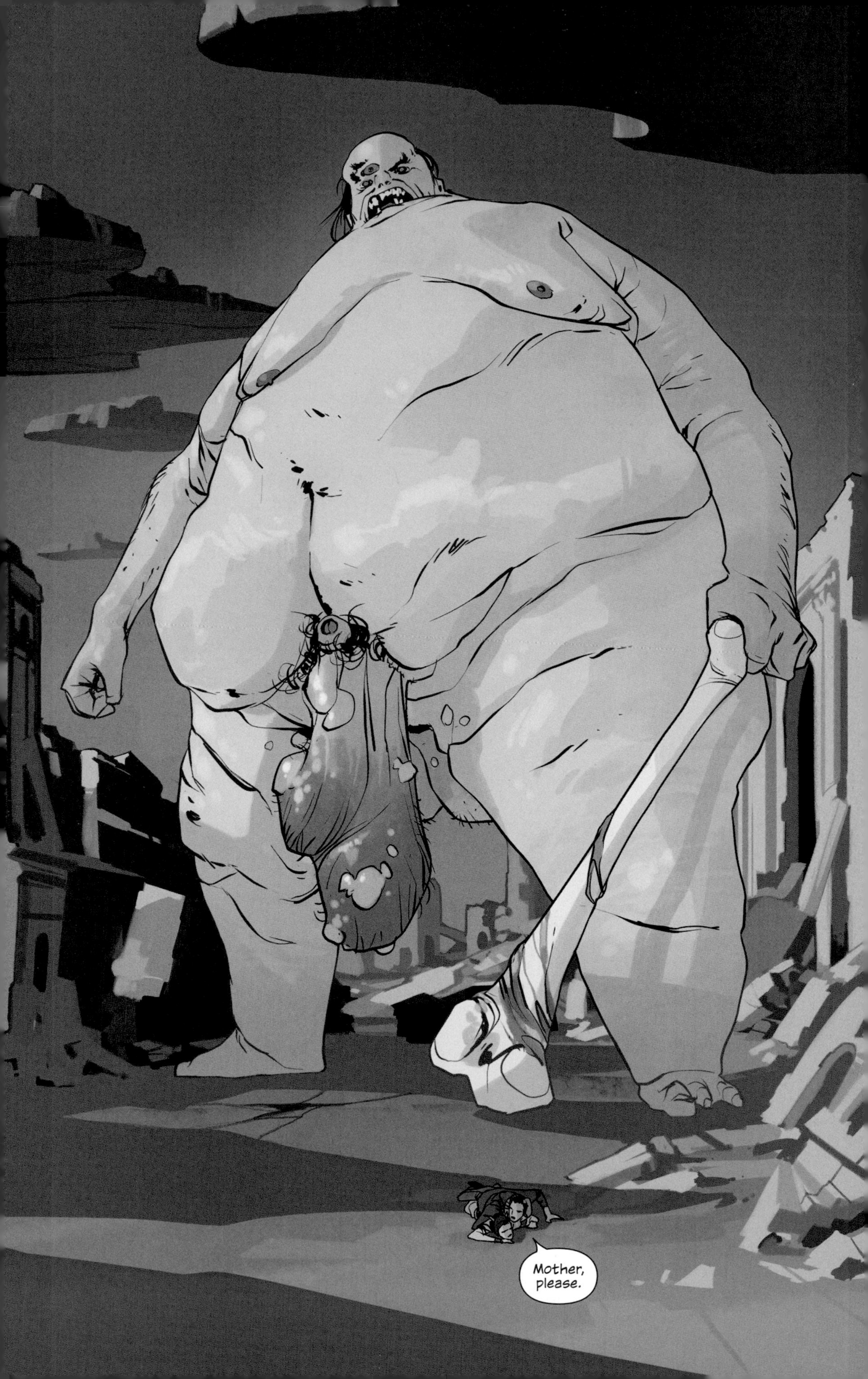
Mother, please.

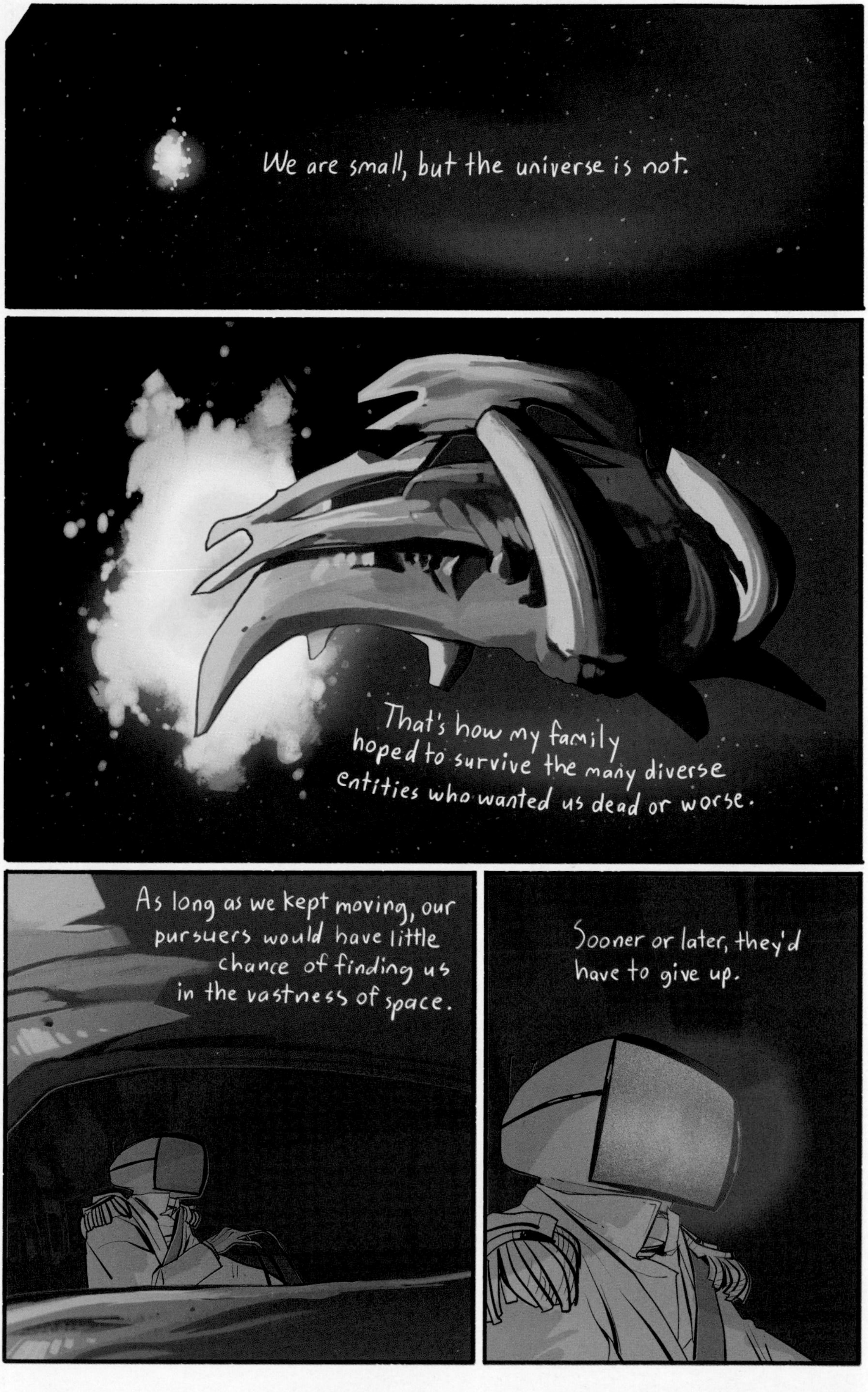

We are small, but the universe is not.

That's how my family hoped to survive the many diverse entities who wanted us dead or worse.

As long as we kept moving, our pursuers would have little chance of finding us in the vastness of space.

Sooner or later, they'd have to give up.

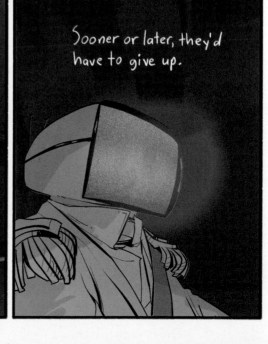

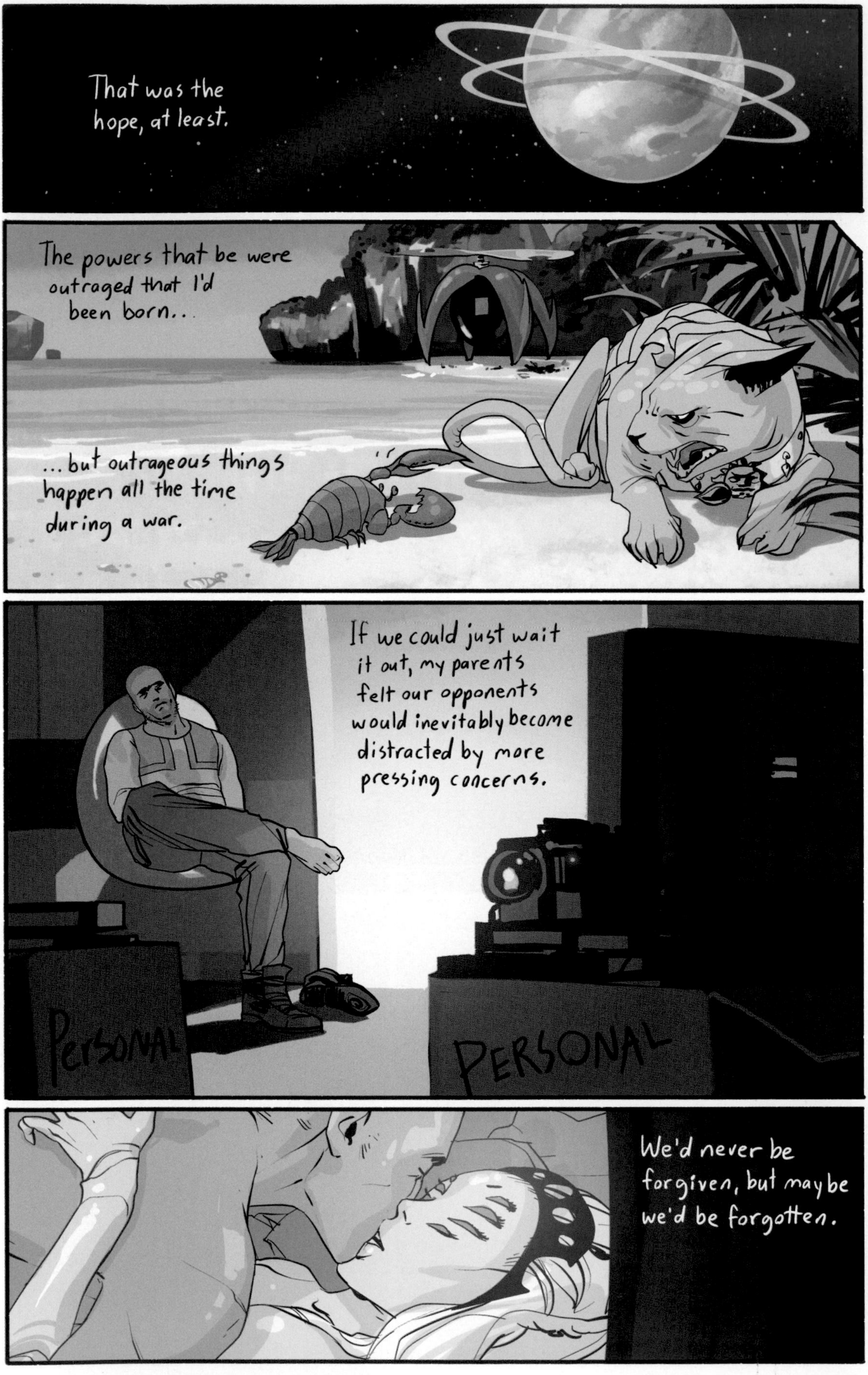
That was the hope, at least.
The powers that be were outraged that I'd been born...
...but outrageous things happen all the time during a war.
If we could just wait it out, my parents felt our opponents would inevitably become distracted by more pressing concerns.
PERSONAL
PERSONAL
We'd never be forgiven, but maybe we'd be forgotten.

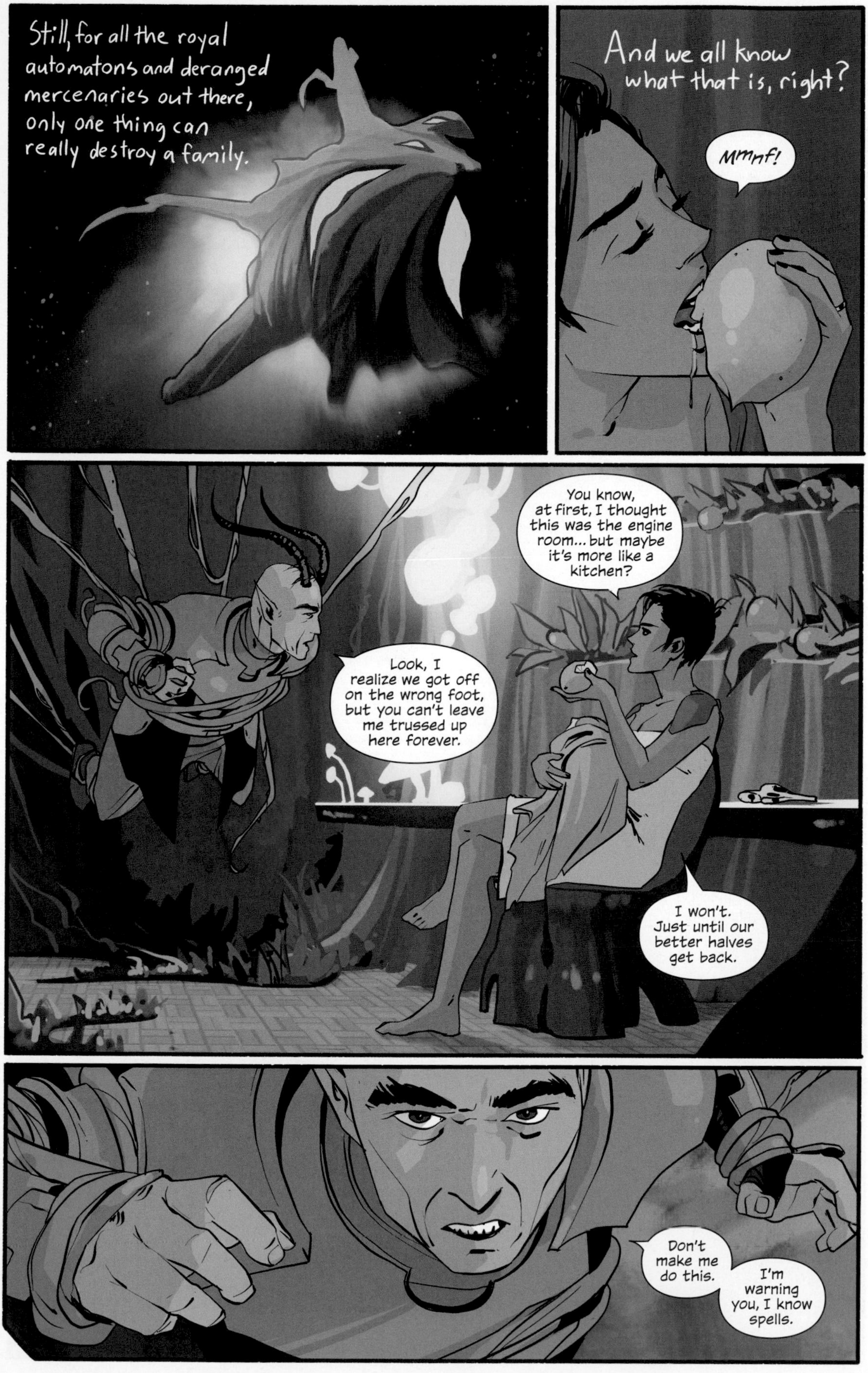
Still, for all the royal automatons and deranged mercenaries out there, only one thing can really destroy a family.
And we all know what that is, right?
Mmmf!
You know, at first, I thought this was the engine room... but maybe it's more like a kitchen?
Look, I realize we got off on the wrong foot, but you can't leave me trussed up here forever.
I won't. Just until our better halves get back.
Don't make me do this.
I'm warning you, I know spells.

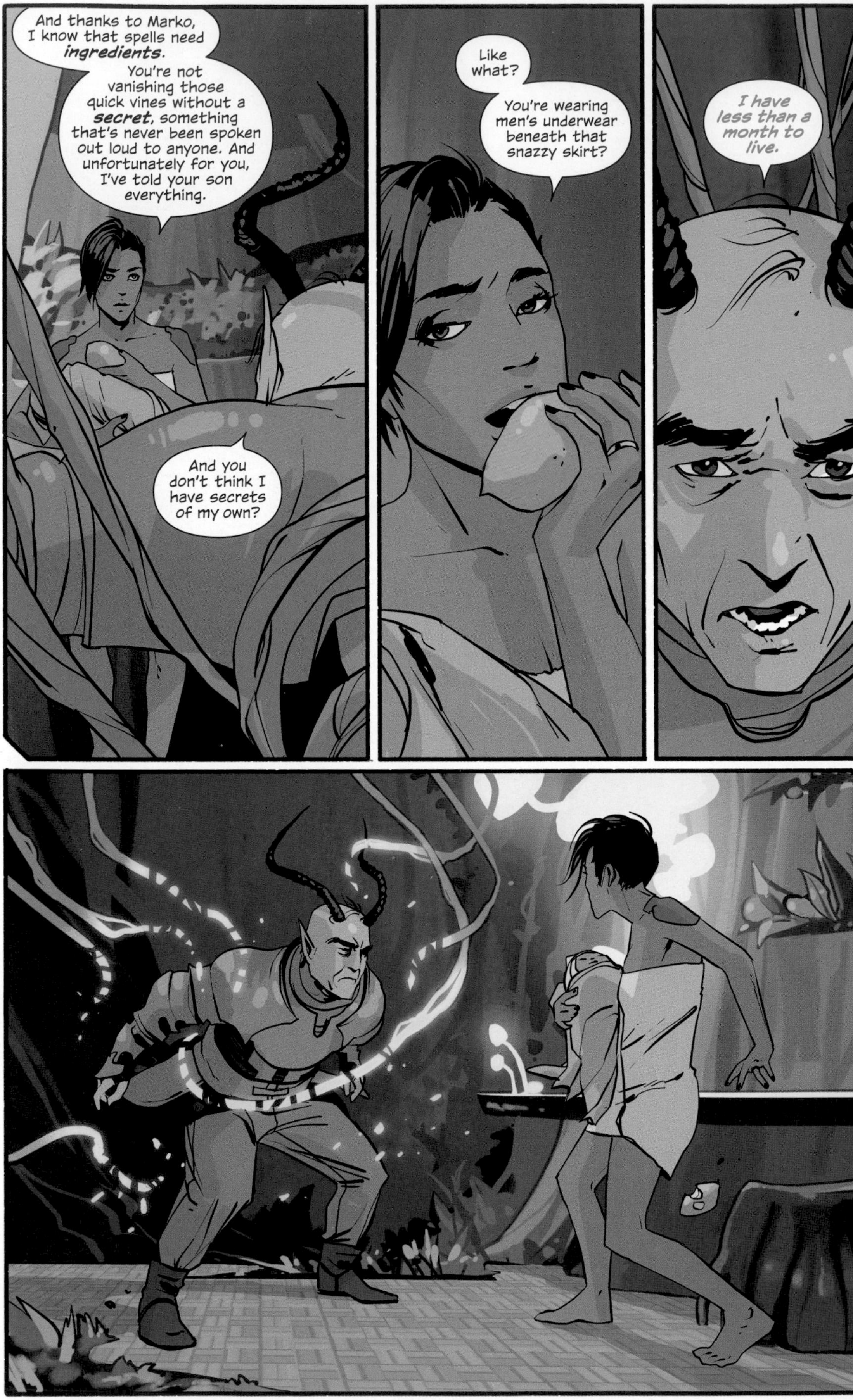
And thanks to Marko, I know that spells need **ingredients**.
You're not vanishing those quick vines without a **secret**, something that's never been spoken out loud to anyone. And unfortunately for you, I've told your son everything.
And you don't think I have secrets of my own?
Like what?
You're wearing men's underwear beneath that snazzy skirt?
I have less than a month to live.

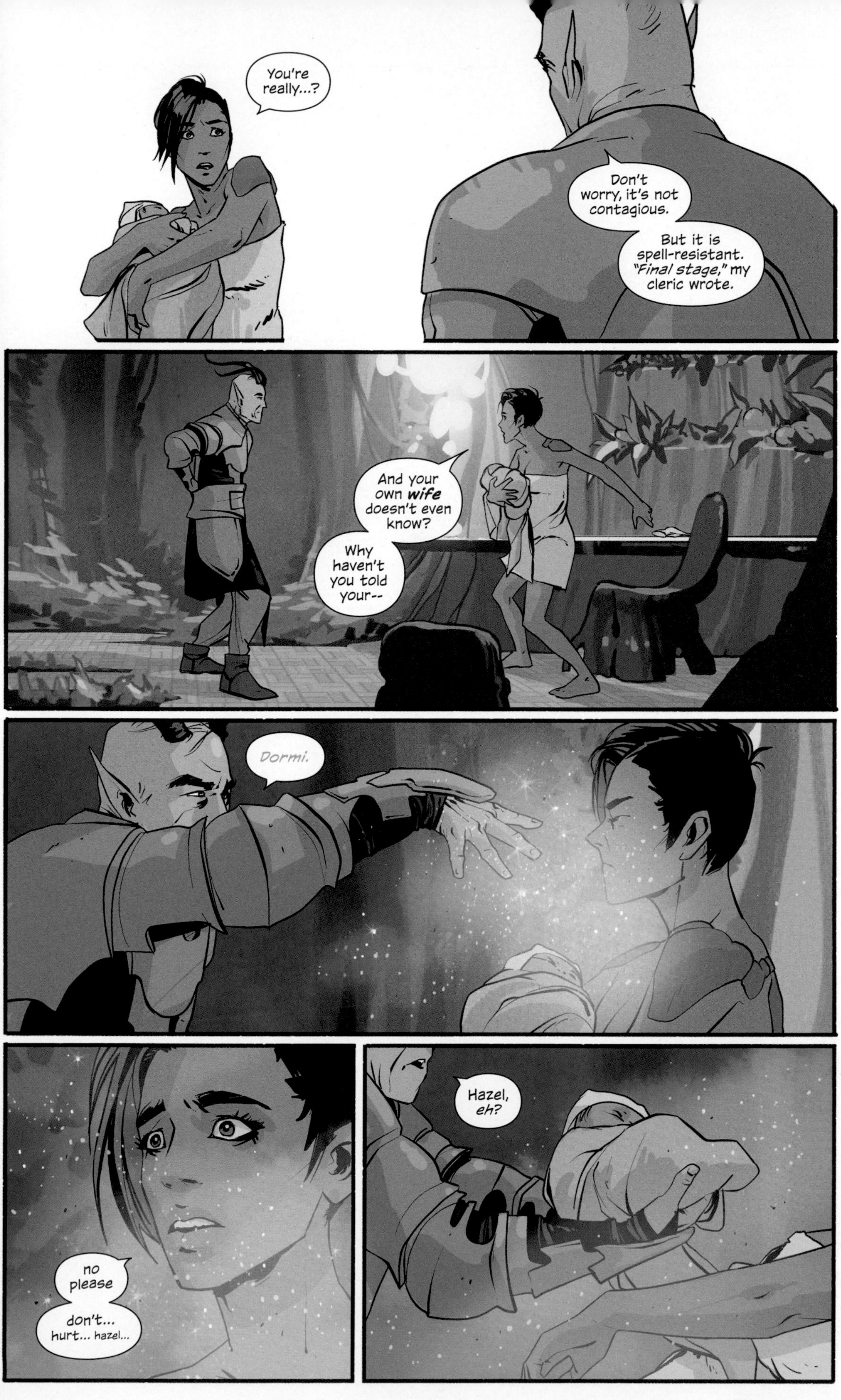
You're really...?
Don't worry, it's not contagious.
But it is spell-resistant. "*Final stage*," my cleric wrote.
And your own **wife** doesn't even know?
Why haven't you told your--
Dormi.
no please
don't... hurt... hazel...
Hazel, *eh?*

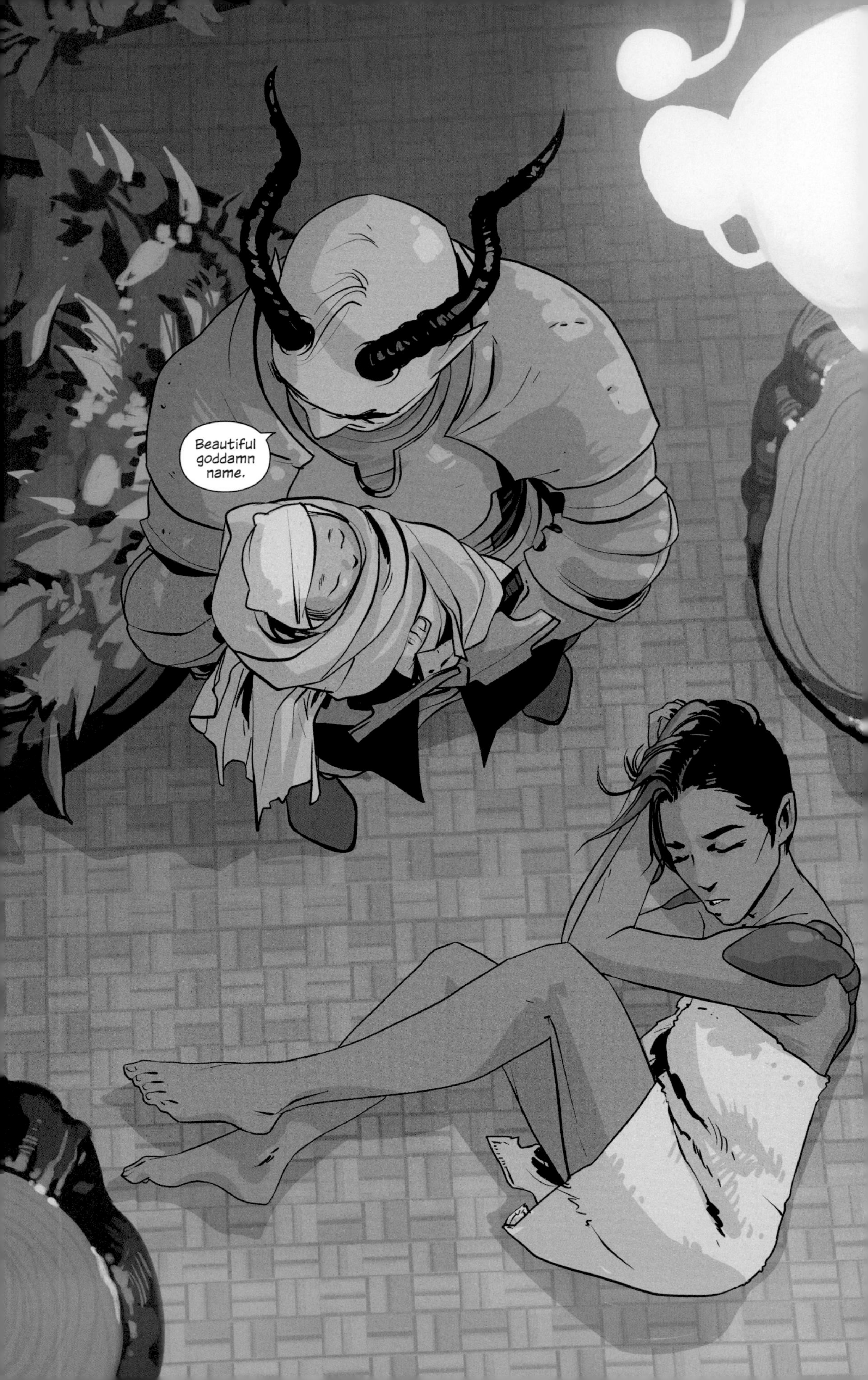
Beautiful goddamn name.

end chapter seven

CHAPTER
EIGHT

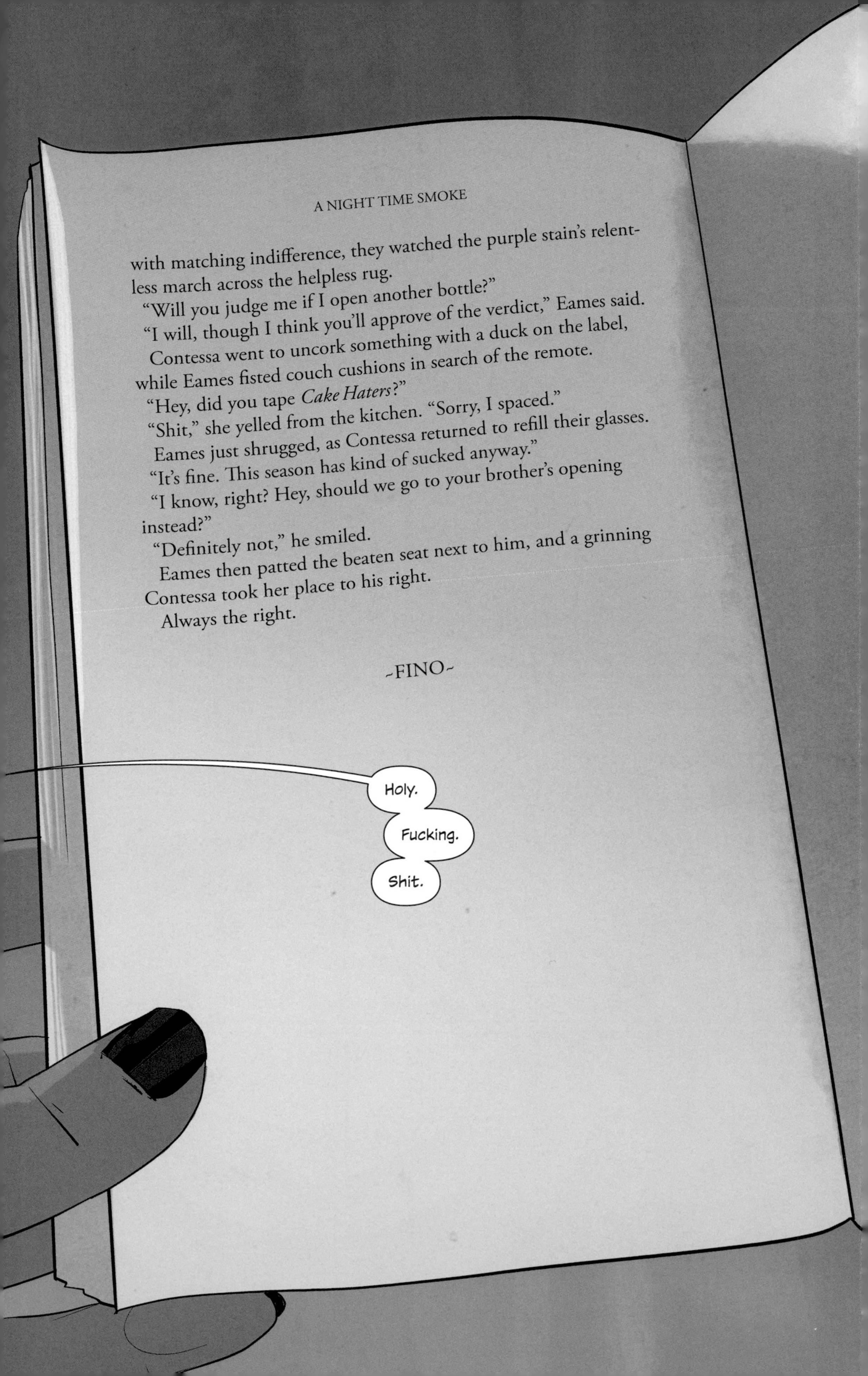

with matching indifference, they watched the purple stain's relentless march across the helpless rug.

"Will you judge me if I open another bottle?"

"I will, though I think you'll approve of the verdict," Eames said.

Contessa went to uncork something with a duck on the label, while Eames fisted couch cushions in search of the remote.

"Hey, did you tape *Cake Haters*?"

"Shit," she yelled from the kitchen. "Sorry, I spaced."

Eames just shrugged, as Contessa returned to refill their glasses.

"It's fine. This season has kind of sucked anyway."

"I know, right? Hey, should we go to your brother's opening instead?"

"Definitely not," he smiled.

Eames then patted the beaten seat next to him, and a grinning Contessa took her place to his right.

Always the right.

~FINO~

Holy.
Fucking.
Shit.

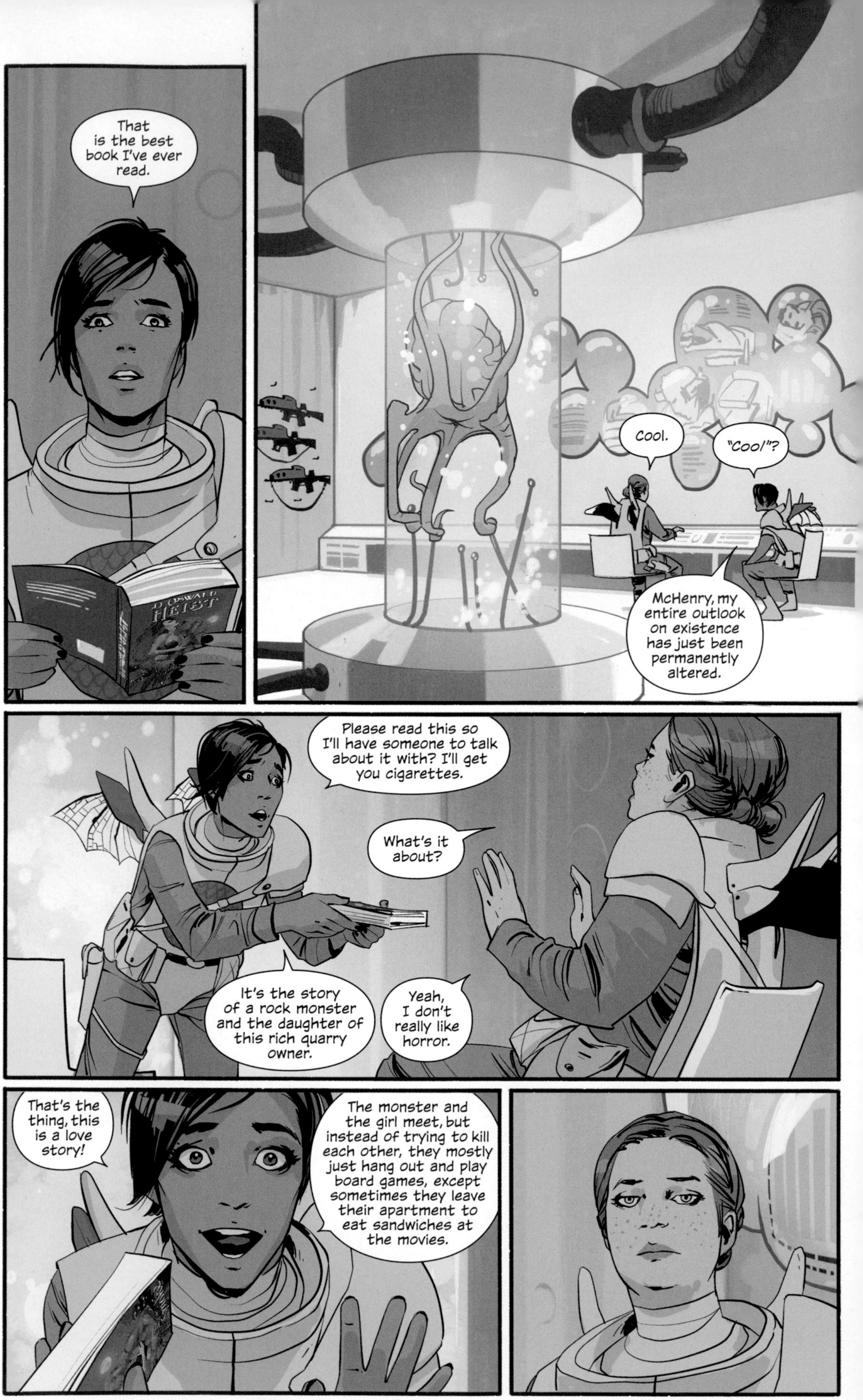
That is the best book I've ever read.
D. OSWALD HEIST
Cool.
"Cool"?
McHenry, my entire outlook on existence has just been permanently altered.
Please read this so I'll have someone to talk about it with? I'll get you cigarettes.
What's it about?
It's the story of a rock monster and the daughter of this rich quarry owner.
Yeah, I don't really like horror.
That's the thing, this is a love story!
The monster and the girl meet, but instead of trying to kill each other, they mostly just hang out and play board games, except sometimes they leave their apartment to eat sandwiches at the movies.

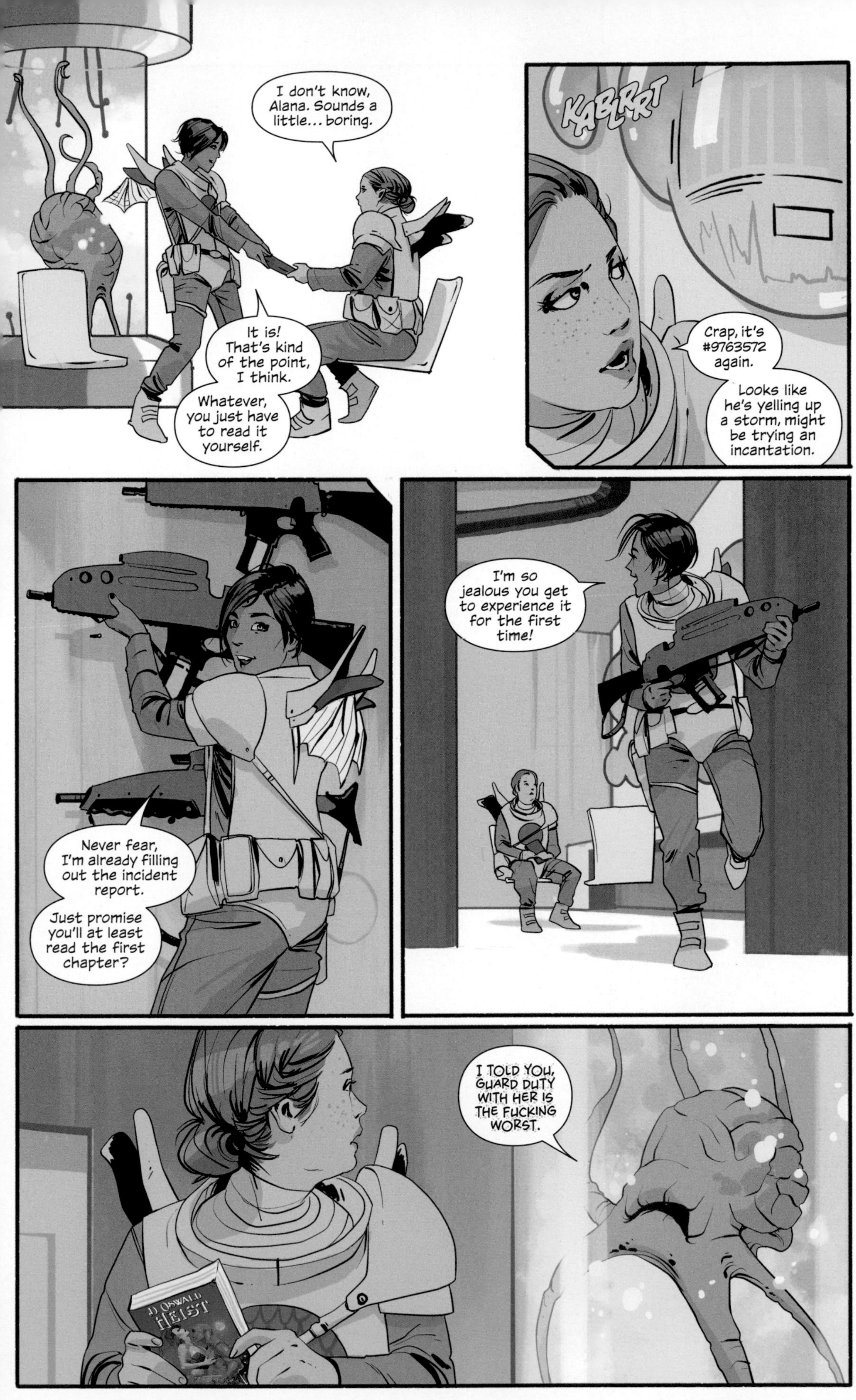
I don't know, Alana. Sounds a little... boring.
It is! That's kind of the point, I think.
Whatever, you just have to read it yourself.
KABLRRT
Crap, it's #9763572 again.
Looks like he's yelling up a storm, might be trying an incantation.
Never fear, I'm already filling out the incident report.
Just promise you'll at least read the first chapter?
I'm so jealous you get to experience it for the first time!
I TOLD YOU, GUARD DUTY WITH HER IS THE FUCKING WORST.
D. OSWALD
HEIST

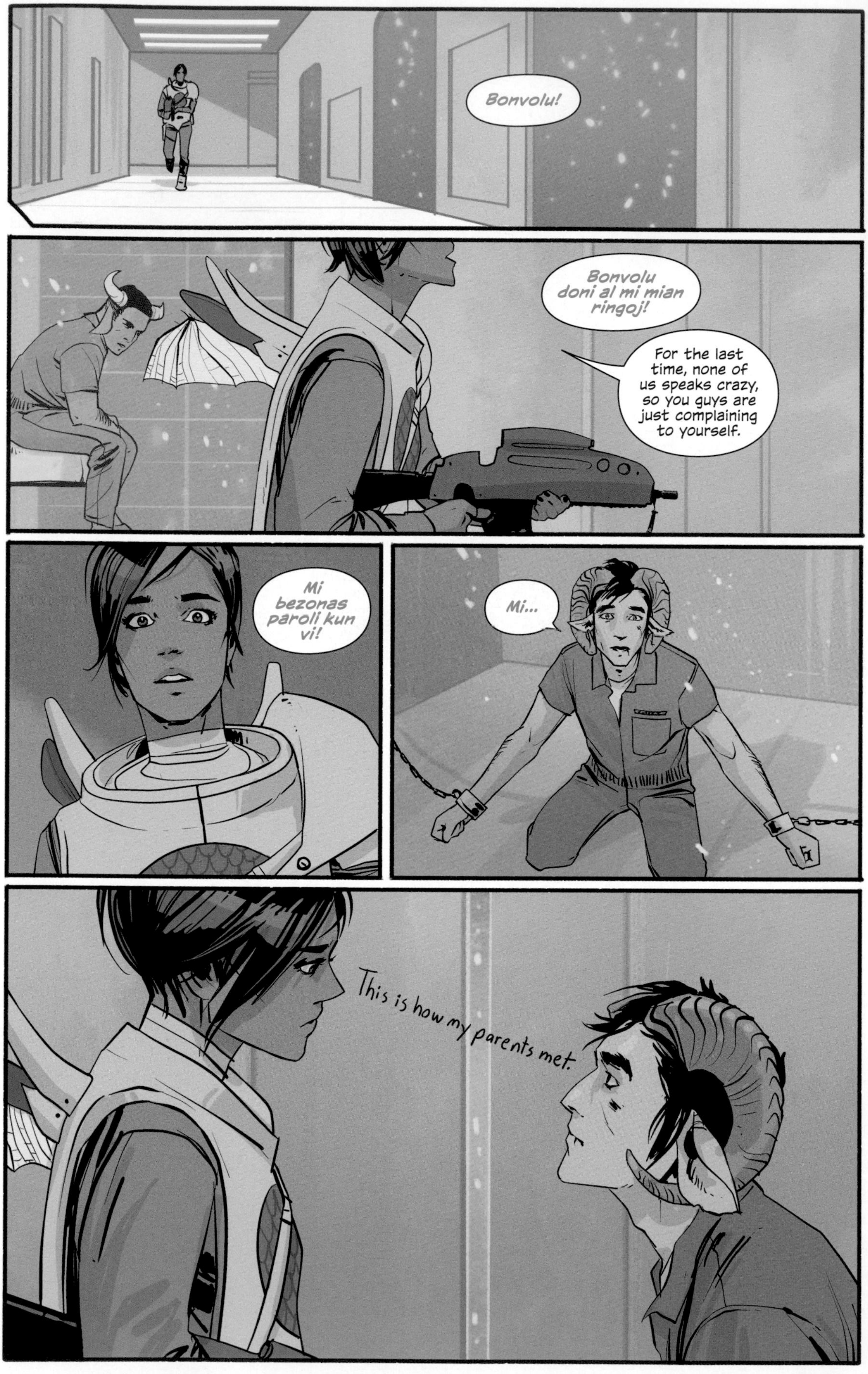
Bonvolu!
Bonvolu doni al mi mian ringoj!
For the last time, none of us speaks crazy, so you guys are just complaining to yourself.
Mi bezonas paroli kun vi!
Mi...
This is how my parents met.

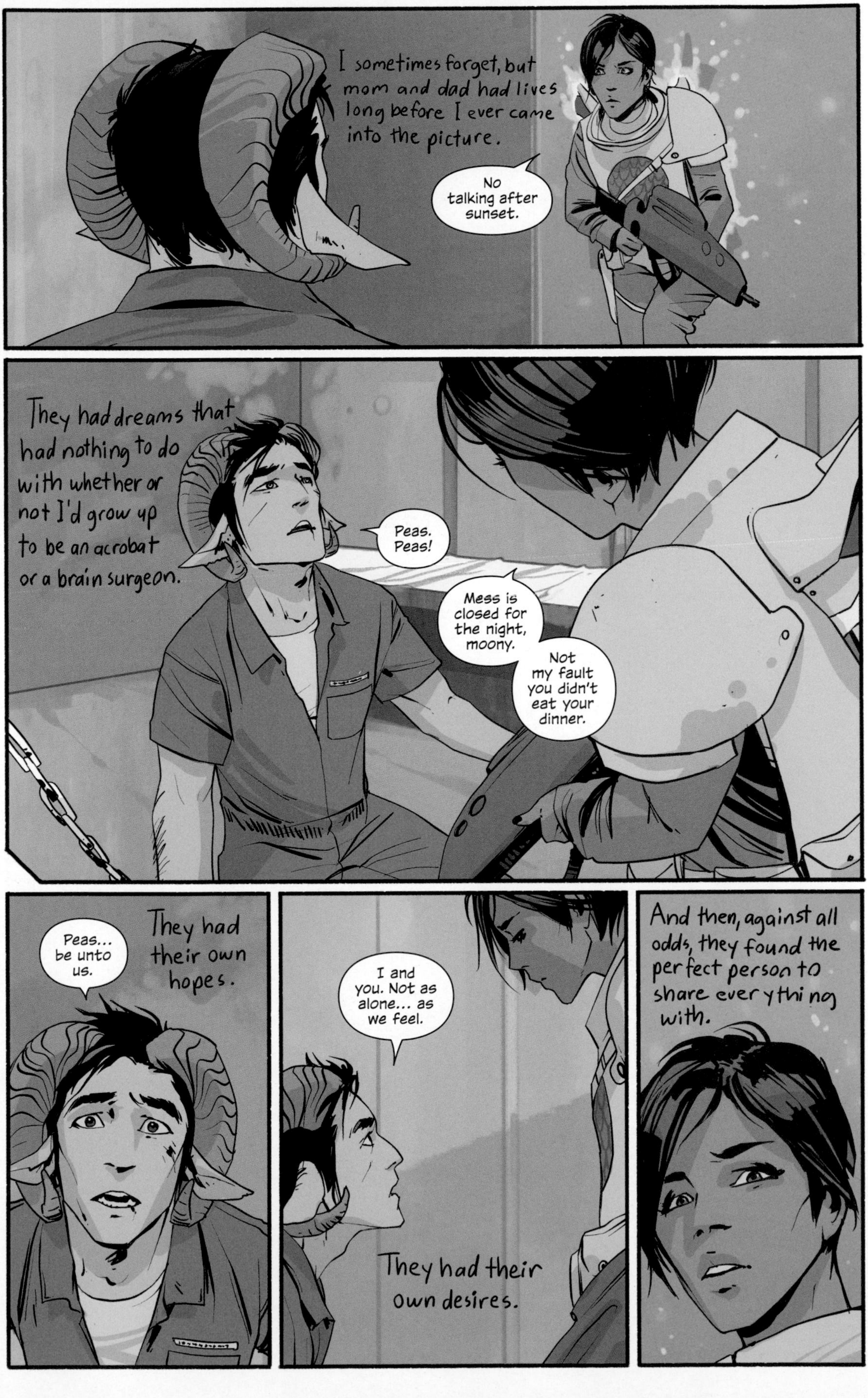

I sometimes forget, but mom and dad had lives long before I ever came into the picture.
No talking after sunset.
They had dreams that had nothing to do with whether or not I'd grow up to be an acrobat or a brain surgeon.
Peas. Peas!
Mess is closed for the night, moony.
Not my fault you didn't eat your dinner.
Peas... be unto us.
They had their own hopes.
I and you. Not as alone... as we feel.
They had their own desires.
And then, against all odds, they found the perfect person to share everything with.

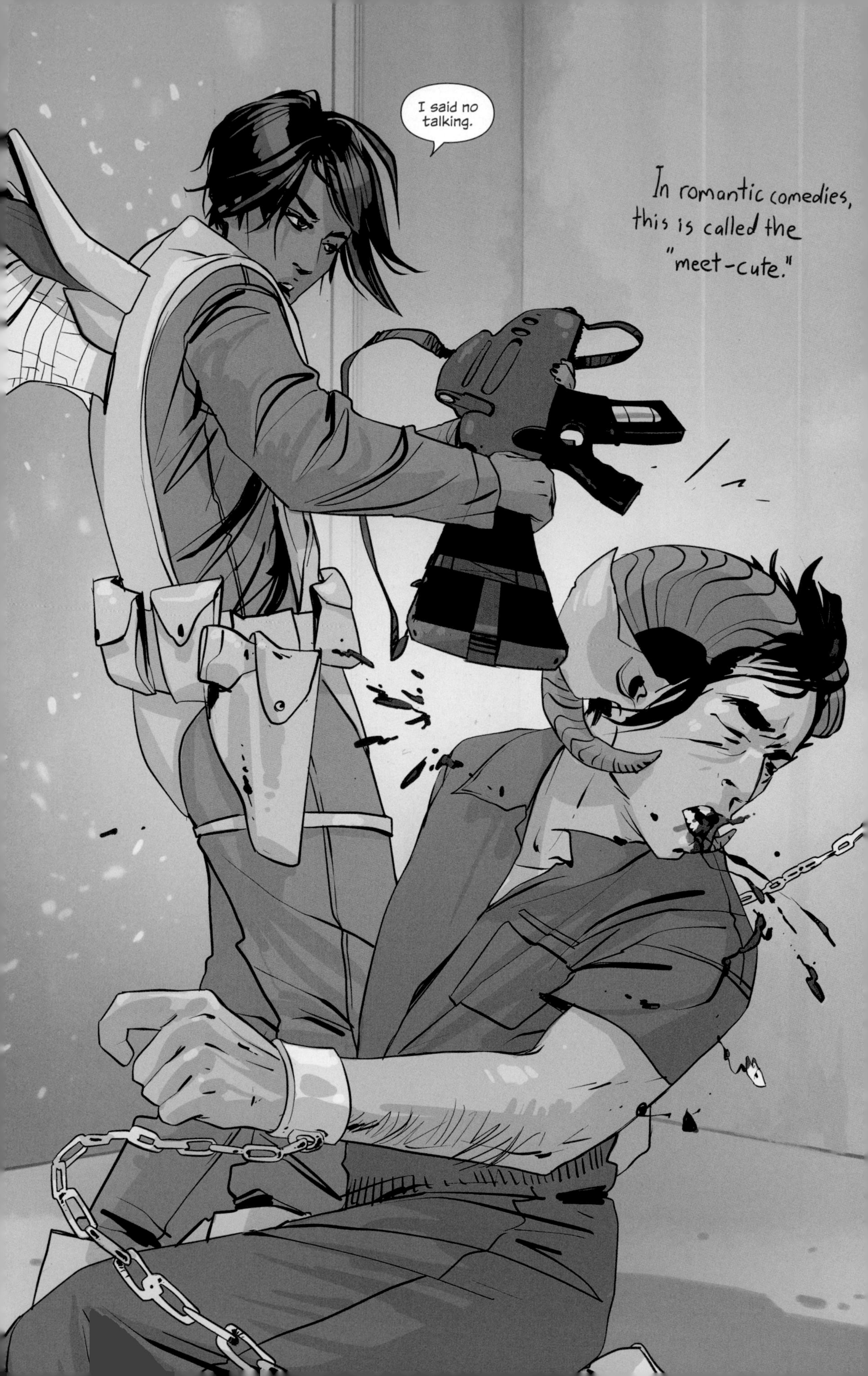
I said no talking.
In romantic comedies, this is called the "meet-cute."

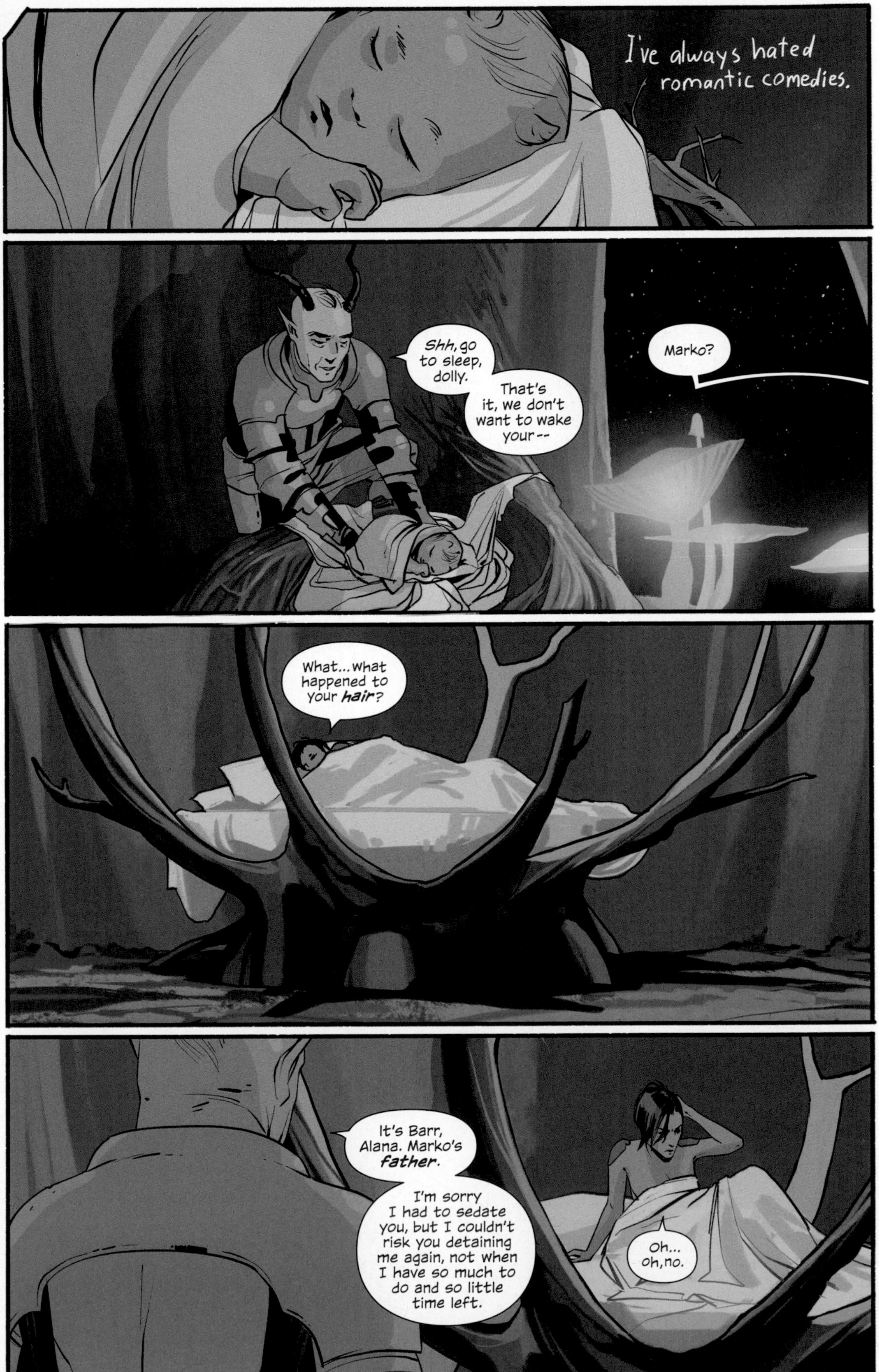
I've always hated romantic comedies.
Shh, go to sleep, dolly.
That's it, we don't want to wake your--
Marko?
What...what happened to your hair?
It's Barr, Alana. Marko's father.
I'm sorry I had to sedate you, but I couldn't risk you detaining me again, not when I have so much to do and so little time left.
Oh... oh, no.

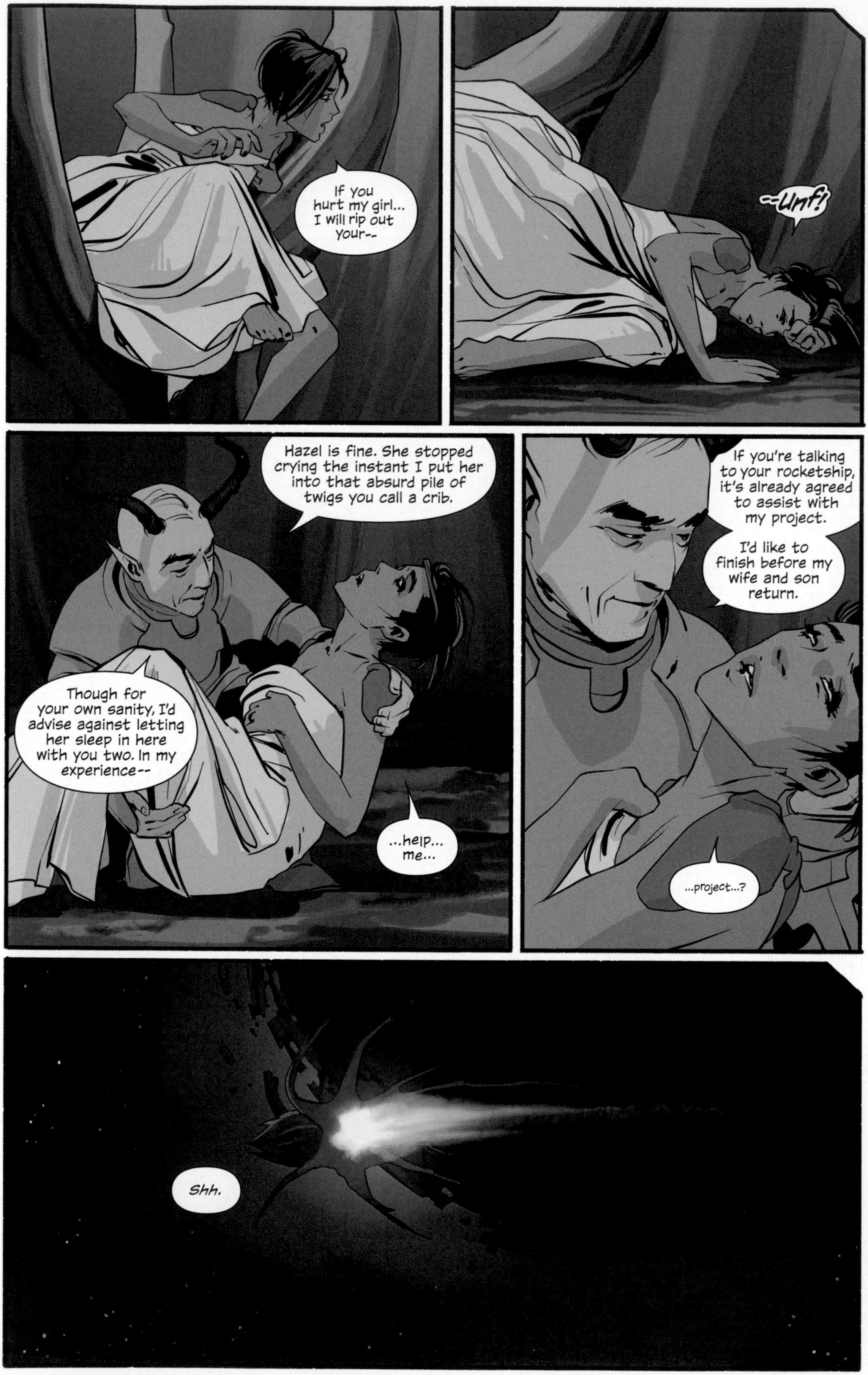
If you hurt my girl... I will rip out your--
--Unf!
Hazel is fine. She stopped crying the instant I put her into that absurd pile of twigs you call a crib.
Though for your own sanity, I'd advise against letting her sleep in here with you two. In my experience--
...help... me...
If you're talking to your rocketship, it's already agreed to assist with my project.
I'd like to finish before my wife and son return.
...project...?
Shh.

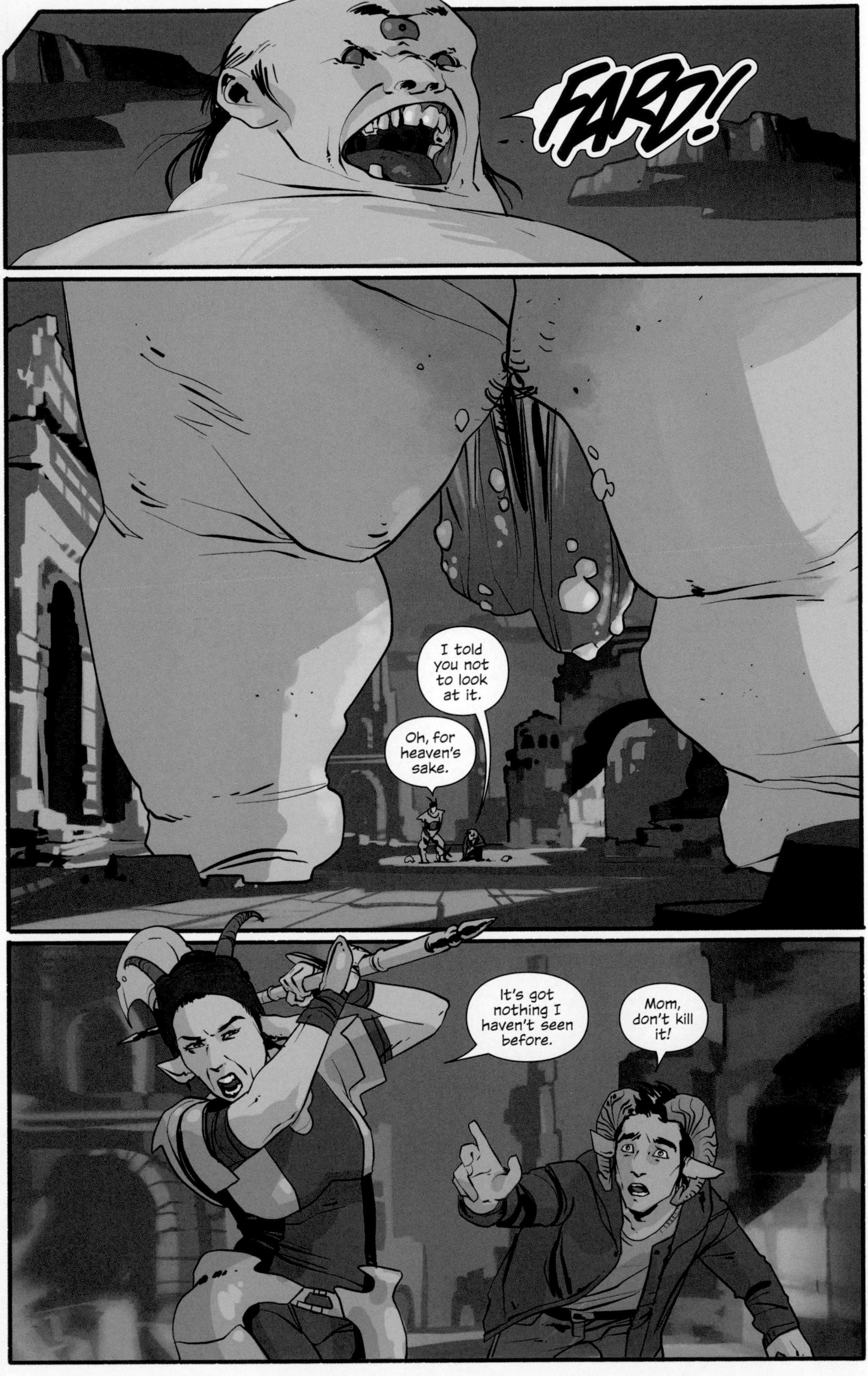
FARD!
I told you not to look at it.
Oh, for heaven's sake.
It's got nothing I haven't seen before.
Mom, don't kill it!

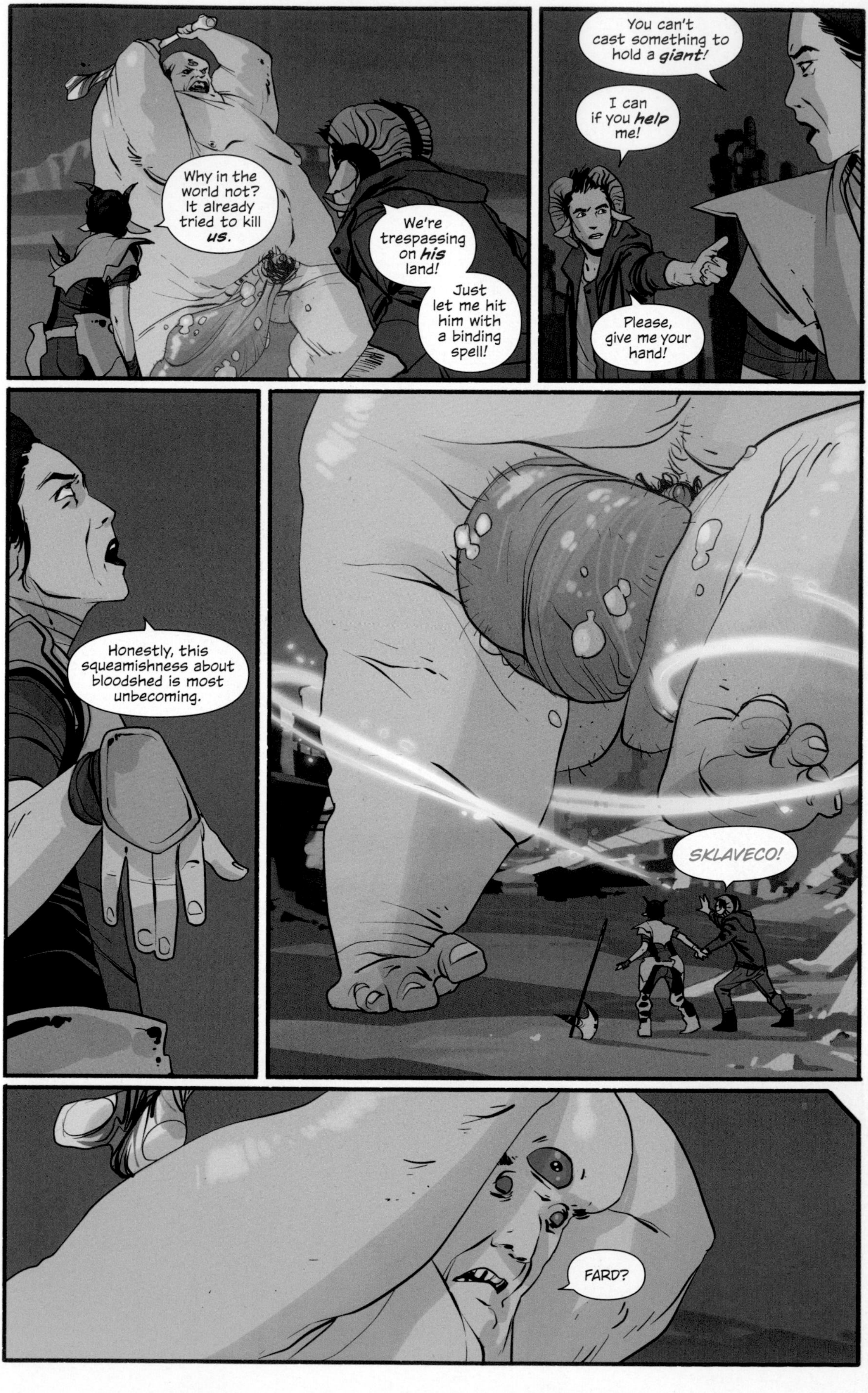
Why in the world not? It already tried to kill *us*.
We're trespassing on *his* land!
Just let me hit him with a binding spell!
You can't cast something to hold a *giant*!
I can if you *help* me!
Please, give me your hand!
Honestly, this squeamishness about bloodshed is most unbecoming.
SKLAVECO!
FARD?

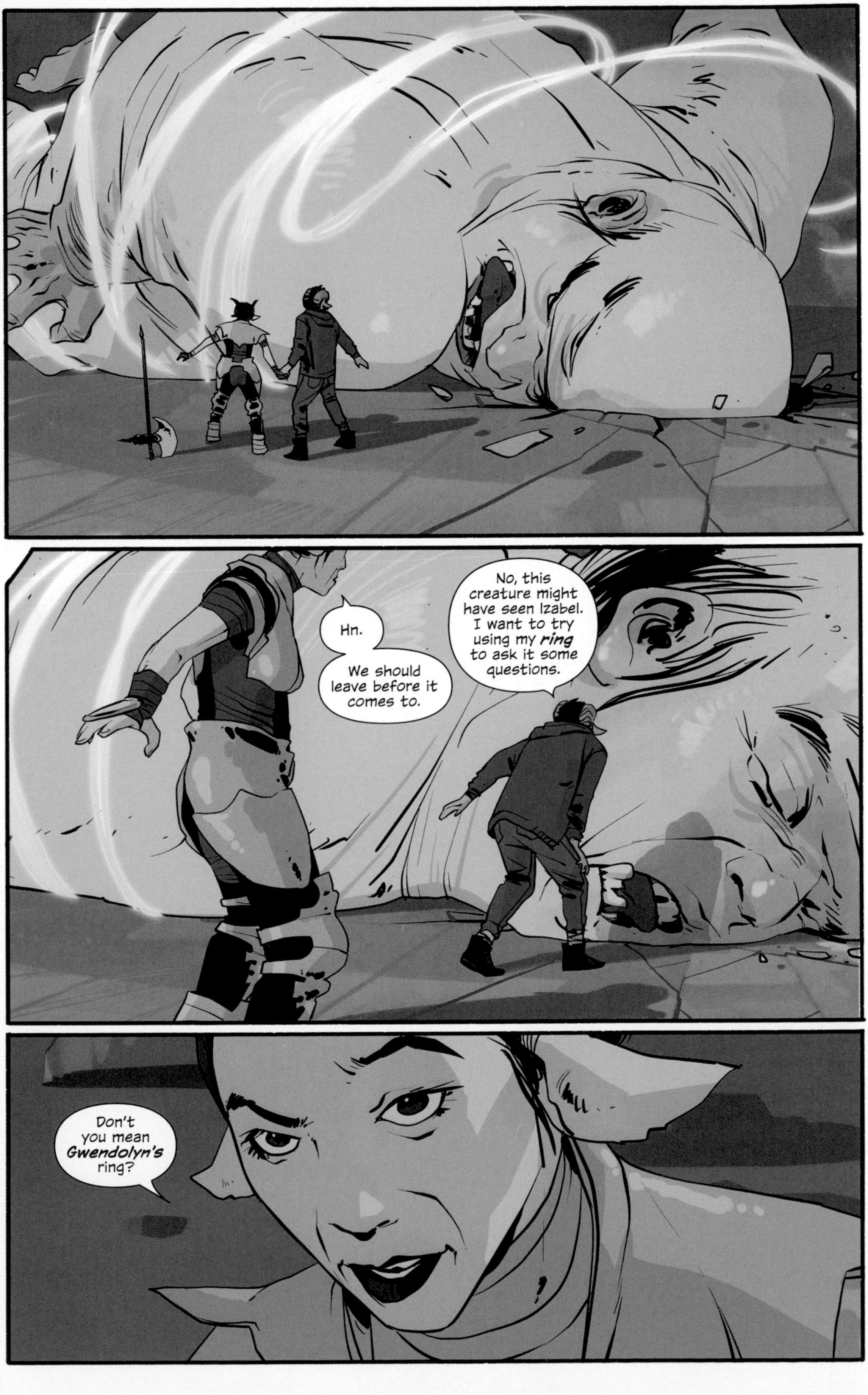
Hn.
We should leave before it comes to.
No, this creature might have seen Izabel. I want to try using my ***ring*** to ask it some questions.
Don't you mean ***Gwendolyn's*** ring?

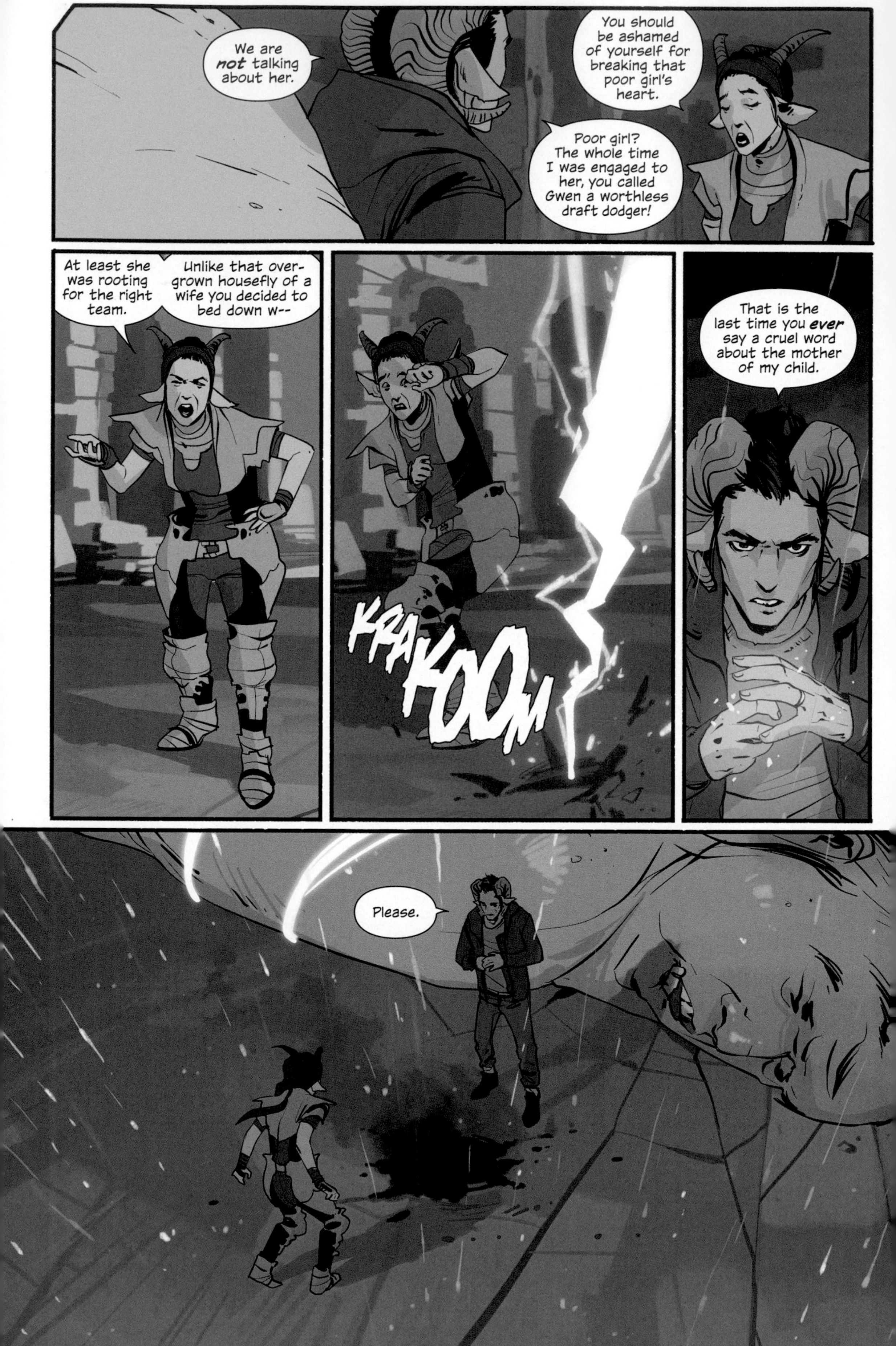

We are not talking about her.
You should be ashamed of yourself for breaking that poor girl's heart.
Poor girl? The whole time I was engaged to her, you called Gwen a worthless draft dodger!
At least she was rooting for the right team.
Unlike that over-grown housefly of a wife you decided to bed down w--
KRAKOOM
That is the last time you ever say a cruel word about the mother of my child.
Please.

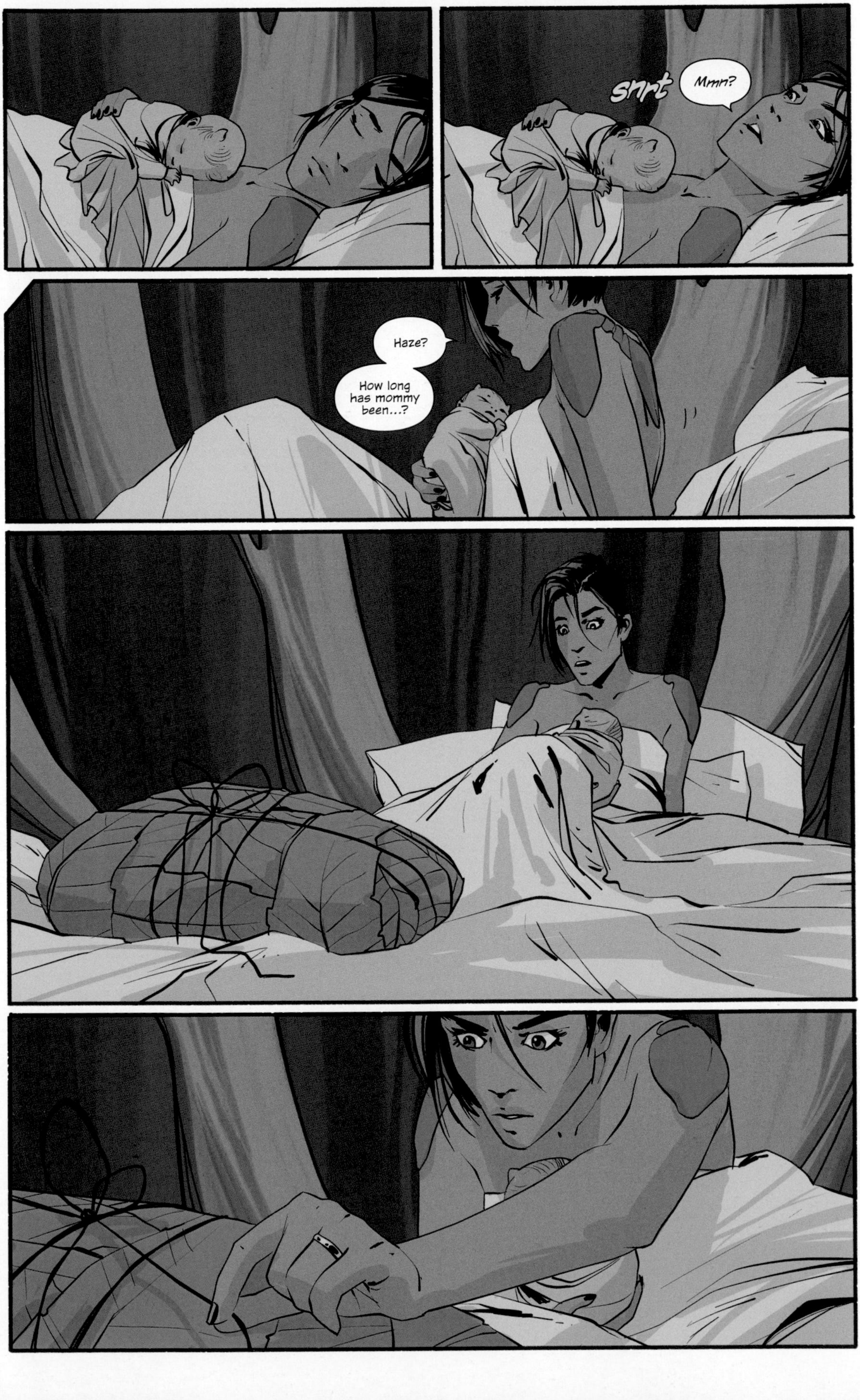
snrt
Mmn?
Haze?
How long has mommy been...?

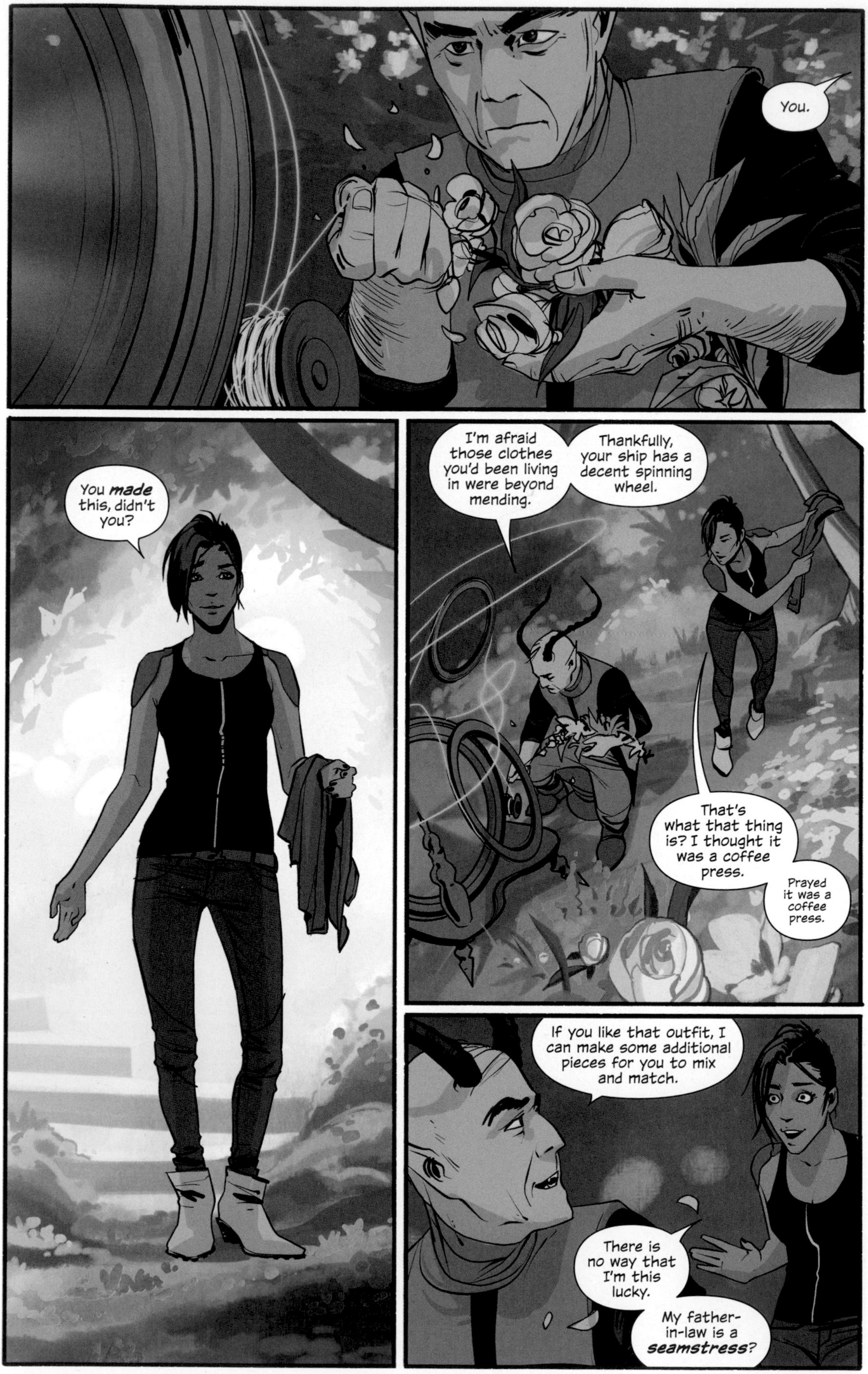
You.
You *made* this, didn't you?
I'm afraid those clothes you'd been living in were beyond mending.
Thankfully, your ship has a decent spinning wheel.
That's what that thing is? I thought it was a coffee press.
Prayed it was a coffee press.
If you like that outfit, I can make some additional pieces for you to mix and match.
There is no way that I'm this lucky.
My father-in-law is a ***seamstress***?

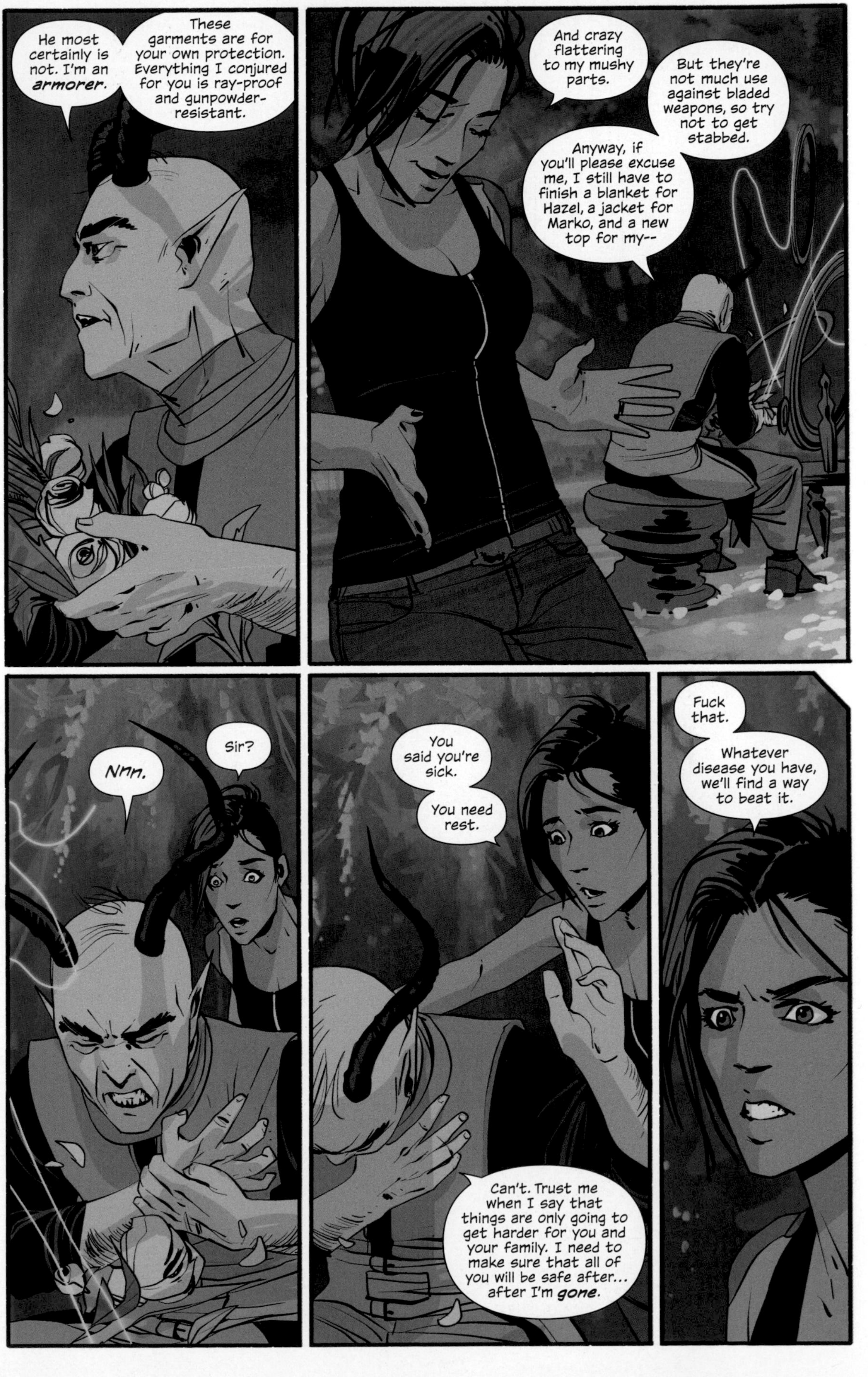
He most certainly is not. I'm an *armorer*.
These garments are for your own protection. Everything I conjured for you is ray-proof and gunpowder-resistant.
And crazy flattering to my mushy parts.
But they're not much use against bladed weapons, so try not to get stabbed.
Anyway, if you'll please excuse me, I still have to finish a blanket for Hazel, a jacket for Marko, and a new top for my--
Nnn.
Sir?
You said you're sick.
You need rest.
Can't. Trust me when I say that things are only going to get harder for you and your family. I need to make sure that all of you will be safe after... after I'm *gone*.
Fuck that.
Whatever disease you have, we'll find a way to beat it.

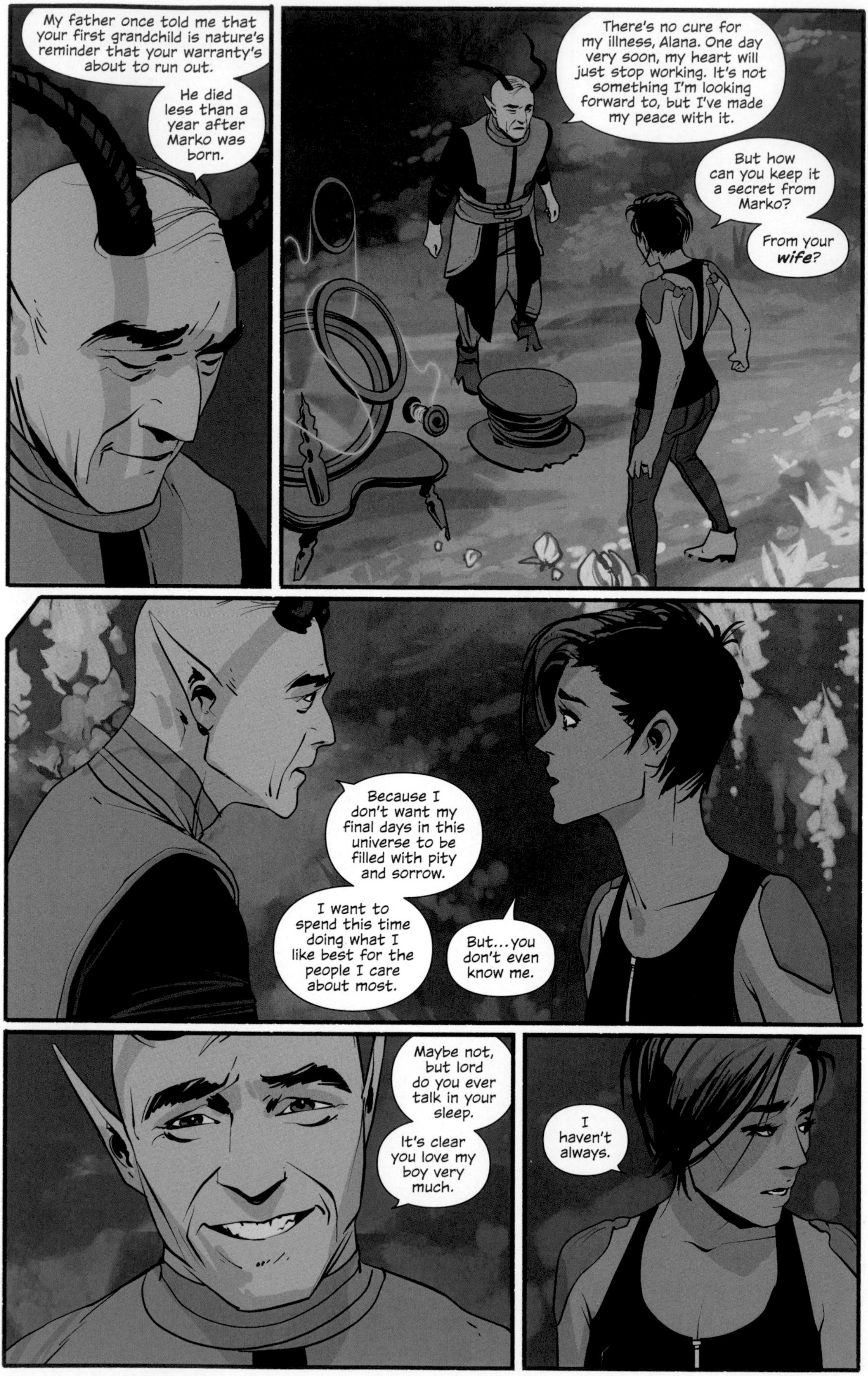
My father once told me that your first grandchild is nature's reminder that your warranty's about to run out.
He died less than a year after Marko was born.
There's no cure for my illness, Alana. One day very soon, my heart will just stop working. It's not something I'm looking forward to, but I've made my peace with it.
But how can you keep it a secret from Marko?
From your ***wife***?
Because I don't want my final days in this universe to be filled with pity and sorrow.
I want to spend this time doing what I like best for the people I care about most.
But...you don't even know me.
Maybe not, but lord do you ever talk in your sleep.
It's clear you love my boy very much.
I haven't always.

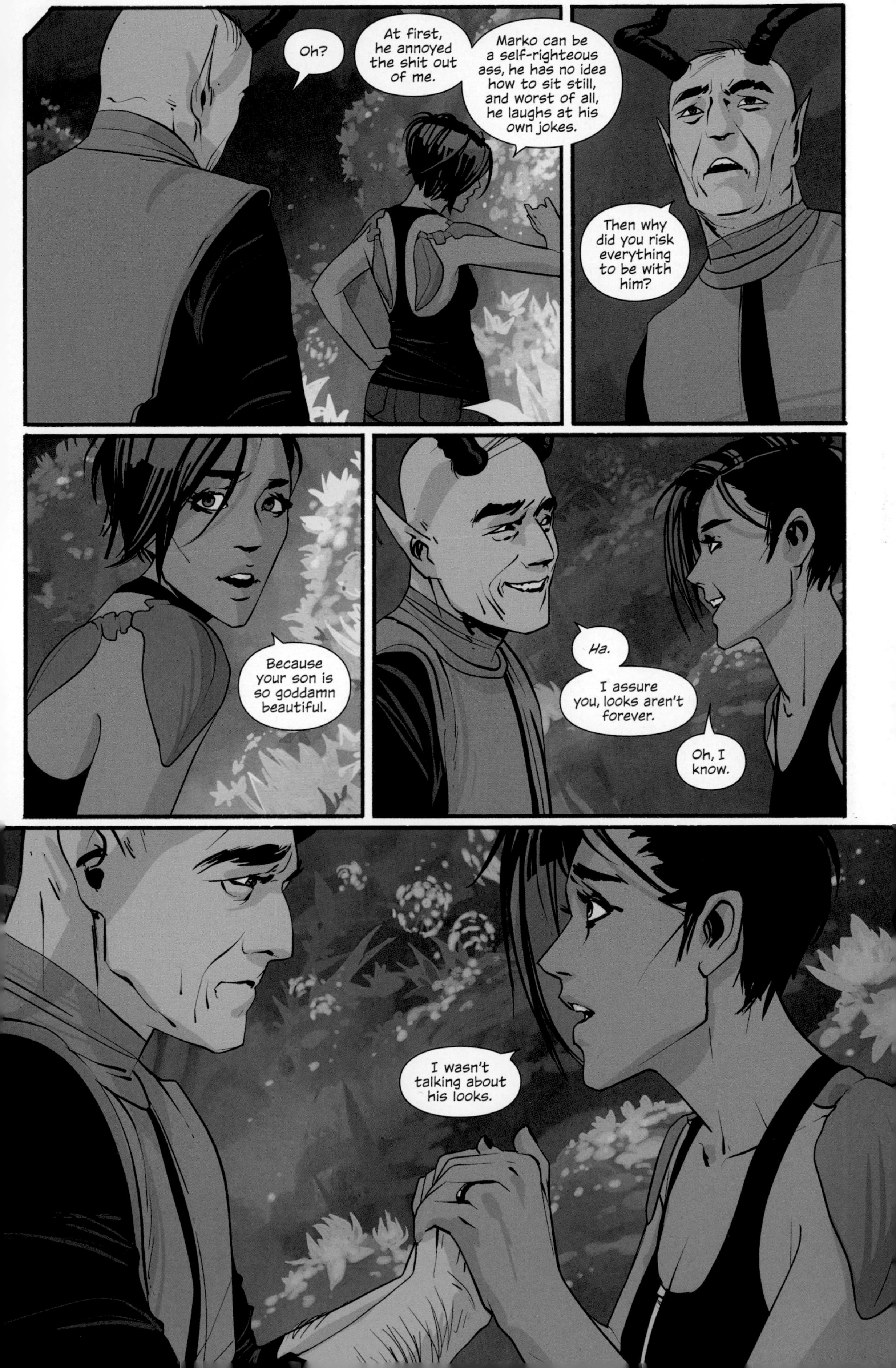
Oh?
At first, he annoyed the shit out of me.
Marko can be a self-righteous ass, he has no idea how to sit still, and worst of all, he laughs at his own jokes.
Then why did you risk everything to be with him?
Because your son is so goddamn beautiful.
Ha.
I assure you, looks aren't forever.
Oh, I know.
I wasn't talking about his looks.

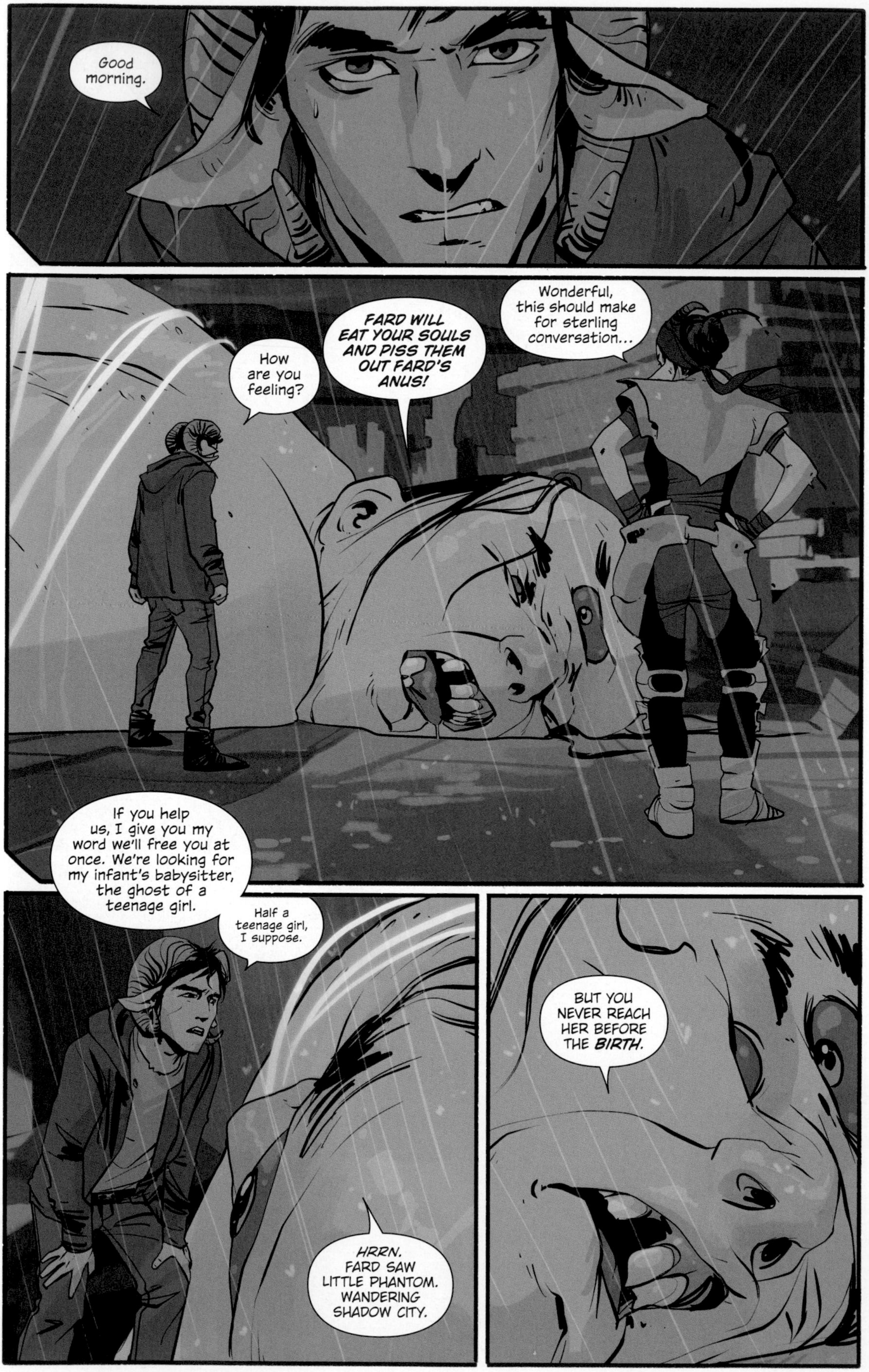
Good morning.
How are you feeling?
FARD WILL EAT YOUR SOULS AND PISS THEM OUT FARD'S ANUS!
Wonderful, this should make for sterling conversation...
If you help us, I give you my word we'll free you at once. We're looking for my infant's babysitter, the ghost of a teenage girl.
Half a teenage girl, I suppose.
HRRN. FARD SAW LITTLE PHANTOM. WANDERING SHADOW CITY.
BUT YOU NEVER REACH HER BEFORE THE BIRTH.

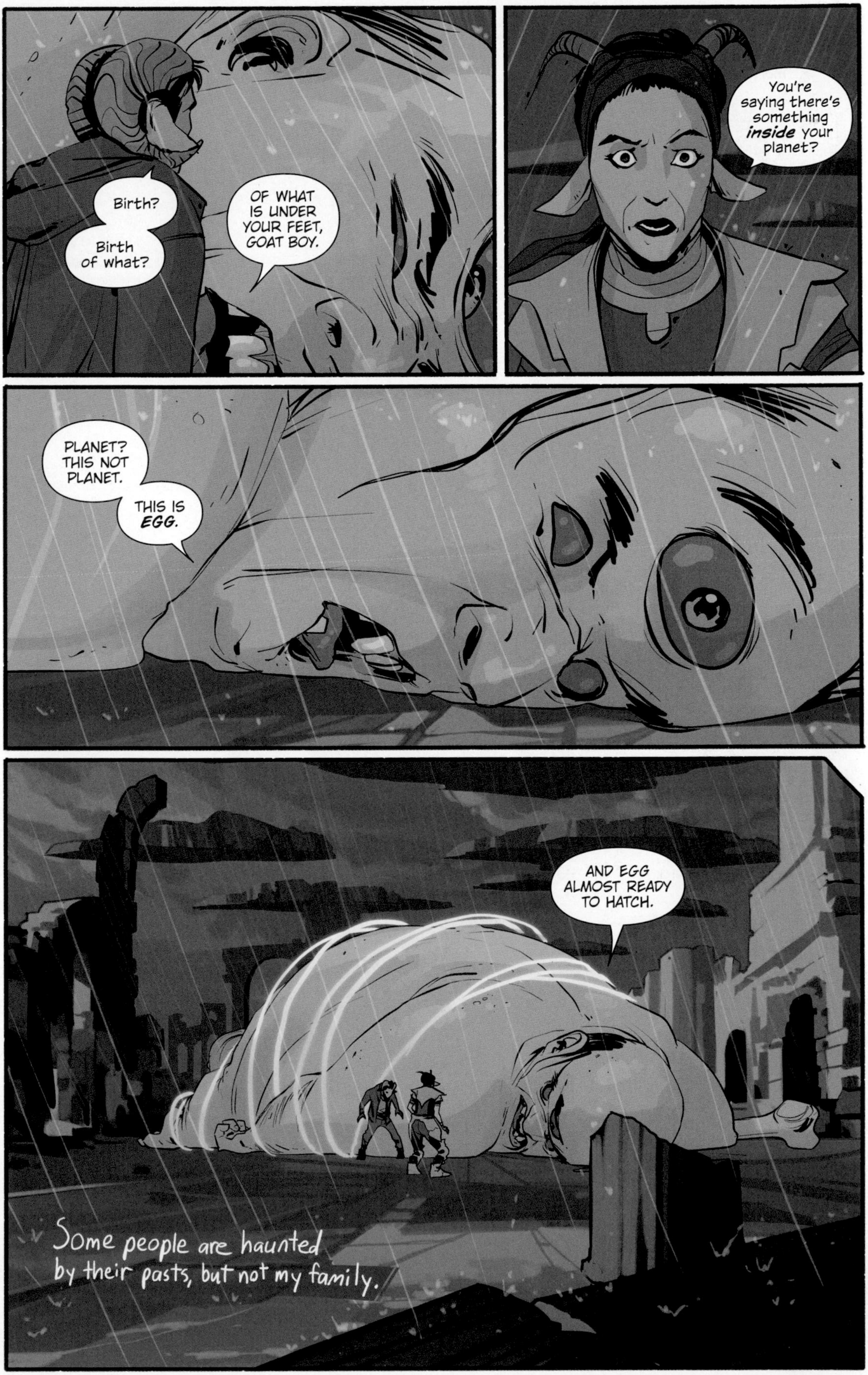
Birth?
Birth of what?
OF WHAT IS UNDER YOUR FEET, GOAT BOY.
You're saying there's something *inside* your planet?
PLANET? THIS NOT PLANET.
THIS IS *EGG*.
AND EGG ALMOST READY TO HATCH.
Some people are haunted by their pasts, but not my family.

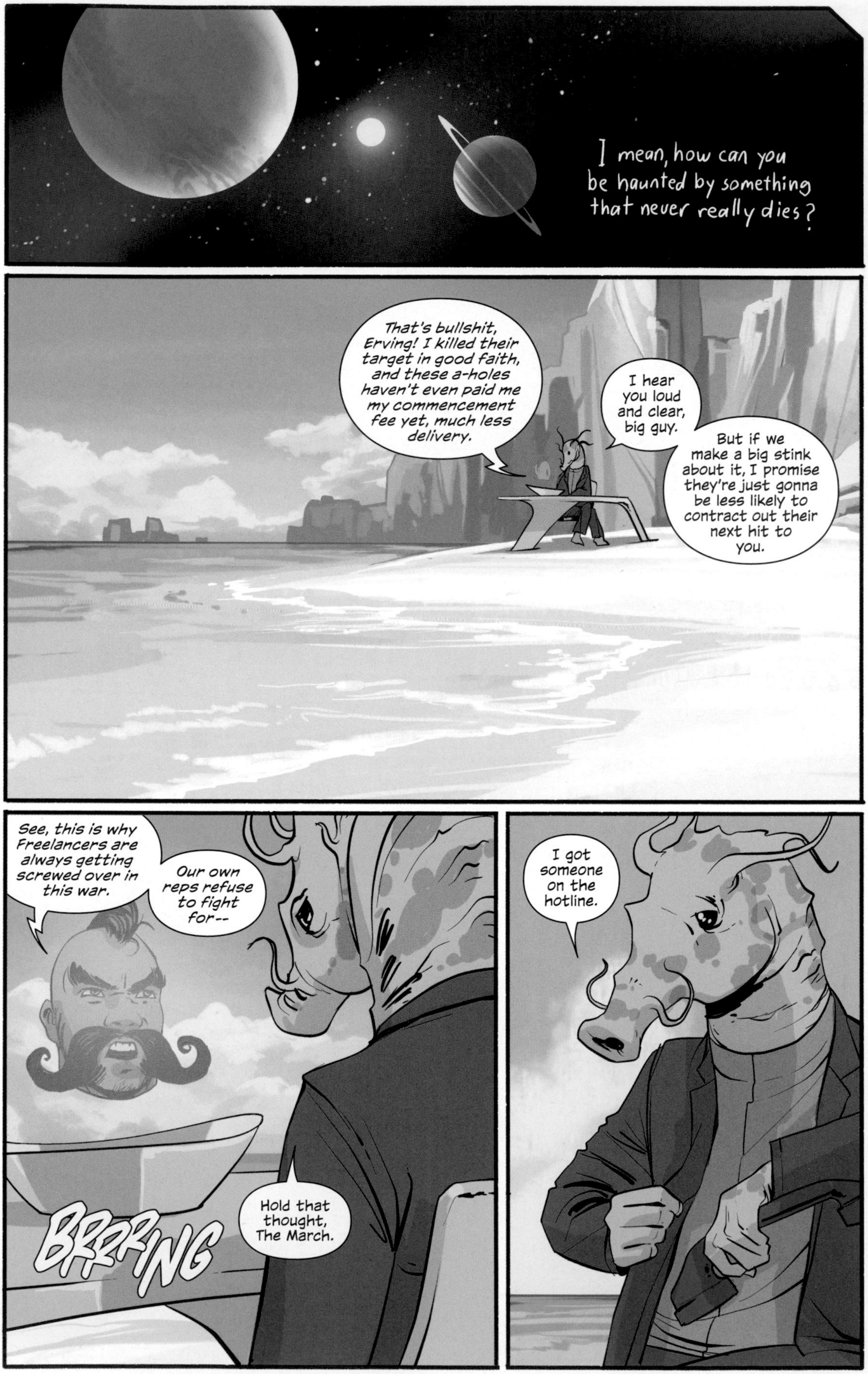
I mean, how can you be haunted by something that never really dies?
That's bullshit, Erving! I killed their target in good faith, and these a-holes haven't even paid me my commencement fee yet, much less delivery.
I hear you loud and clear, big guy.
But if we make a big stink about it, I promise they're just gonna be less likely to contract out their next hit to you.
See, this is why Freelancers are always getting screwed over in this war.
Our own reps refuse to fight for--
BRRRING
Hold that thought, The March.
I got someone on the hotline.

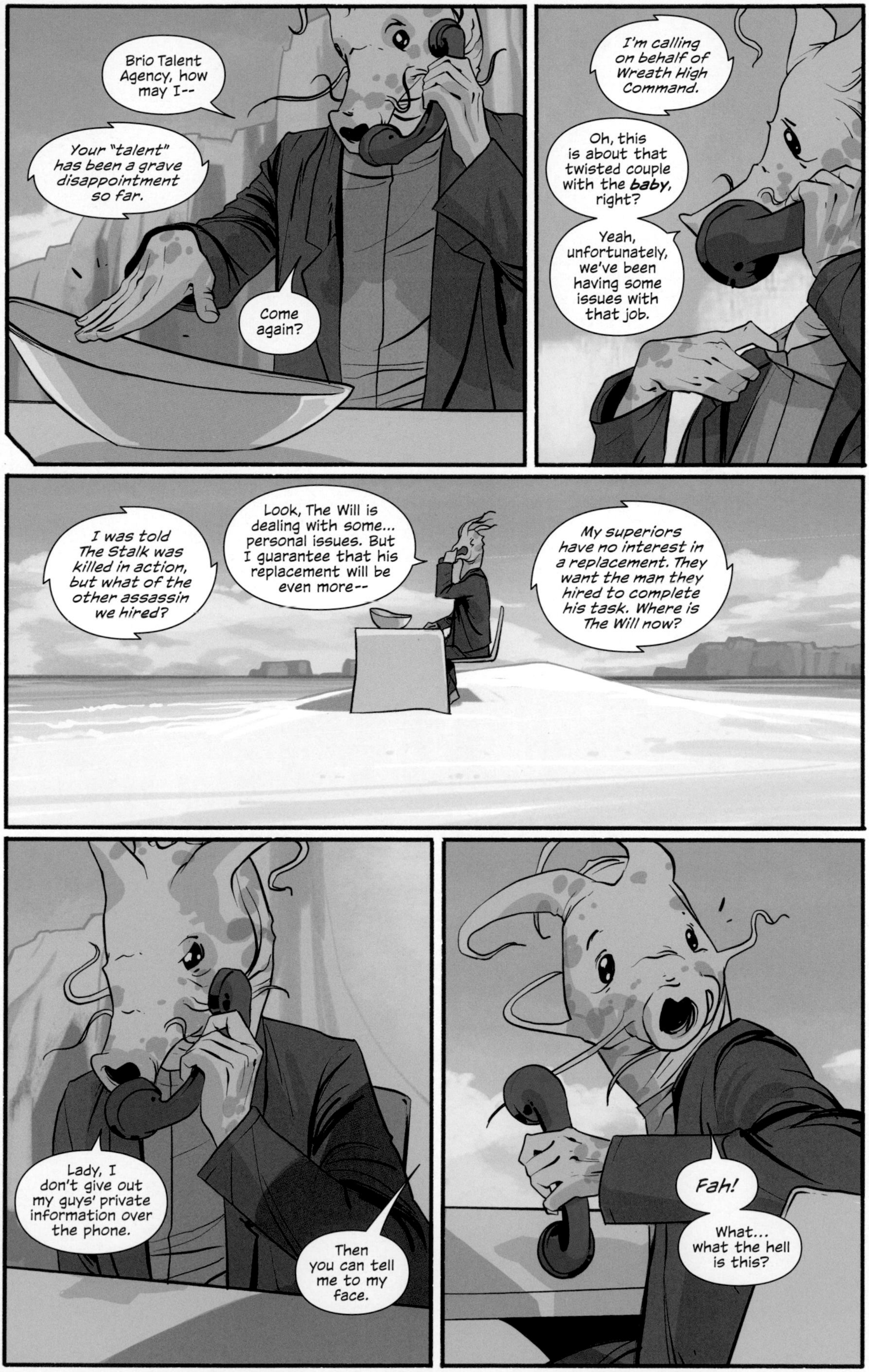

Brio Talent Agency, how may I--
Your "talent" has been a grave disappointment so far.
Come again?
I'm calling on behalf of Wreath High Command.
Oh, this is about that twisted couple with the *baby*, right?
Yeah, unfortunately, we've been having some issues with that job.
I was told The Stalk was killed in action, but what of the other assassin we hired?
Look, The Will is dealing with some... personal issues. But I guarantee that his replacement will be even more--
My superiors have no interest in a replacement. They want the man they hired to complete his task. Where is The Will now?
Lady, I don't give out my guys' private information over the phone.
Then you can tell me to my face.
Fah!
What... what the hell is this?

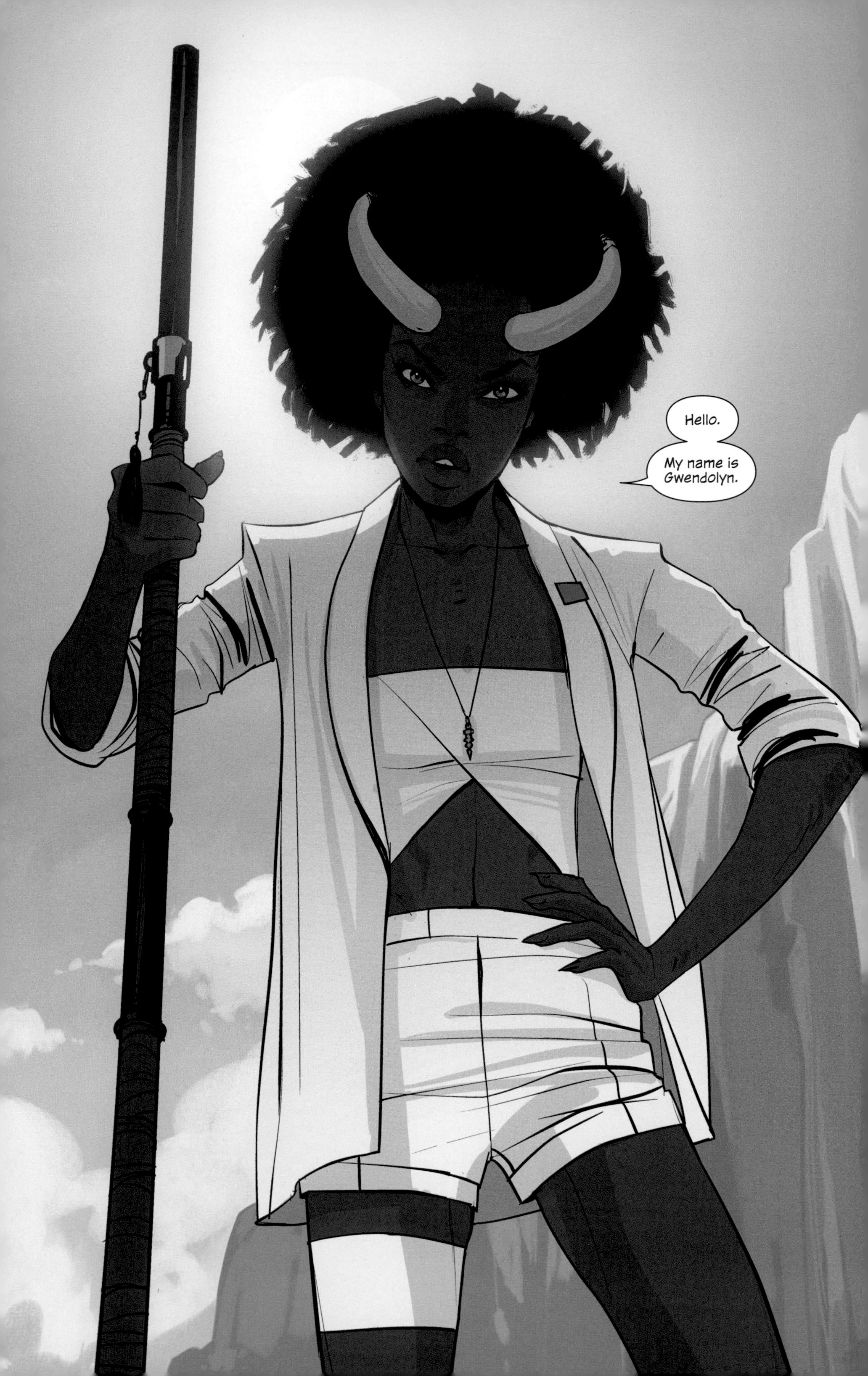
Hello.
My name is Gwendolyn.

end chapter eight

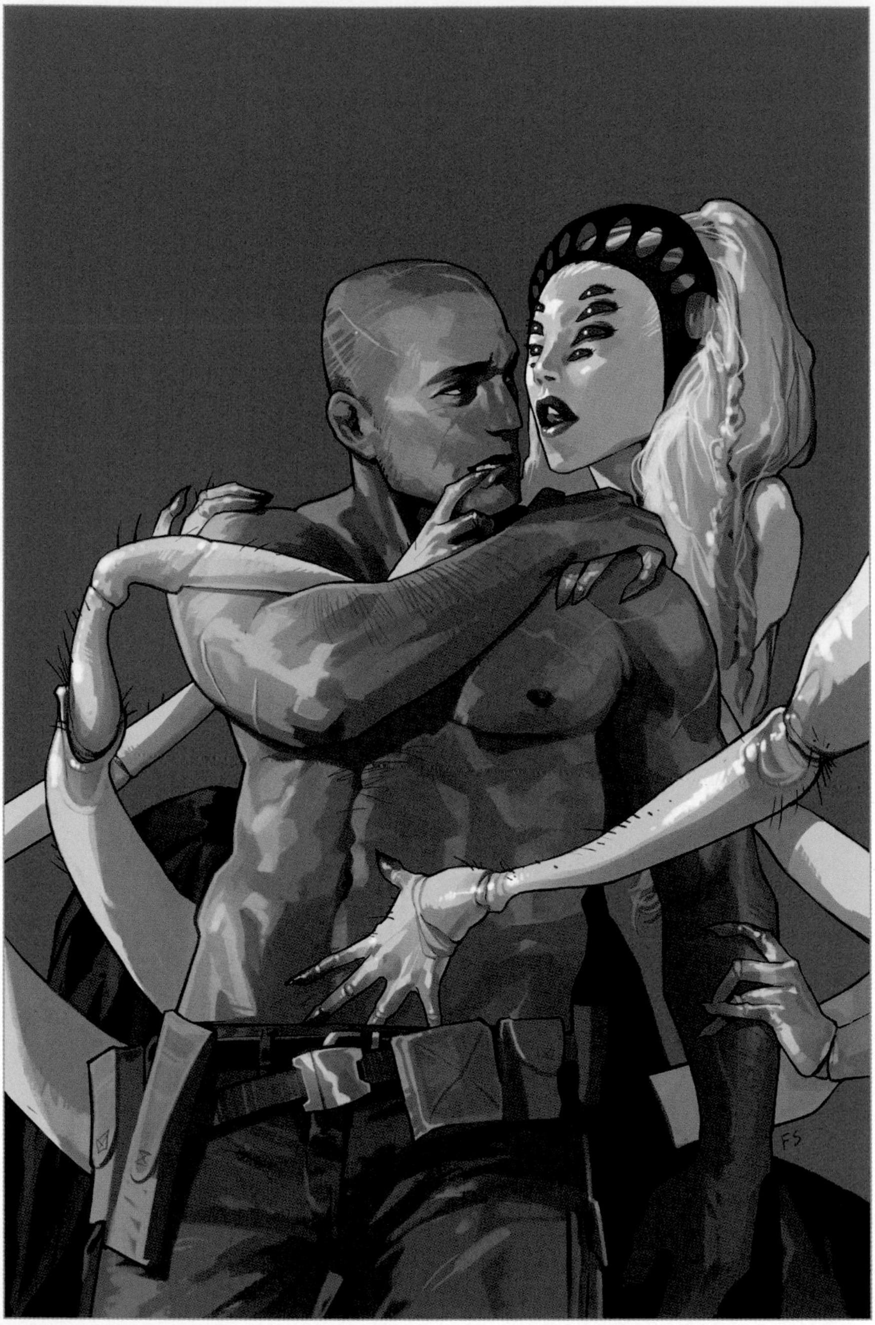
FS

CHAPTER
NINE

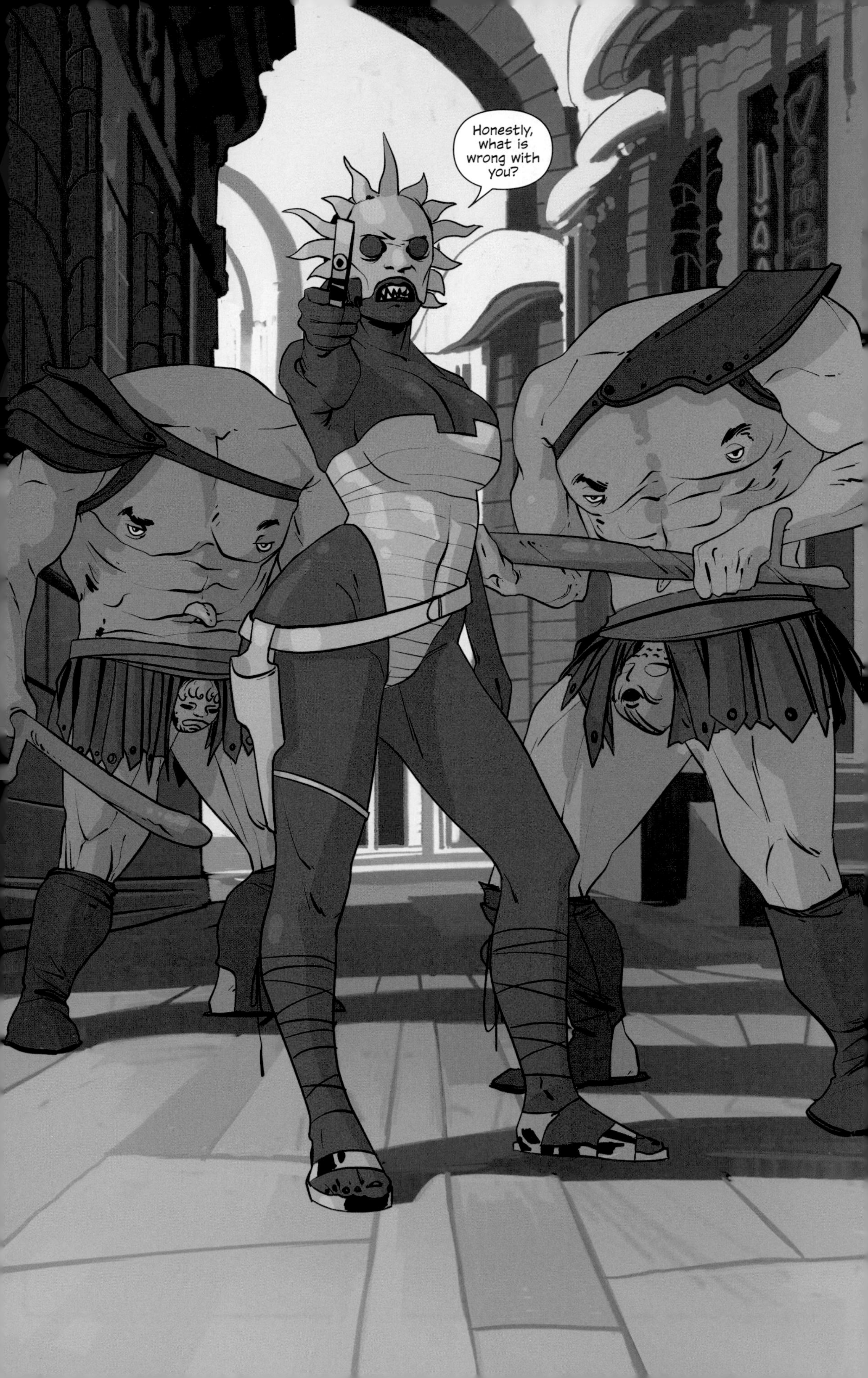
Honestly, what is wrong with you?

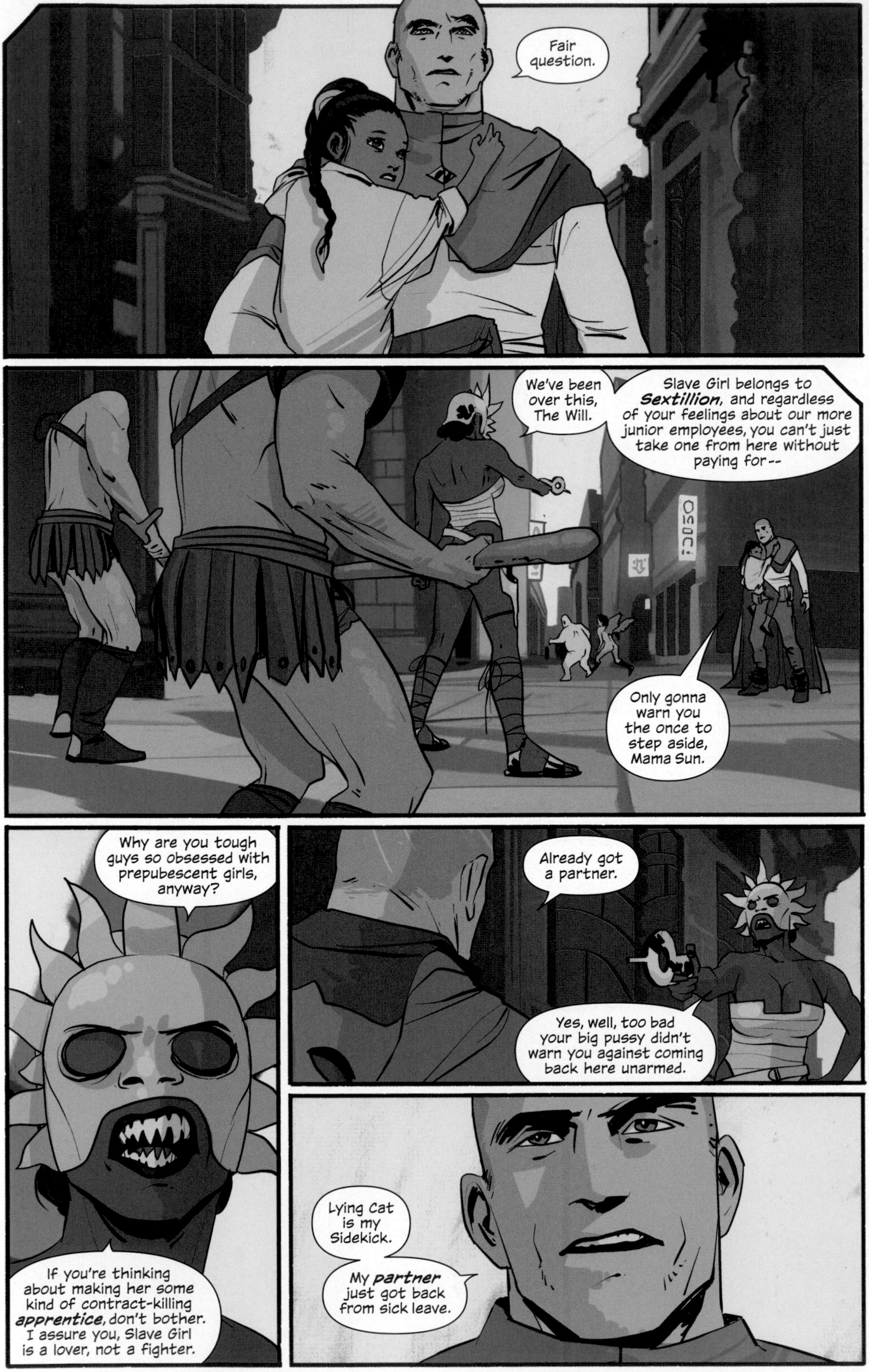
Fair question.
We've been over this, The Will.
Slave Girl belongs to *Sextillion*, and regardless of your feelings about our more junior employees, you can't just take one from here without paying for--
Only gonna warn you the once to step aside, Mama Sun.
Why are you tough guys so obsessed with prepubescent girls, anyway?
If you're thinking about making her some kind of contract-killing *apprentice*, don't bother. I assure you, Slave Girl is a lover, not a fighter.
Already got a partner.
Yes, well, too bad your big pussy didn't warn you against coming back here unarmed.
Lying Cat is my Sidekick.
My *partner* just got back from sick leave.

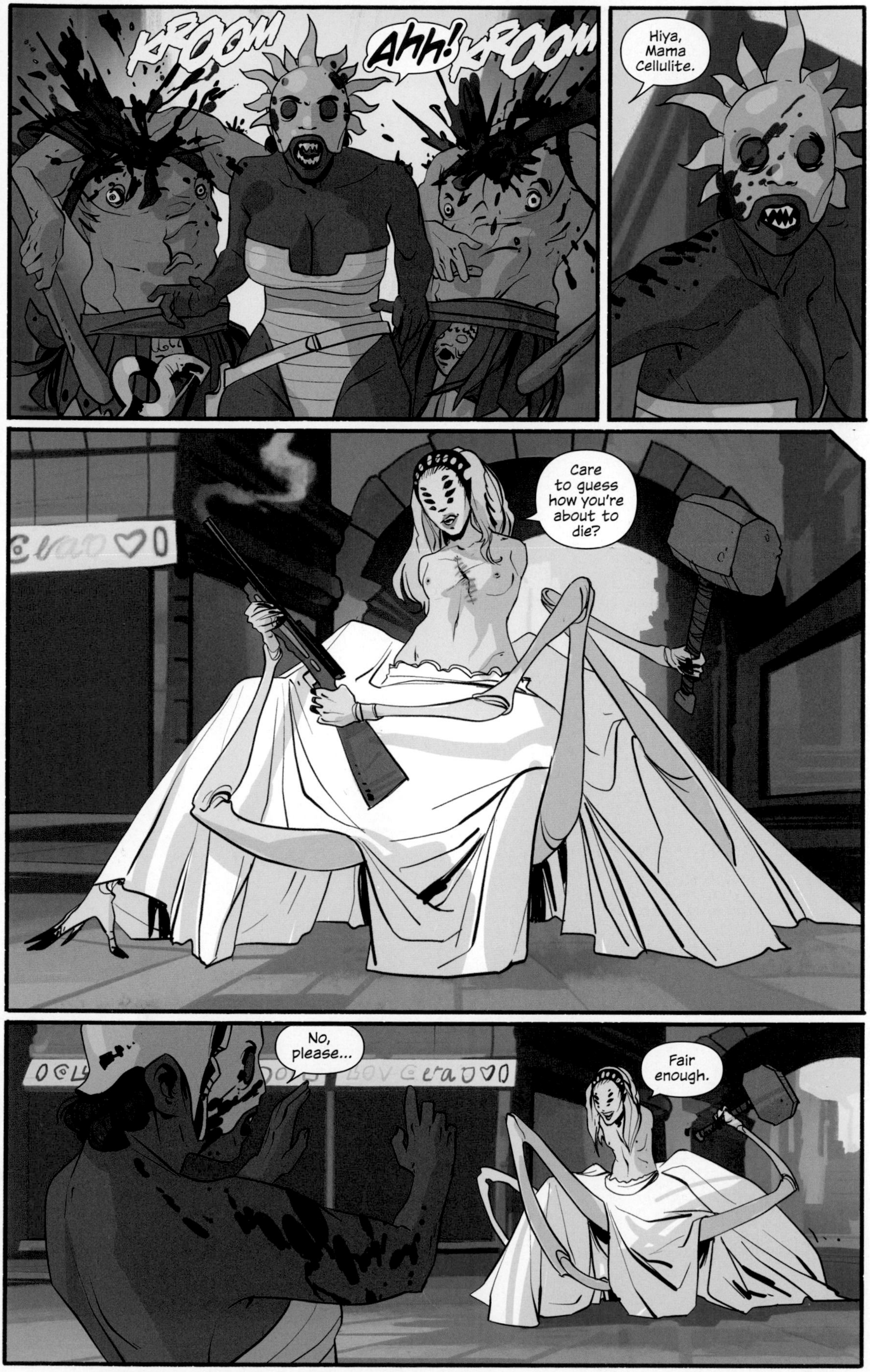
KROOM
Ahh!
KROOM
Hiya, Mama Cellulite.
Care to guess how you're about to die?
No, please...
Fair enough.

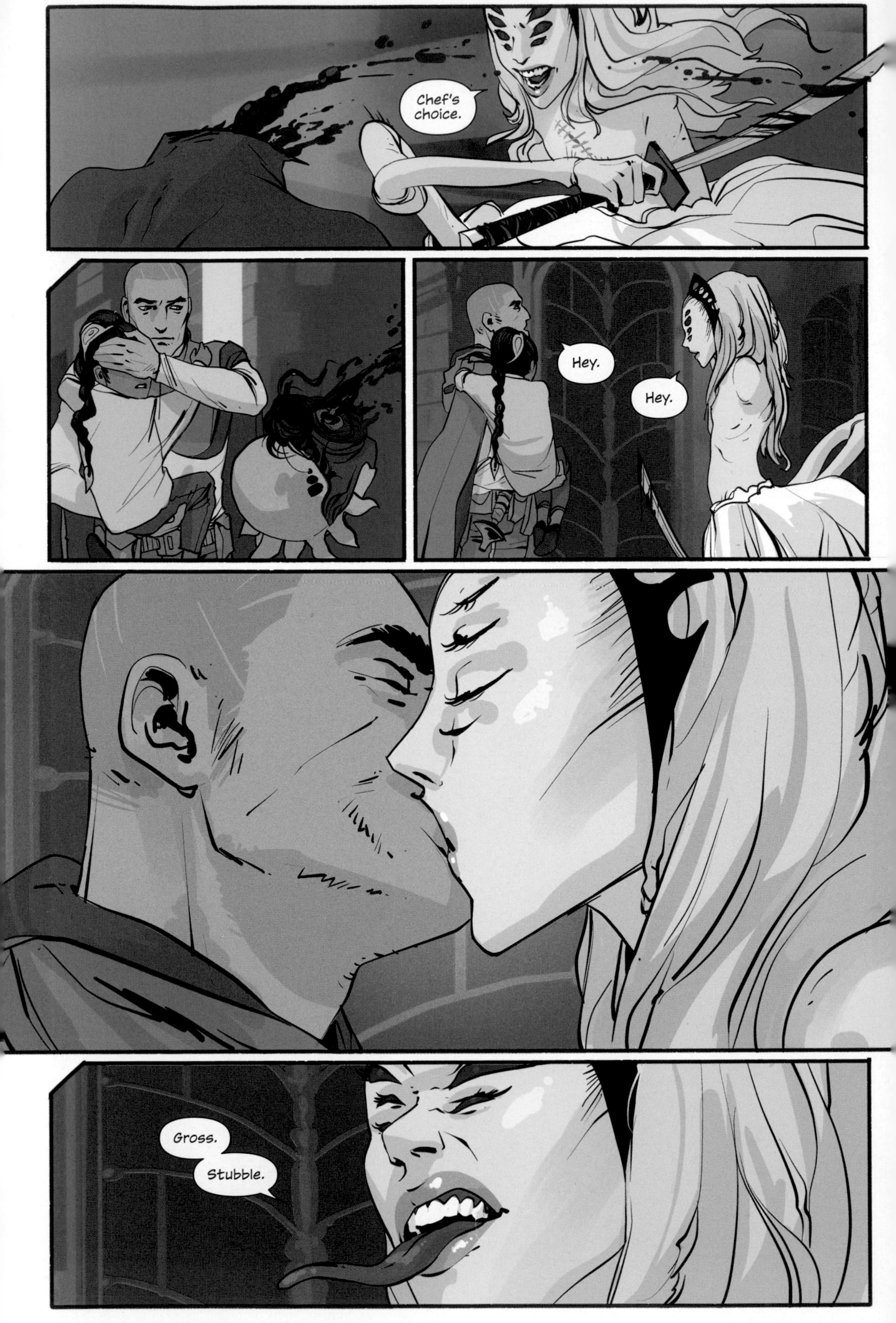
Chef's choice.
Hey.
Hey.
Gross.
Stubble.

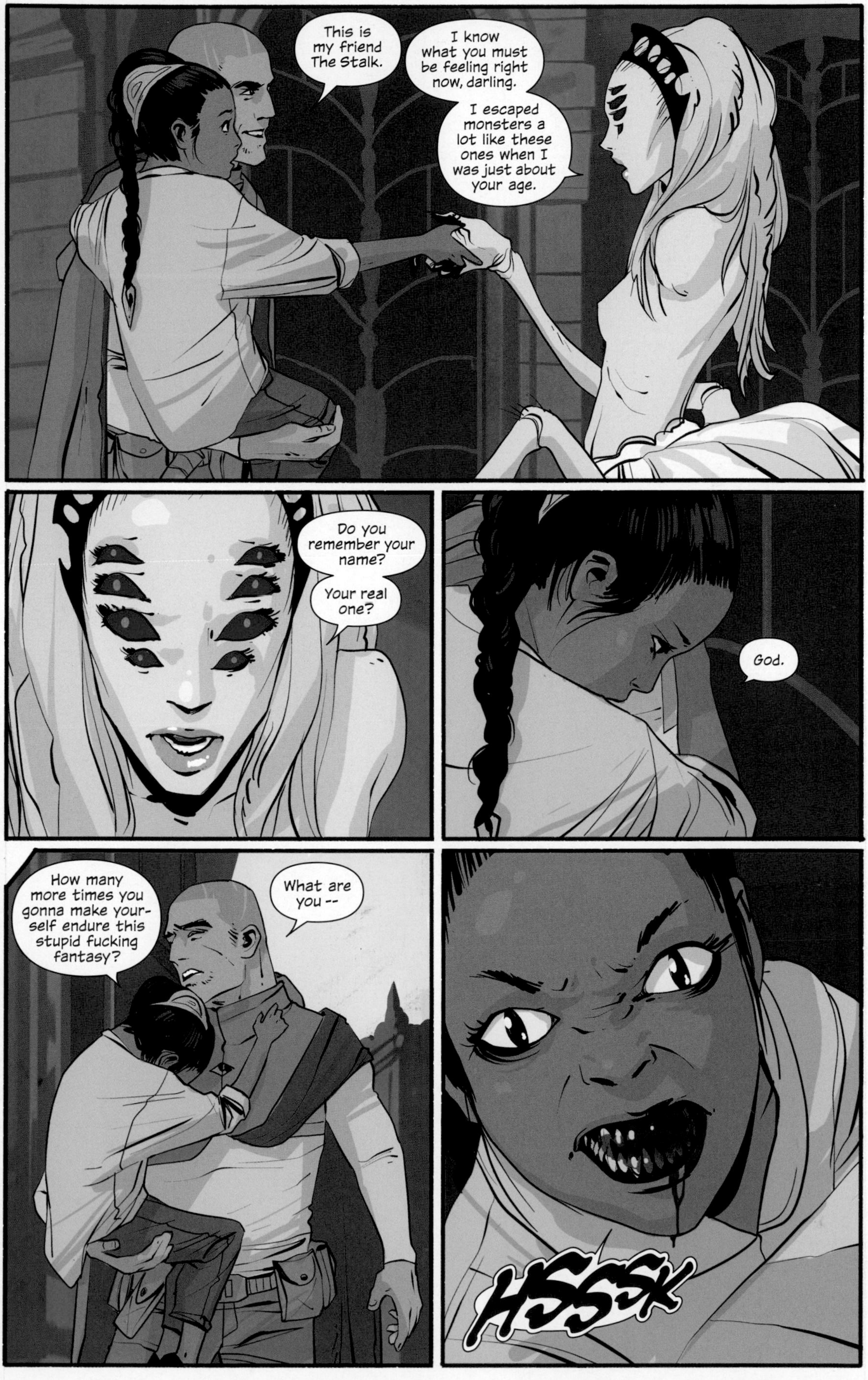
This is my friend The Stalk.
I know what you must be feeling right now, darling.
I escaped monsters a lot like these ones when I was just about your age.
Do you remember your name?
Your real one?
God.
How many more times you gonna make your-self endure this stupid fucking fantasy?
What are you --
HSSSK

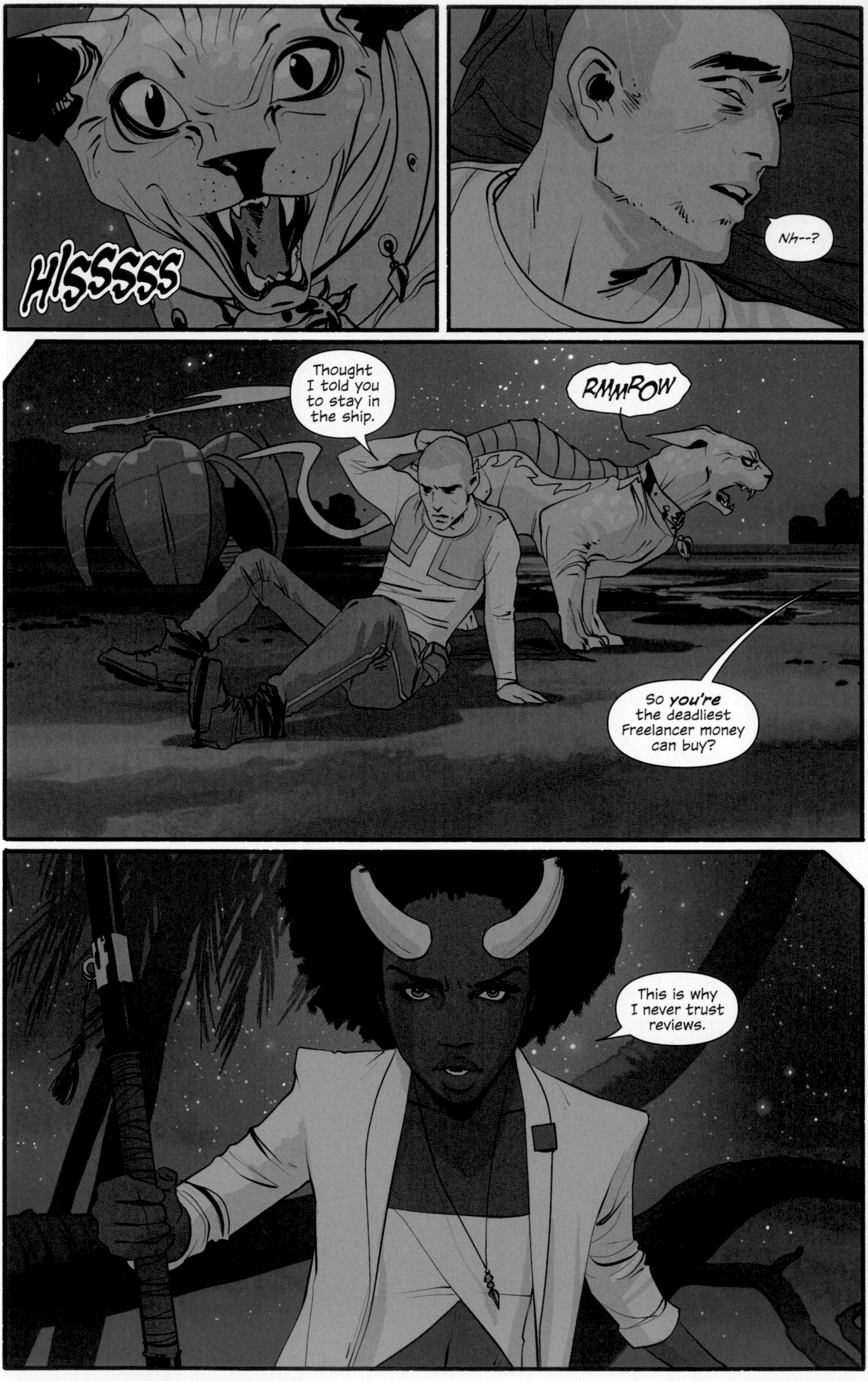
HISSSSS
Nh--?
Thought I told you to stay in the ship.
RMMROW
So *you're* the deadliest Freelancer money can buy?
This is why I never trust reviews.

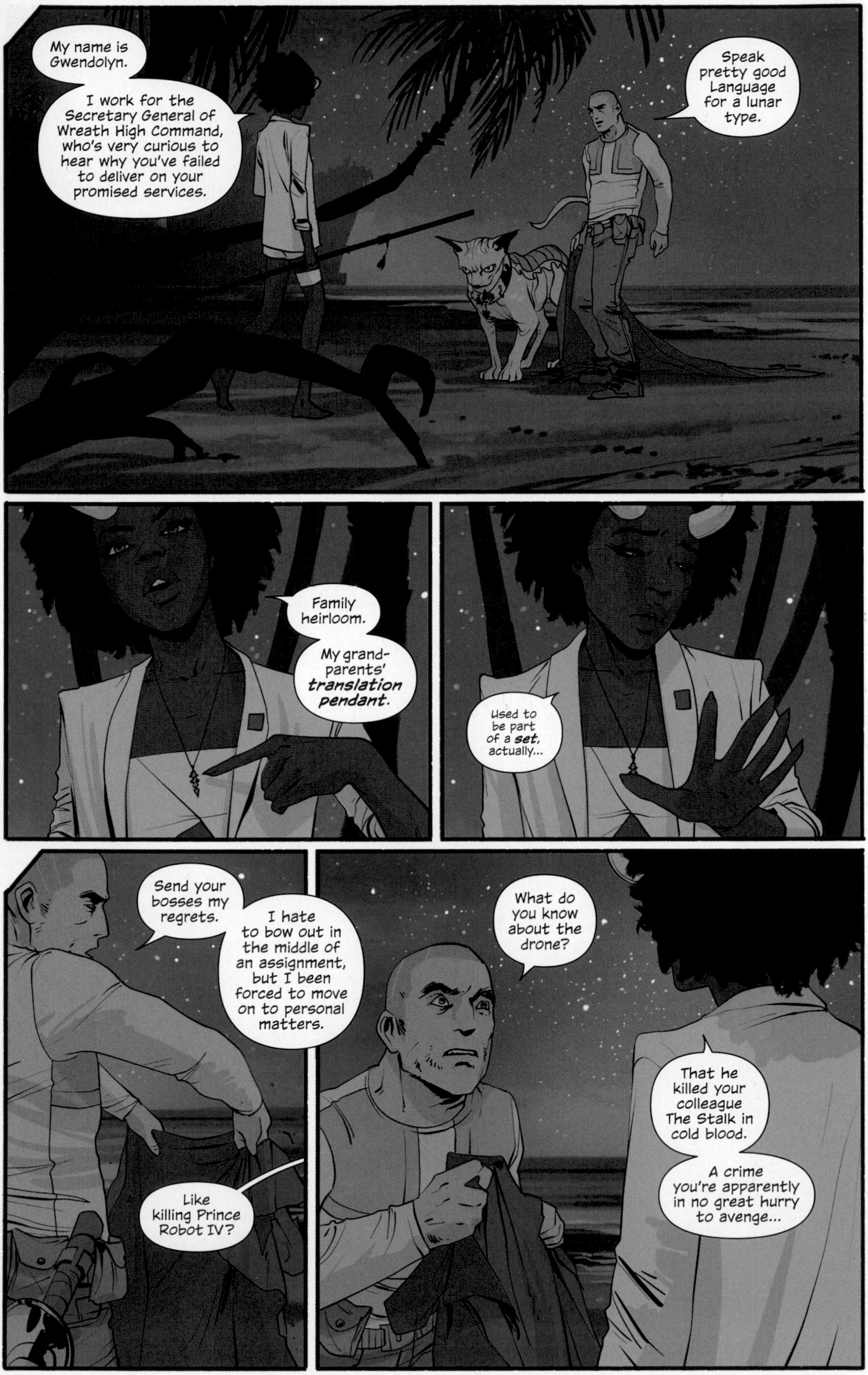

My name is Gwendolyn.
I work for the Secretary General of Wreath High Command, who's very curious to hear why you've failed to deliver on your promised services.
Speak pretty good Language for a lunar type.
Family heirloom.
My grand-parents' ***translation pendant***.
Used to be part of a ***set***, actually...
Send your bosses my regrets.
I hate to bow out in the middle of an assignment, but I been forced to move on to personal matters.
Like killing Prince Robot IV?
What do you know about the drone?
That he killed your colleague The Stalk in cold blood.
A crime you're apparently in no great hurry to avenge...

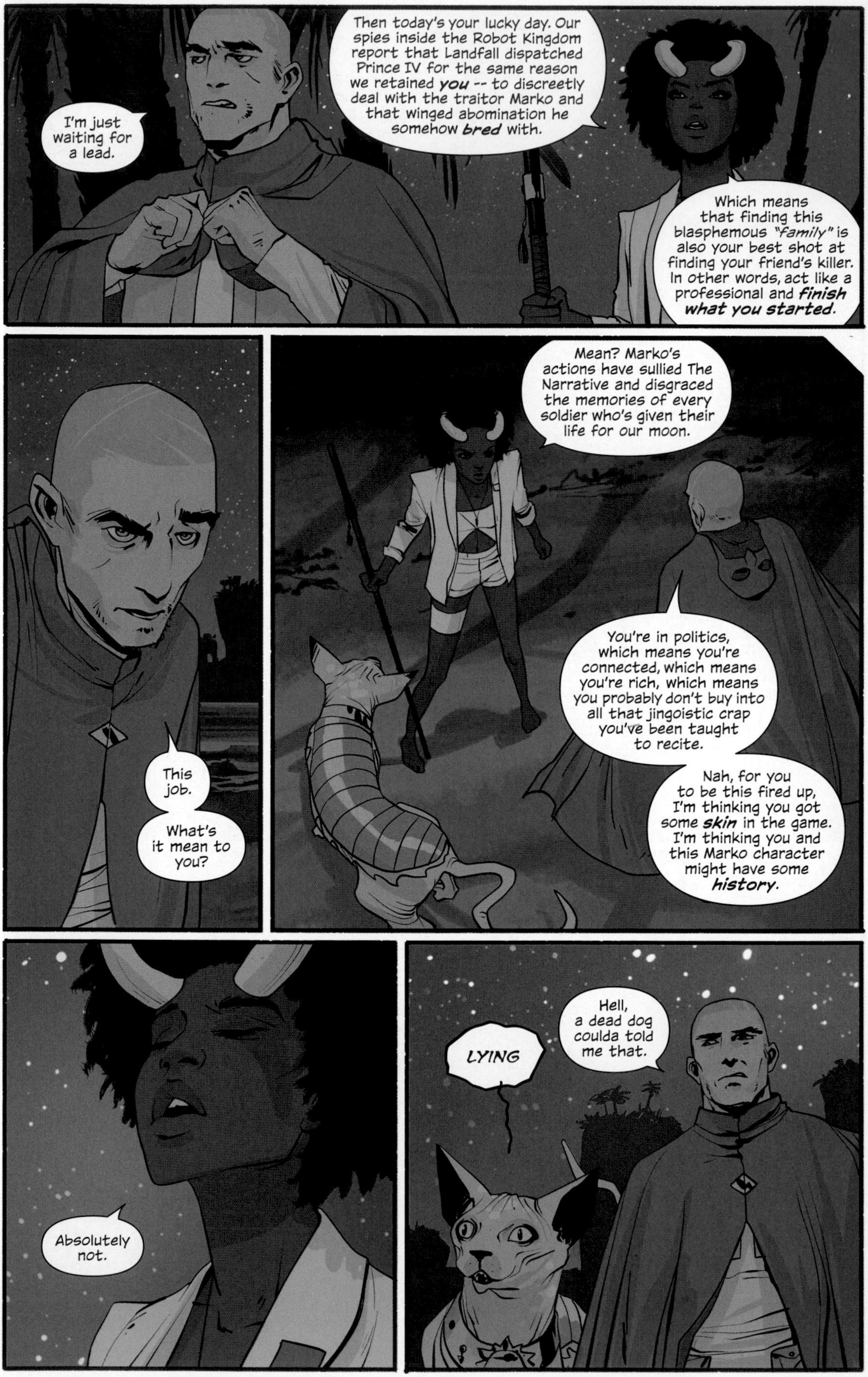
I'm just waiting for a lead.
Then today's your lucky day. Our spies inside the Robot Kingdom report that Landfall dispatched Prince IV for the same reason we retained *you* -- to discreetly deal with the traitor Marko and that winged abomination he somehow *bred* with.
Which means that finding this blasphemous *"family"* is also your best shot at finding your friend's killer. In other words, act like a professional and ***finish what you started***.
This job.
What's it mean to you?
Mean? Marko's actions have sullied The Narrative and disgraced the memories of every soldier who's given their life for our moon.
You're in politics, which means you're connected, which means you're rich, which means you probably don't buy into all that jingoistic crap you've been taught to recite.
Nah, for you to be this fired up, I'm thinking you got some ***skin*** in the game. I'm thinking you and this Marko character might have some ***history***.
Absolutely not.
LYING
Hell, a dead dog coulda told me that.

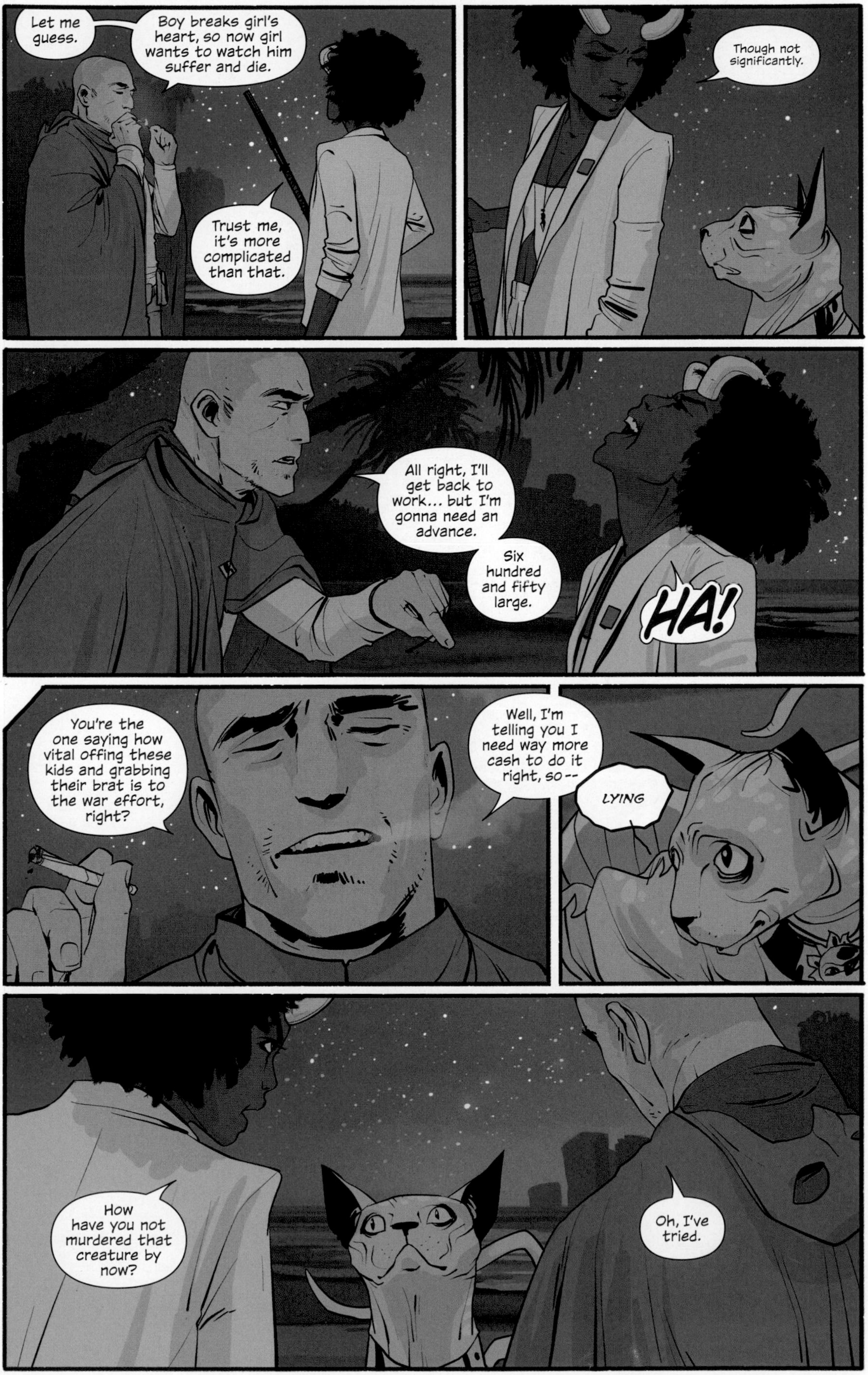

Let me guess.
Boy breaks girl's heart, so now girl wants to watch him suffer and die.
Trust me, it's more complicated than that.
Though not significantly.
All right, I'll get back to work... but I'm gonna need an advance.
Six hundred and fifty large.
HA!
You're the one saying how vital offing these kids and grabbing their brat is to the war effort, right?
Well, I'm telling you I need way more cash to do it right, so --
LYING
How have you not murdered that creature by now?
Oh, I've tried.

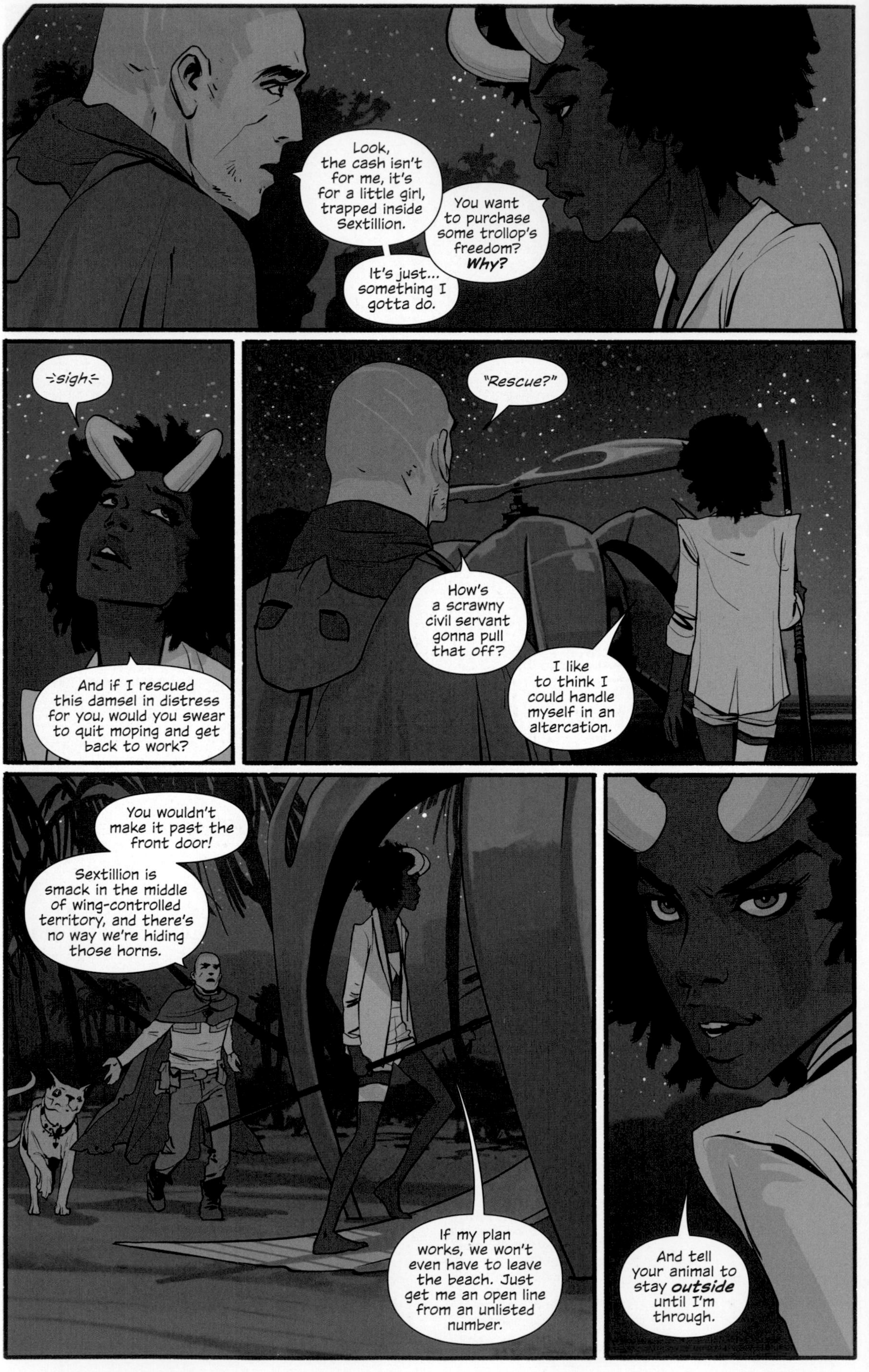
Look, the cash isn't for me, it's for a little girl, trapped inside Sextillion.
You want to purchase some trollop's freedom? **Why?**
It's just... something I gotta do.
-sigh-
And if I rescued this damsel in distress for you, would you swear to quit moping and get back to work?
"Rescue?"
How's a scrawny civil servant gonna pull that off?
I like to think I could handle myself in an altercation.
You wouldn't make it past the front door!
Sextillion is smack in the middle of wing-controlled territory, and there's no way we're hiding those horns.
If my plan works, we won't even have to leave the beach. Just get me an open line from an unlisted number.
And tell your animal to stay ***outside*** until I'm through.

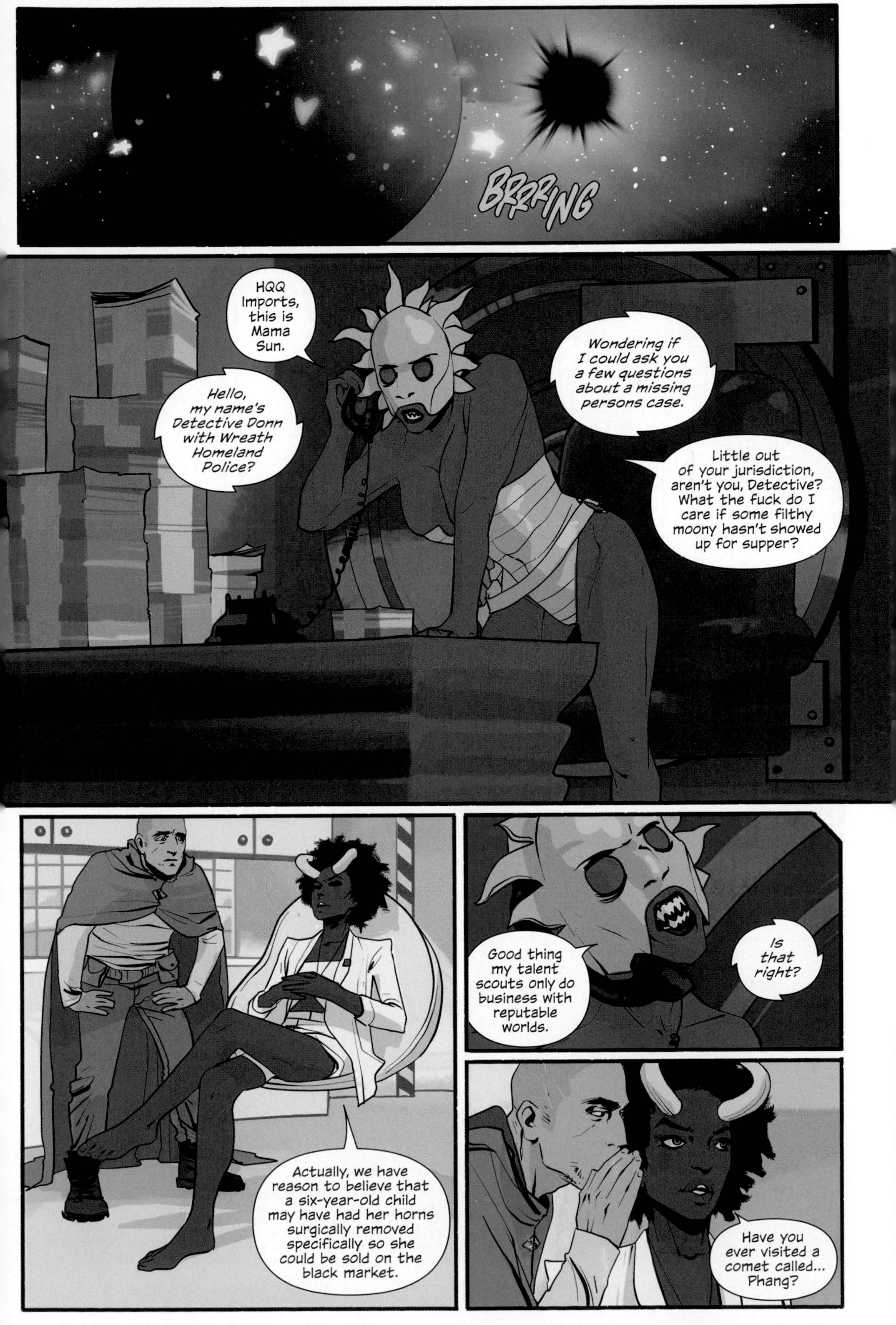
BRRRING
HQQ Imports, this is Mama Sun.
Hello, my name's Detective Donn with Wreath Homeland Police?
Wondering if I could ask you a few questions about a missing persons case.
Little out of your jurisdiction, aren't you, Detective? What the fuck do I care if some filthy moony hasn't showed up for supper?
Actually, we have reason to believe that a six-year-old child may have had her horns surgically removed specifically so she could be sold on the black market.
Good thing my talent scouts only do business with reputable worlds.
Is that right?
Have you ever visited a comet called... Phang?

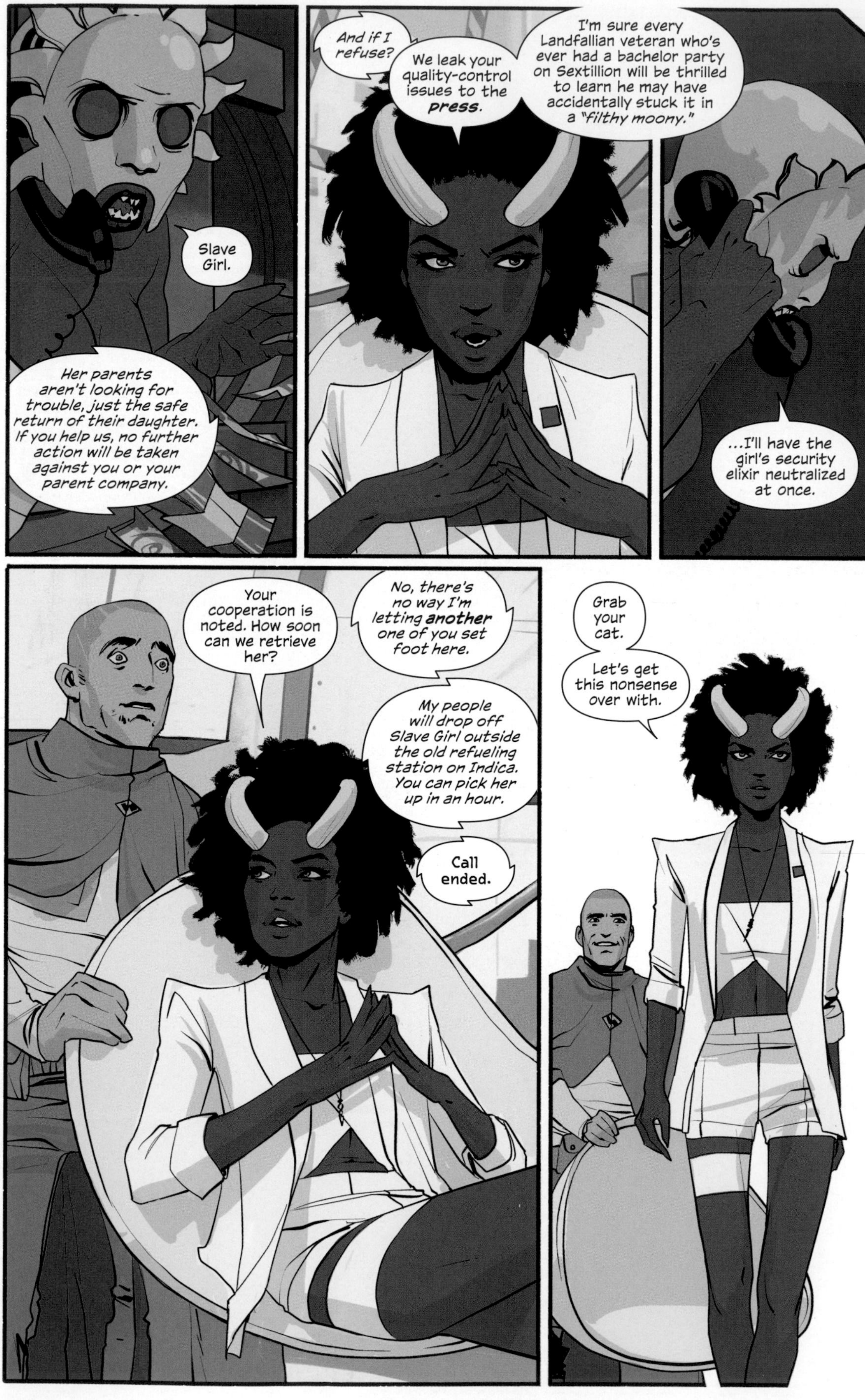
Slave Girl.
Her parents aren't looking for trouble, just the safe return of their daughter. If you help us, no further action will be taken against you or your parent company.
And if I refuse?
We leak your quality-control issues to the press.
I'm sure every Landfallian veteran who's ever had a bachelor party on Sextillion will be thrilled to learn he may have accidentally stuck it in a "filthy moony."
...I'll have the girl's security elixir neutralized at once.
Your cooperation is noted. How soon can we retrieve her?
No, there's no way I'm letting another one of you set foot here.
My people will drop off Slave Girl outside the old refueling station on Indica. You can pick her up in an hour.
Call ended.
Grab your cat.
Let's get this nonsense over with.

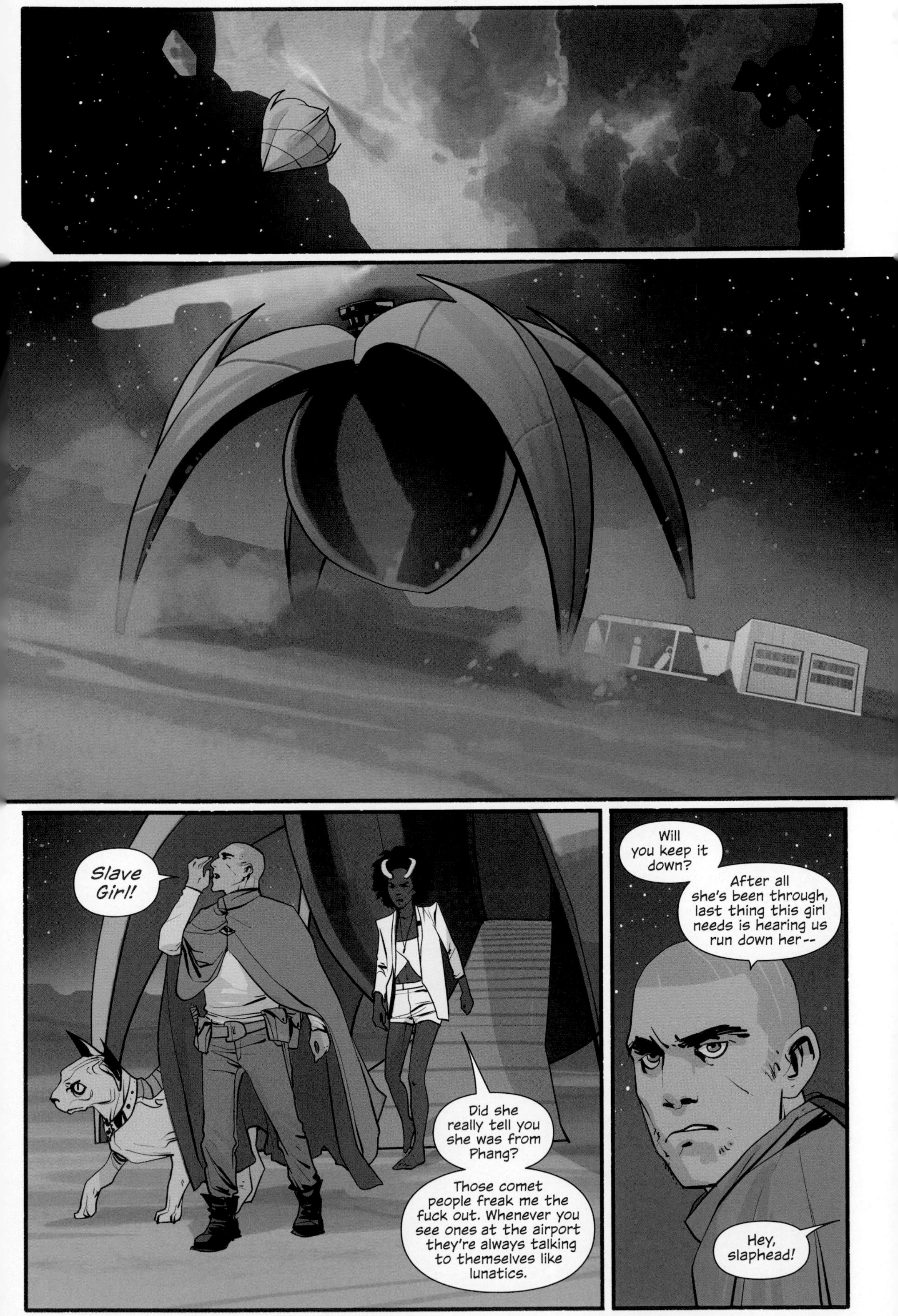
Slave Girl!
Did she really tell you she was from Phang?
Those comet people freak me the fuck out. Whenever you see ones at the airport they're always talking to themselves like lunatics.
Will you keep it down?
After all she's been through, last thing this girl needs is hearing us run down her--
Hey, slaphead!

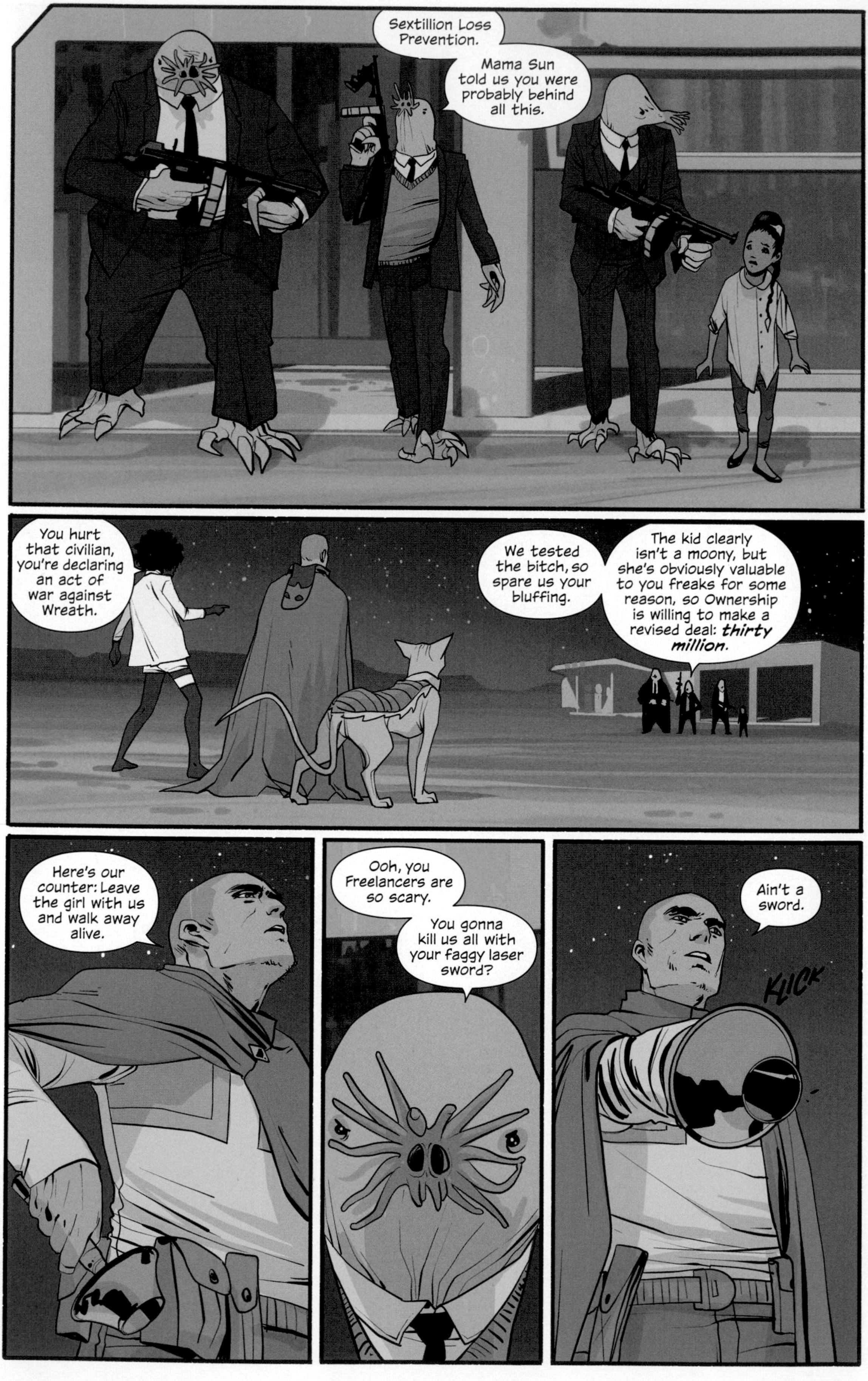
Sextillion Loss Prevention.
Mama Sun told us you were probably behind all this.
You hurt that civilian, you're declaring an act of war against Wreath.
We tested the bitch, so spare us your bluffing.
The kid clearly isn't a moony, but she's obviously valuable to you freaks for some reason, so Ownership is willing to make a revised deal: thirty million.
Here's our counter: Leave the girl with us and walk away alive.
Ooh, you Freelancers are so scary.
You gonna kill us all with your faggy laser sword?
Ain't a sword.
KLICK

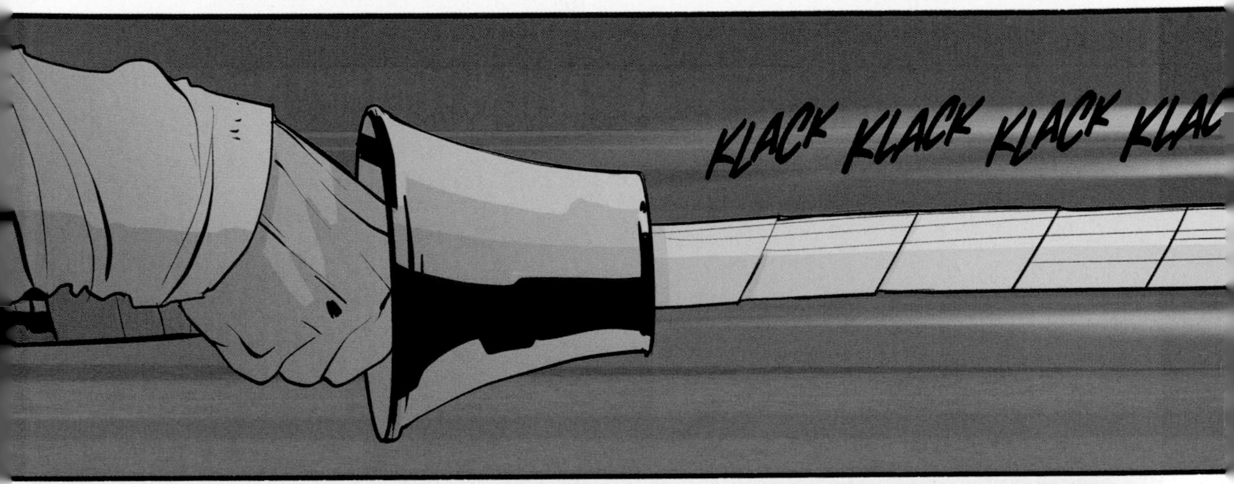
KLACK KLACK KLACK KLAC

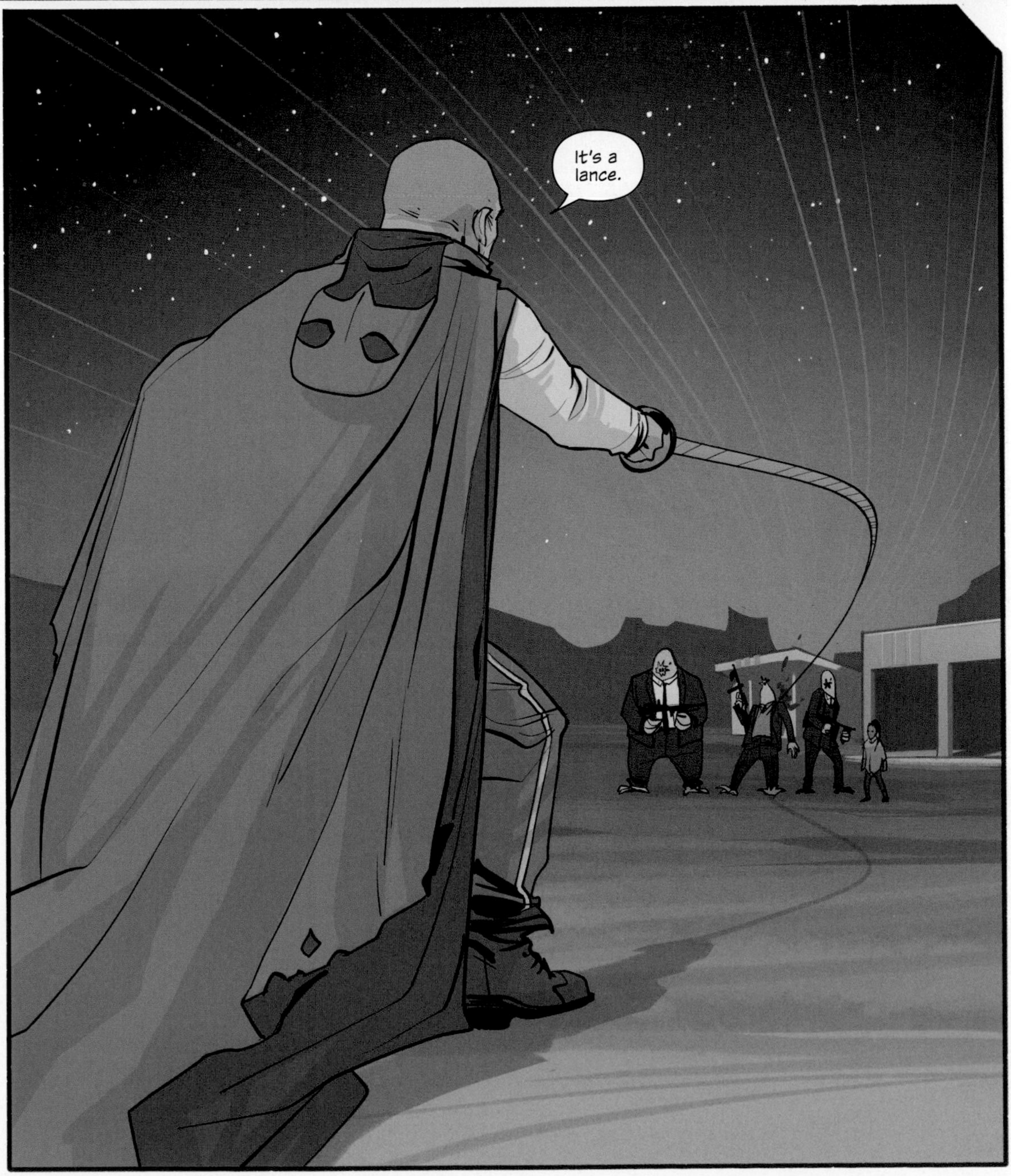
It's a lance.

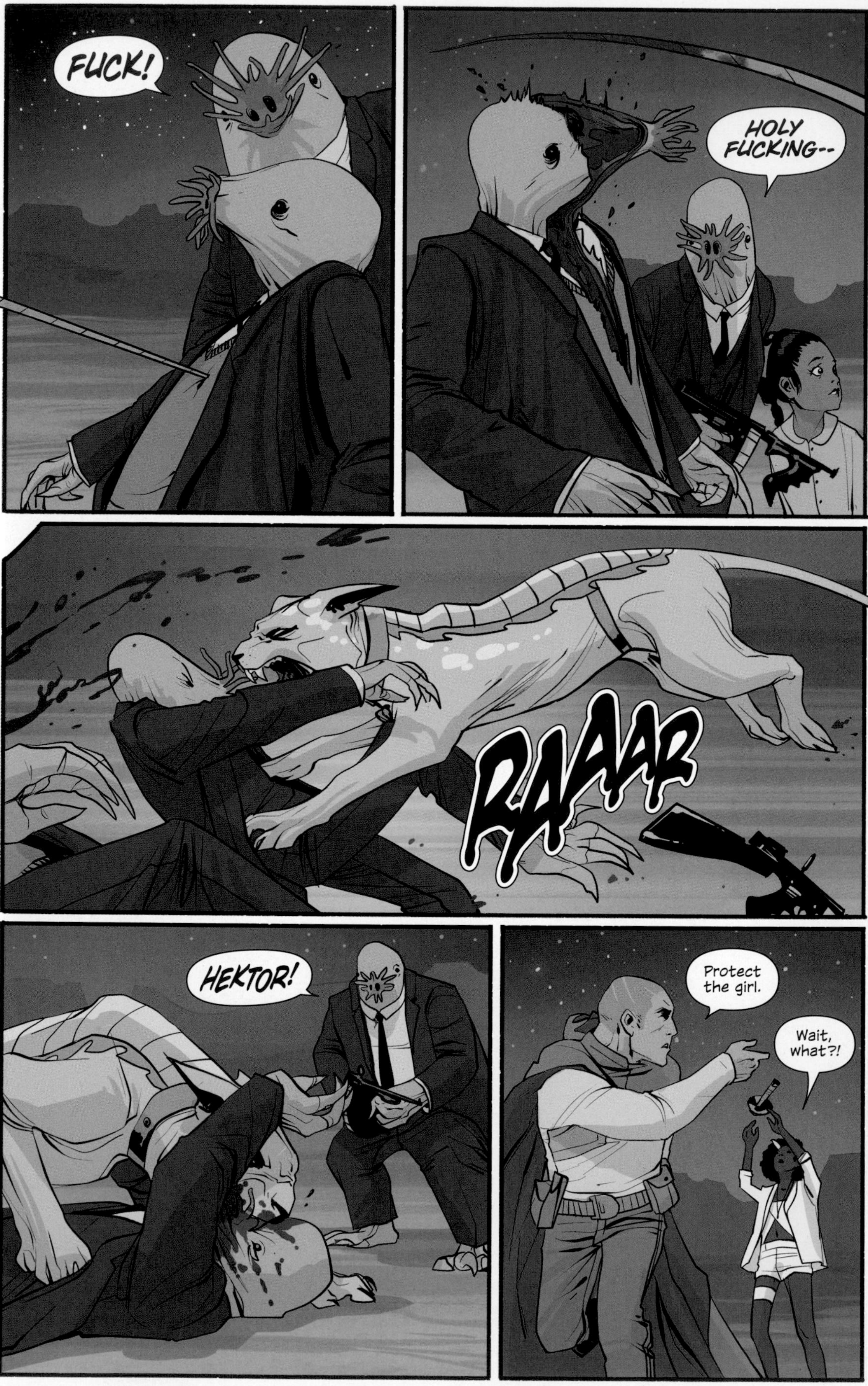
FUCK!
HOLY FUCKING--
RAAAR
HEKTOR!
Protect the girl.
Wait, what?!

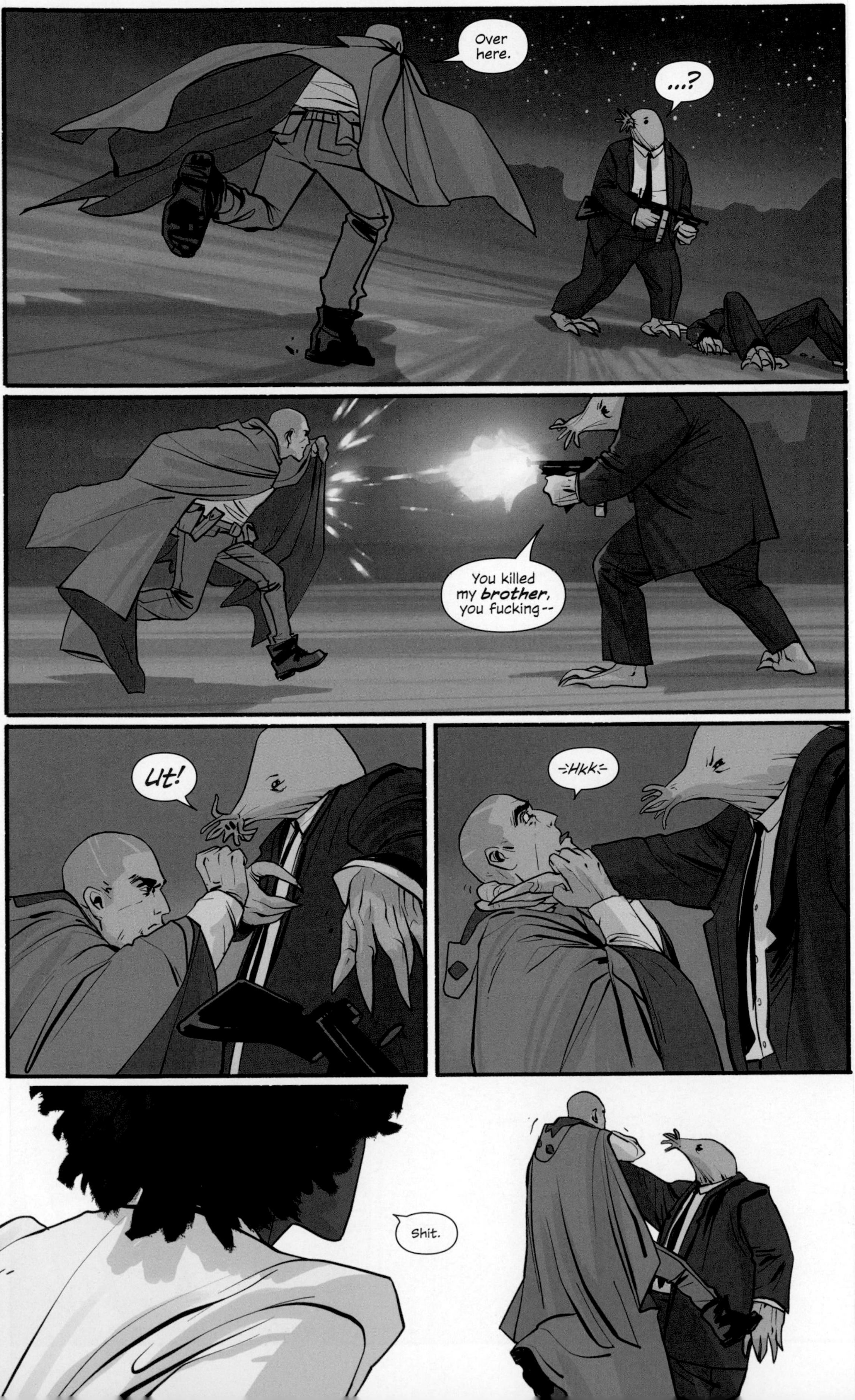
Over here.
...?
You killed my *brother*, you fucking--
Ut!
-HKK-
Shit.

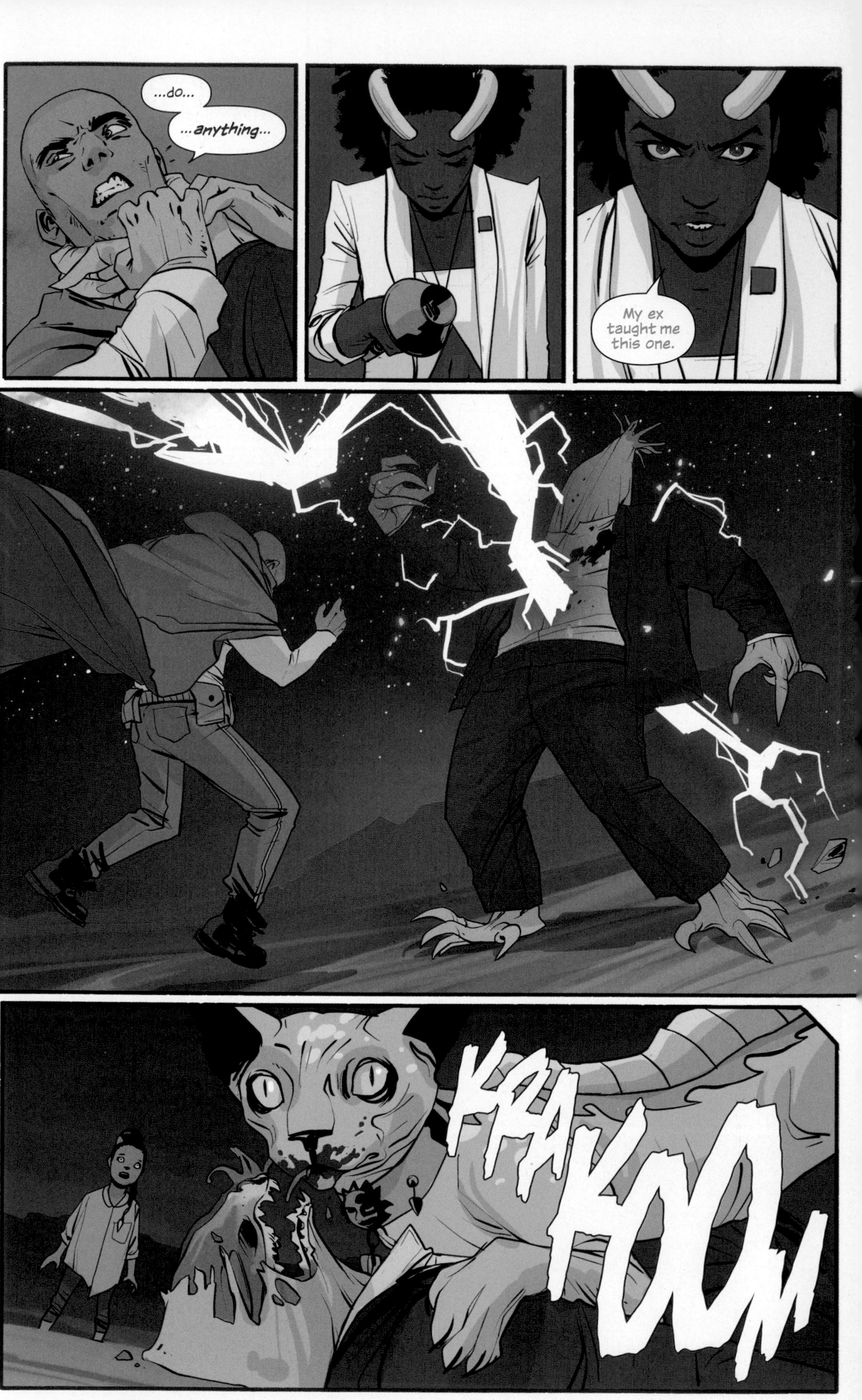
...do...
...anything...
My ex taught me this one.
KRAKOOM

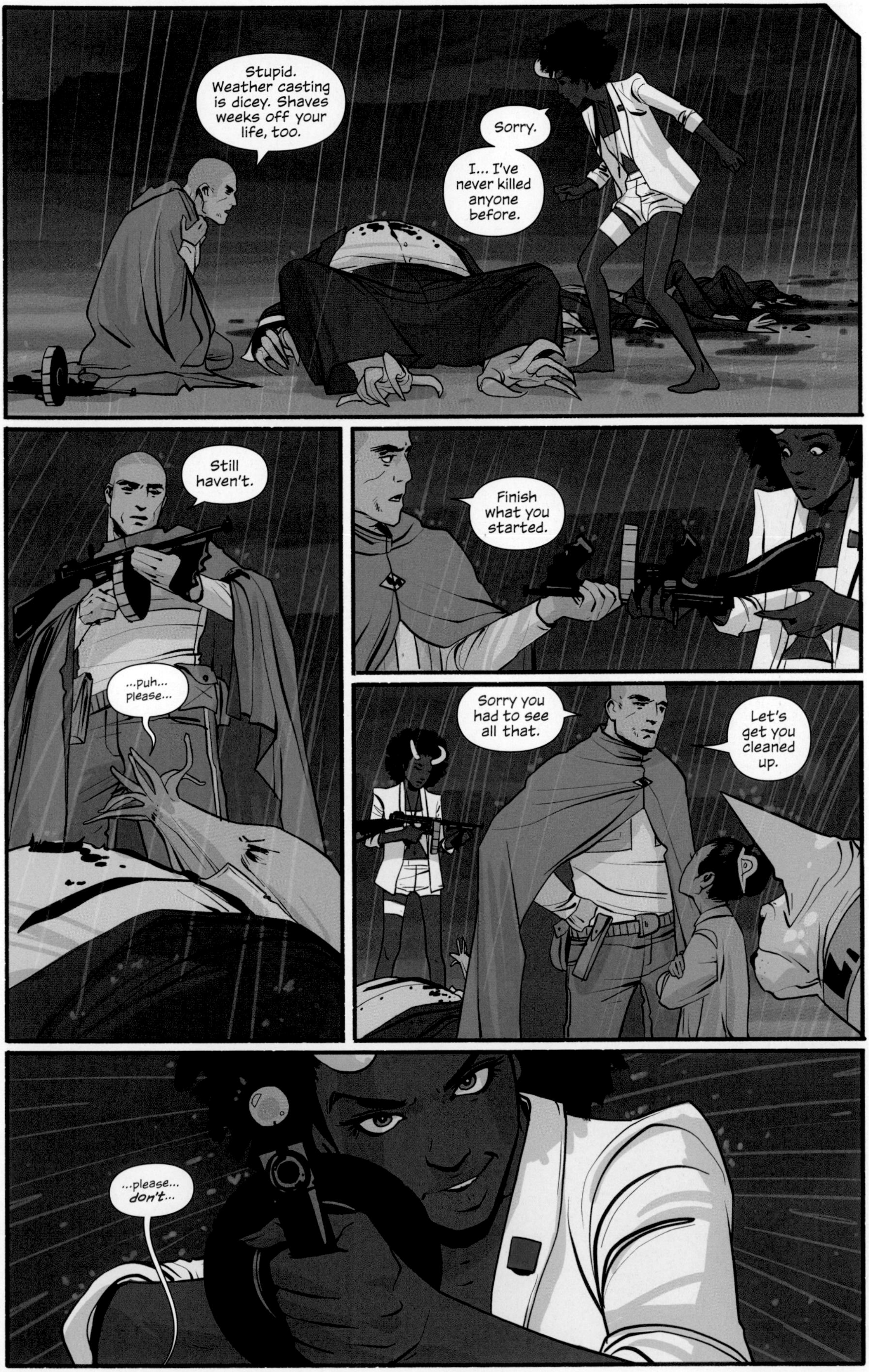
Stupid. Weather casting is dicey. Shaves weeks off your life, too.
Sorry.
I... I've never killed anyone before.
Still haven't.
...puh... please...
Finish what you started.
Sorry you had to see all that.
Let's get you cleaned up.
...please... *don't*...

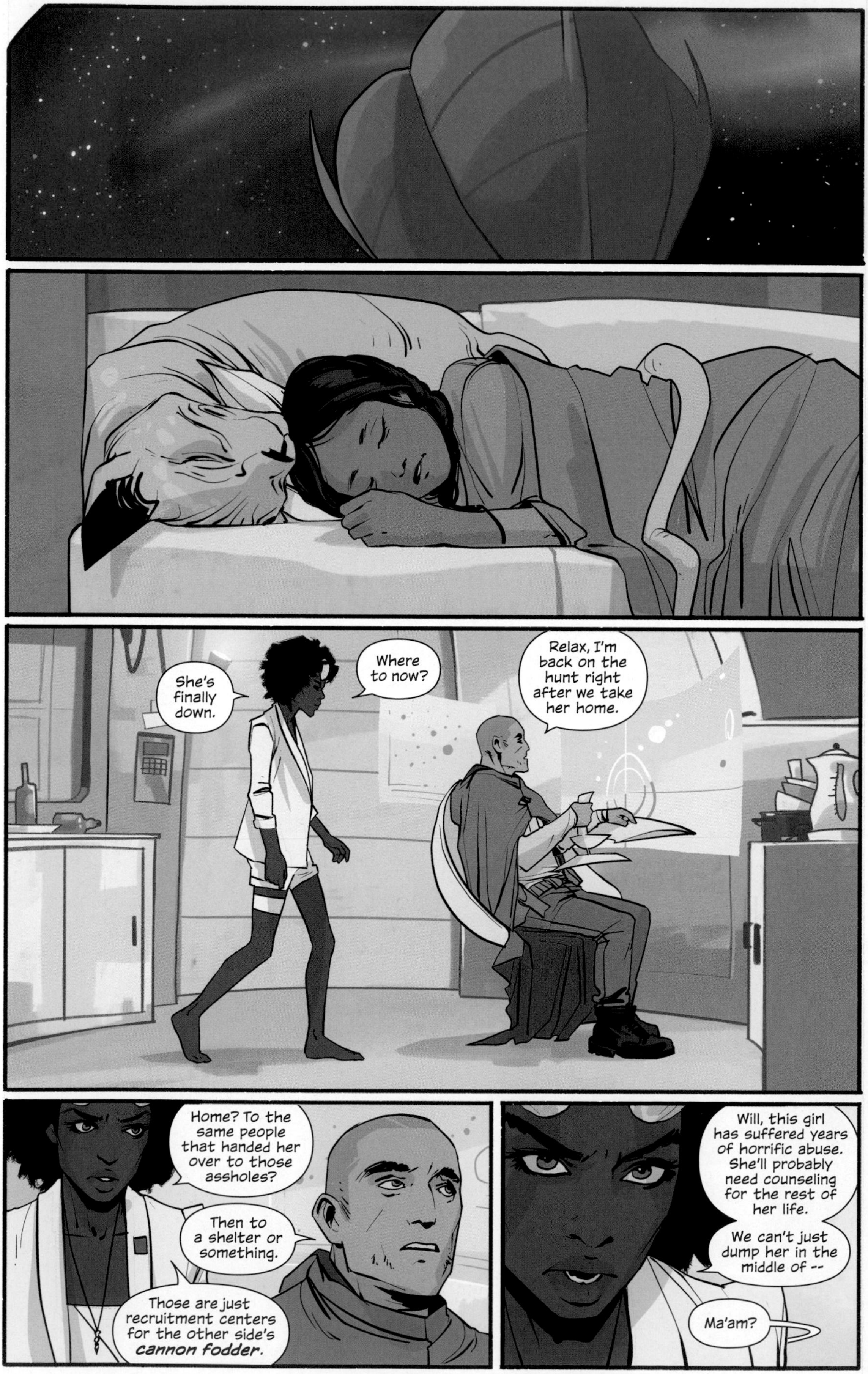

She's finally down.
Where to now?
Relax, I'm back on the hunt right after we take her home.
Home? To the same people that handed her over to those assholes?
Then to a shelter or something.
Those are just recruitment centers for the other side's ***cannon fodder***.
Will, this girl has suffered years of horrific abuse. She'll probably need counseling for the rest of her life.
We can't just dump her in the middle of --
Ma'am?

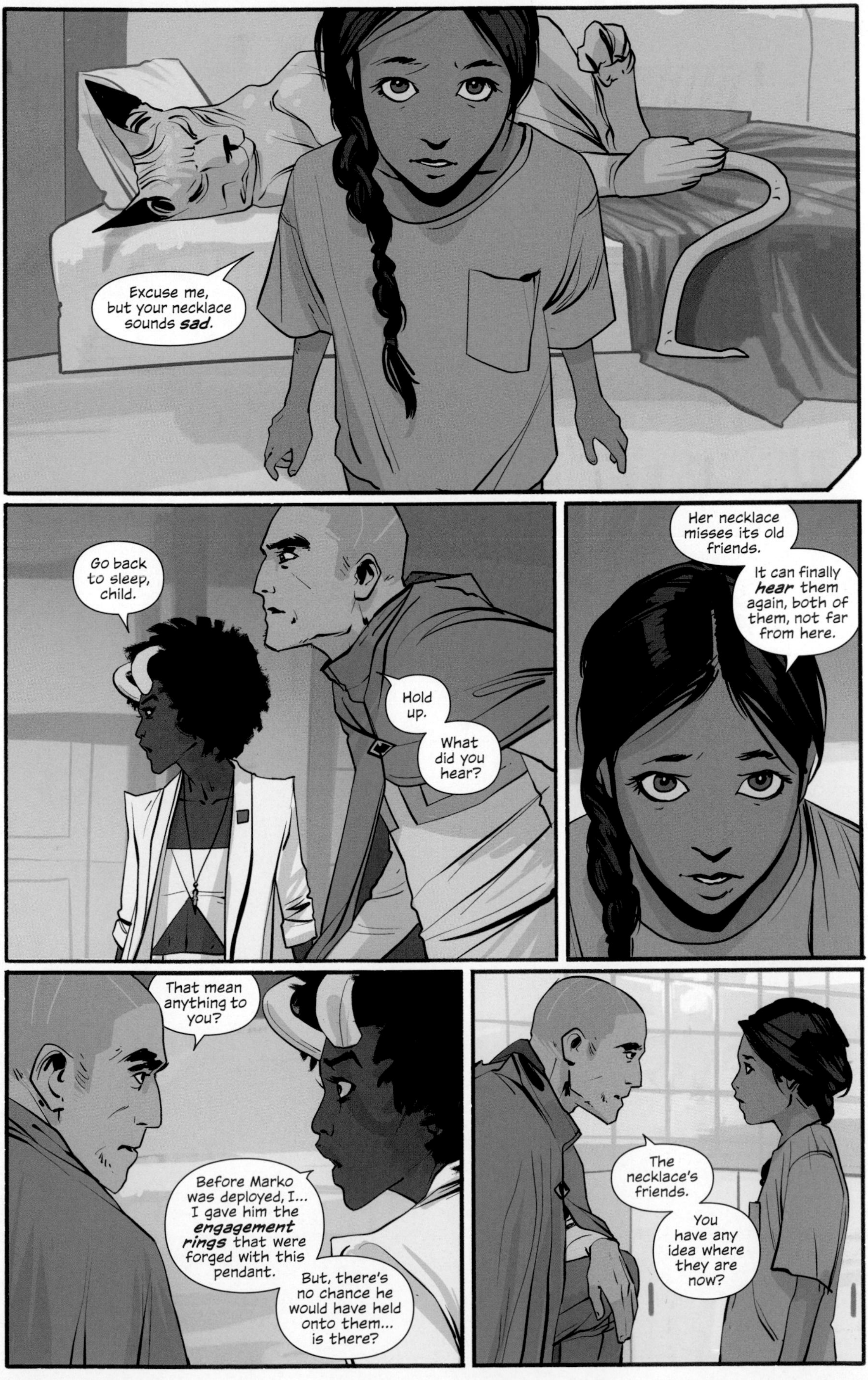

Excuse me, but your necklace sounds *sad*.
Go back to sleep, child.
Hold up.
What did you hear?
Her necklace misses its old friends.
It can finally *hear* them again, both of them, not far from here.
That mean anything to you?
Before Marko was deployed, I... I gave him the *engagement rings* that were forged with this pendant.
But, there's no chance he would have held onto them... is there?
The necklace's friends.
You have any idea where they are now?

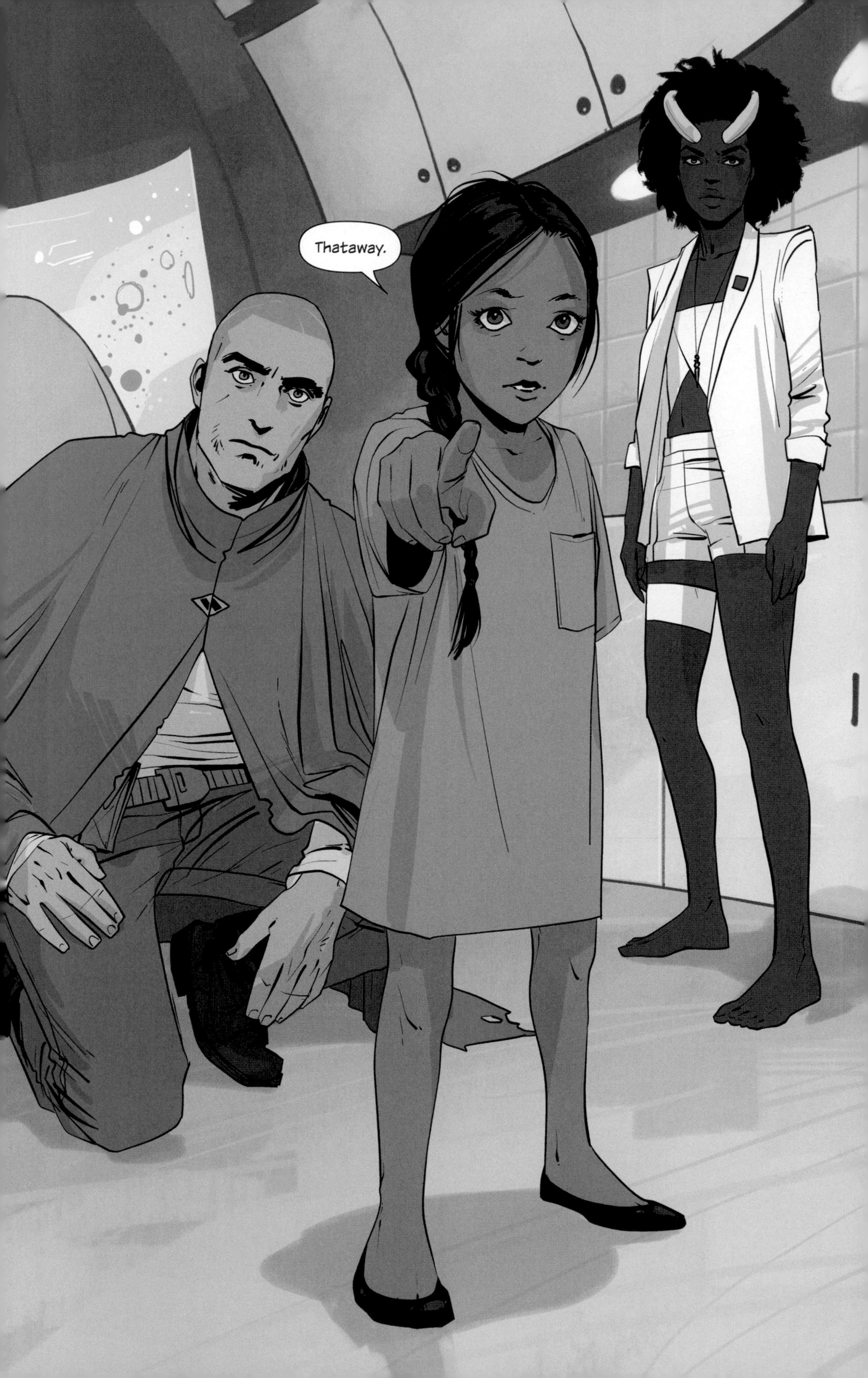
Thataway.

end chapter nine

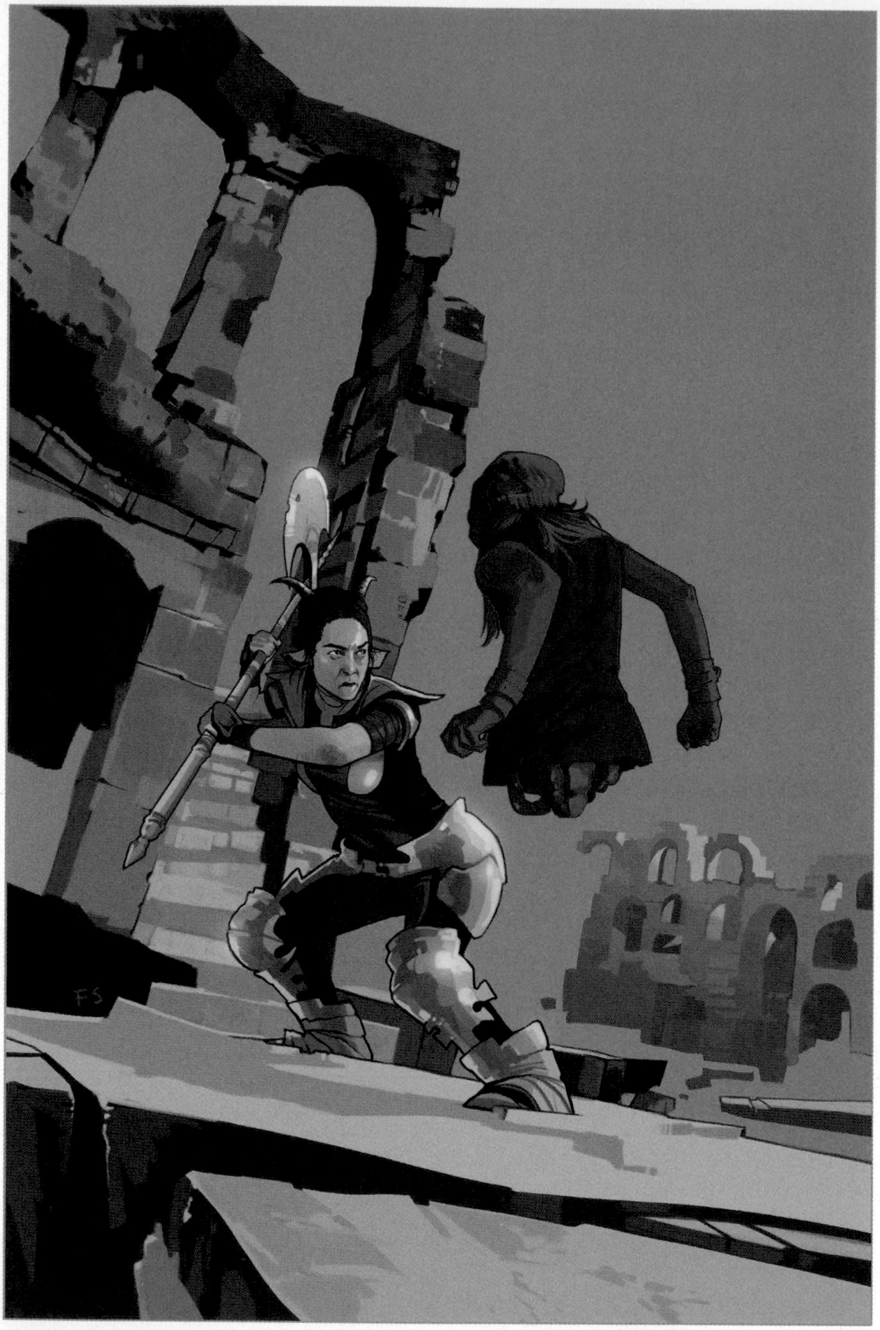
FS

CHAPTER TEN

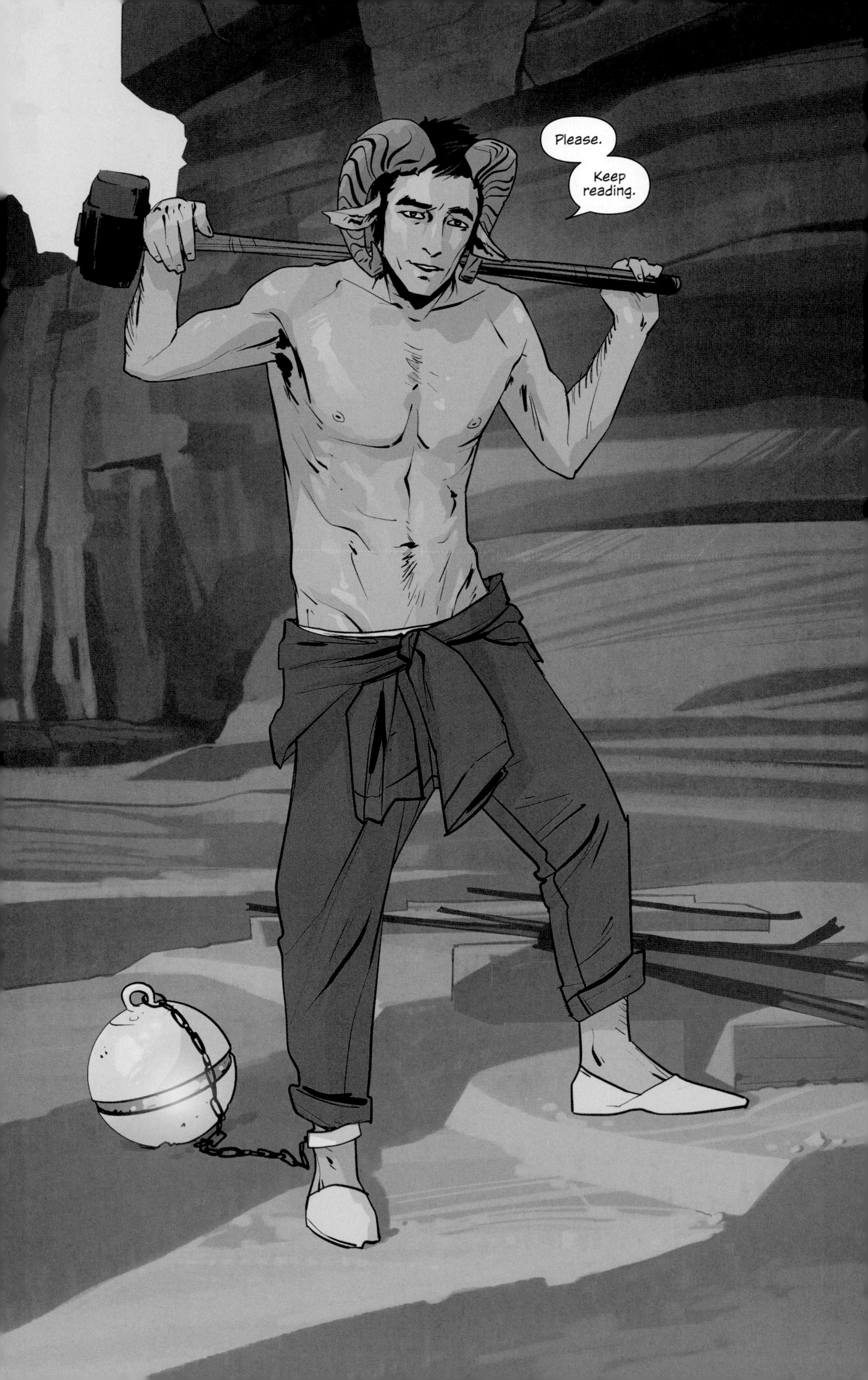
Please.
Keep reading.

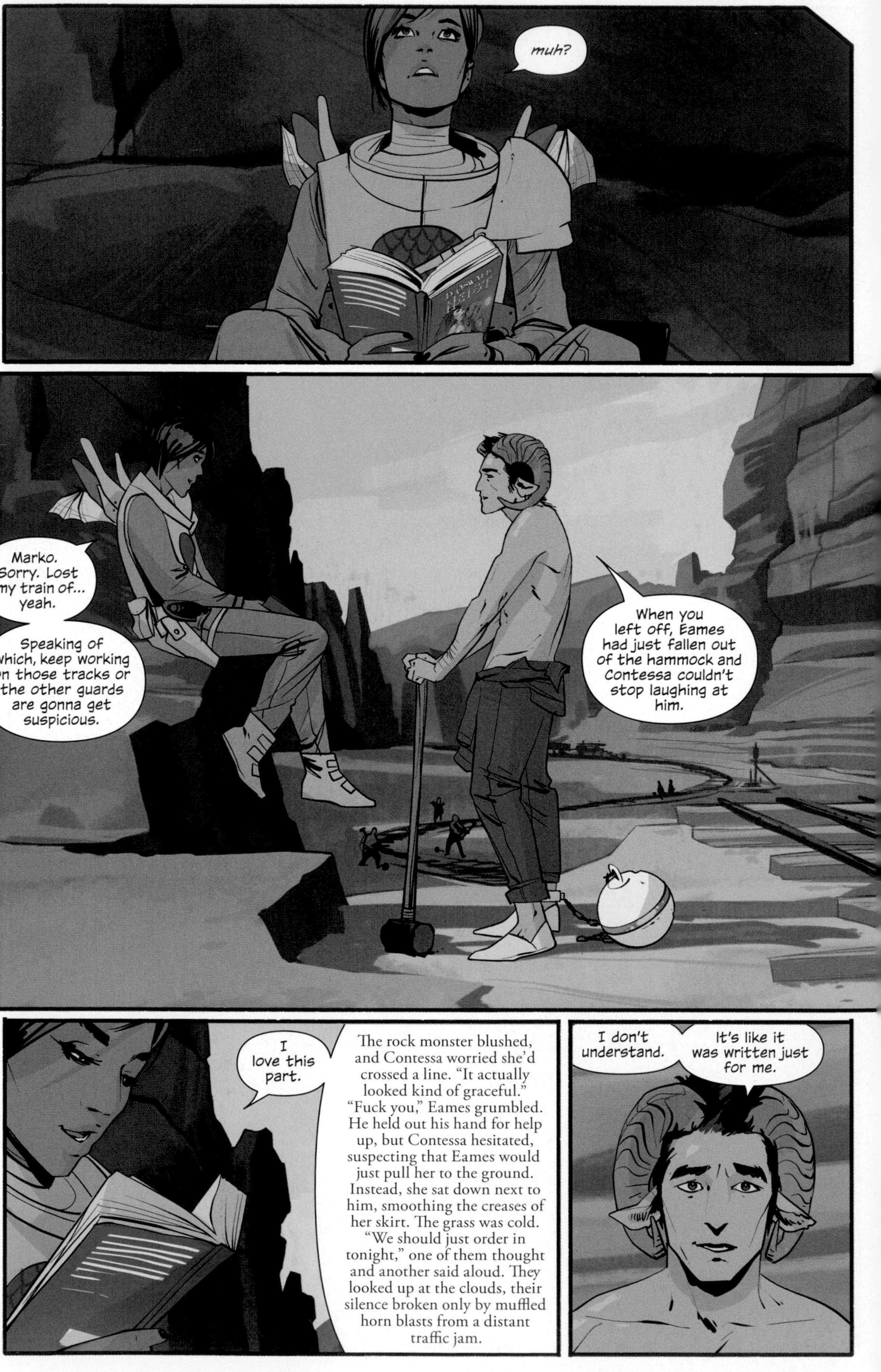
muh?
Marko. Sorry. Lost my train of... yeah.
Speaking of which, keep working on those tracks or the other guards are gonna get suspicious.
When you left off, Eames had just fallen out of the hammock and Contessa couldn't stop laughing at him.
I love this part.
The rock monster blushed, and Contessa worried she'd crossed a line. "It actually looked kind of graceful." "Fuck you," Eames grumbled. He held out his hand for help up, but Contessa hesitated, suspecting that Eames would just pull her to the ground. Instead, she sat down next to him, smoothing the creases of her skirt. The grass was cold. "We should just order in tonight," one of them thought and another said aloud. They looked up at the clouds, their silence broken only by muffled horn blasts from a distant traffic jam.
I don't understand.
It's like it was written just for me.

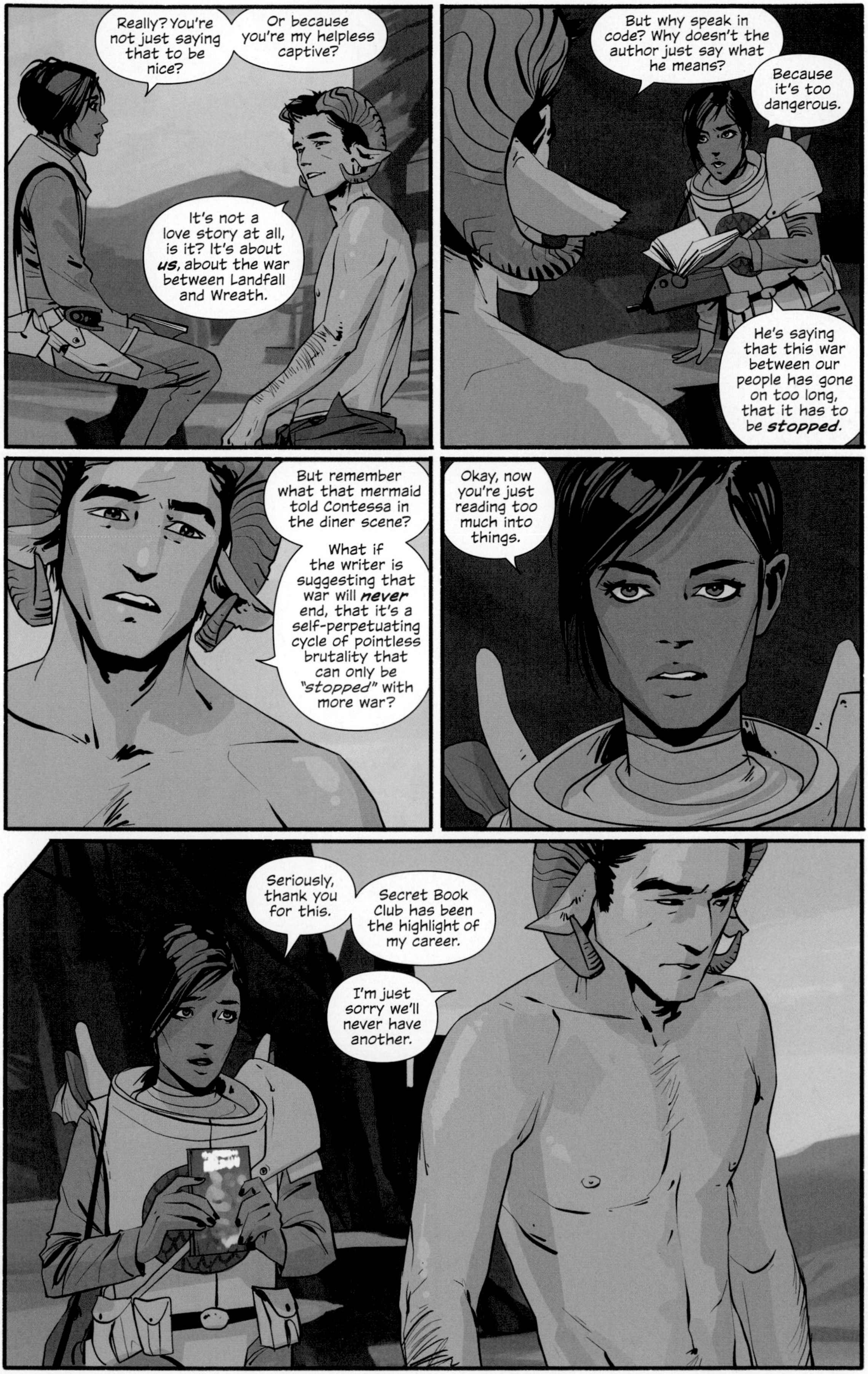
Really? You're not just saying that to be nice?
Or because you're my helpless captive?
It's not a love story at all, is it? It's about *us*, about the war between Landfall and Wreath.
But why speak in code? Why doesn't the author just say what he means?
Because it's too dangerous.
He's saying that this war between our people has gone on too long, that it has to be *stopped*.
But remember what that mermaid told Contessa in the diner scene?
What if the writer is suggesting that war will *never* end, that it's a self-perpetuating cycle of pointless brutality that can only be *"stopped"* with more war?
Okay, now you're just reading too much into things.
Seriously, thank you for this.
Secret Book Club has been the highlight of my career.
I'm just sorry we'll never have another.

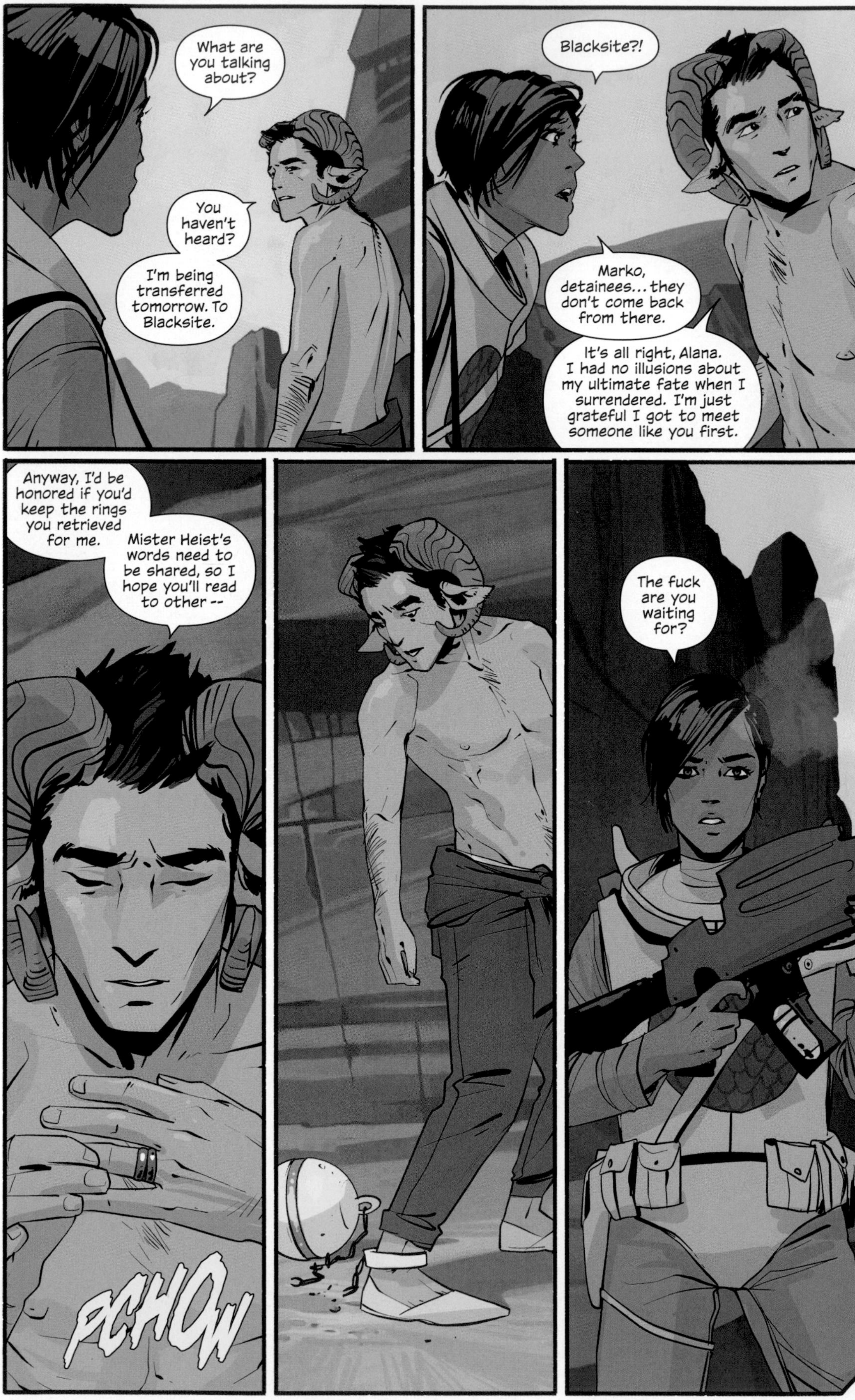
What are you talking about?
You haven't heard?
I'm being transferred tomorrow. To Blacksite.
Blacksite?!
Marko, detainees... they don't come back from there.
It's all right, Alana. I had no illusions about my ultimate fate when I surrendered. I'm just grateful I got to meet someone like you first.
Anyway, I'd be honored if you'd keep the rings you retrieved for me.
Mister Heist's words need to be shared, so I hope you'll read to other --
PCHOW
The fuck are you waiting for?

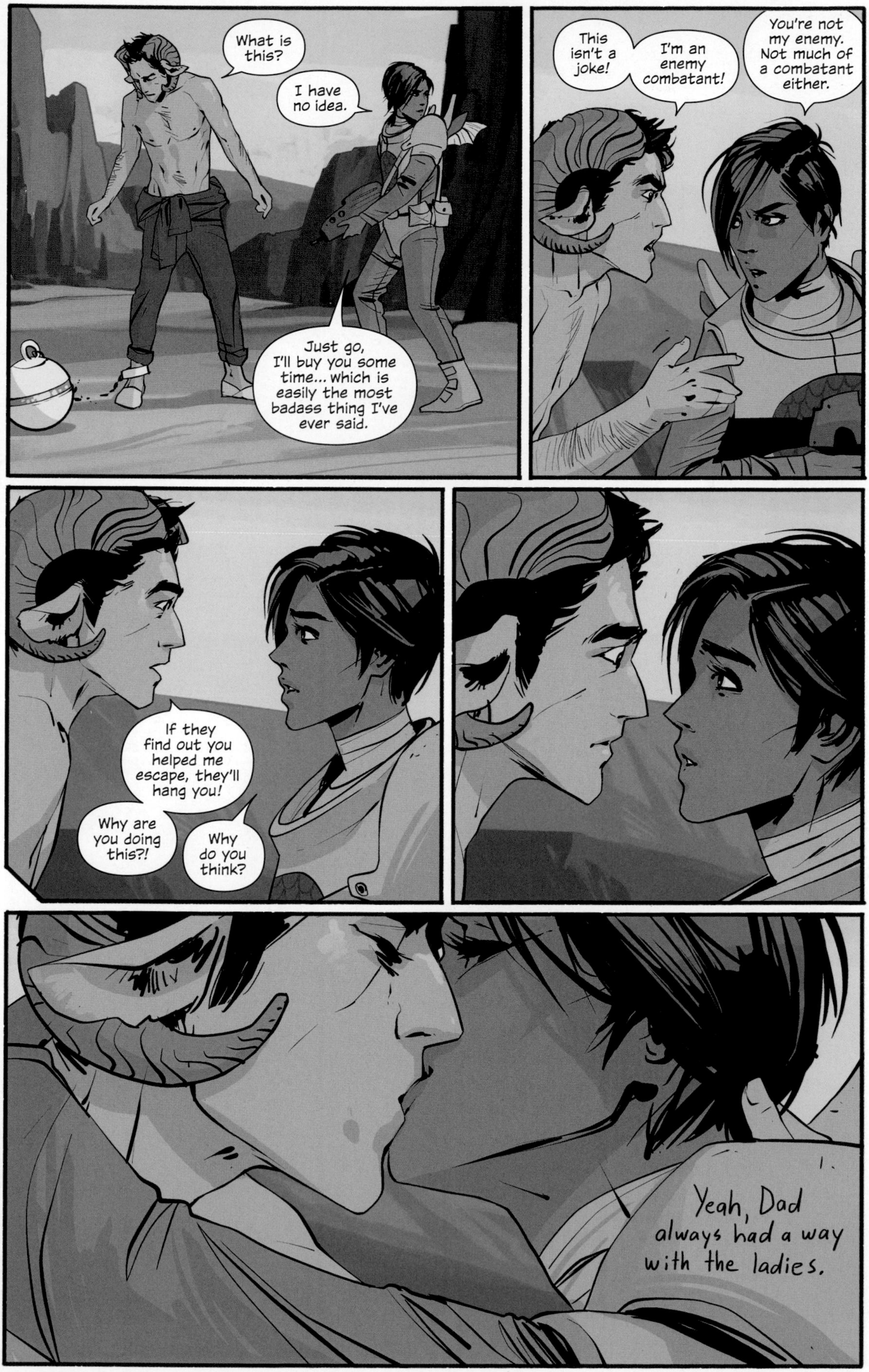
What is this?
I have no idea.
Just go, I'll buy you some time... which is easily the most badass thing I've ever said.
This isn't a joke!
I'm an enemy combatant!
You're not my enemy. Not much of a combatant either.
If they find out you helped me escape, they'll hang you!
Why are you doing this?!
Why do you think?
Yeah, Dad always had a way with the ladies.

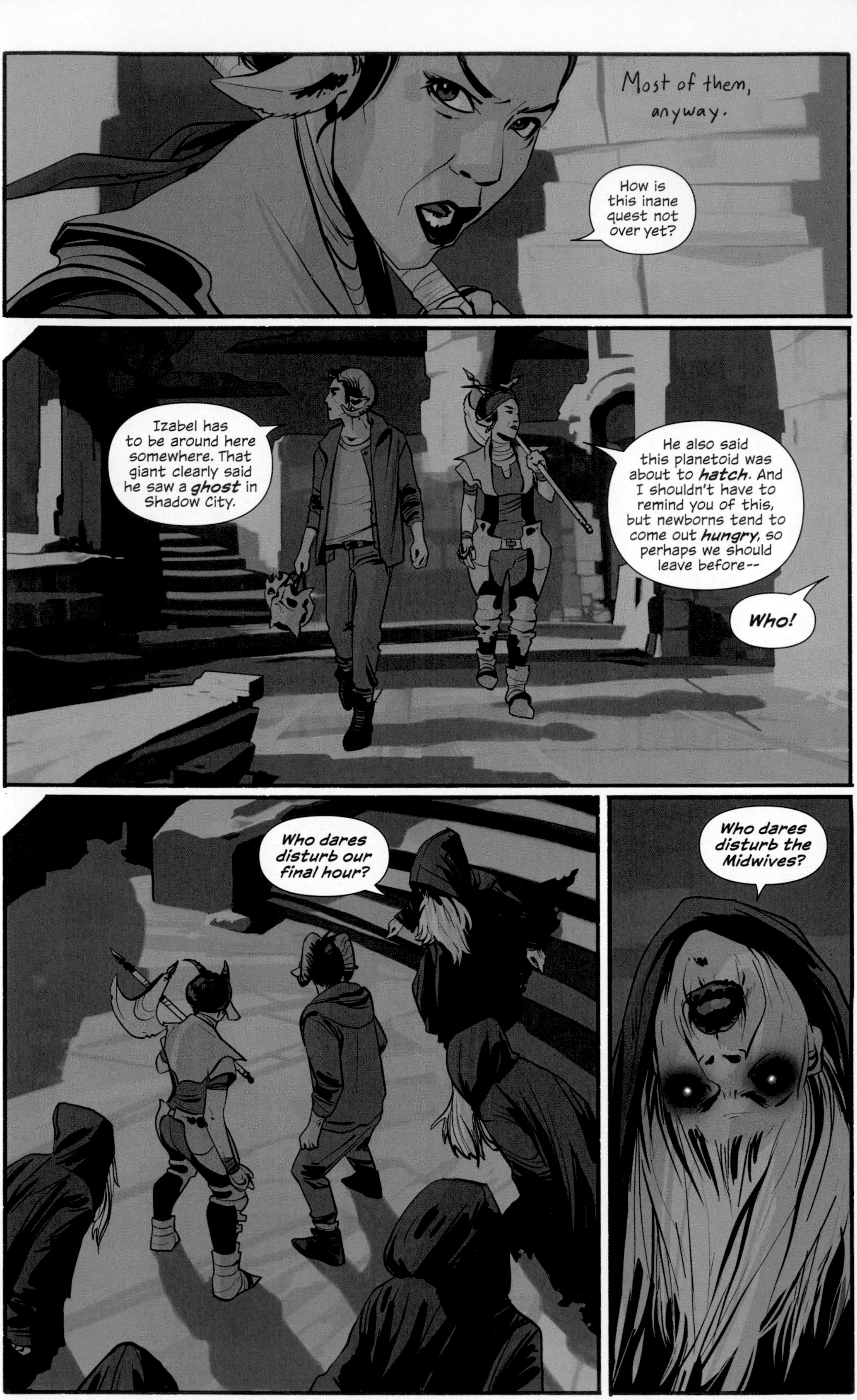
Most of them, anyway.
How is this inane quest not over yet?
Izabel has to be around here somewhere. That giant clearly said he saw a *ghost* in Shadow City.
He also said this planetoid was about to *hatch*. And I shouldn't have to remind you of this, but newborns tend to come out *hungry*, so perhaps we should leave before--
Who!
Who dares disturb our final hour?
Who dares disturb the Midwives?

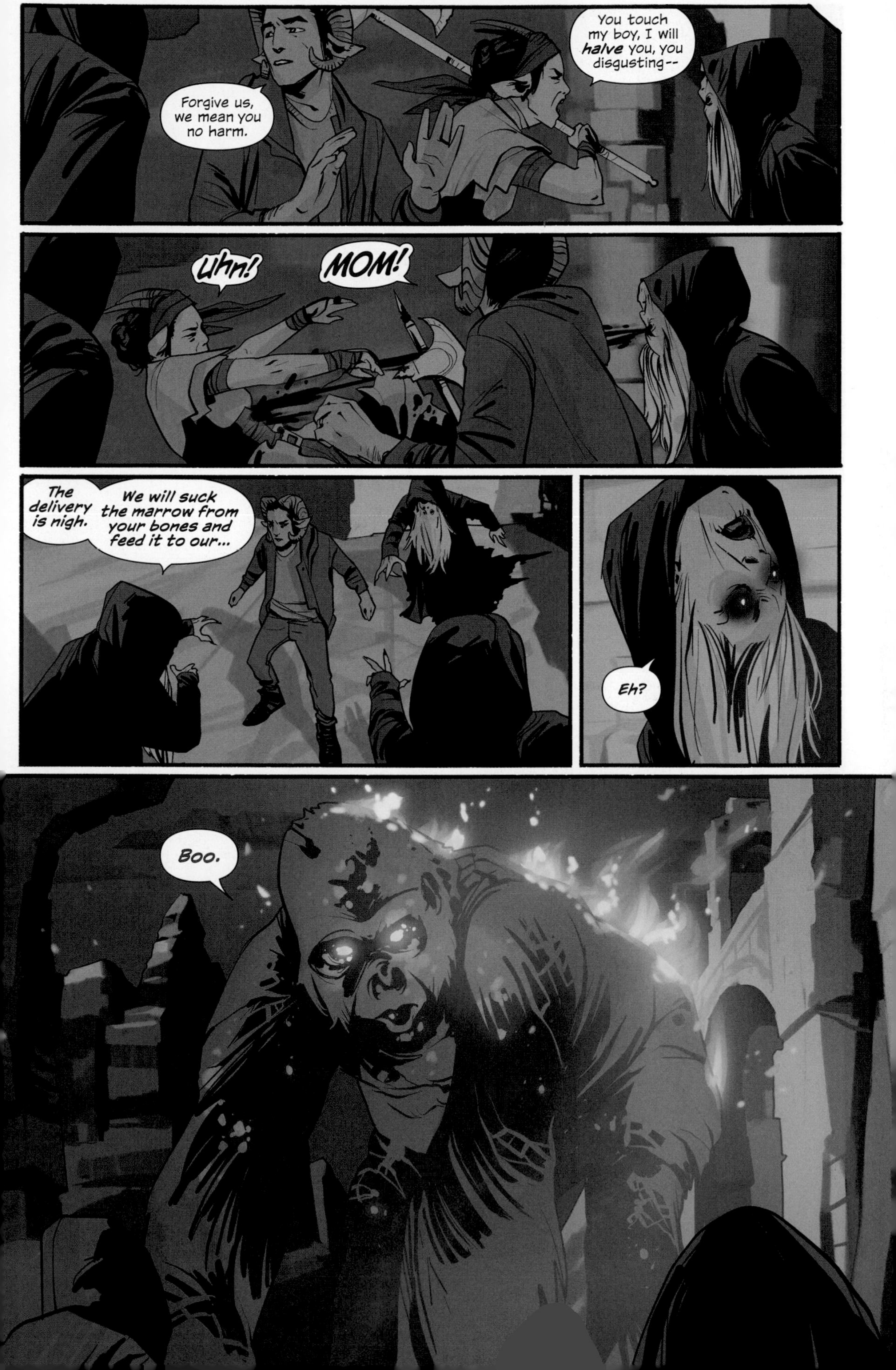
Forgive us, we mean you no harm.
You touch my boy, I will *halve* you, you disgusting--
Uhn!
MOM!
The delivery is nigh.
We will suck the marrow from your bones and feed it to our...
Eh?
Boo.

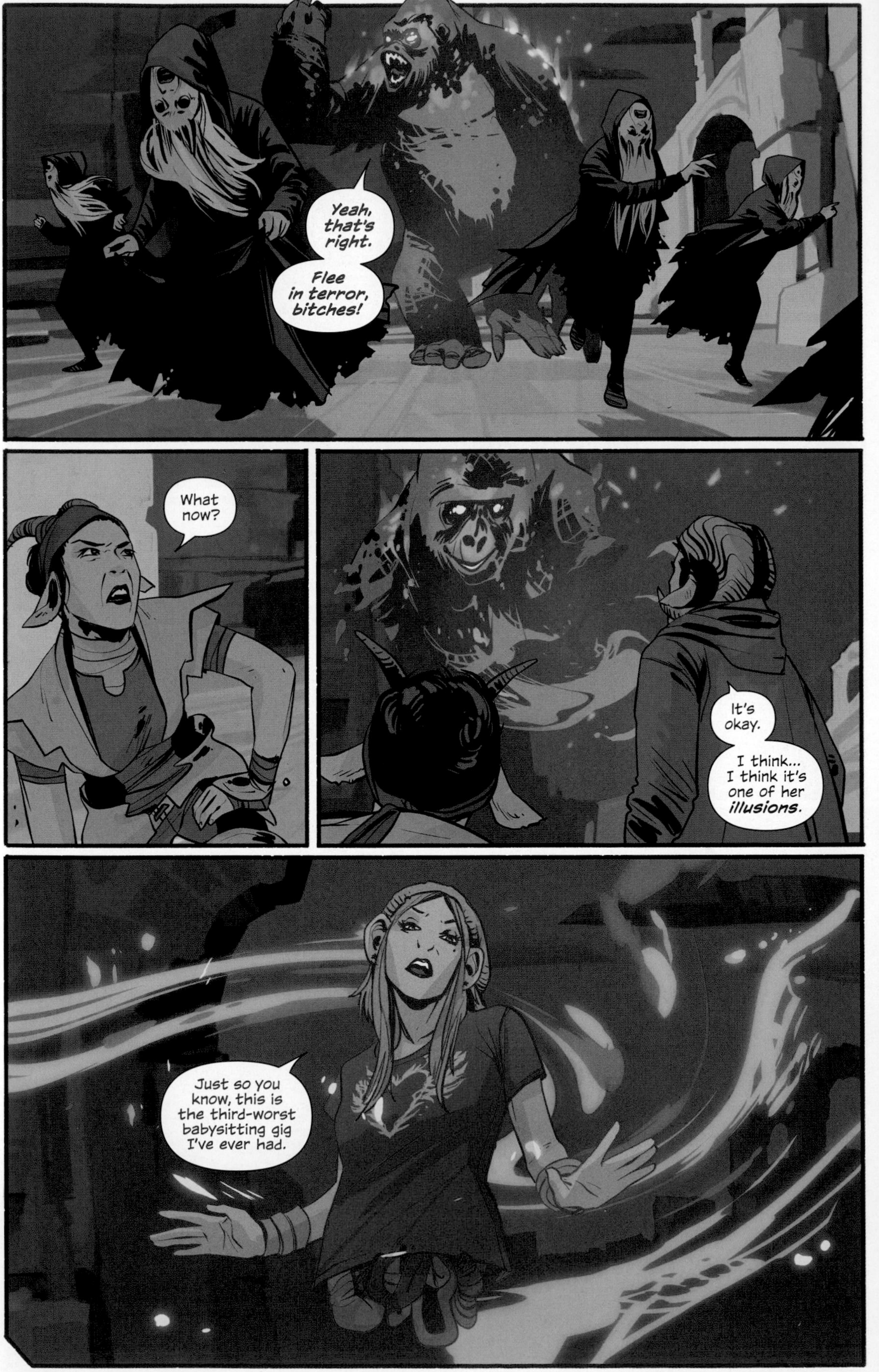
Yeah, that's right.
Flee in terror, bitches!
What now?
It's okay.
I think... I think it's one of her *illusions*.
Just so you know, this is the third-worst babysitting gig I've ever had.

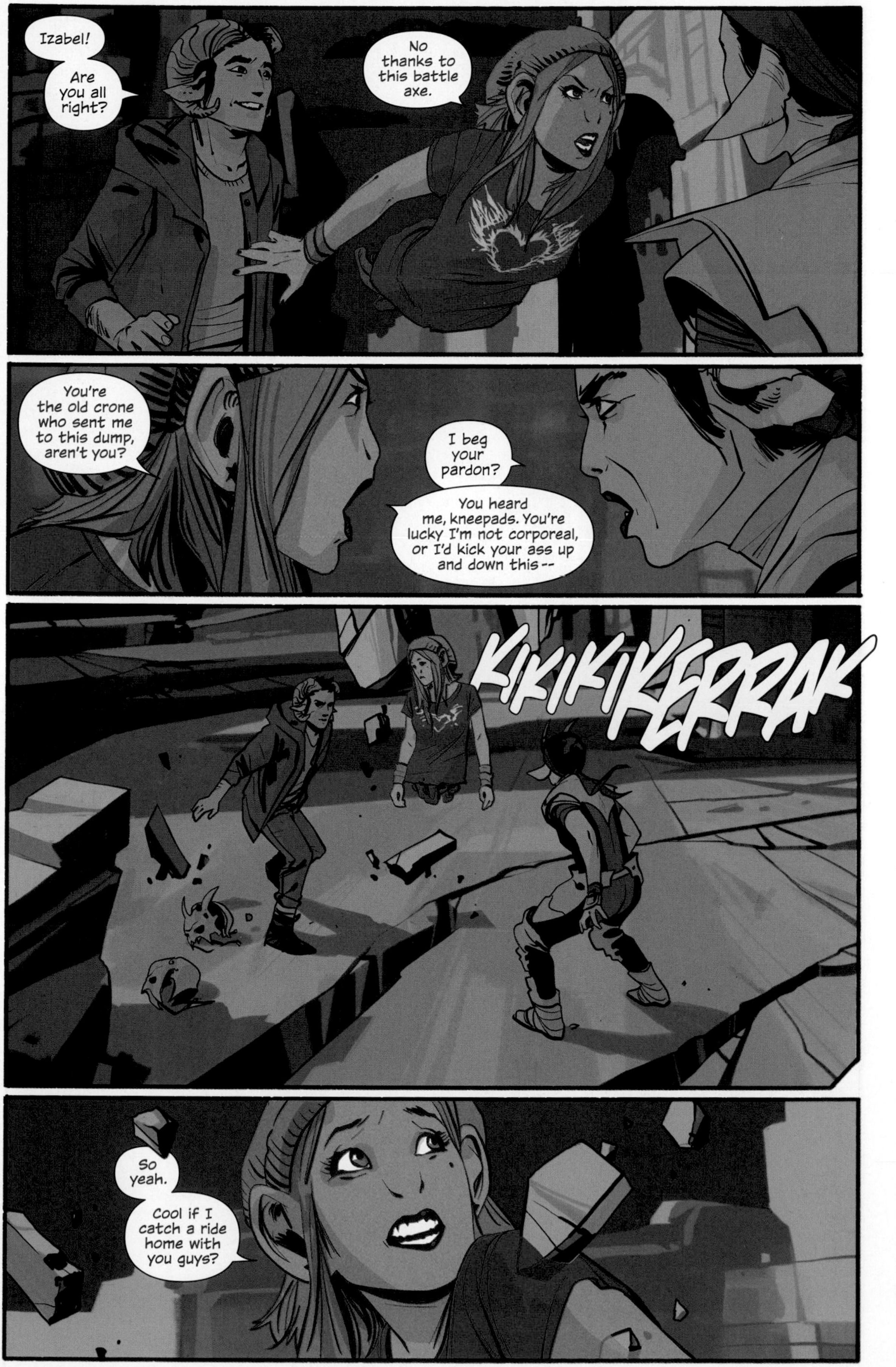

Izabel!
Are you all right?
No thanks to this battle axe.
You're the old crone who sent me to this dump, aren't you?
I beg your pardon?
You heard me, kneepads. You're lucky I'm not corporeal, or I'd kick your ass up and down this --
KIKIKIKERRAK
So yeah.
Cool if I catch a ride home with you guys?

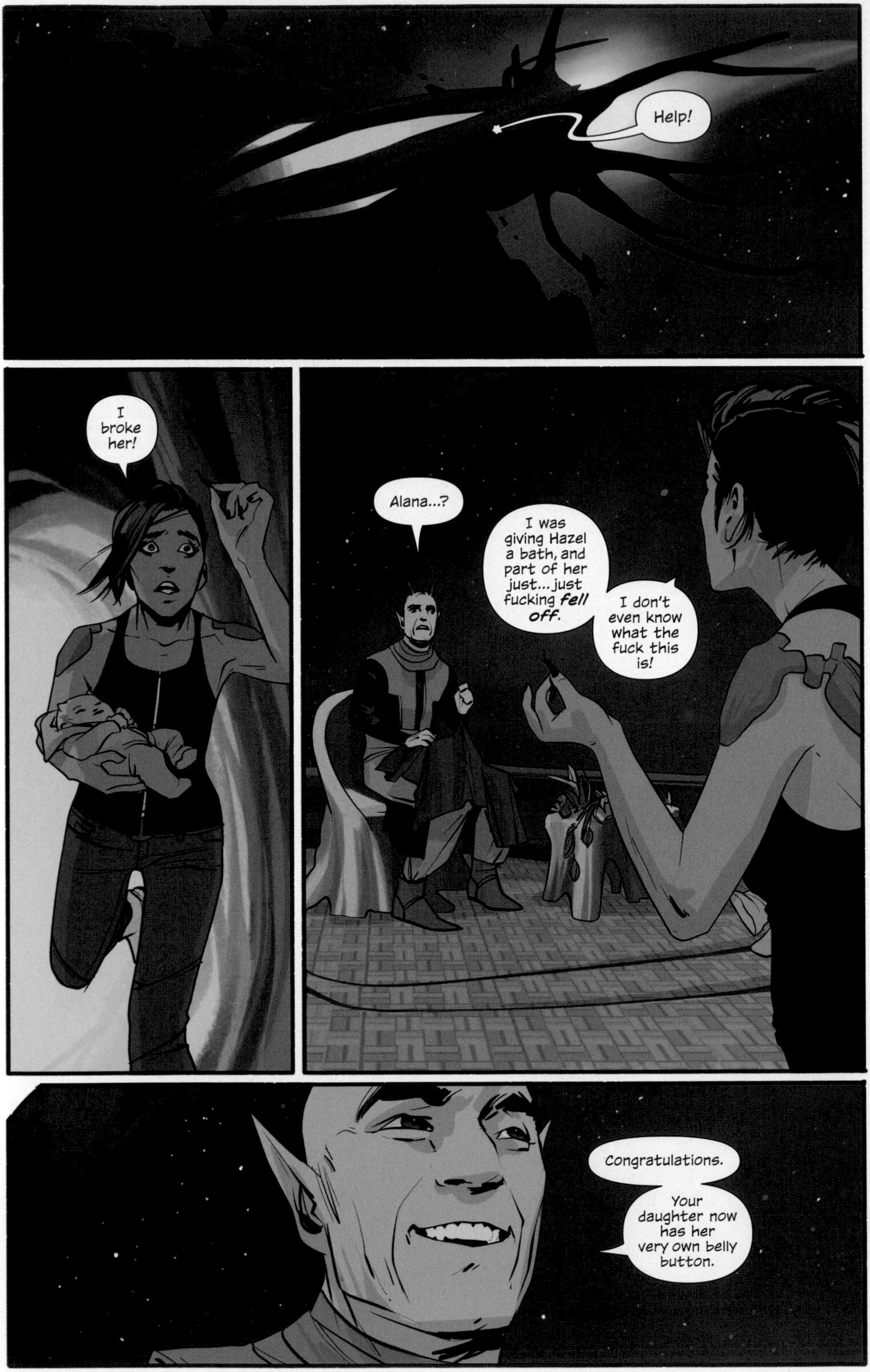
Help!
I broke her!
Alana...?
I was giving Hazel a bath, and part of her just... just fucking *fell off*.
I don't even know what the fuck this is!
Congratulations.
Your daughter now has her very own belly button.

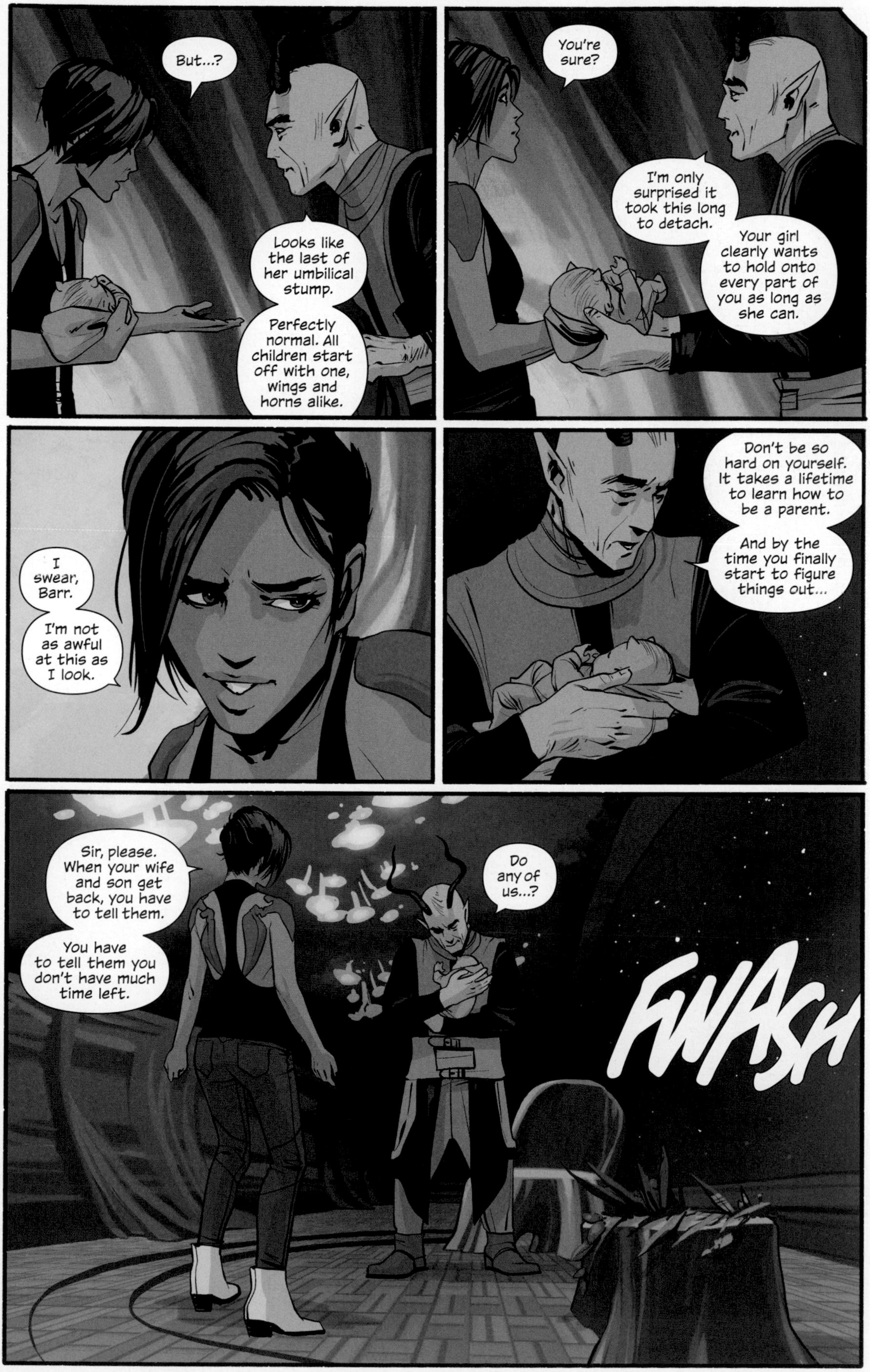
But...?
Looks like the last of her umbilical stump.
Perfectly normal. All children start off with one, wings and horns alike.
You're sure?
I'm only surprised it took this long to detach.
Your girl clearly wants to hold onto every part of you as long as she can.
I swear, Barr.
I'm not as awful at this as I look.
Don't be so hard on yourself. It takes a lifetime to learn how to be a parent.
And by the time you finally start to figure things out...
Sir, please. When your wife and son get back, you have to tell them.
You have to tell them you don't have much time left.
Do any of us...?
FWASH

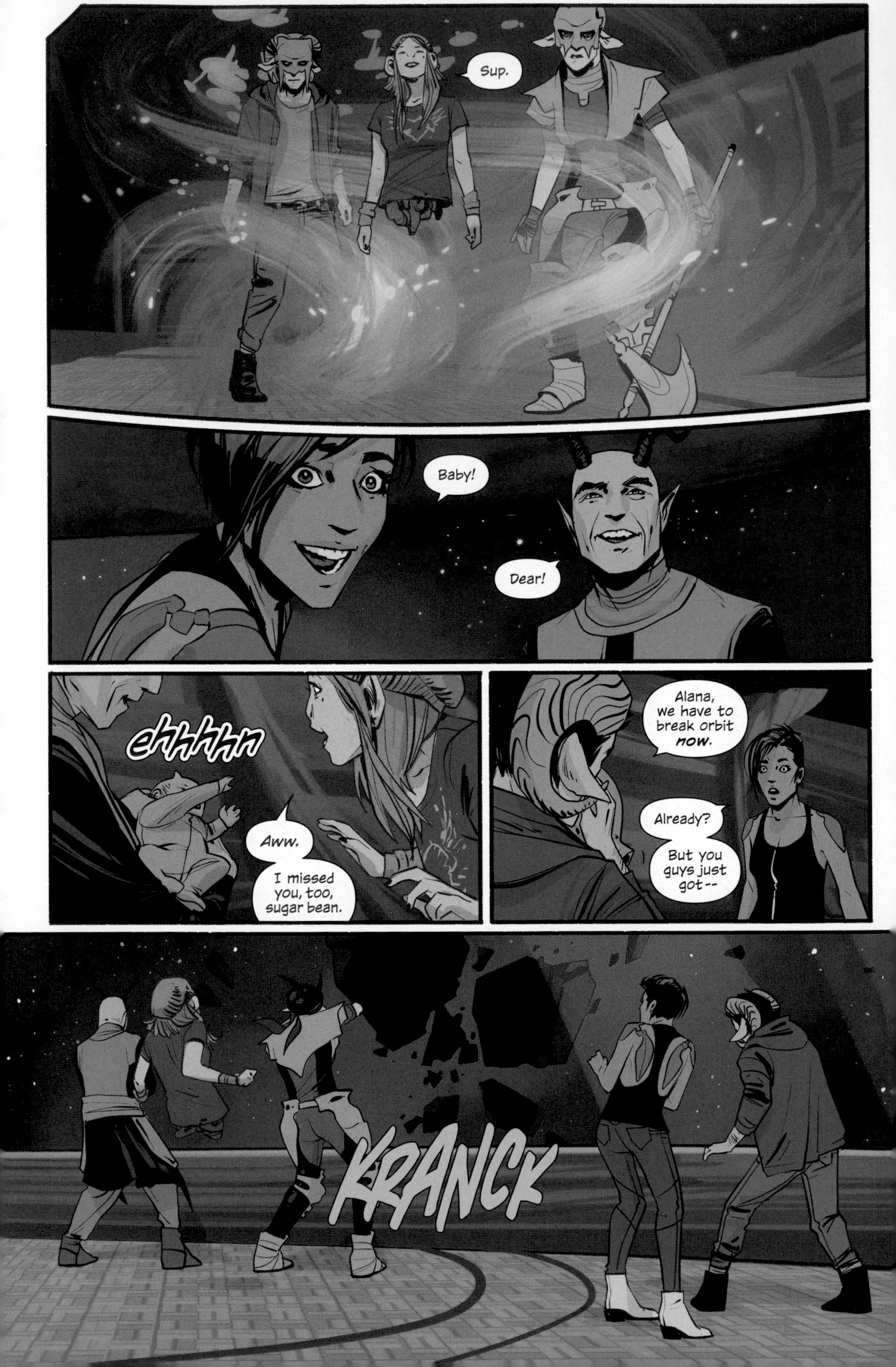
Sup.
Baby!
Dear!
ehhhhn
Aww.
I missed you, too, sugar bean.
Alana, we have to break orbit now.
Already?
But you guys just got--
KRANCK

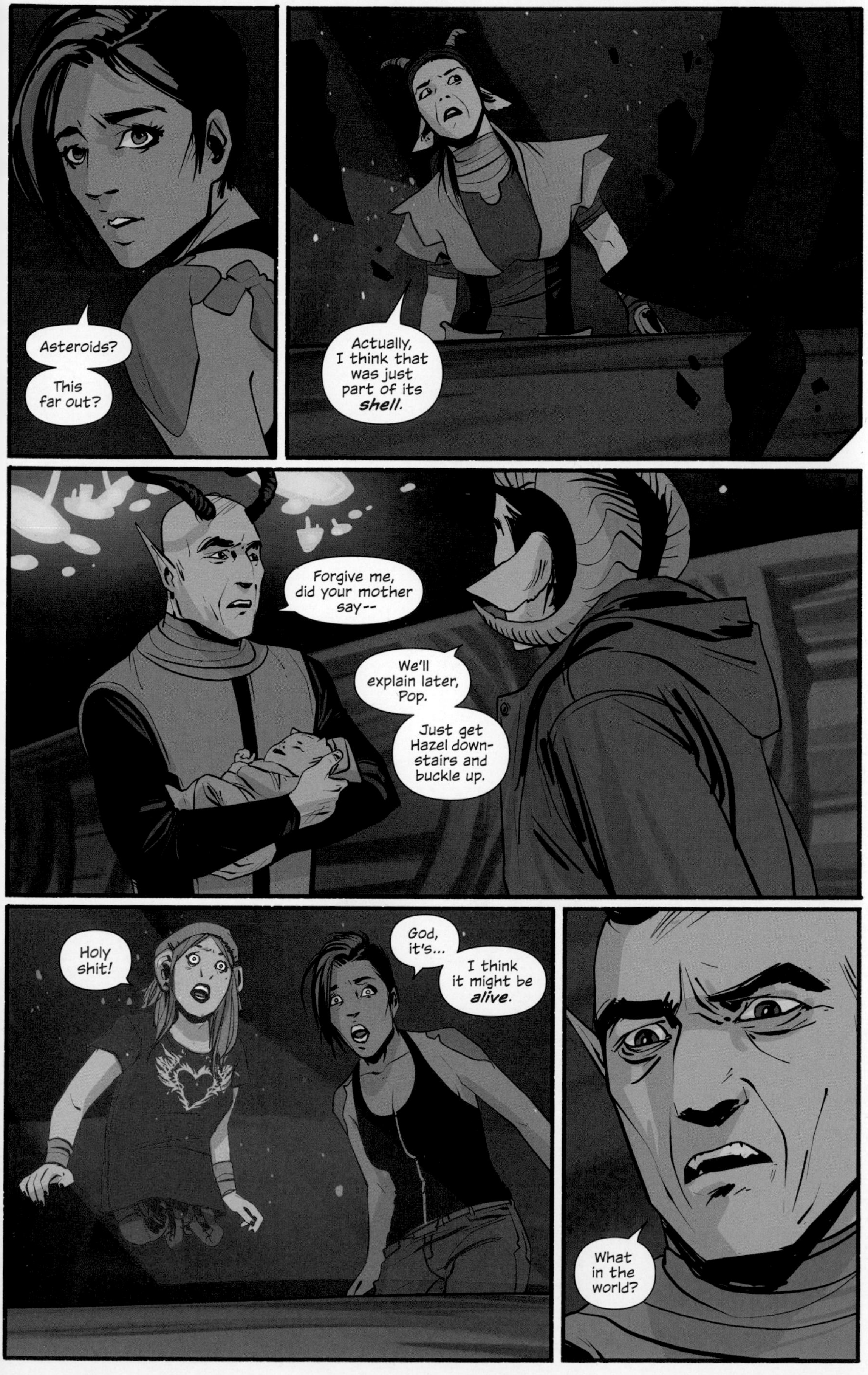
Asteroids?
This far out?
Actually, I think that was just part of its *shell*.
Forgive me, did your mother say--
We'll explain later, Pop.
Just get Hazel down-stairs and buckle up.
Holy shit!
God, it's...
I think it might be *alive*.
What in the world?

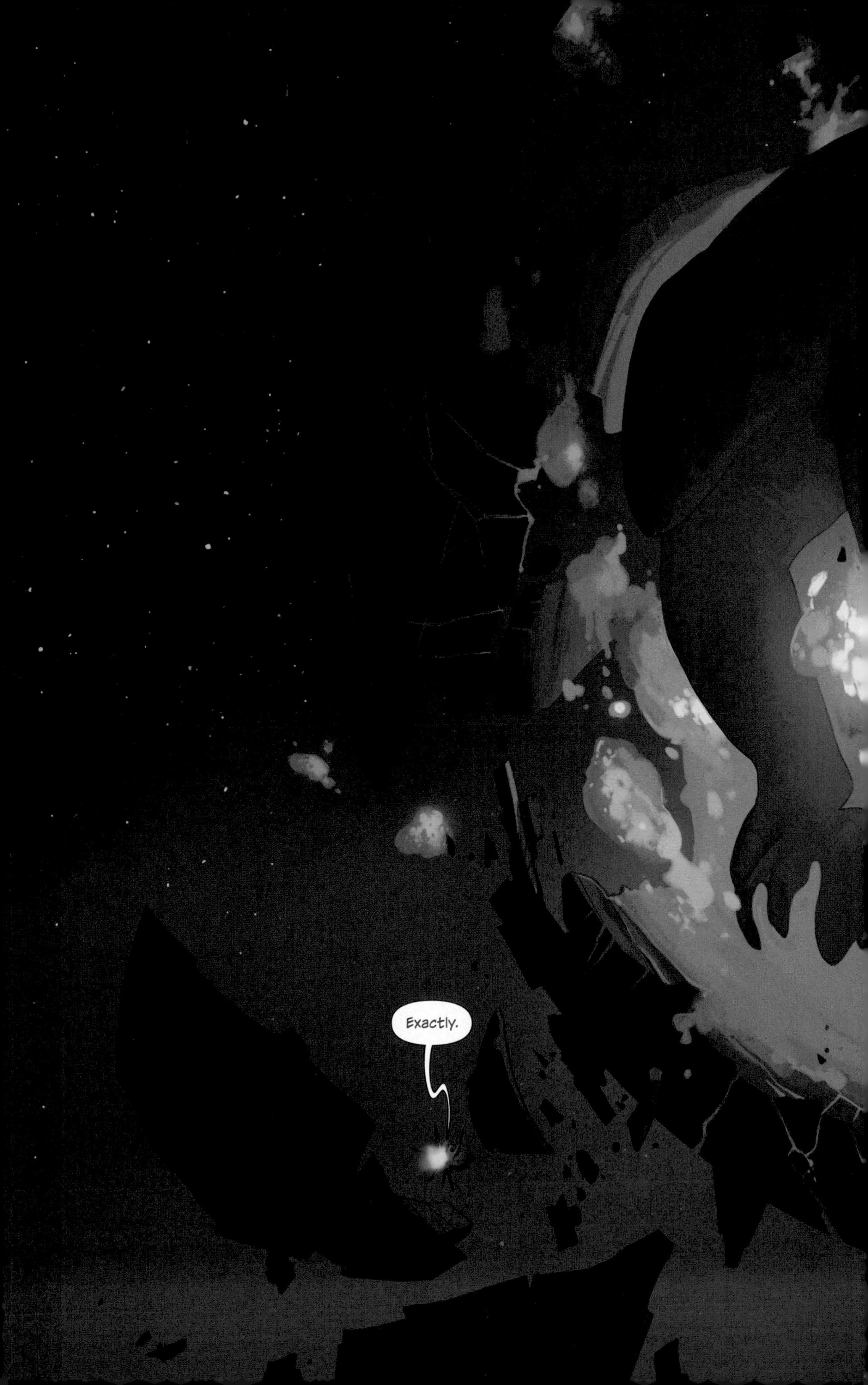
Exactly.

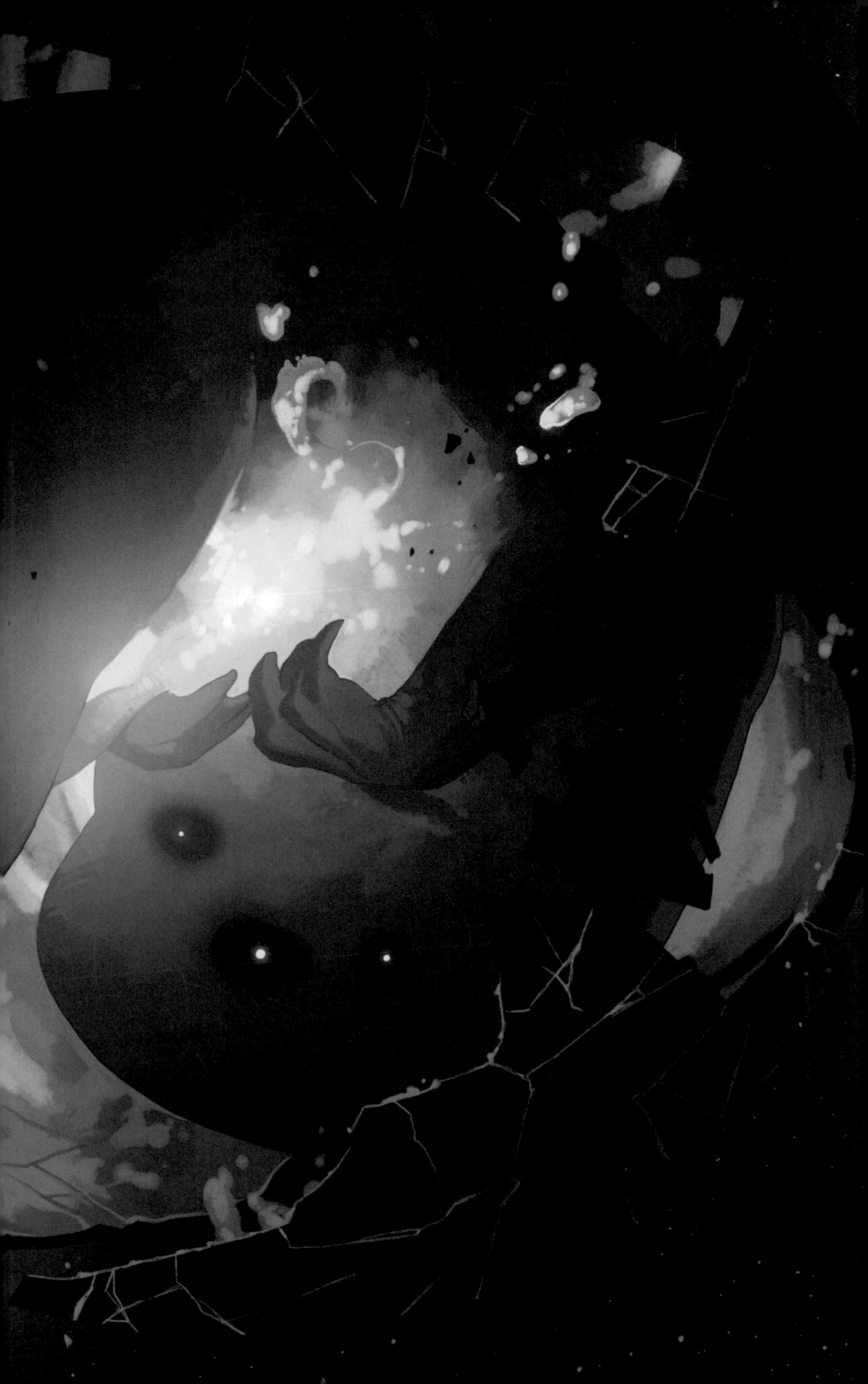

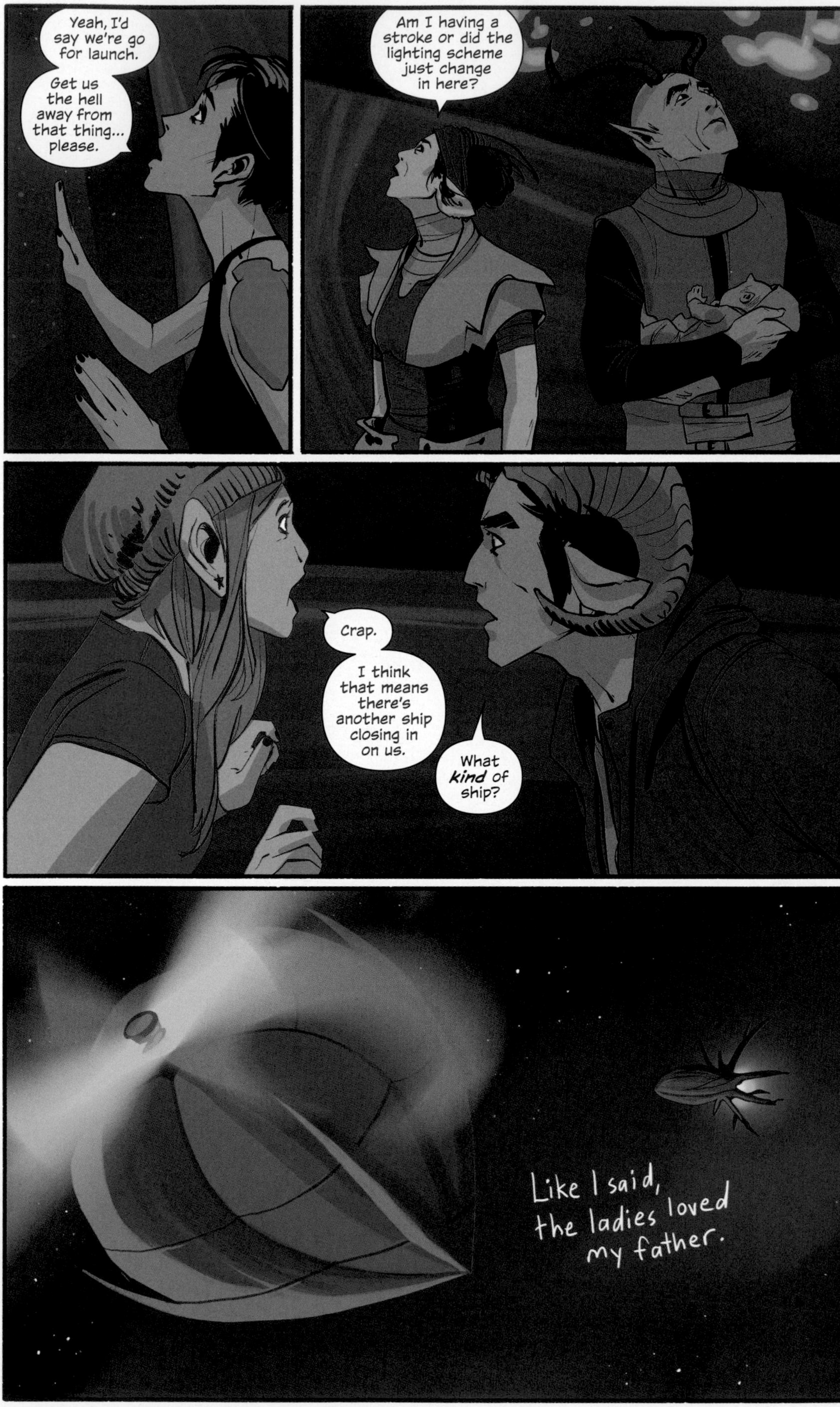
Yeah, I'd say we're go for launch.
Get us the hell away from that thing... please.
Am I having a stroke or did the lighting scheme just change in here?
Crap.
I think that means there's another ship closing in on us.
What *kind* of ship?
Like I said, the ladies loved my father.

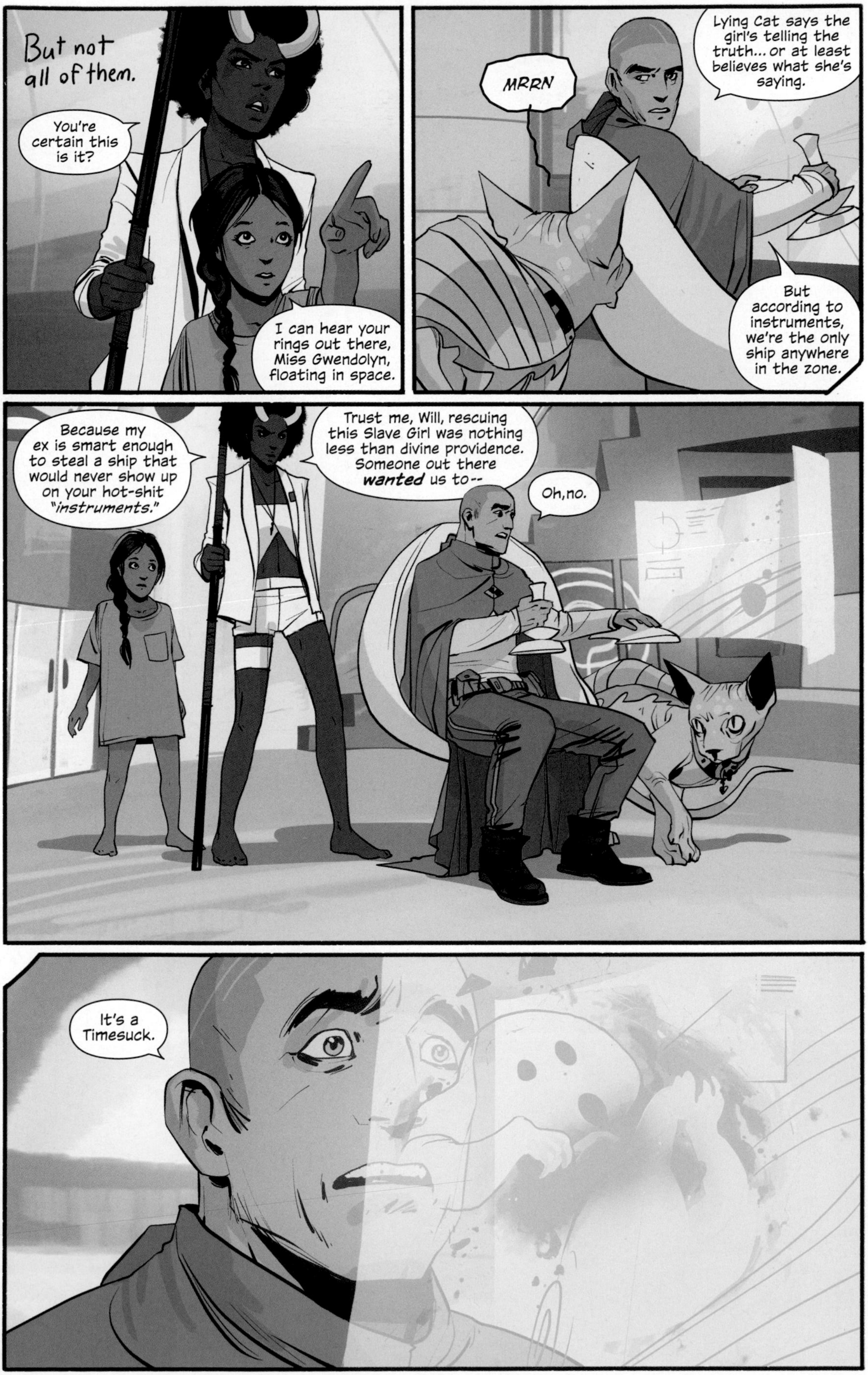
But not all of them.
You're certain this is it?
I can hear your rings out there, Miss Gwendolyn, floating in space.
MRRN
Lying Cat says the girl's telling the truth... or at least believes what she's saying.
But according to instruments, we're the only ship anywhere in the zone.
Because my ex is smart enough to steal a ship that would never show up on your hot-shit "instruments."
Trust me, Will, rescuing this Slave Girl was nothing less than divine providence. Someone out there wanted us to--
Oh, no.
It's a Timesuck.

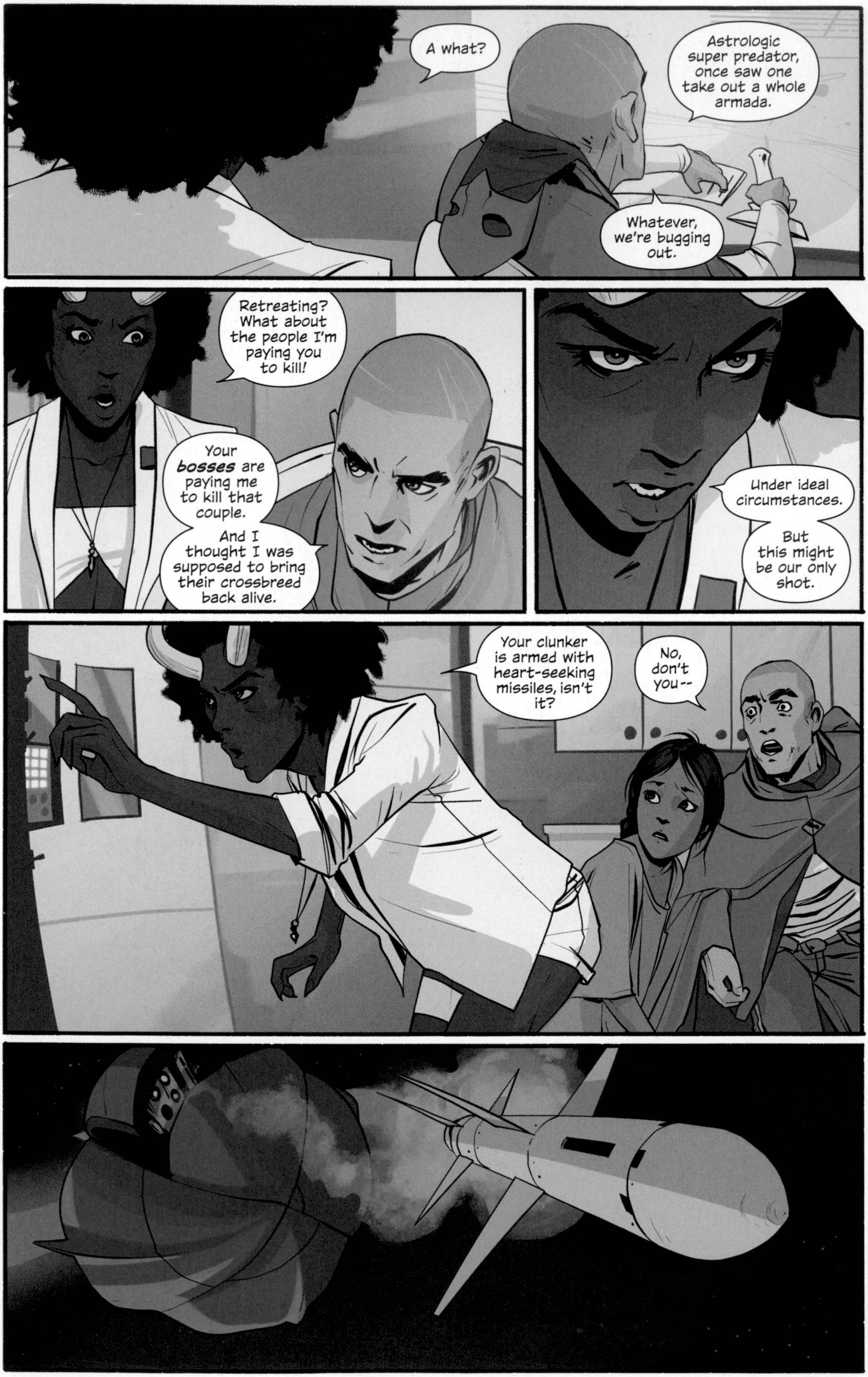
A what?
Astrologic super predator, once saw one take out a whole armada.
Whatever, we're bugging out.
Retreating? What about the people I'm paying you to kill!
Your **bosses** are paying me to kill that couple.
And I thought I was supposed to bring their crossbreed back alive.
Under ideal circumstances.
But this might be our only shot.
Your clunker is armed with heart-seeking missiles, isn't it?
No, don't you--

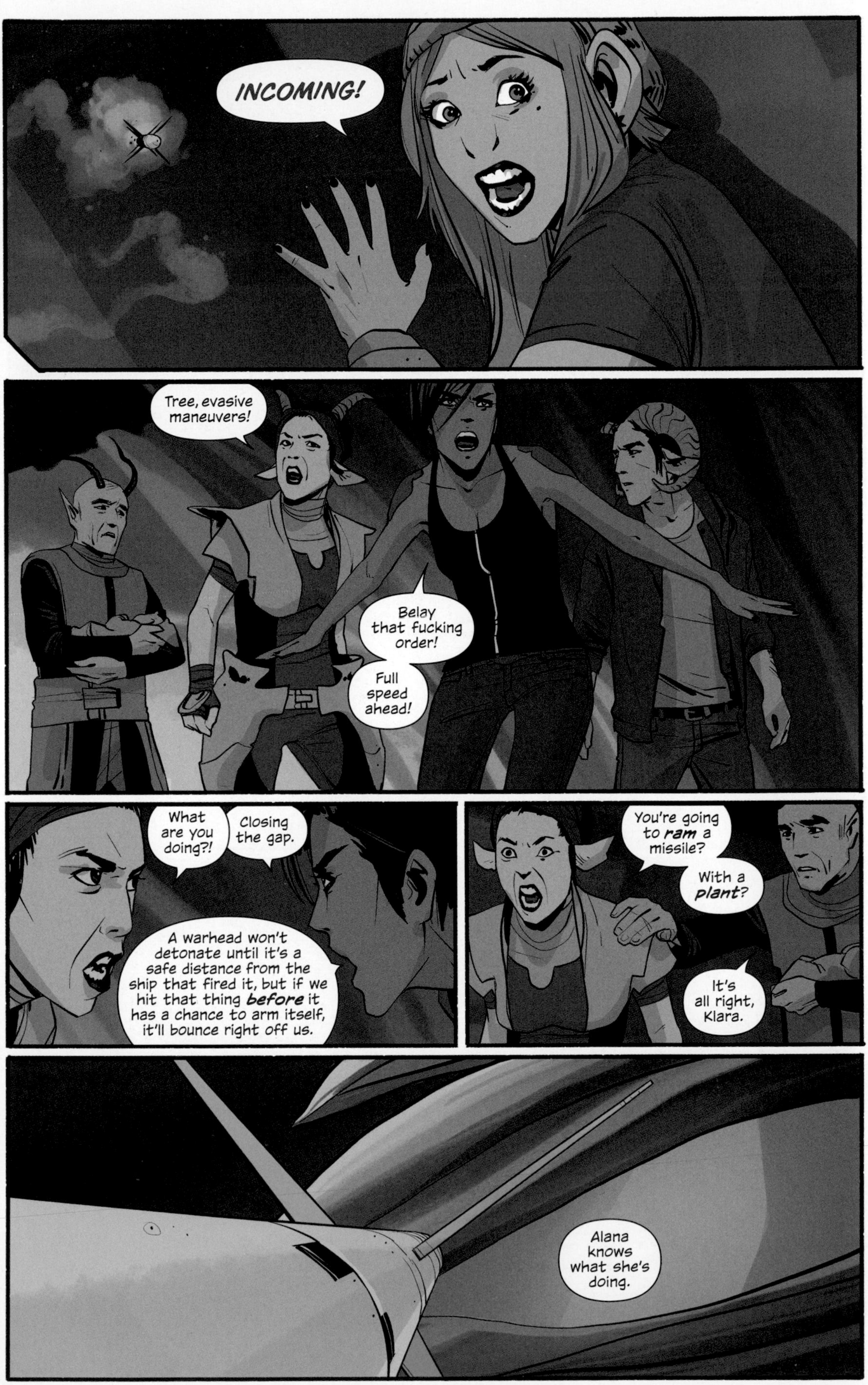
INCOMING!
Tree, evasive maneuvers!
Belay that fucking order!
Full speed ahead!
What are you doing?!
Closing the gap.
A warhead won't detonate until it's a safe distance from the ship that fired it, but if we hit that thing *before* it has a chance to arm itself, it'll bounce right off us.
You're going to *ram* a missile?
With a *plant*?
It's all right, Klara.
Alana knows what she's doing.

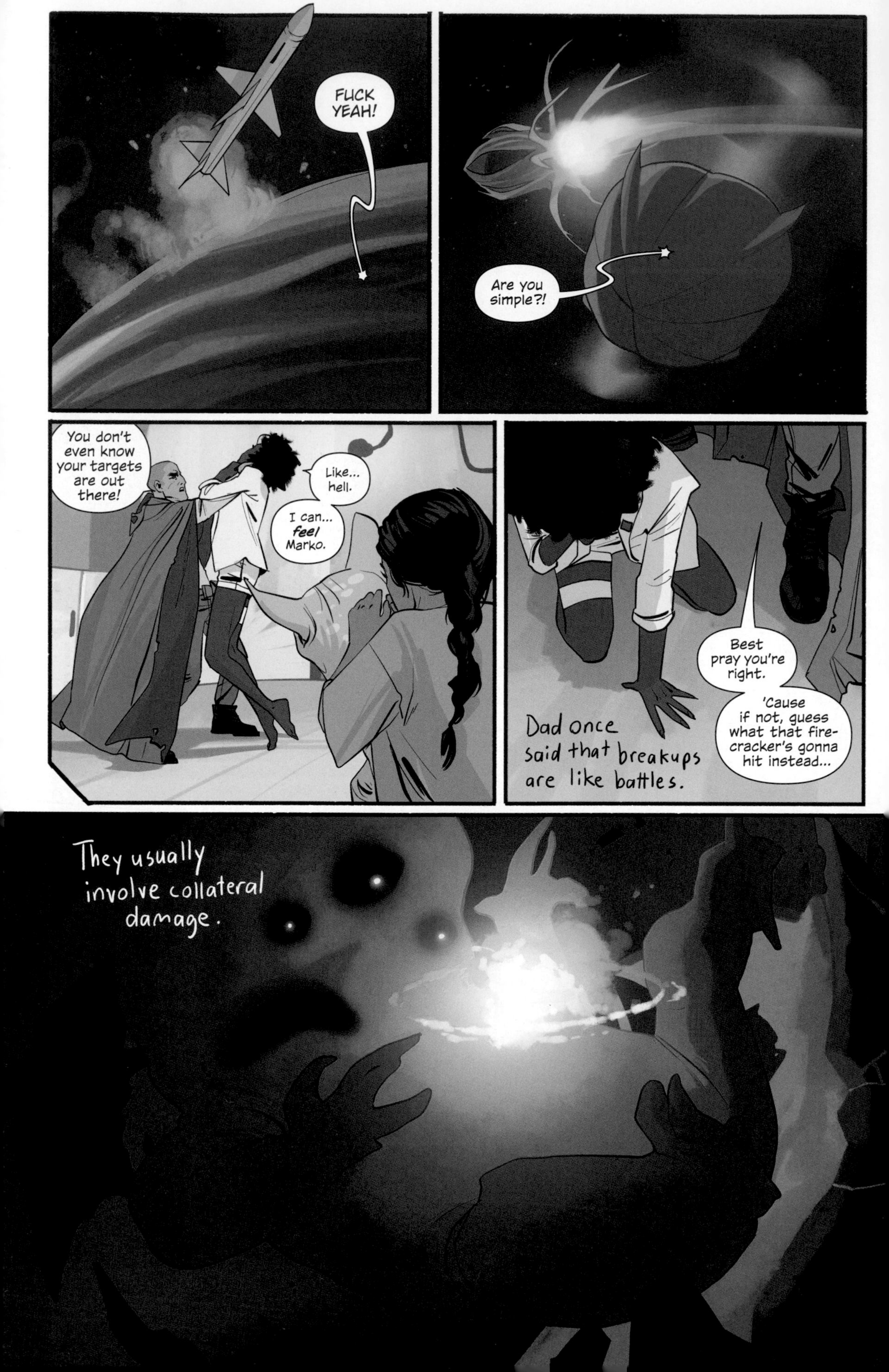
FUCK YEAH!
Are you simple?!
You don't even know your targets are out there!
Like... hell.
I can... *feel* Marko.
Dad once said that breakups are like battles.
Best pray you're right.
'Cause if not, guess what that fire-cracker's gonna hit instead...
They usually involve collateral damage.

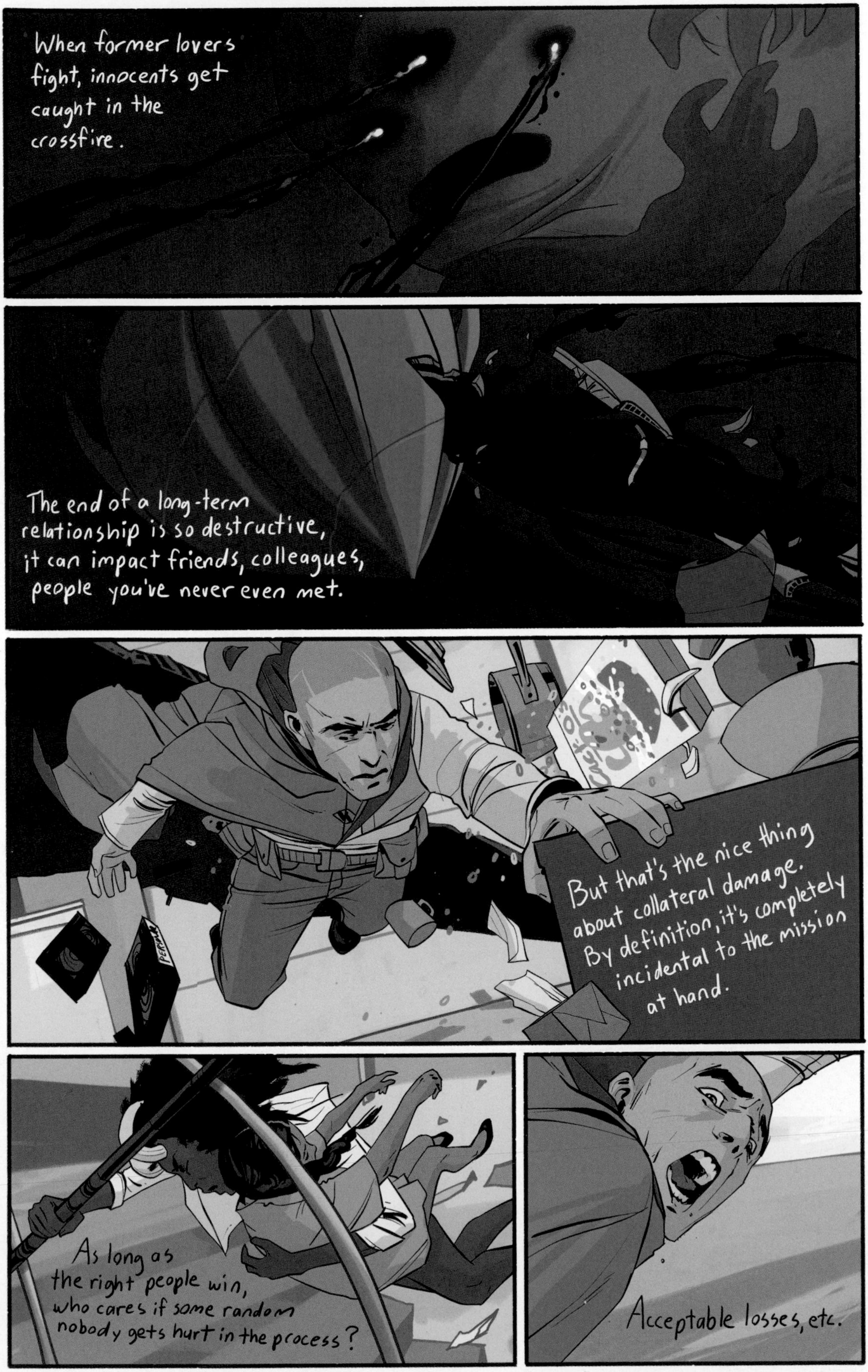
When former lovers fight, innocents get caught in the crossfire.
The end of a long-term relationship is so destructive, it can impact friends, colleagues, people you've never even met.
But that's the nice thing about collateral damage. By definition, it's completely incidental to the mission at hand.
As long as the right people win, who cares if some random nobody gets hurt in the process?
Acceptable losses, etc.

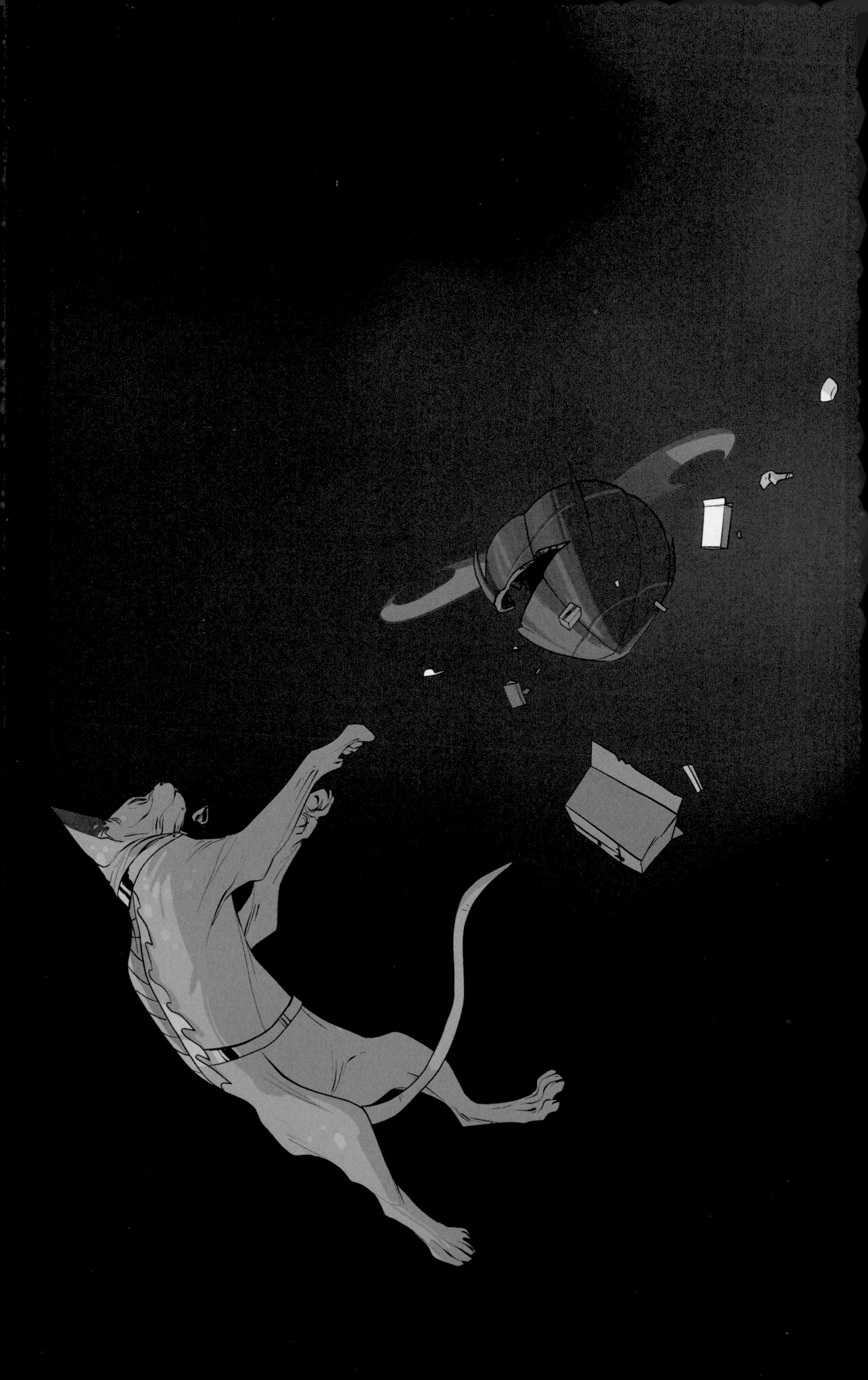

end chapter ten

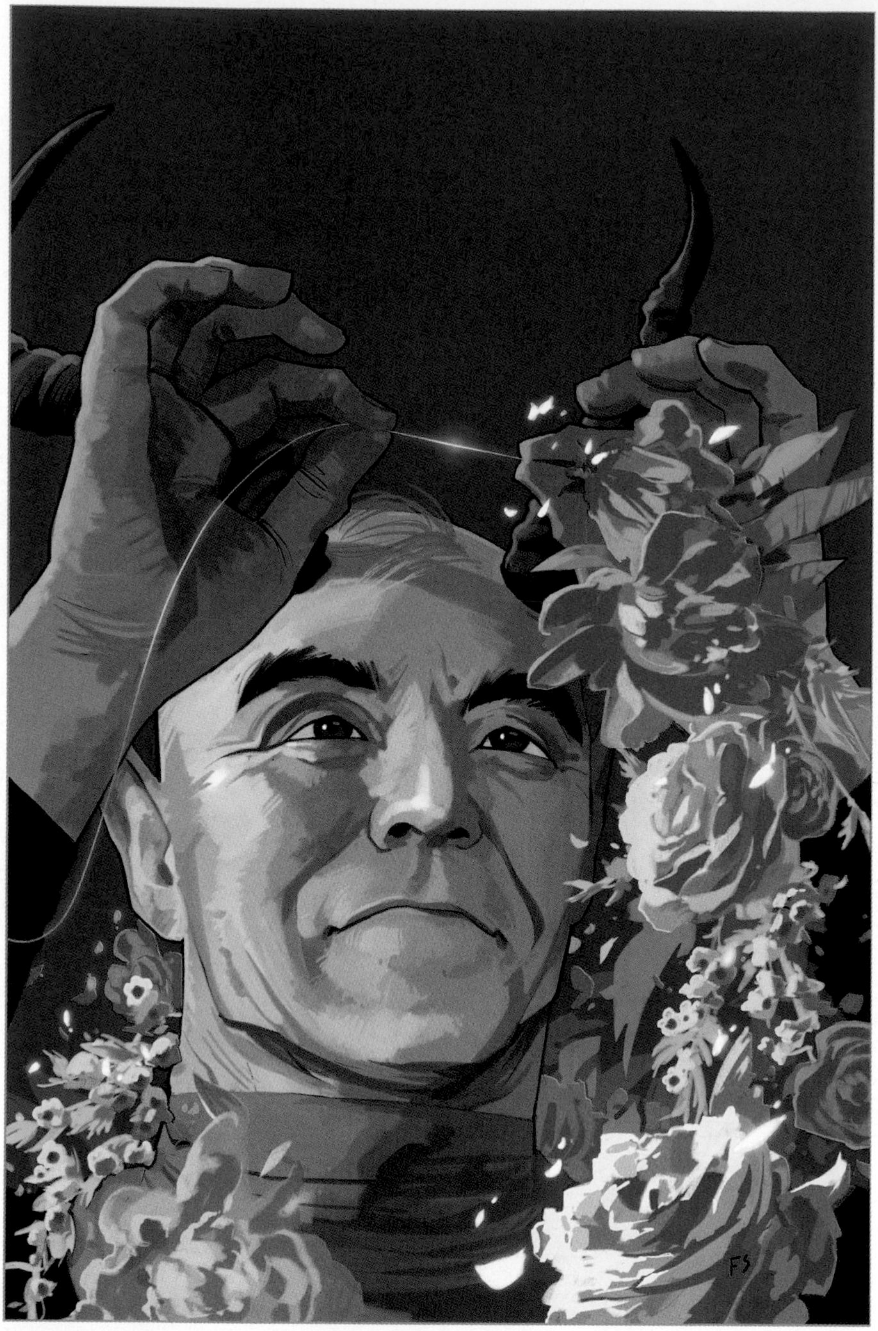
FS

CHAPTER ELEVEN

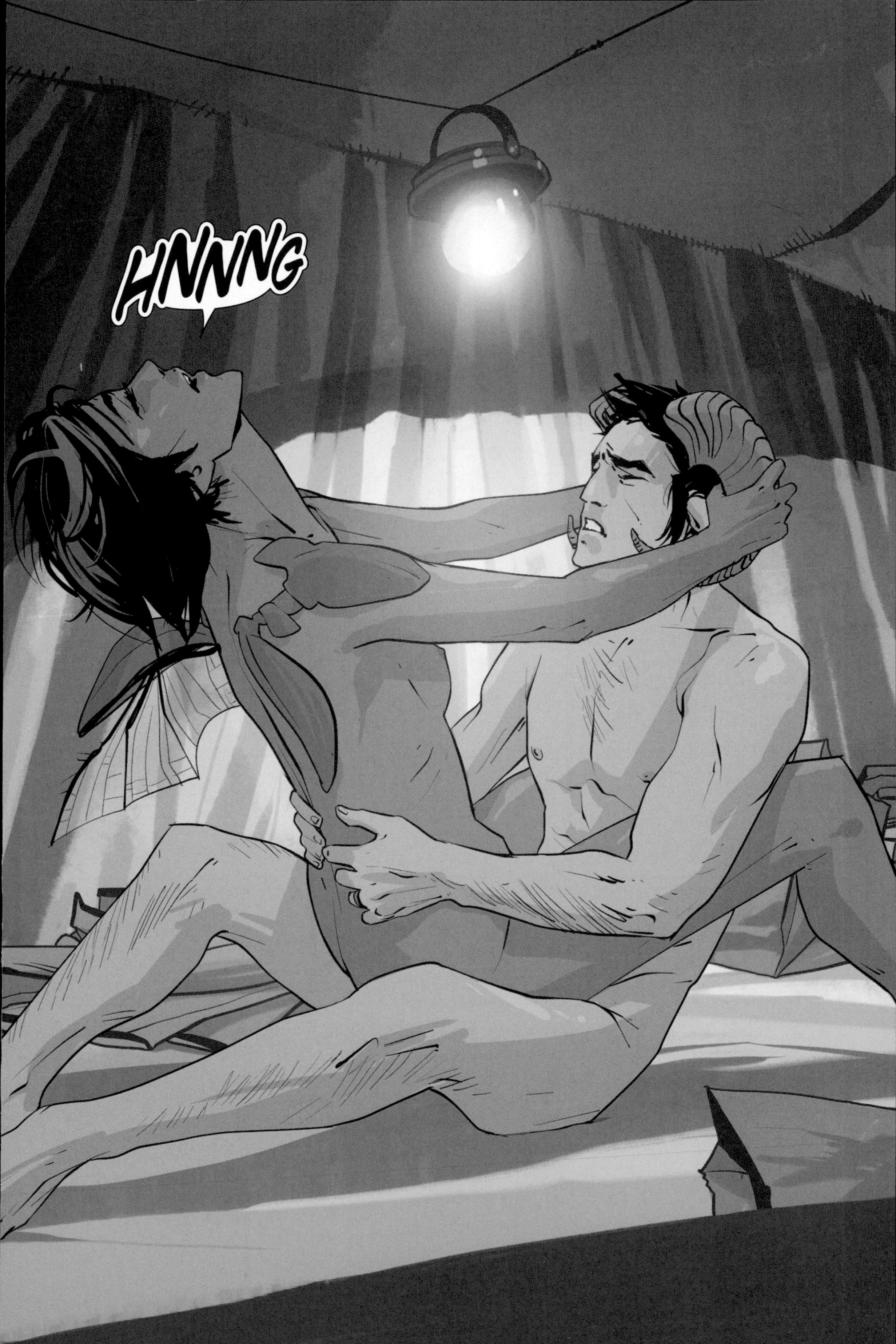
HNNNG

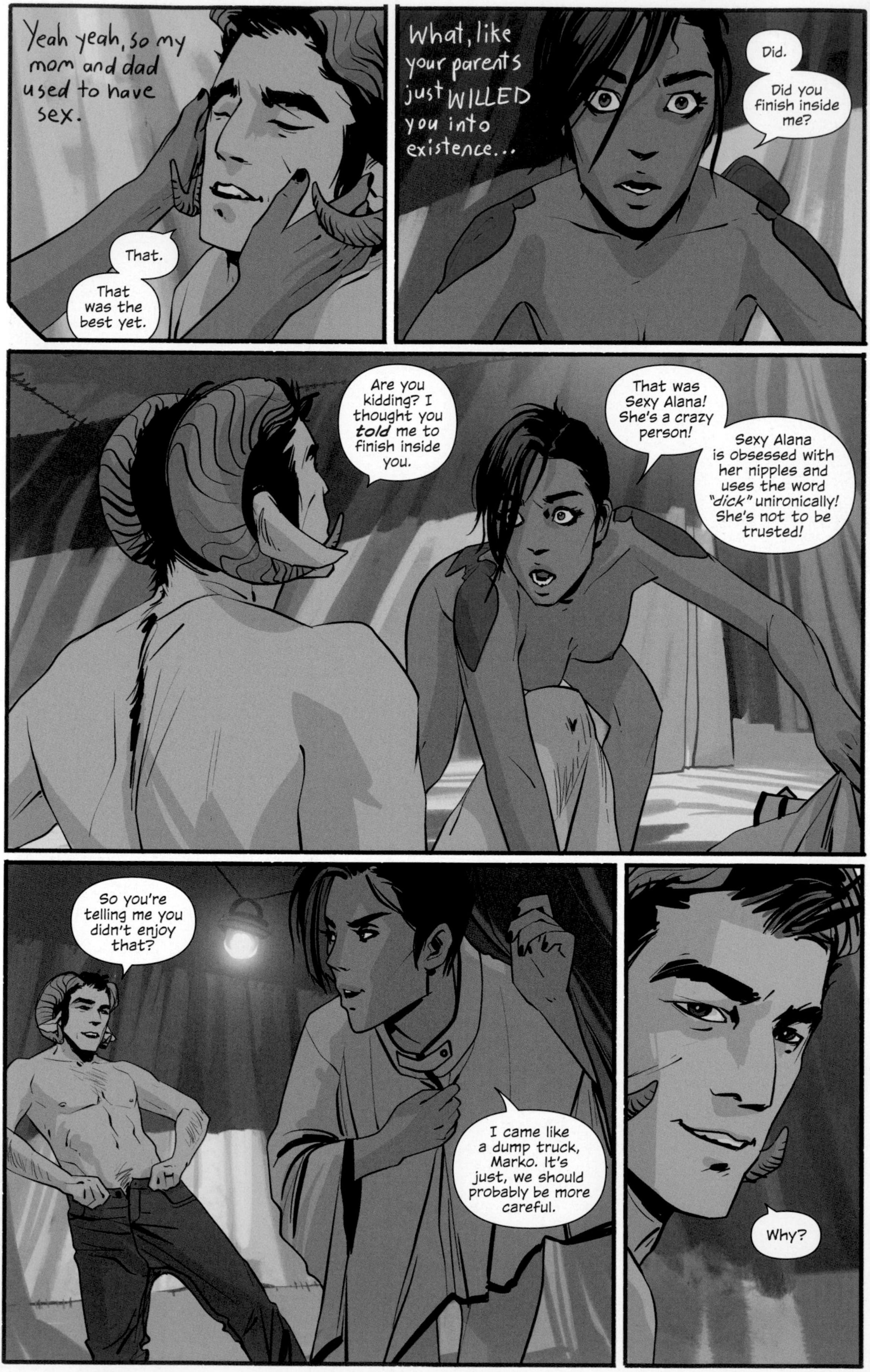
Yeah yeah, so my mom and dad used to have sex.
That.
That was the best yet.
What, like your parents just WILLED you into existence...
Did.
Did you finish inside me?
Are you kidding? I thought you *told* me to finish inside you.
That was Sexy Alana! She's a crazy person!
Sexy Alana is obsessed with her nipples and uses the word "*dick*" unironically! She's not to be trusted!
So you're telling me you didn't enjoy that?
I came like a dump truck, Marko. It's just, we should probably be more careful.
Why?

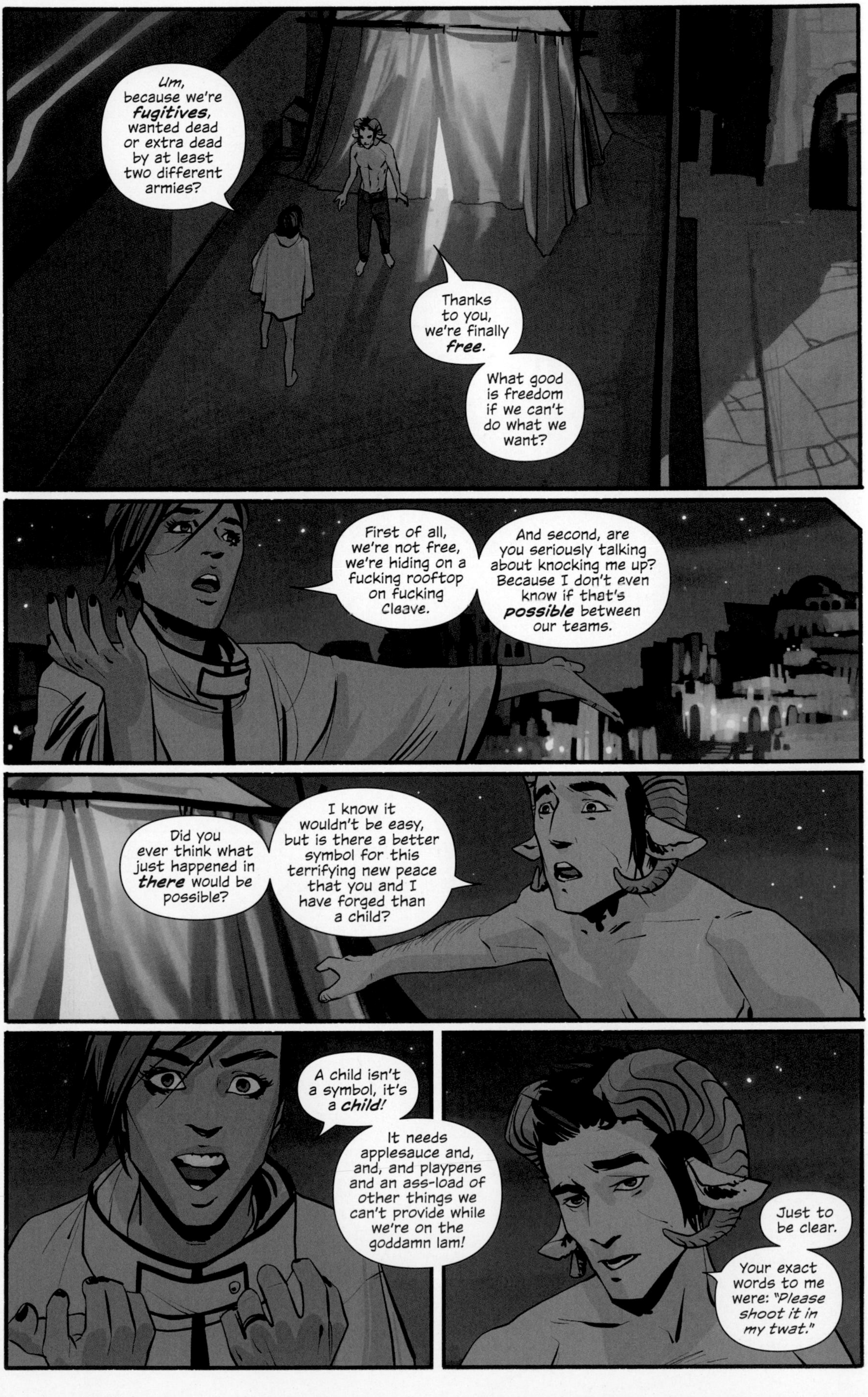
Um, because we're *fugitives*, wanted dead or extra dead by at least two different armies?
Thanks to you, we're finally *free*.
What good is freedom if we can't do what we want?
First of all, we're not free, we're hiding on a fucking rooftop on fucking Cleave.
And second, are you seriously talking about knocking me up? Because I don't even know if that's *possible* between our teams.
Did you ever think what just happened in *there* would be possible?
I know it wouldn't be easy, but is there a better symbol for this terrifying new peace that you and I have forged than a child?
A child isn't a symbol, it's a *child*!
It needs applesauce and, and, and playpens and an ass-load of other things we can't provide while we're on the goddamn lam!
Just to be clear.
Your exact words to me were: *"Please shoot it in my twat."*

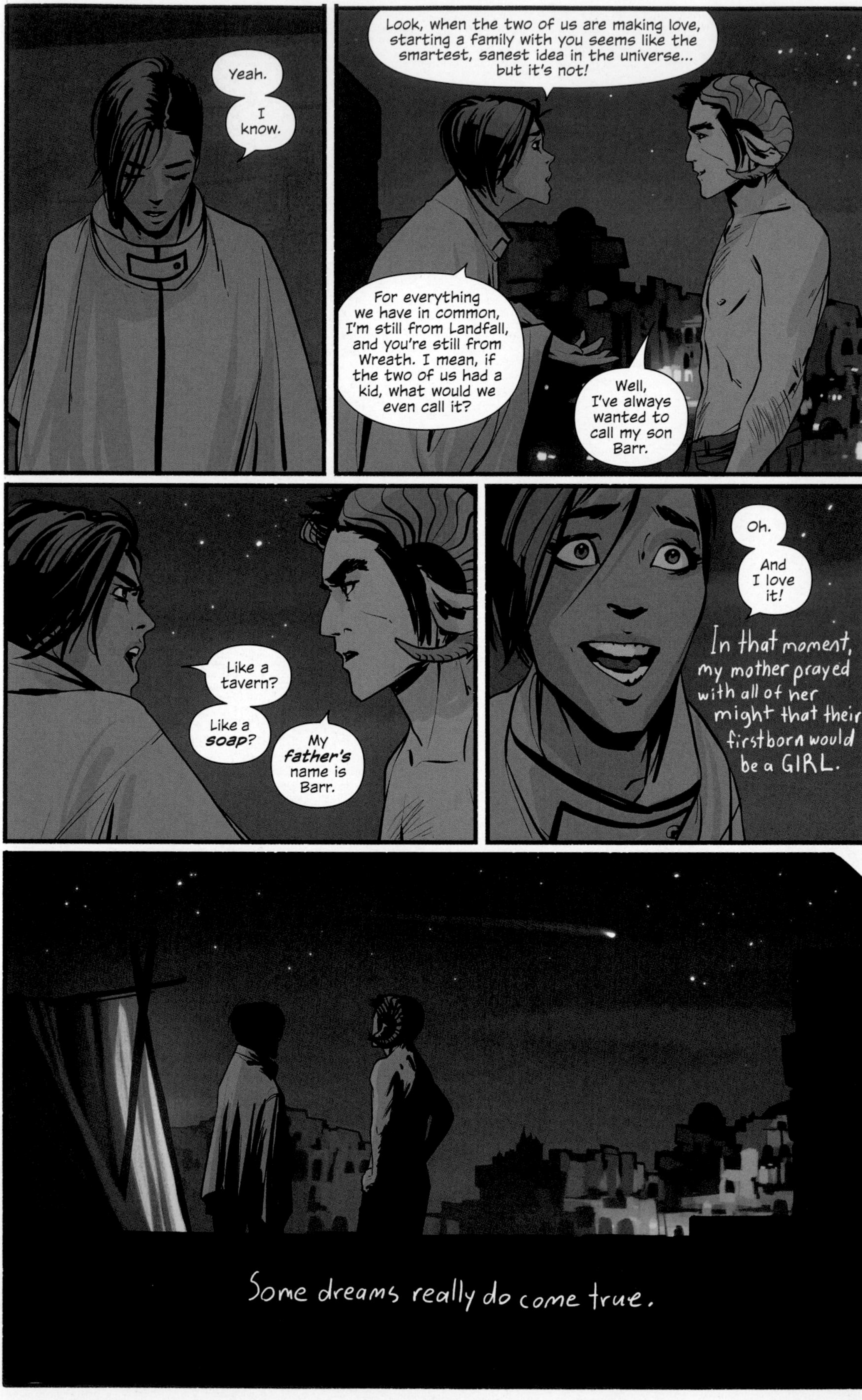
Yeah.
I know.
Look, when the two of us are making love, starting a family with you seems like the smartest, sanest idea in the universe... but it's not!
For everything we have in common, I'm still from Landfall, and you're still from Wreath. I mean, if the two of us had a kid, what would we even call it?
Well, I've always wanted to call my son Barr.
Like a tavern?
Like a soap?
My father's name is Barr.
Oh.
And I love it!
In that moment, my mother prayed with all of her might that their firstborn would be a GIRL.
Some dreams really do come true.

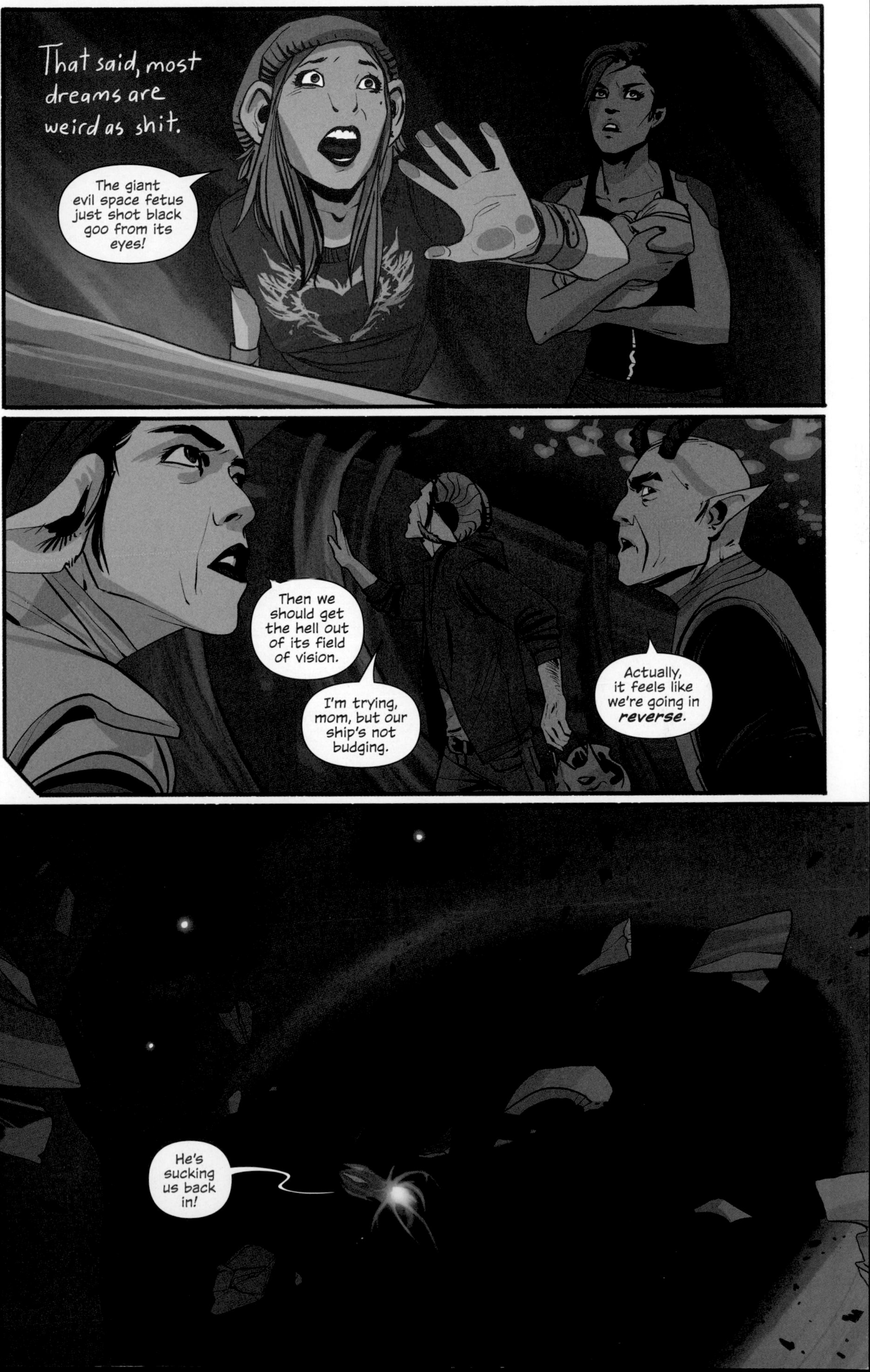
That said, most dreams are weird as shit.
The giant evil space fetus just shot black goo from its eyes!
Then we should get the hell out of its field of vision.
I'm trying, mom, but our ship's not budging.
Actually, it feels like we're going in **reverse**.
He's sucking us back in!

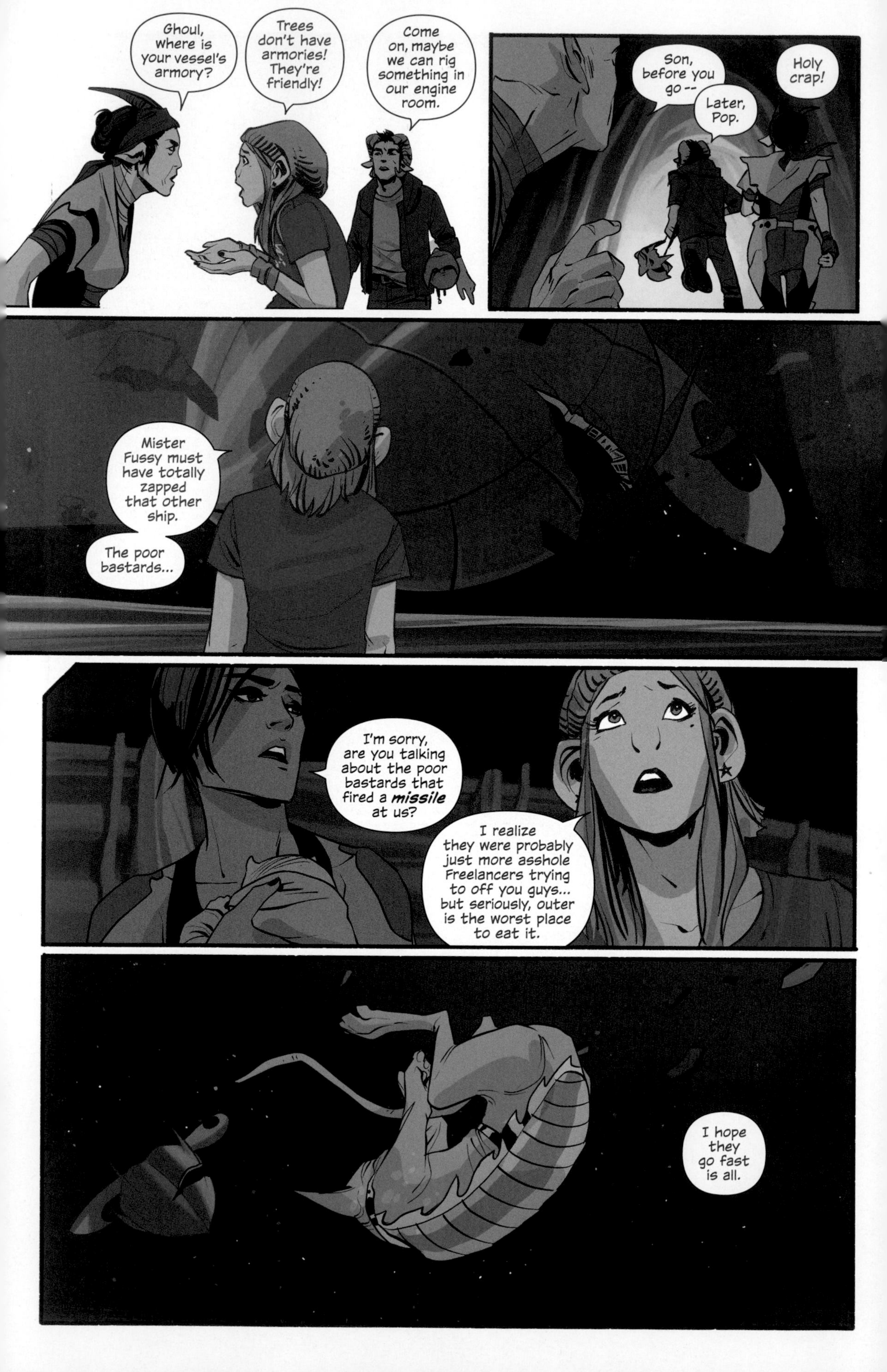
Ghoul, where is your vessel's armory?
Trees don't have armories! They're friendly!
Come on, maybe we can rig something in our engine room.
Son, before you go --
Holy crap!
Later, Pop.
Mister Fussy must have totally zapped that other ship.
The poor bastards...
I'm sorry, are you talking about the poor bastards that fired a *missile* at us?
I realize they were probably just more asshole Freelancers trying to off you guys... but seriously, outer is the worst place to eat it.
I hope they go fast is all.

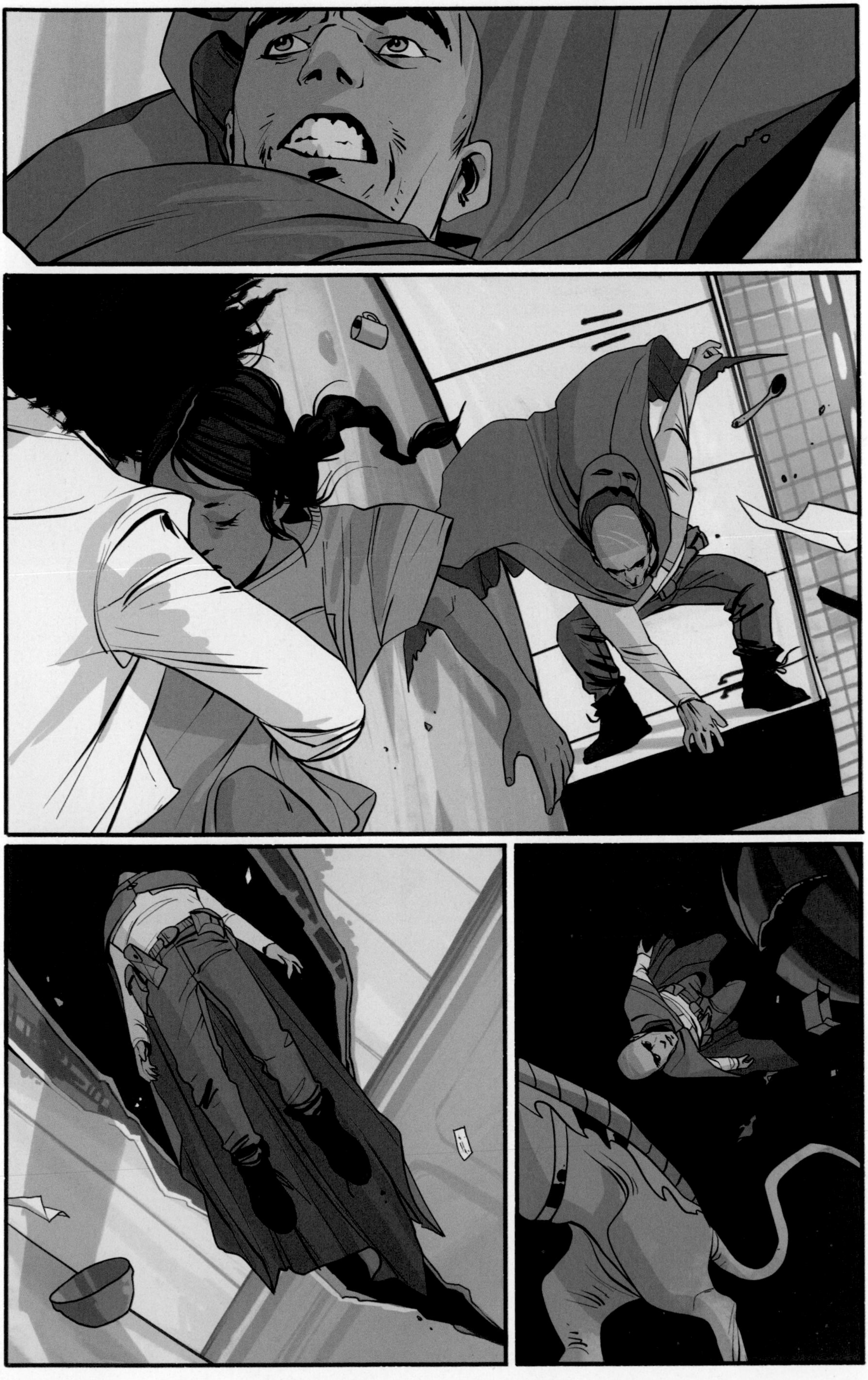

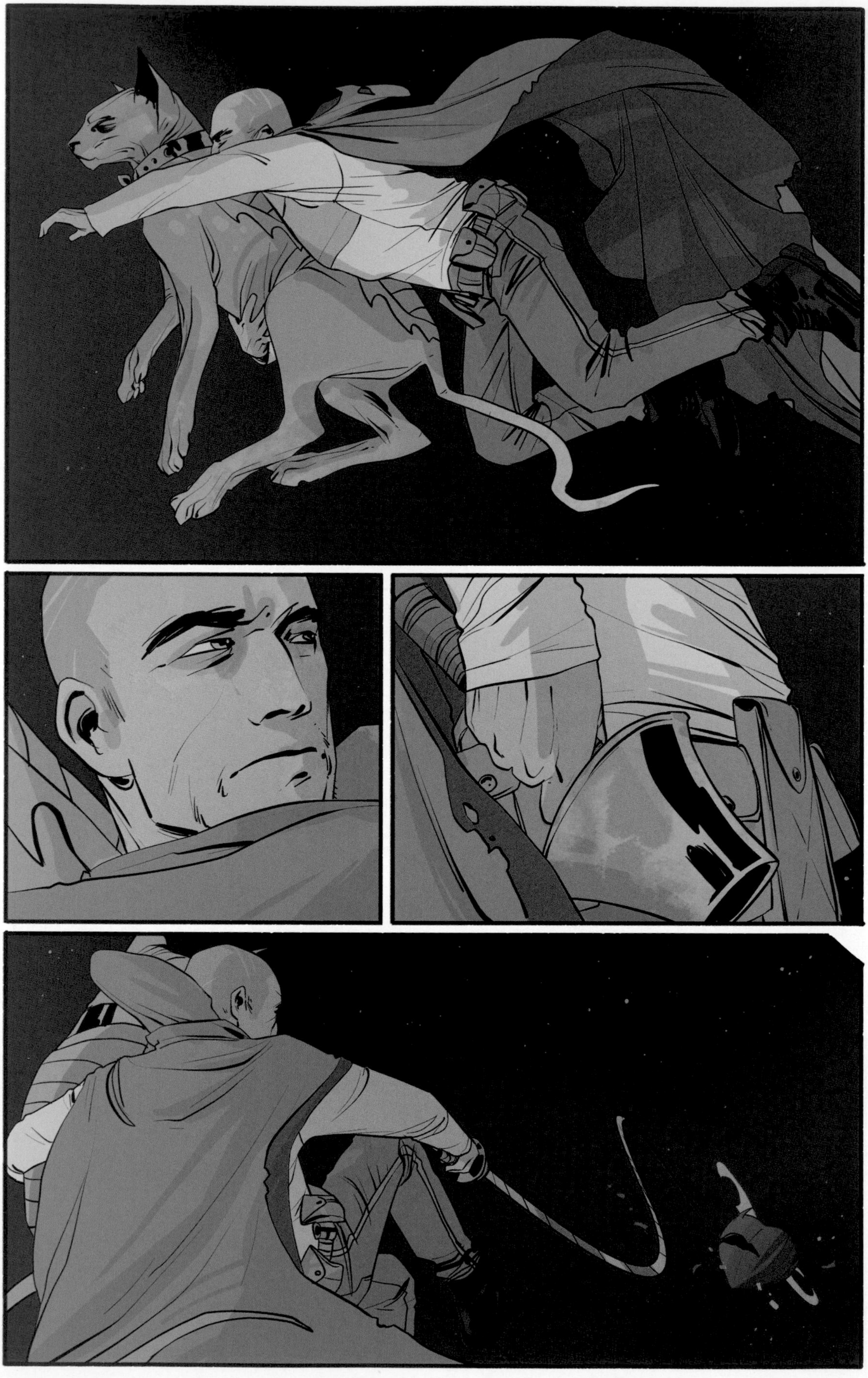

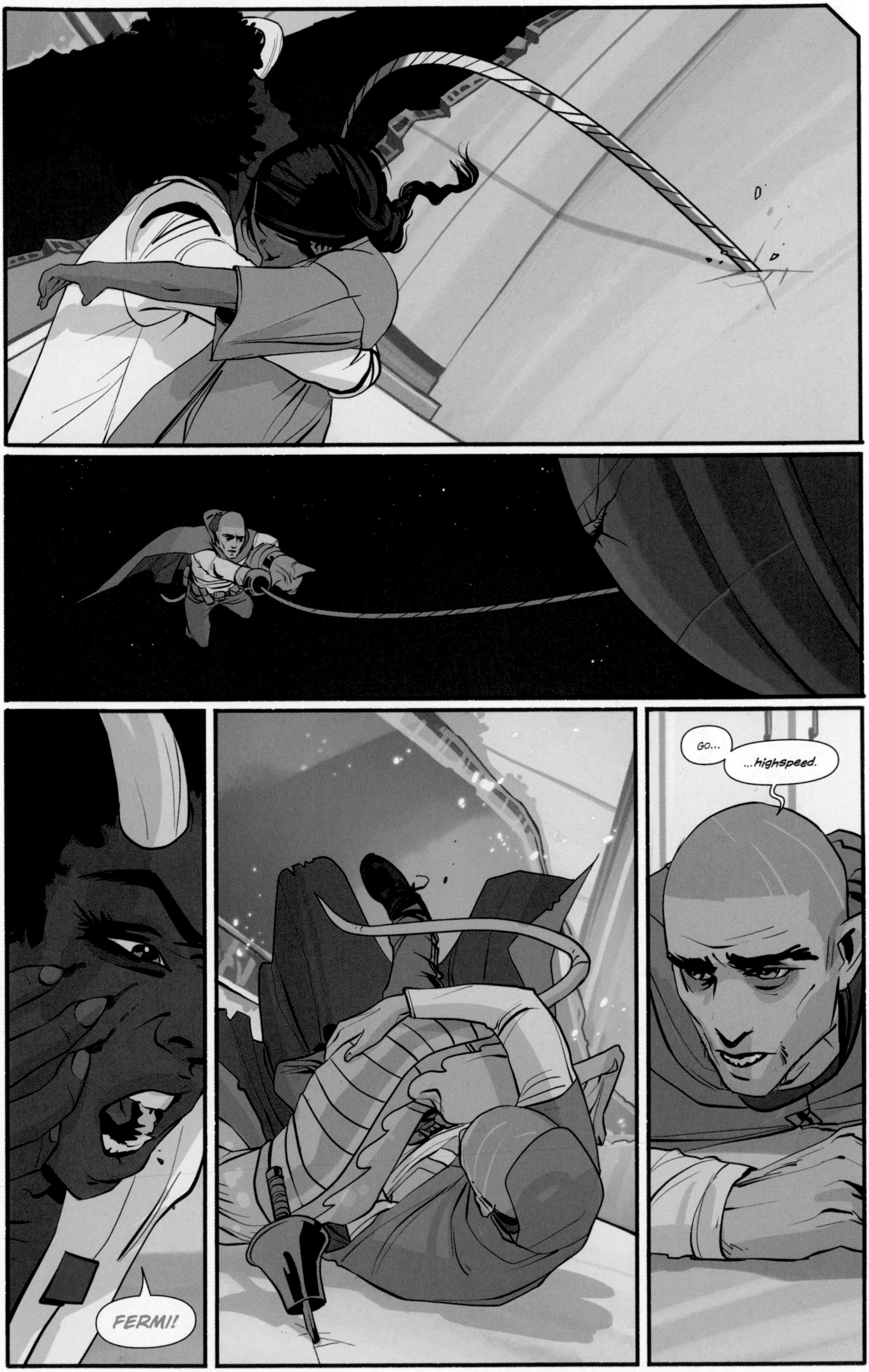
FERMI!
GO...
...highspeed.

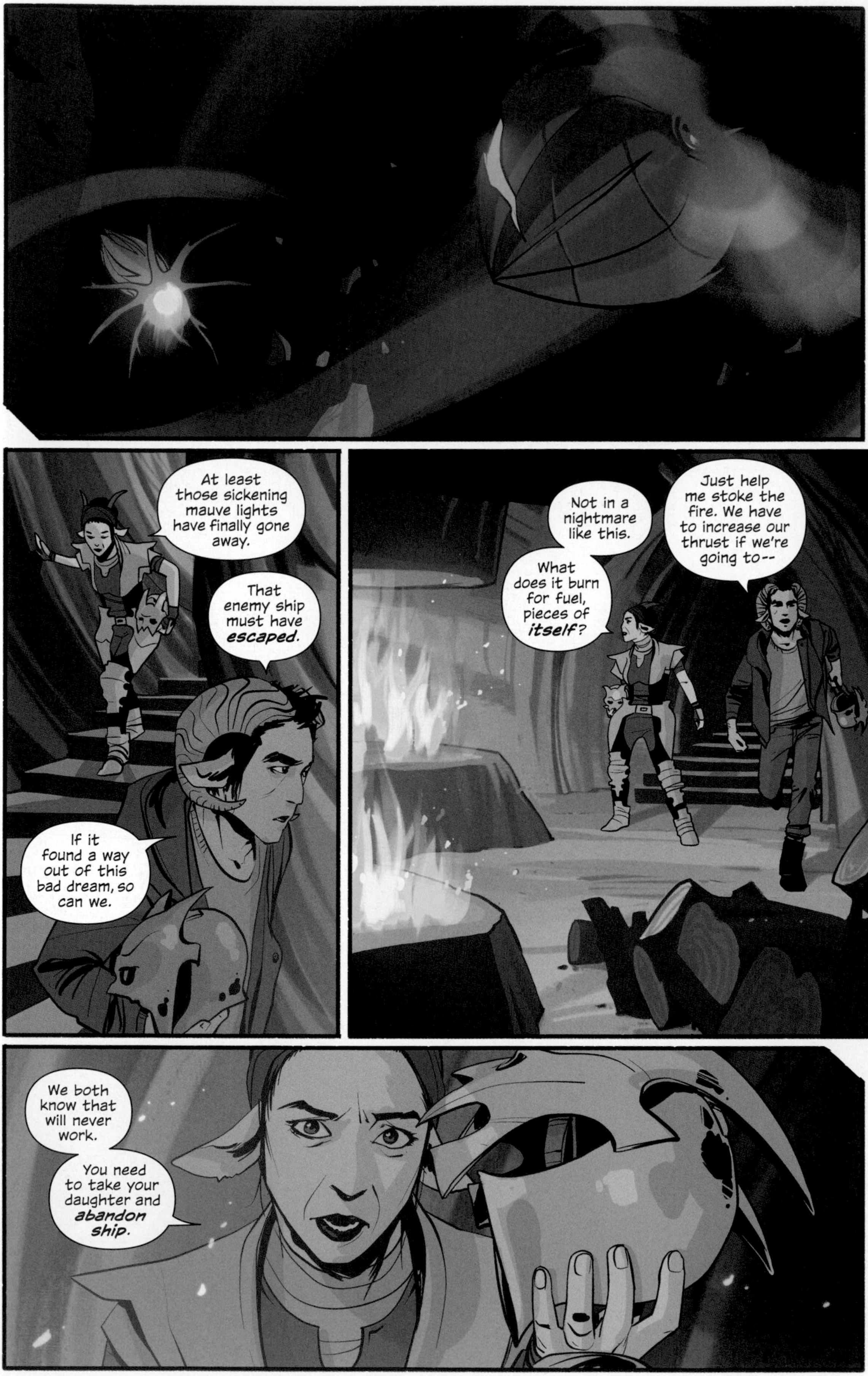
At least those sickening mauve lights have finally gone away.
That enemy ship must have *escaped*.
If it found a way out of this bad dream, so can we.
Not in a nightmare like this.
What does it burn for fuel, pieces of *itself*?
Just help me stoke the fire. We have to increase our thrust if we're going to--
We both know that will never work.
You need to take your daughter and *abandon ship*.

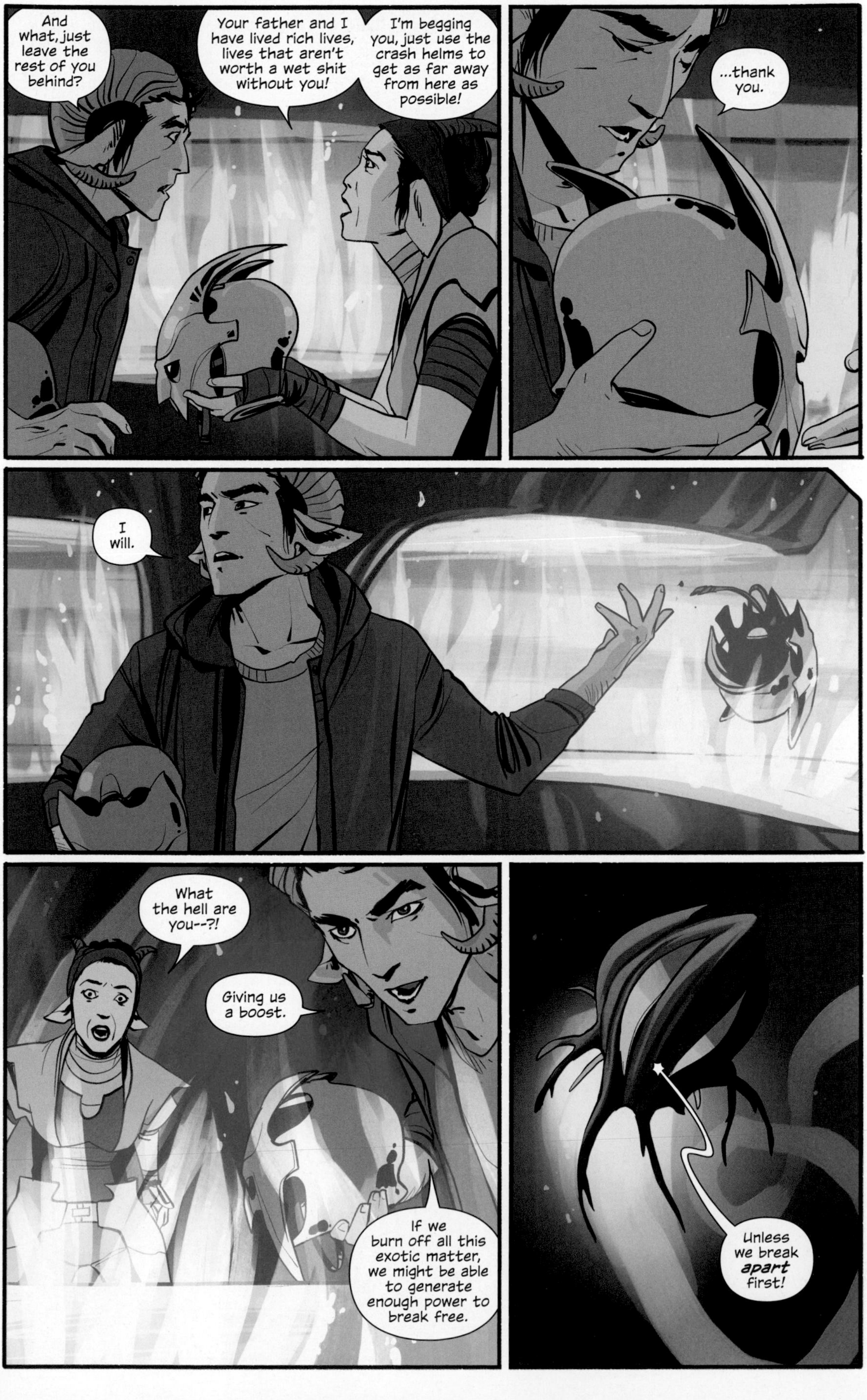
And what, just leave the rest of you behind?
Your father and I have lived rich lives, lives that aren't worth a wet shit without you!
I'm begging you, just use the crash helms to get as far away from here as possible!
...thank you.
I will.
What the hell are you--?!
Giving us a boost.
If we burn off all this exotic matter, we might be able to generate enough power to break free.
Unless we break *apart* first!

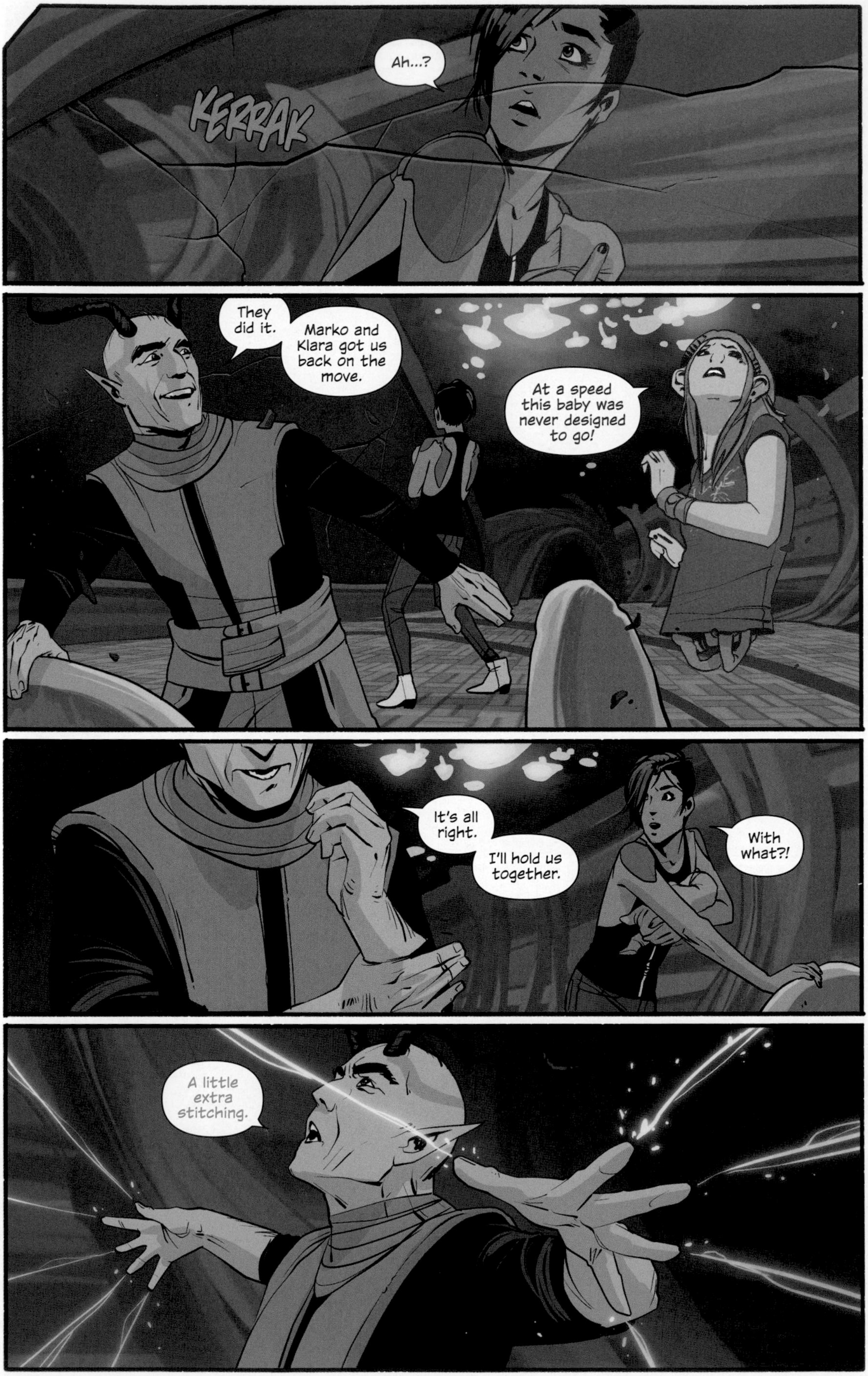
Ah...?
KERRAK
They did it.
Marko and Klara got us back on the move.
At a speed this baby was never designed to go!
It's all right.
I'll hold us together.
With what?!
A little extra stitching.

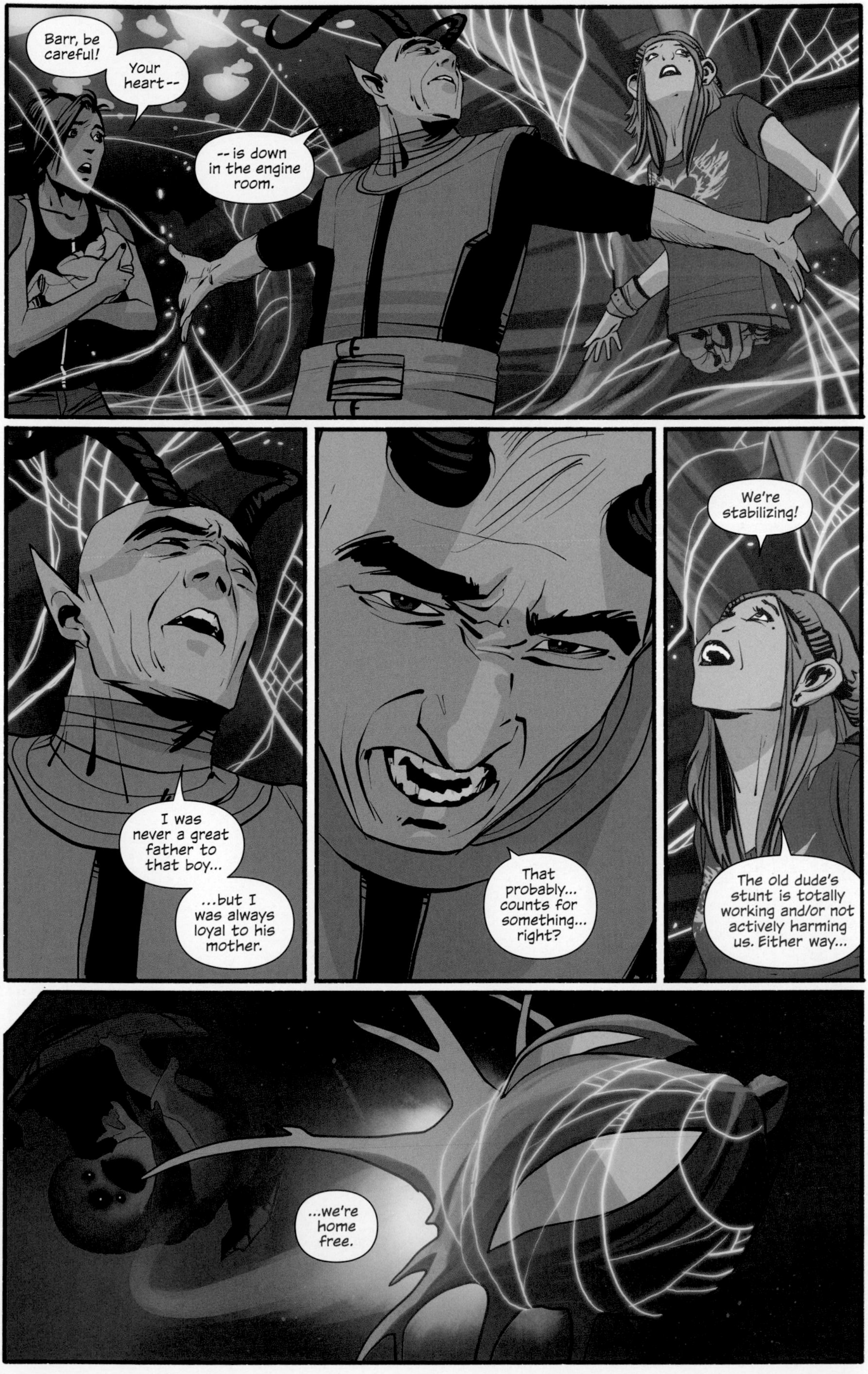
Barr, be careful!
Your heart--
--is down in the engine room.
I was never a great father to that boy...
...but I was always loyal to his mother.
That probably... counts for something... right?
We're stabilizing!
The old dude's stunt is totally working and/or not actively harming us. Either way...
...we're home free.

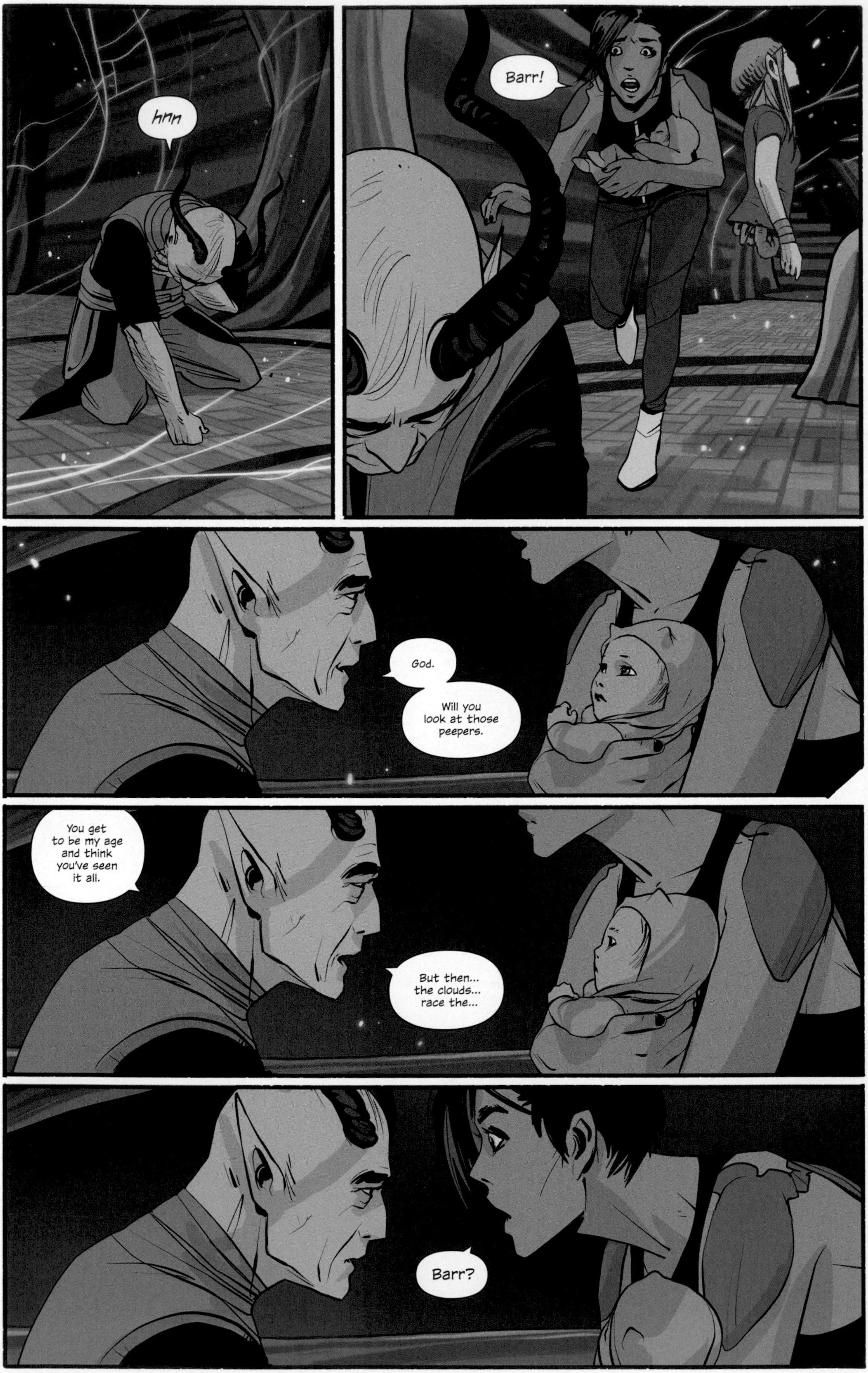
hnn
Barr!
God.
Will you look at those peepers.
You get to be my age and think you've seen it all.
But then... the clouds... race the...
Barr?

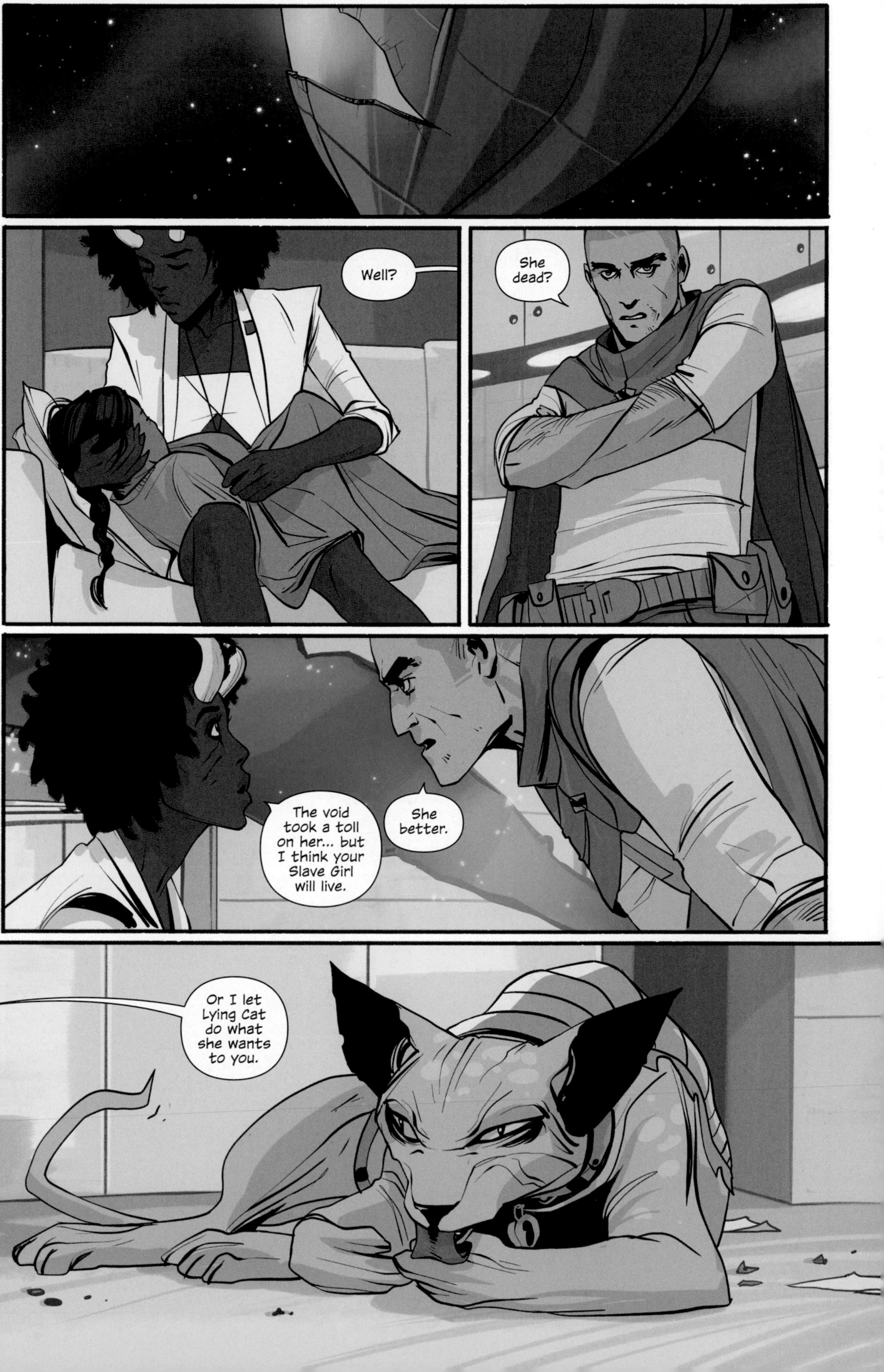
Well?
She dead?
The void took a toll on her... but I think your Slave Girl will live.
She better.
Or I let Lying Cat do what she wants to you.

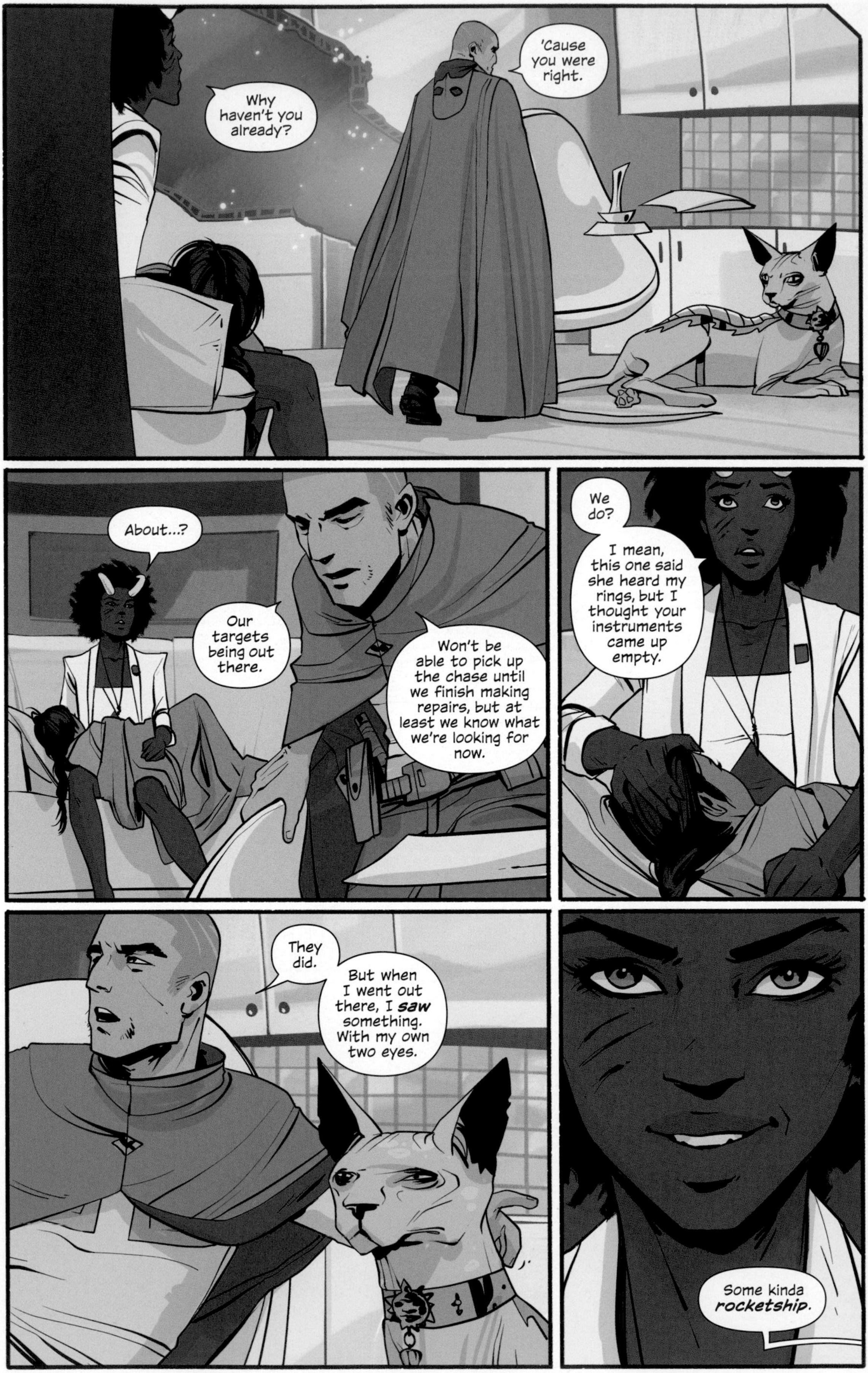
Why haven't you already?
'Cause you were right.
About...?
Our targets being out there.
Won't be able to pick up the chase until we finish making repairs, but at least we know what we're looking for now.
We do?
I mean, this one said she heard my rings, but I thought your instruments came up empty.
They did.
But when I went out there, I *saw* something. With my own two eyes.
Some kinda ***rocketship***.

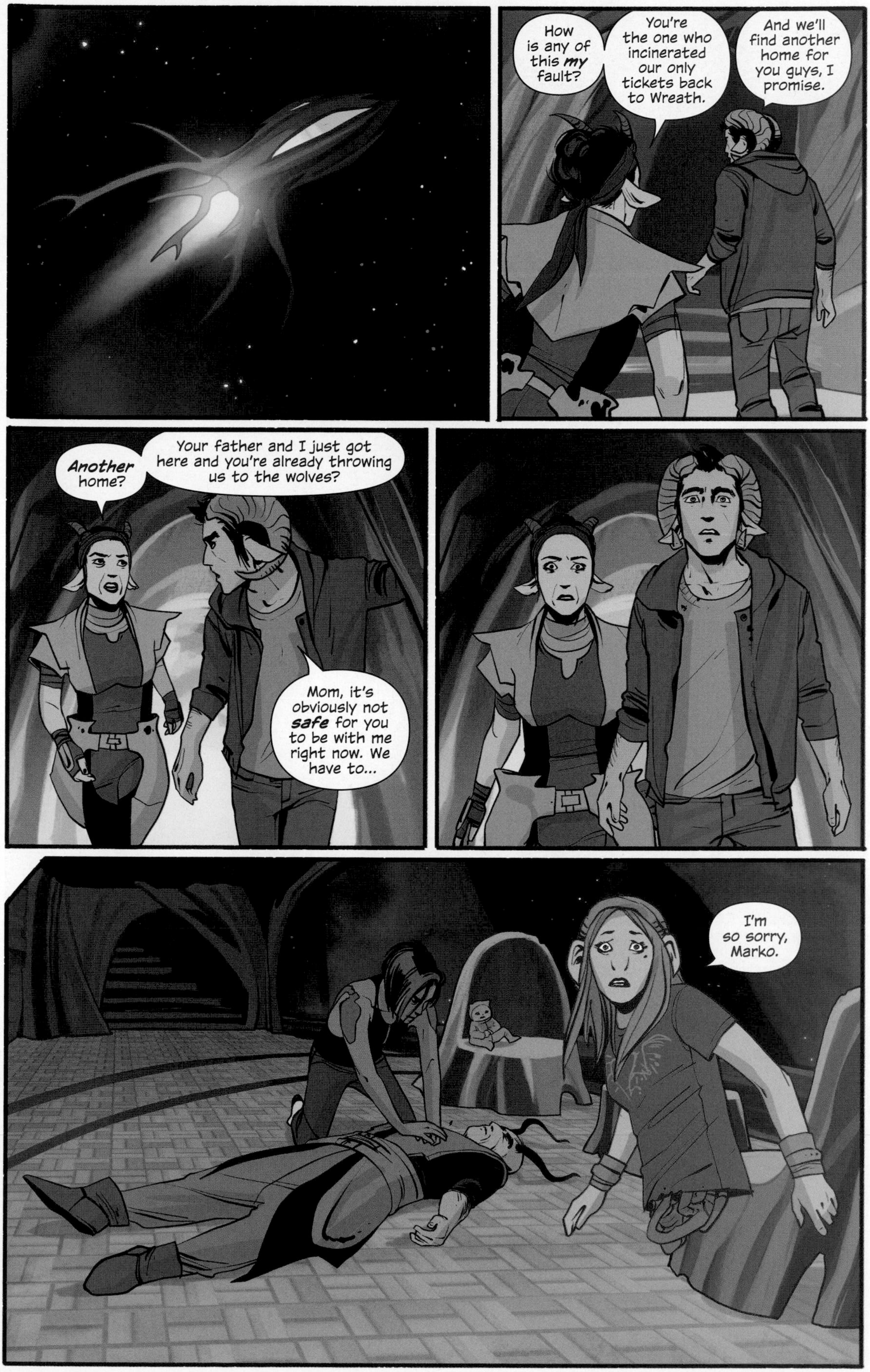
How is any of this *my* fault?
You're the one who incinerated our only tickets back to Wreath.
And we'll find another home for you guys, I promise.
Another home?
Your father and I just got here and you're already throwing us to the wolves?
Mom, it's obviously not *safe* for you to be with me right now. We have to...
I'm so sorry, Marko.

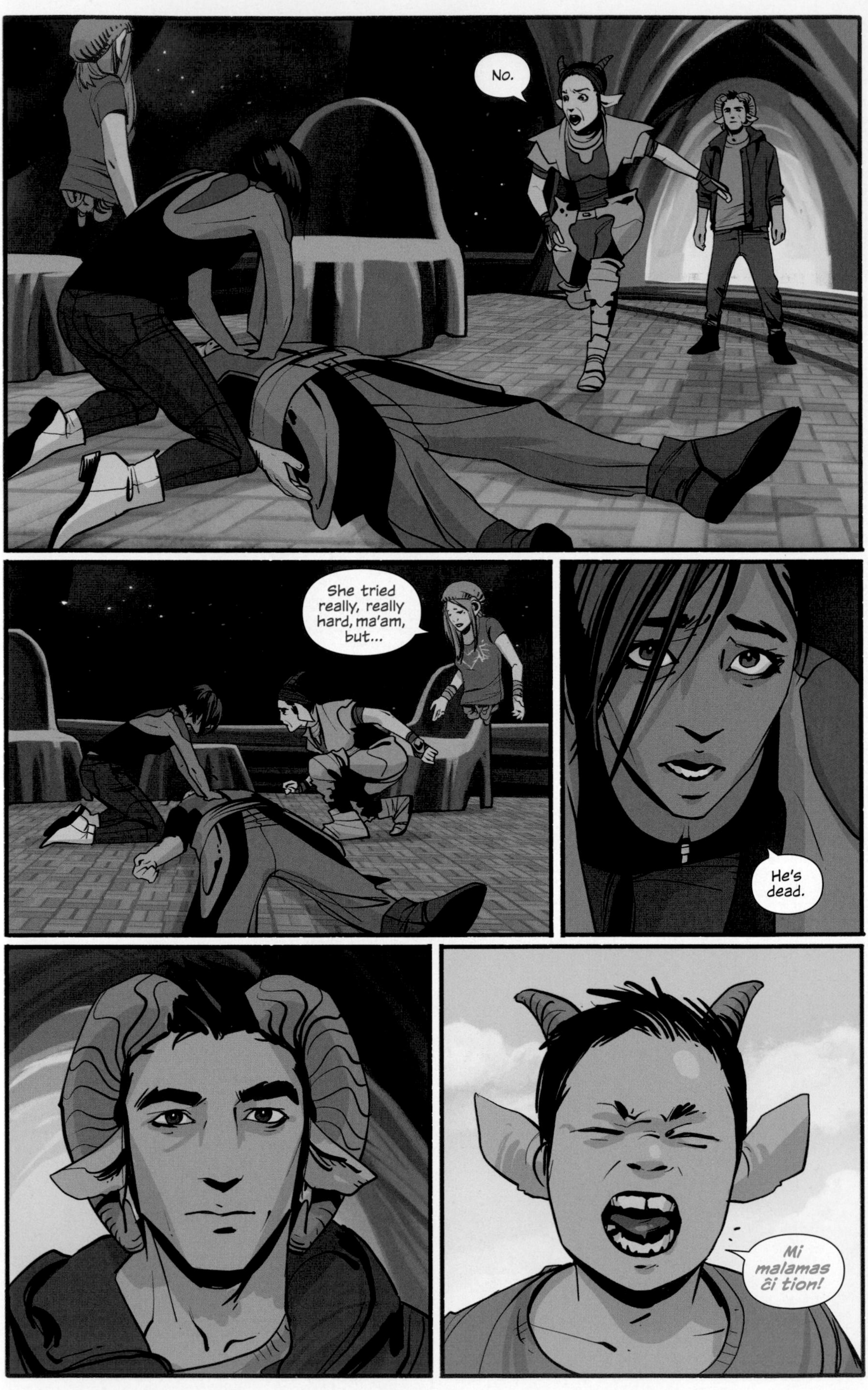
No.
She tried really, really hard, ma'am, but...
He's dead.
Mi malamas ĉi tion!

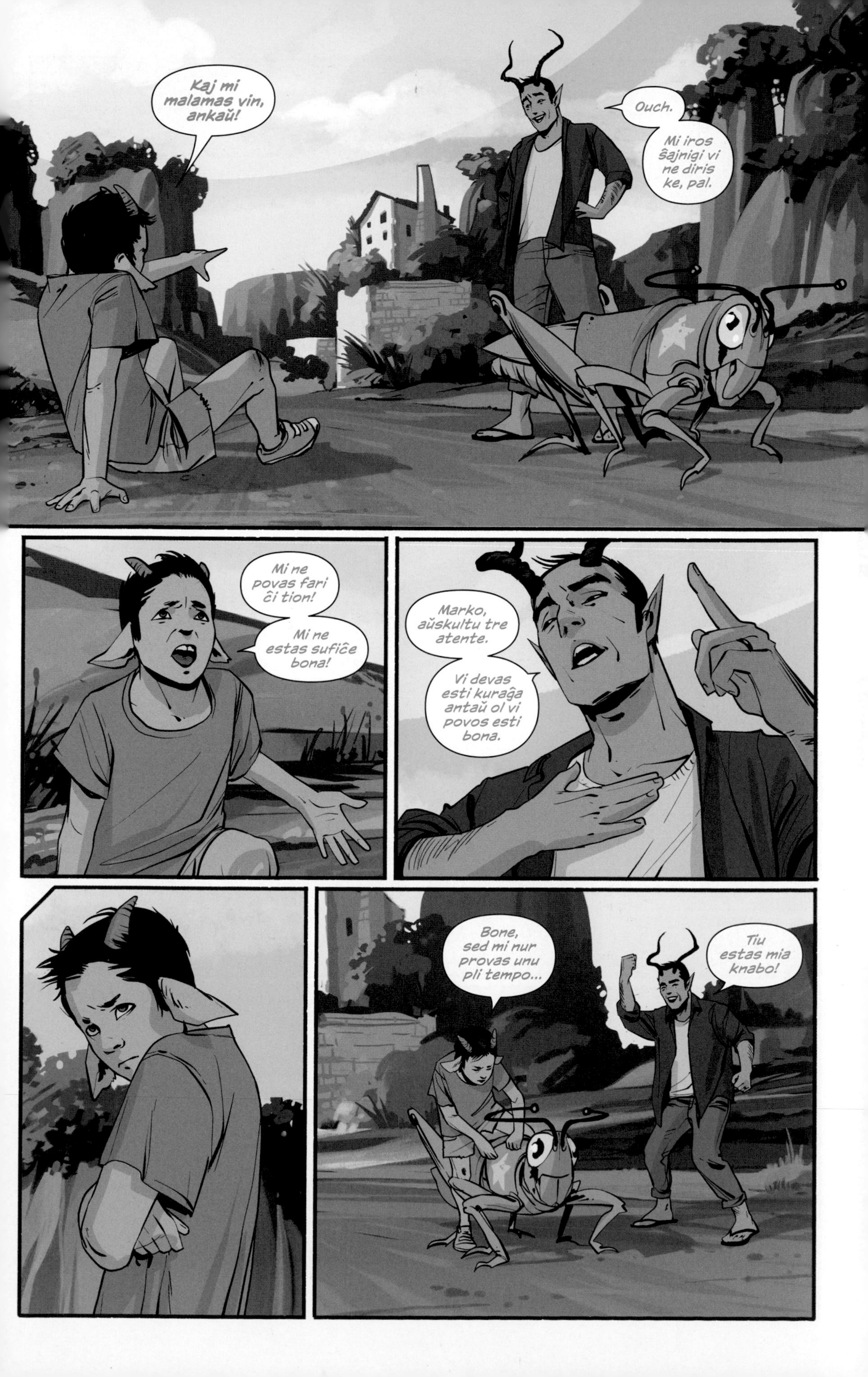
Kaj mi malamas vin, ankaŭ!
Ouch.
Mi iros ŝajnigi vi ne diris ke, pal.
Mi ne povas fari ĉi tion!
Mi ne estas sufiĉe bona!
Marko, aŭskultu tre atente.
Vi devas esti kuraĝa antaŭ ol vi povos esti bona.
Bone, sed mi nur provas unu pli tempo...
Tiu estas mia knabo!

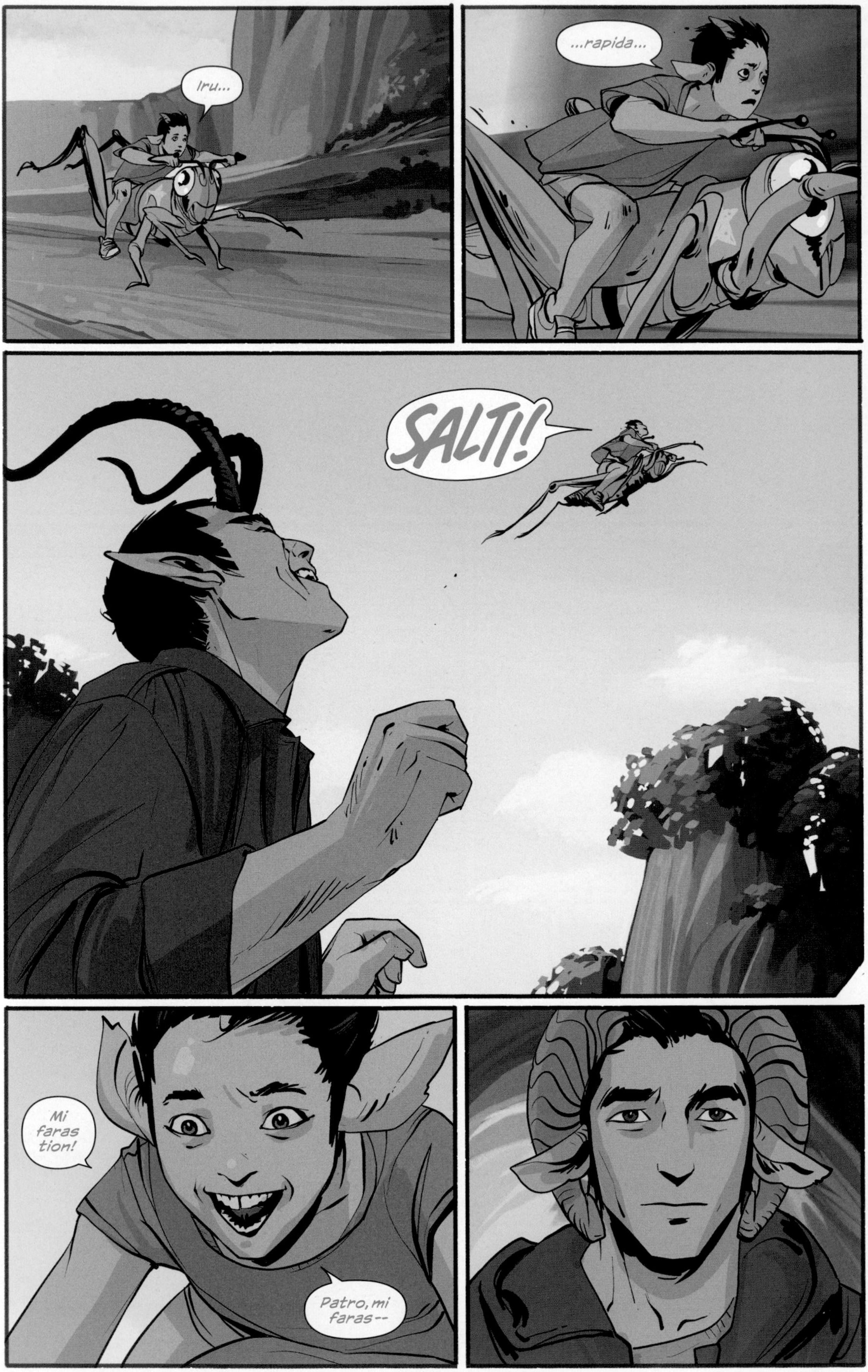
Iru...
...rapida...
SALTI!
Mi faras tion!
Patro, mi faras--

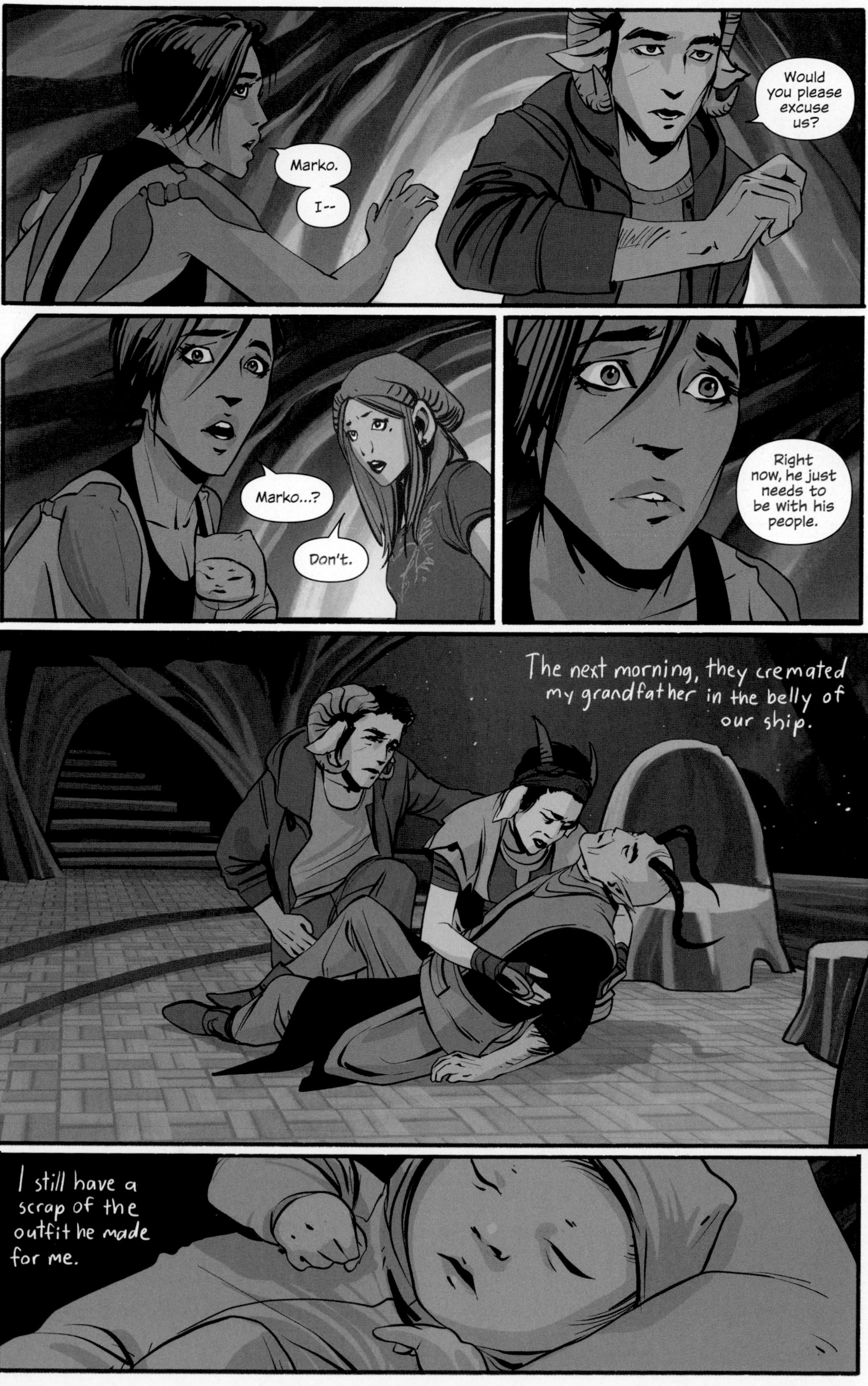
Marko.
I--
Would you please excuse us?
Marko...?
Don't.
Right now, he just needs to be with his people.
The next morning, they cremated my grandfather in the belly of our ship.
I still have a scrap of the outfit he made for me.

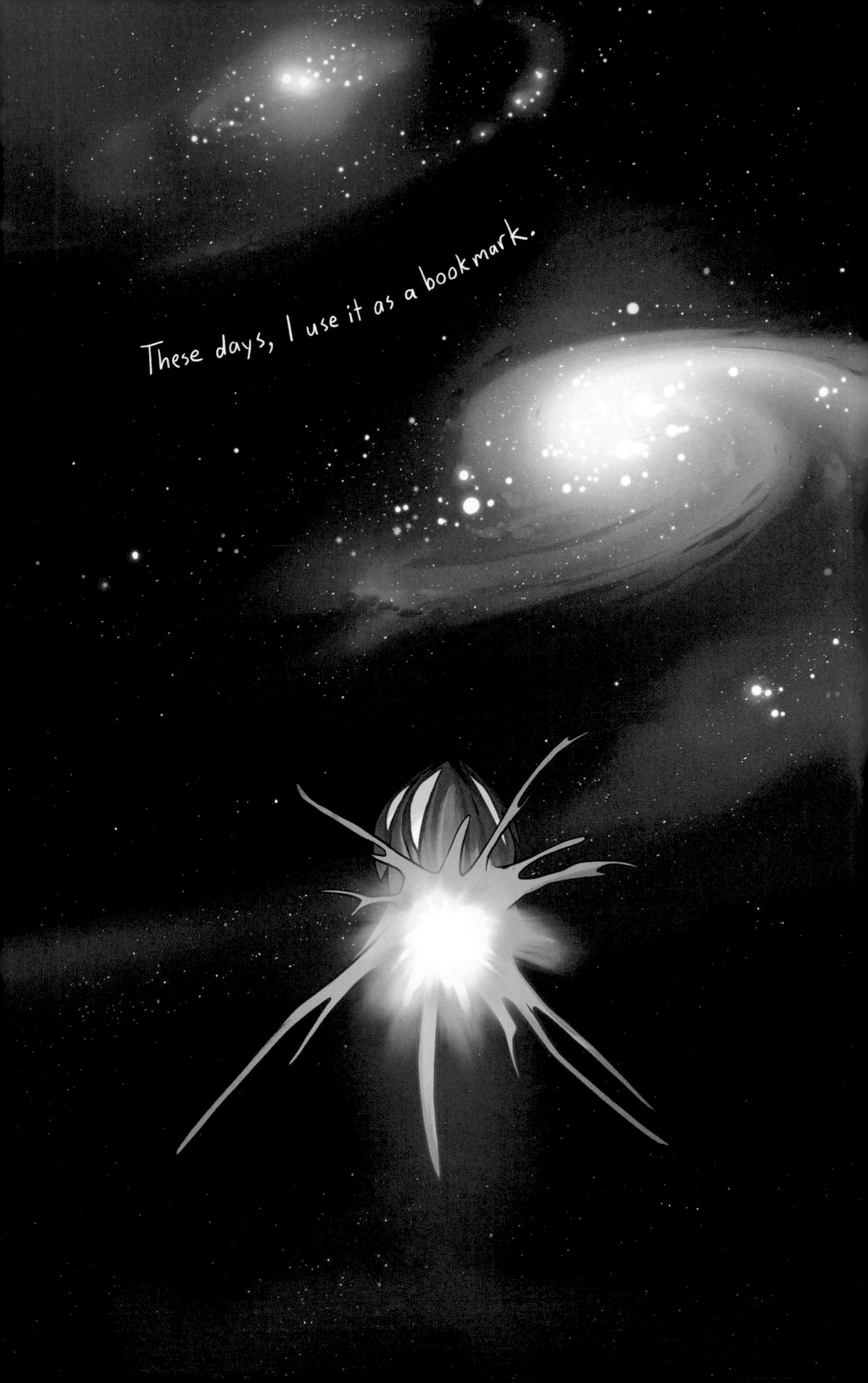
These days, I use it as a bookmark.

end chapter eleven

CHAPTER
TWELVE

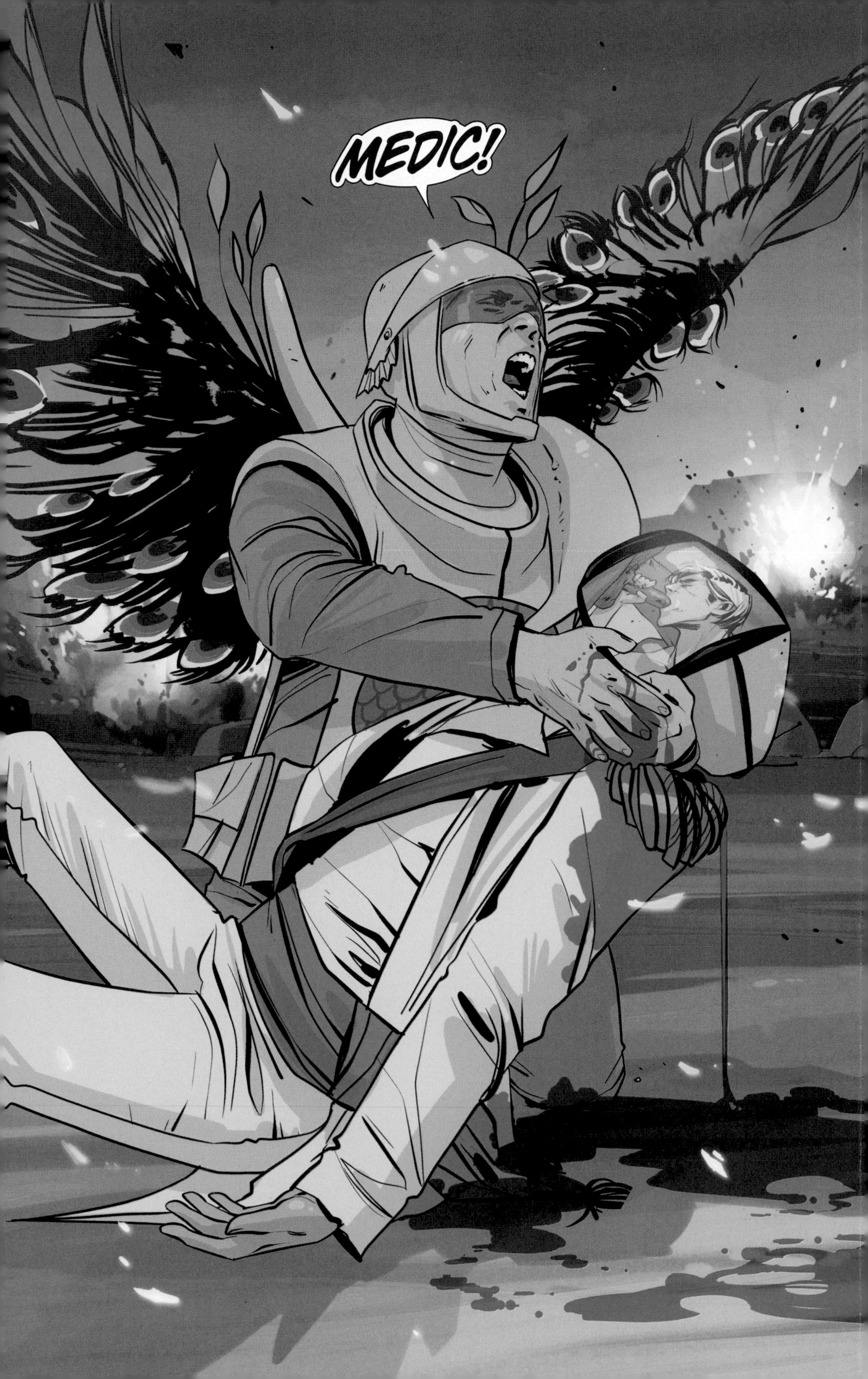
MEDIC!

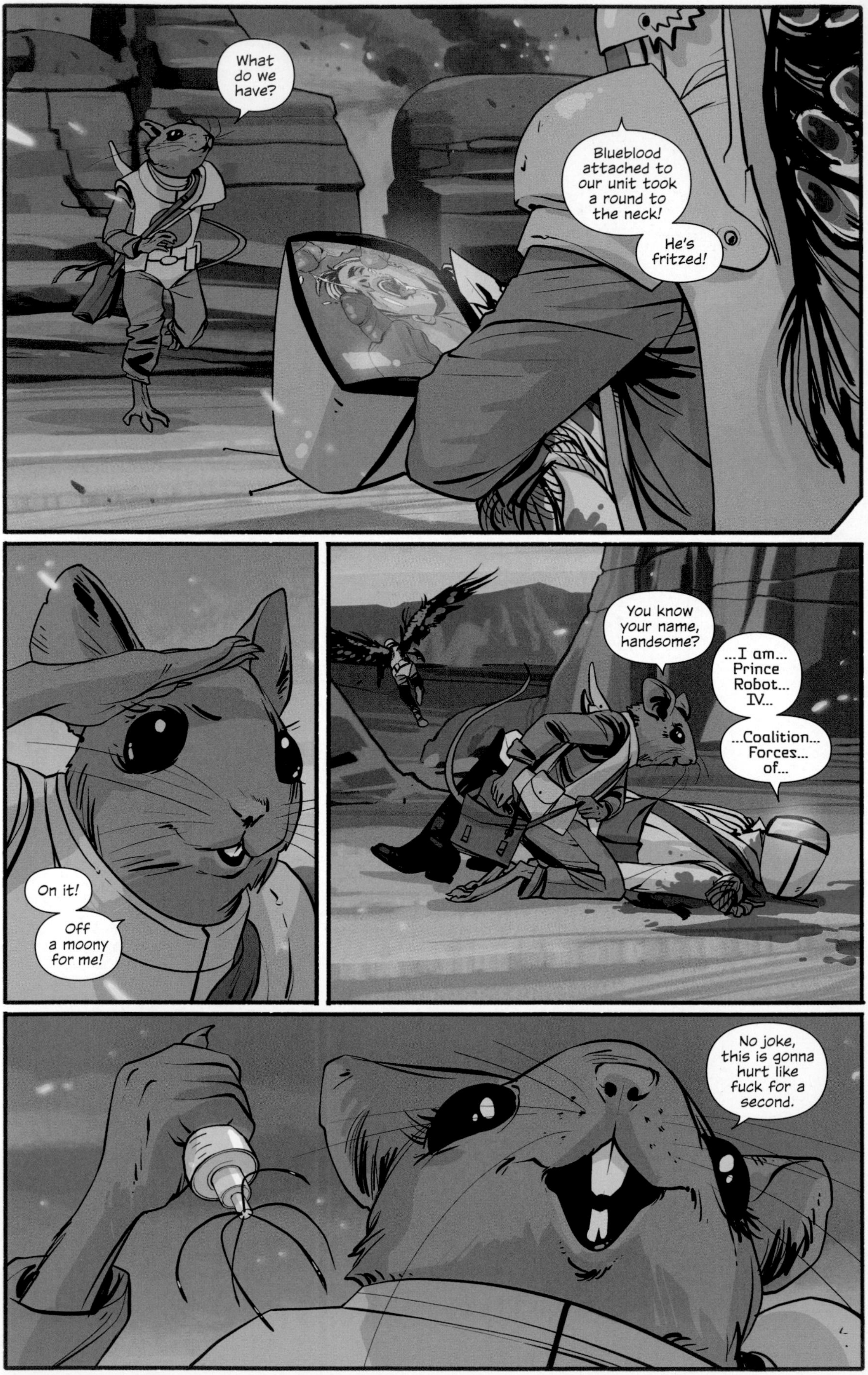
What do we have?
Blueblood attached to our unit took a round to the neck!
He's fritzed!
On it!
Off a moony for me!
You know your name, handsome?
...I am... Prince Robot... IV...
...Coalition... Forces... of...
No joke, this is gonna hurt like fuck for a second.

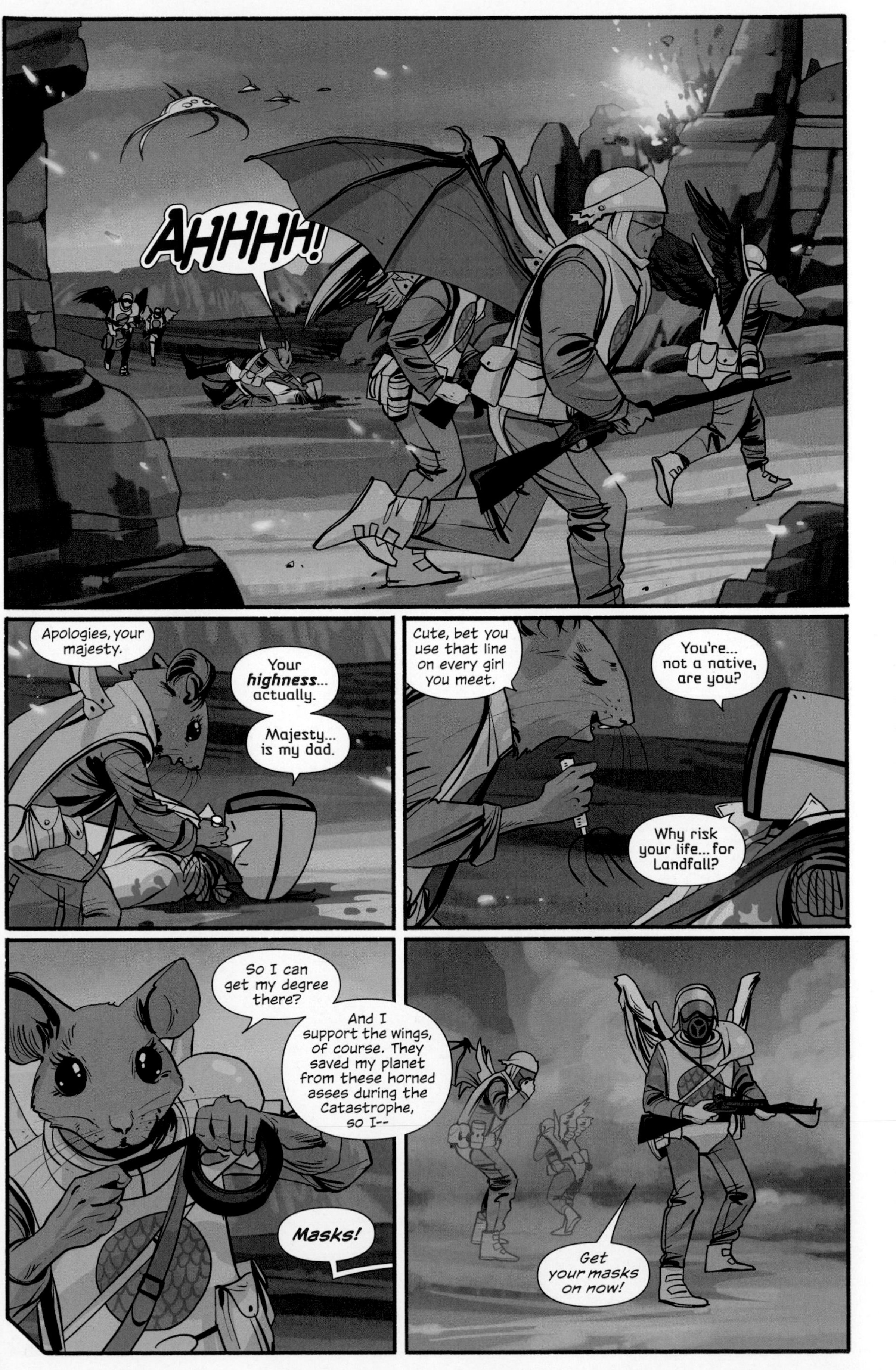
AHHHH!
Apologies, your majesty.
Your *highness*... actually.
Majesty... is my dad.
Cute, bet you use that line on every girl you meet.
You're... not a native, are you?
Why risk your life... for Landfall?
So I can get my degree there?
And I support the wings, of course. They saved my planet from these horned asses during the Catastrophe, so I--
Masks!
Get your masks on now!

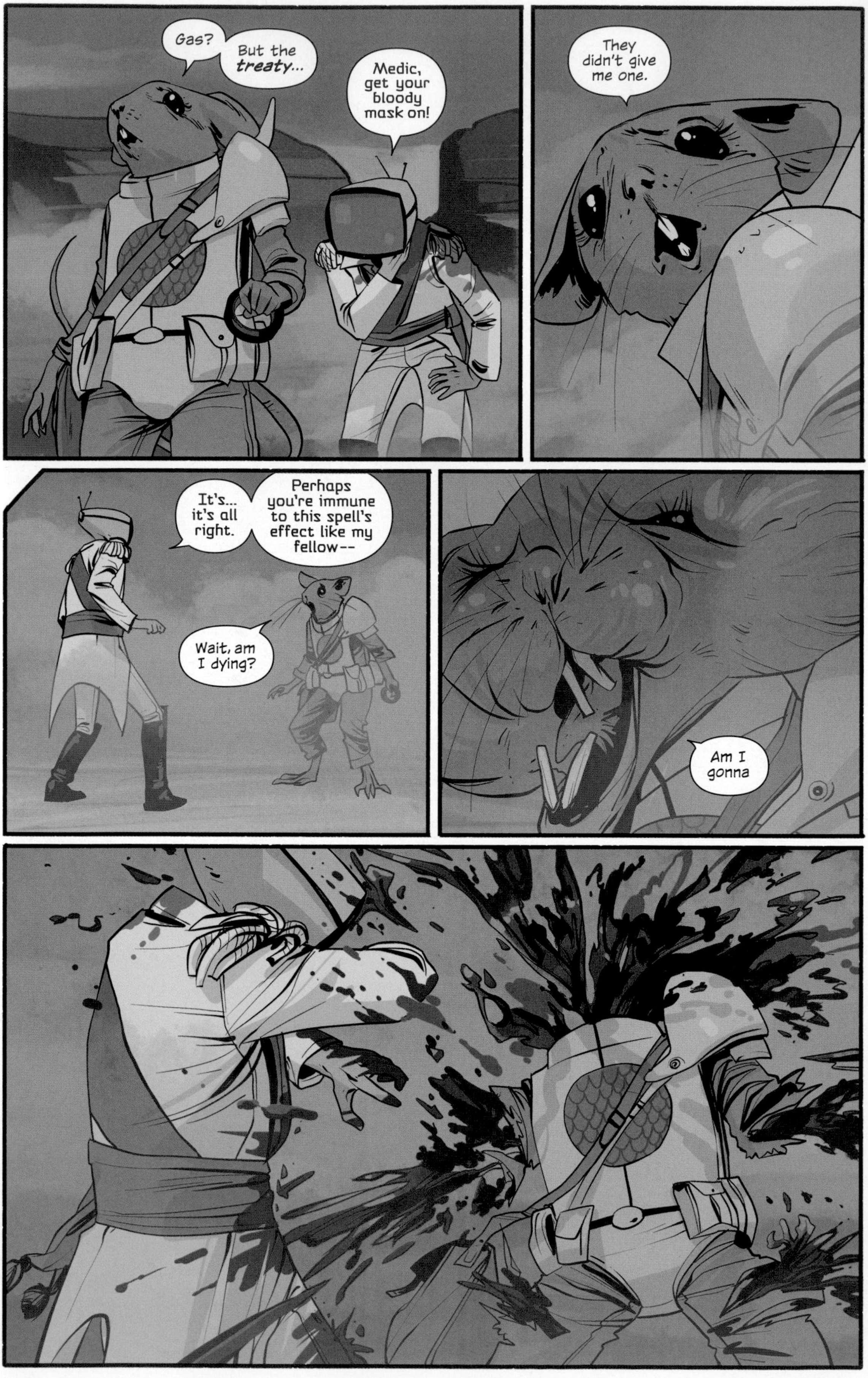
Gas?
But the *treaty*...
Medic, get your bloody mask on!
They didn't give me one.
It's... it's all right.
Perhaps you're immune to this spell's effect like my fellow--
Wait, am I dying?
Am I gonna

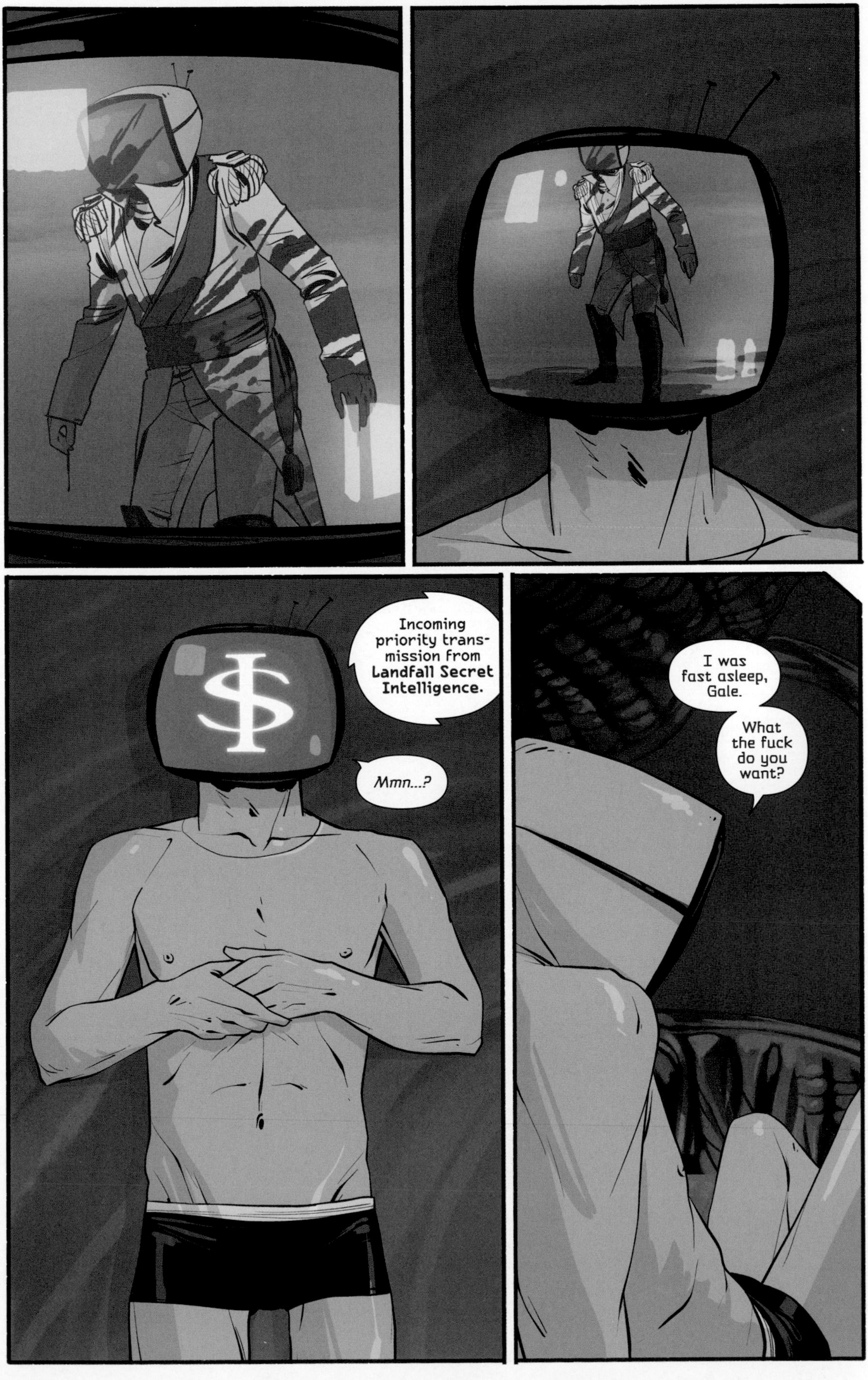
Incoming priority transmission from Landfall Secret Intelligence.
Mmn...?
I was fast asleep, Gale.
What the fuck do you want?

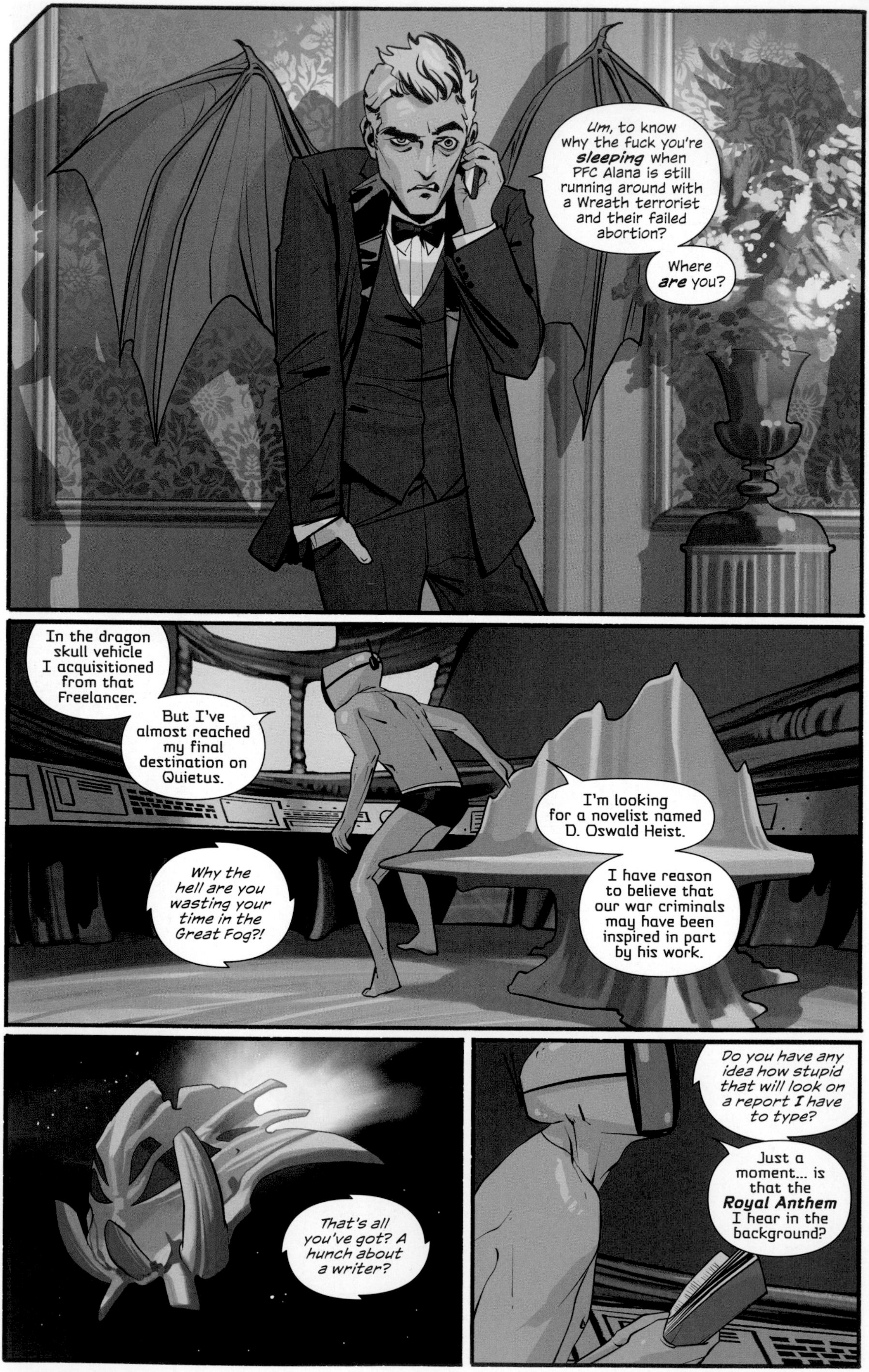
Um, to know why the fuck you're sleeping when PFC Alana is still running around with a Wreath terrorist and their failed abortion?
Where are you?
In the dragon skull vehicle I acquisitioned from that Freelancer.
But I've almost reached my final destination on Quietus.
Why the hell are you wasting your time in the Great Fog?!
I'm looking for a novelist named D. Oswald Heist.
I have reason to believe that our war criminals may have been inspired in part by his work.
That's all you've got? A hunch about a writer?
Do you have any idea how stupid that will look on a report I have to type?
Just a moment... is that the Royal Anthem I hear in the background?

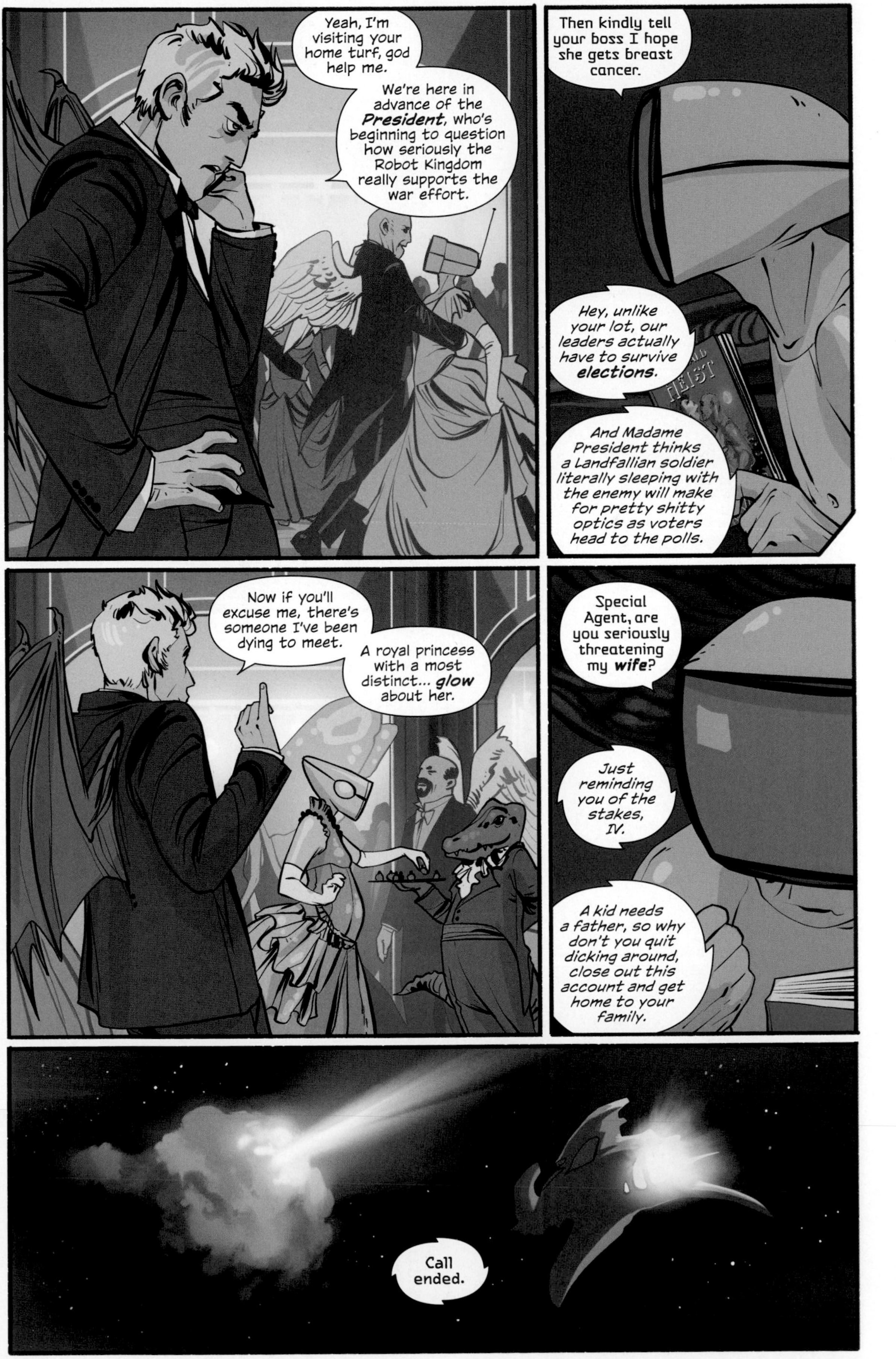

Yeah, I'm visiting your home turf, god help me.
We're here in advance of the **President**, who's beginning to question how seriously the Robot Kingdom really supports the war effort.
Then kindly tell your boss I hope she gets breast cancer.
*Hey, unlike your lot, our leaders actually have to survive **elections**.*
And Madame President thinks a Landfallian soldier literally sleeping with the enemy will make for pretty shitty optics as voters head to the polls.
Now if you'll excuse me, there's someone I've been dying to meet.
A royal princess with a most distinct... **glow** about her.
Special Agent, are you seriously threatening my **wife**?
Just reminding you of the stakes, IV.
A kid needs a father, so why don't you quit dicking around, close out this account and get home to your family.
Call ended.

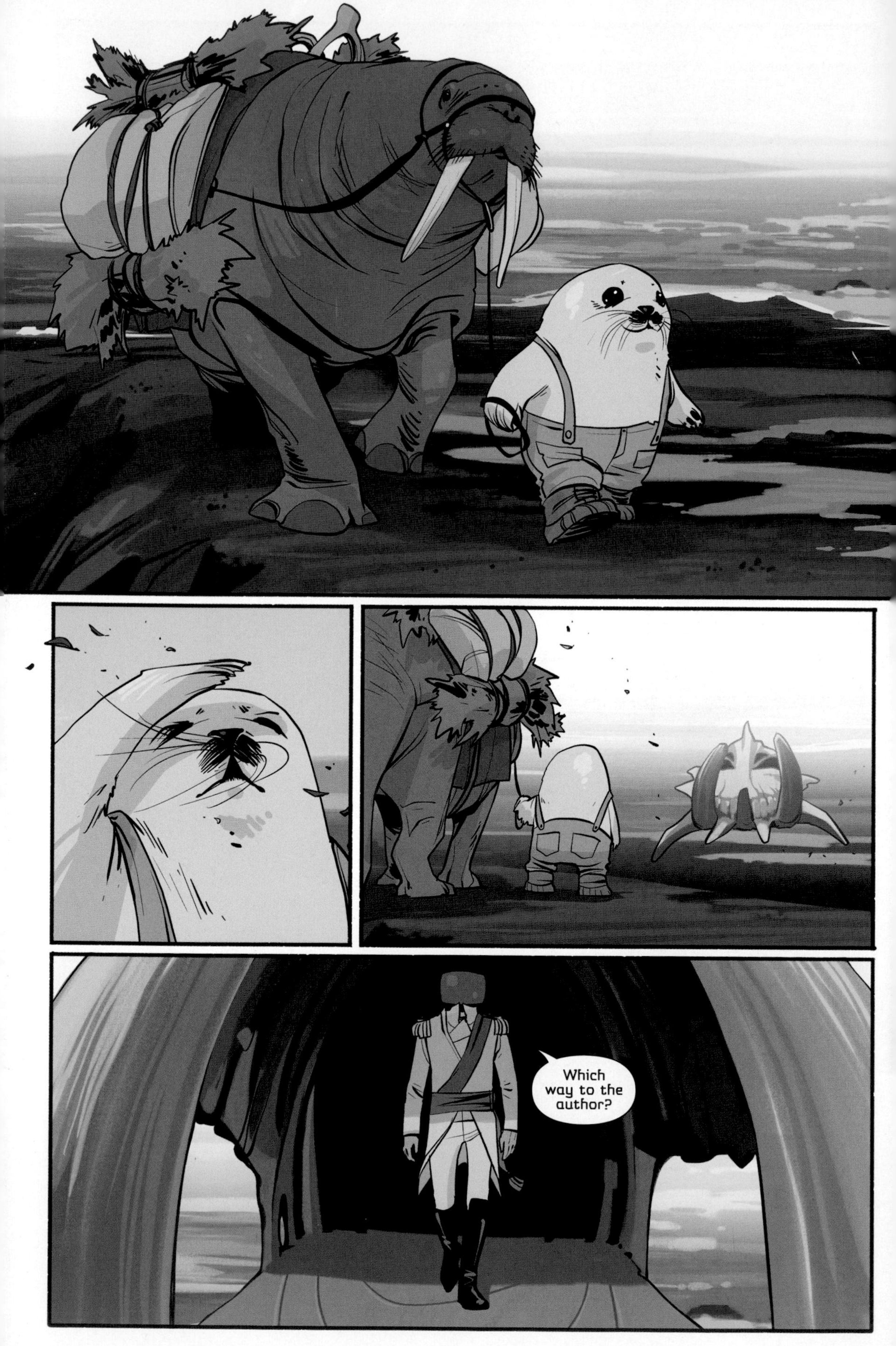
Which way to the author?

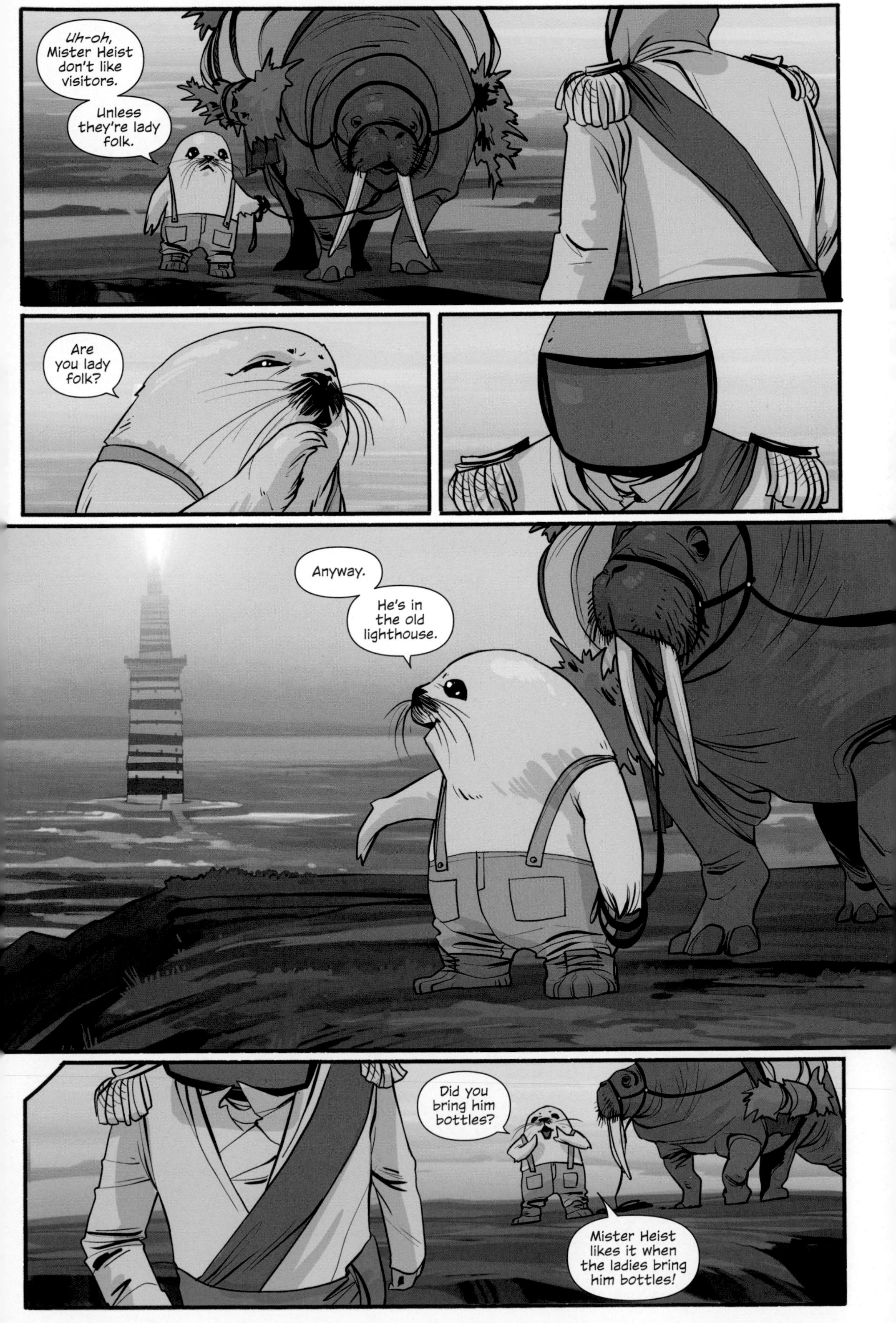
Uh-oh, Mister Heist don't like visitors.
Unless they're lady folk.
Are you lady folk?
Anyway.
He's in the old lighthouse.
Did you bring him bottles?
Mister Heist likes it when the ladies bring him bottles!

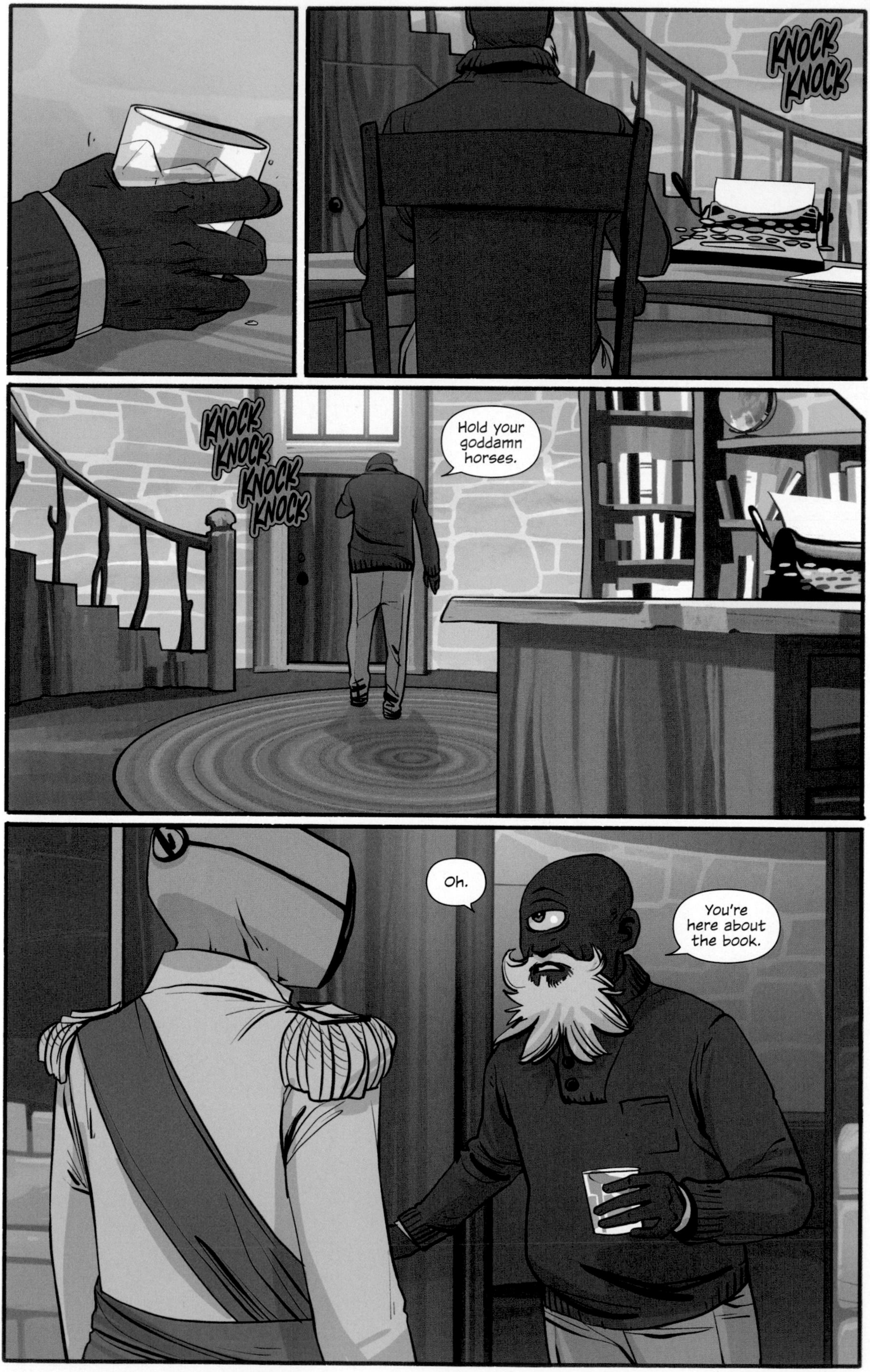

KNOCK KNOCK
KNOCK KNOCK KNOCK KNOCK
Hold your goddamn horses.
Oh.
You're here about the book.

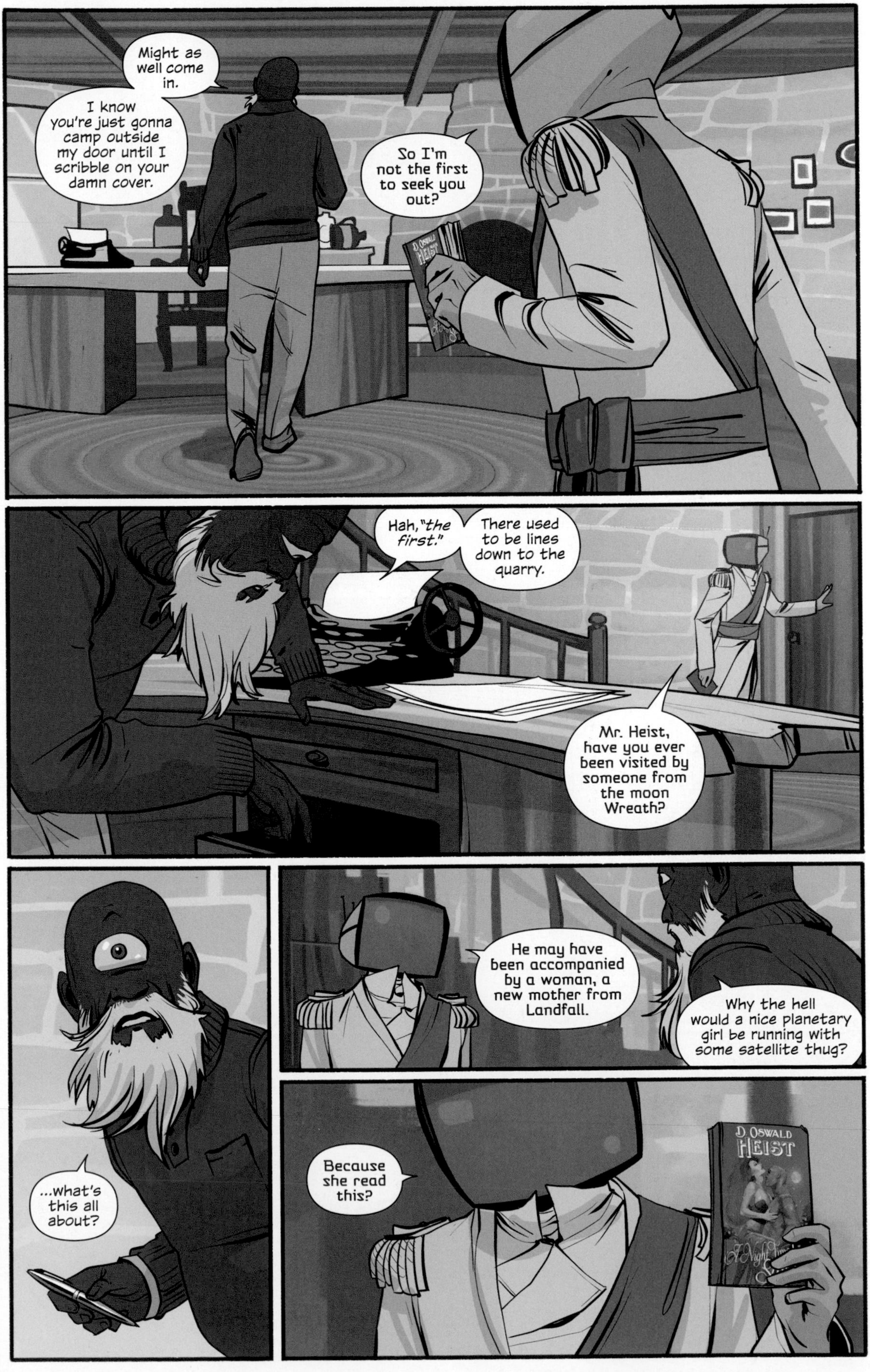

Might as well come in.
I know you're just gonna camp outside my door until I scribble on your damn cover.
So I'm not the first to seek you out?
D. OSWALD HEIST
Hah, "the first."
There used to be lines down to the quarry.
Mr. Heist, have you ever been visited by someone from the moon Wreath?
...what's this all about?
He may have been accompanied by a woman, a new mother from Landfall.
Why the hell would a nice planetary girl be running with some satellite thug?
Because she read this?
D. OSWALD HEIST

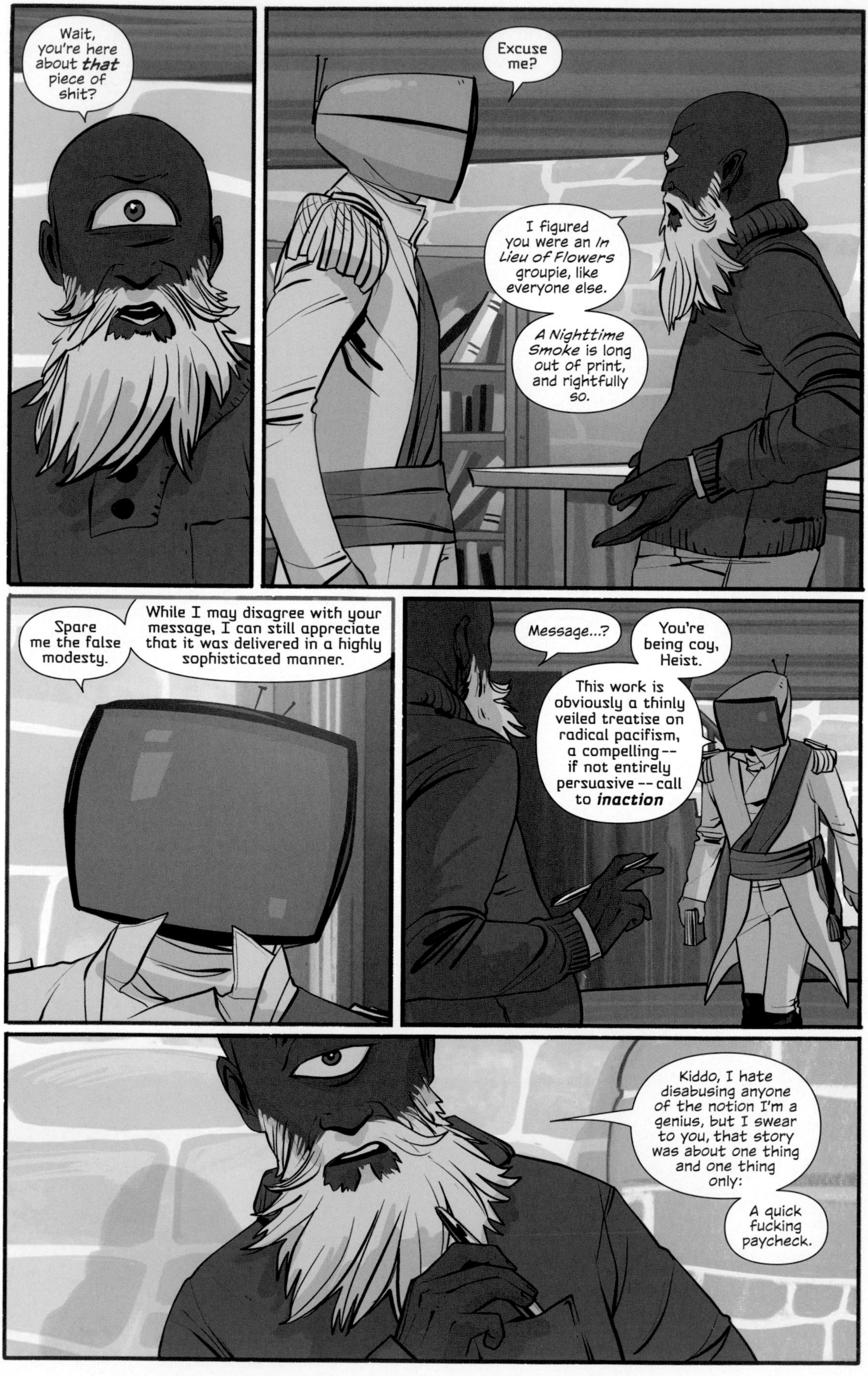
Wait, you're here about *that* piece of shit?
Excuse me?
I figured you were an *In Lieu of Flowers* groupie, like everyone else.
A Nighttime Smoke is long out of print, and rightfully so.
Spare me the false modesty.
While I may disagree with your message, I can still appreciate that it was delivered in a highly sophisticated manner.
Message...?
You're being coy, Heist.
This work is obviously a thinly veiled treatise on radical pacifism, a compelling -- if not entirely persuasive -- call to ***inaction***
Kiddo, I hate disabusing anyone of the notion I'm a genius, but I swear to you, that story was about one thing and one thing only:
A quick fucking paycheck.

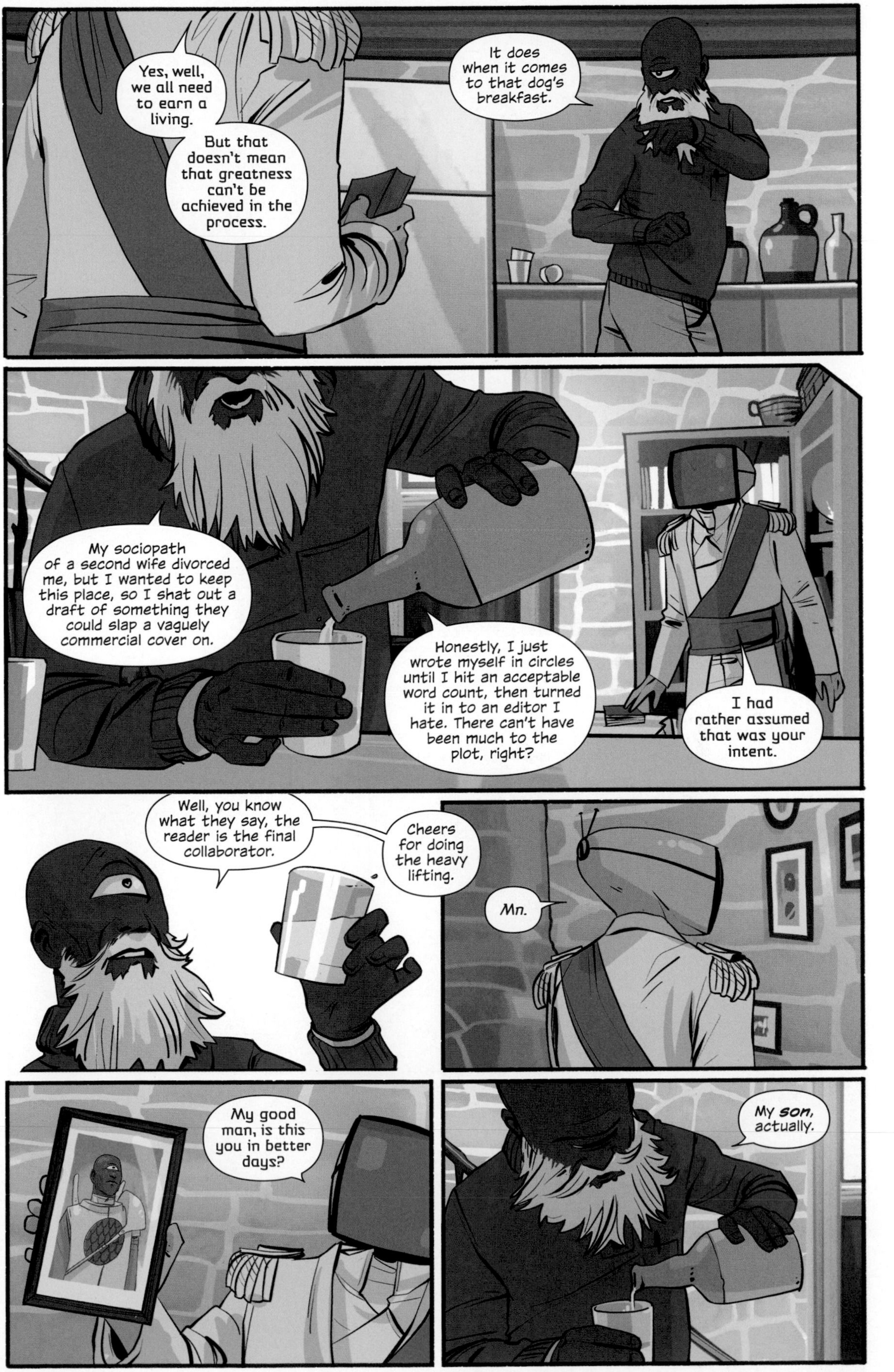

Yes, well, we all need to earn a living.
But that doesn't mean that greatness can't be achieved in the process.
It does when it comes to that dog's breakfast.
My sociopath of a second wife divorced me, but I wanted to keep this place, so I shat out a draft of something they could slap a vaguely commercial cover on.
Honestly, I just wrote myself in circles until I hit an acceptable word count, then turned it in to an editor I hate. There can't have been much to the plot, right?
I had rather assumed that was your intent.
Well, you know what they say, the reader is the final collaborator.
Cheers for doing the heavy lifting.
Mn.
My good man, is this you in better days?
My ***son,*** actually.

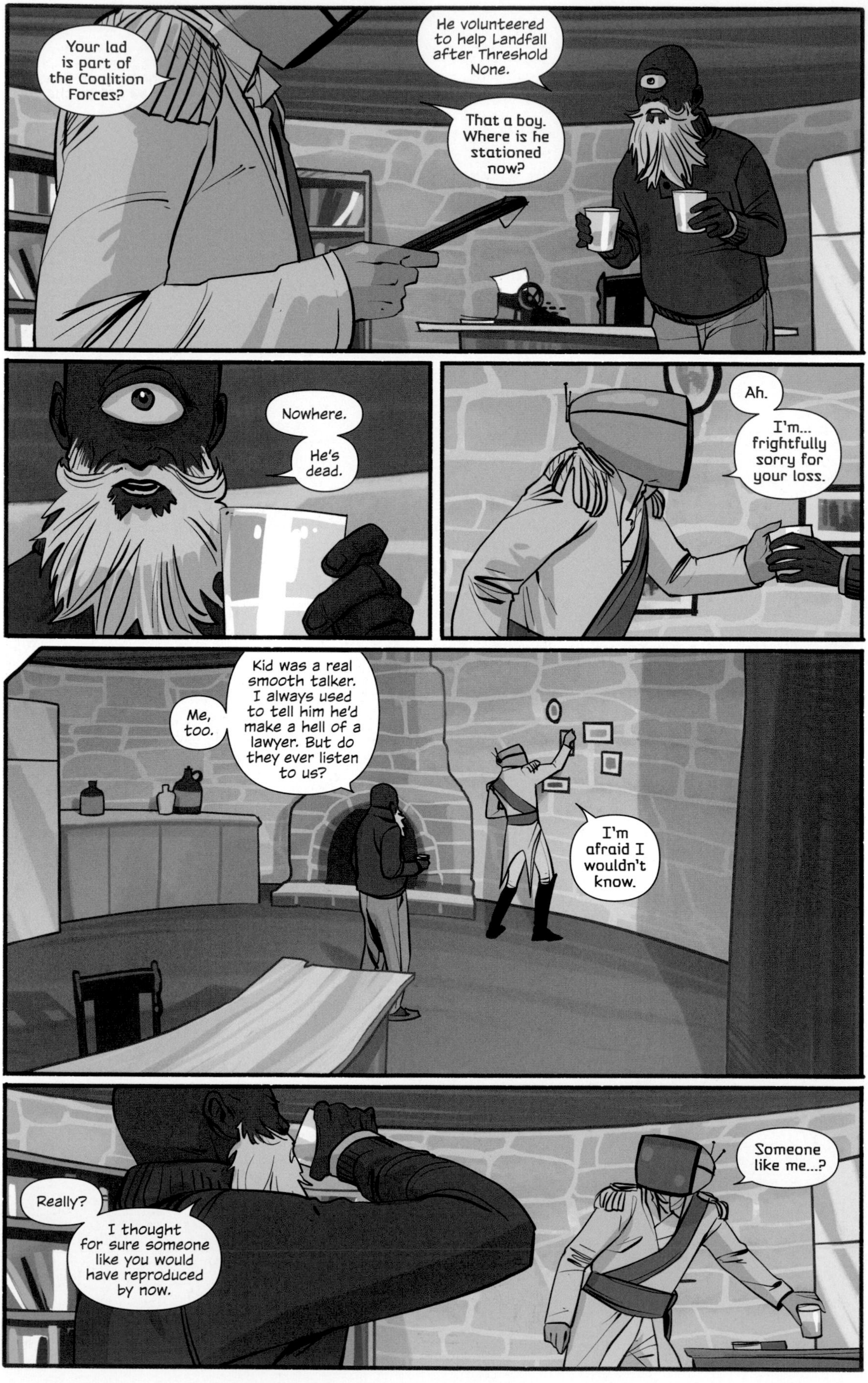
Your lad is part of the Coalition Forces?
He volunteered to help Landfall after Threshold None.
That a boy. Where is he stationed now?
Nowhere.
He's dead.
Ah.
I'm... frightfully sorry for your loss.
Kid was a real smooth talker. I always used to tell him he'd make a hell of a lawyer. But do they ever listen to us?
Me, too.
I'm afraid I wouldn't know.
Really?
I thought for sure someone like you would have reproduced by now.
Someone like me...?

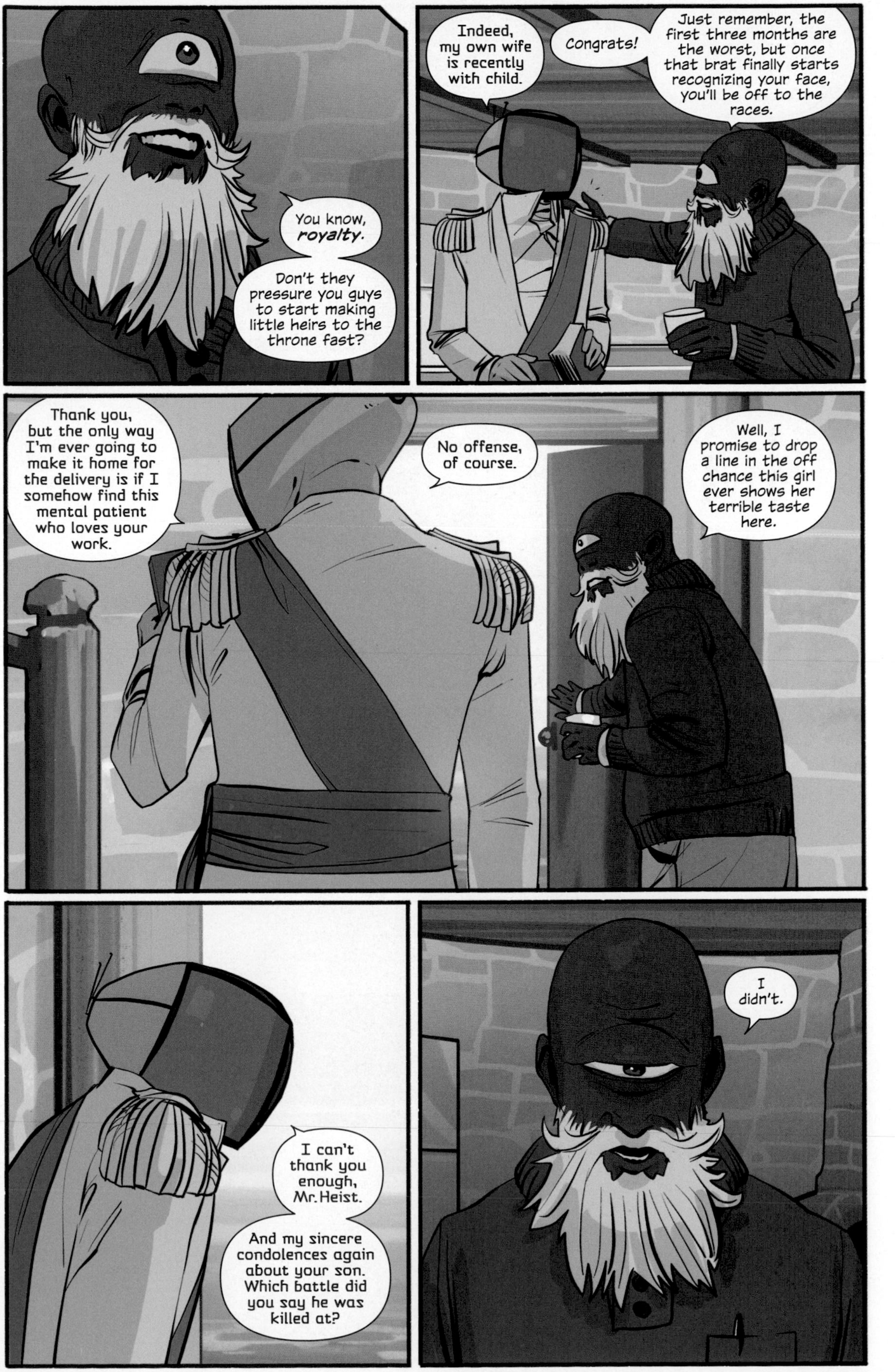
You know, *royalty*.
Don't they pressure you guys to start making little heirs to the throne fast?
Indeed, my own wife is recently with child.
Congrats!
Just remember, the first three months are the worst, but once that brat finally starts recognizing your face, you'll be off to the races.
Thank you, but the only way I'm ever going to make it home for the delivery is if I somehow find this mental patient who loves your work.
No offense, of course.
Well, I promise to drop a line in the off chance this girl ever shows her terrible taste here.
I can't thank you enough, Mr. Heist.
And my sincere condolences again about your son. Which battle did you say he was killed at?
I didn't.

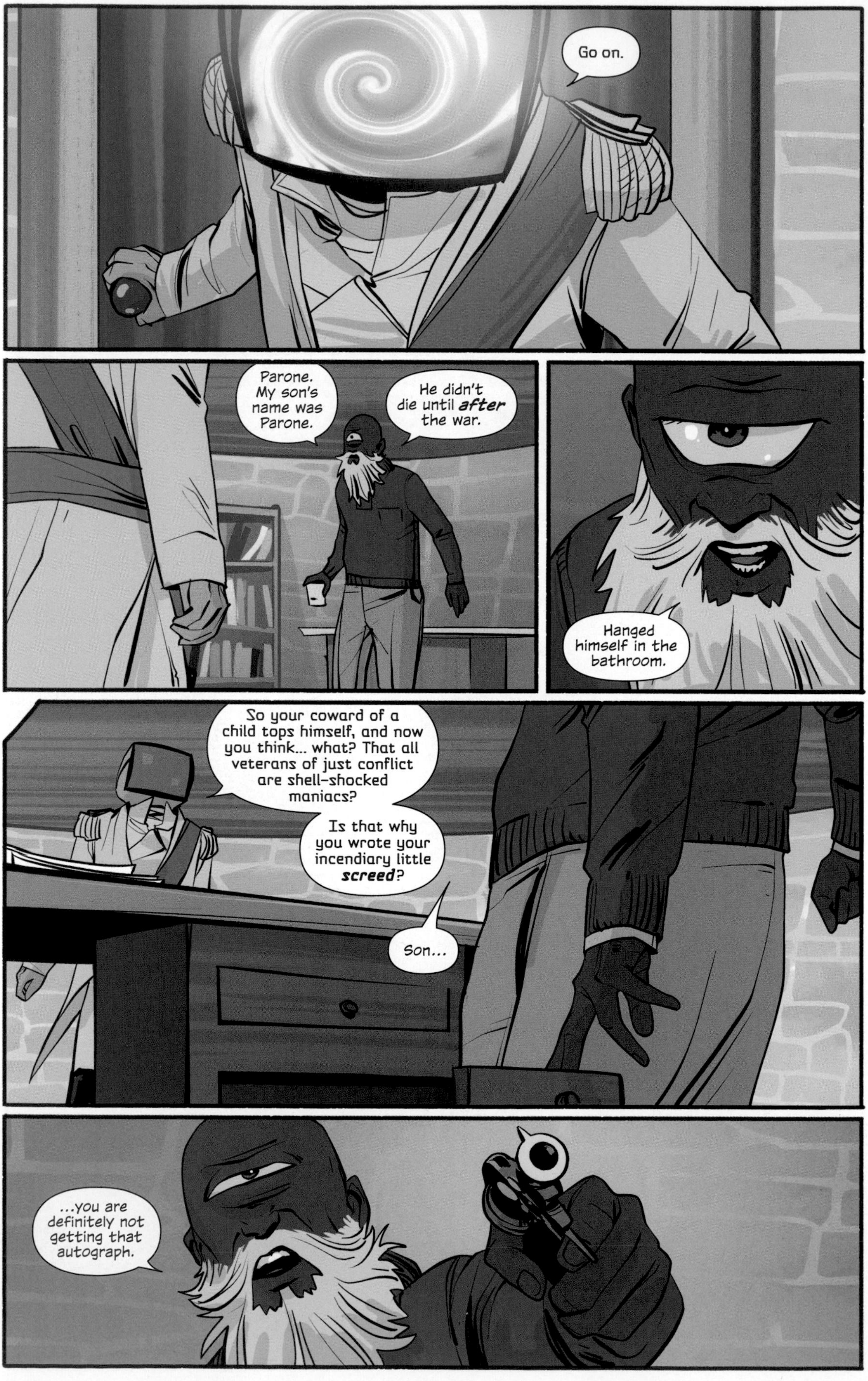
Go on.
Parone. My son's name was Parone.
He didn't die until *after* the war.
Hanged himself in the bathroom.
So your coward of a child tops himself, and now you think... what? That all veterans of just conflict are shell-shocked maniacs?
Is that why you wrote your incendiary little *screed*?
Son...
...you are definitely not getting that autograph.

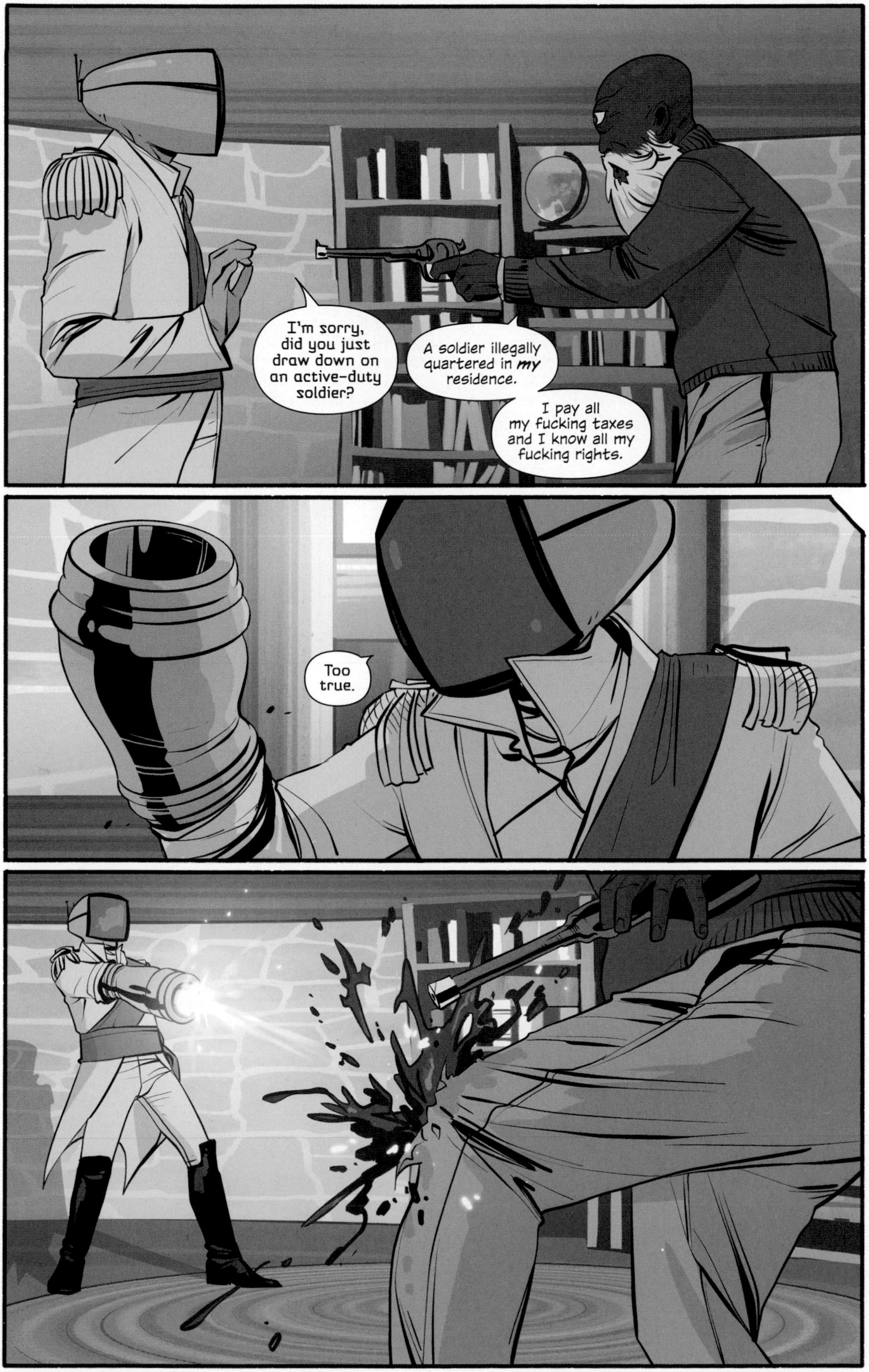
I'm sorry, did you just draw down on an active-duty soldier?
A soldier illegally quartered in *my* residence.
I pay all my fucking taxes and I know all my fucking rights.
Too true.

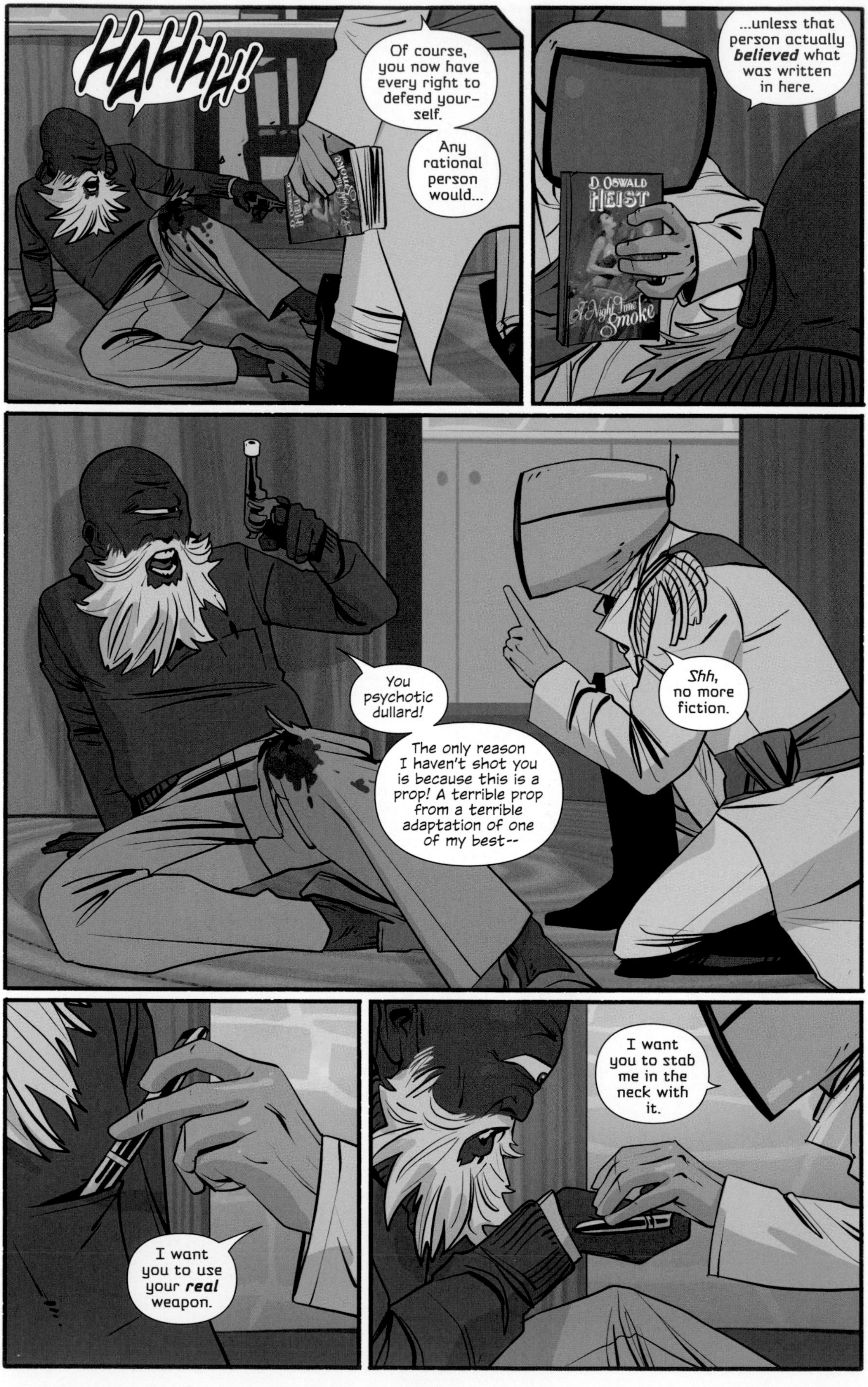
HAHHH!
Of course, you now have every right to defend your-self.
Any rational person would...
...unless that person actually **believed** what was written in here.
D. OSWALD HEIST
A Night Time Smoke
You psychotic dullard!
The only reason I haven't shot you is because this is a prop! A terrible prop from a terrible adaptation of one of my best--
Shh, no more fiction.
I want you to use your ***real*** weapon.
I want you to stab me in the neck with it.

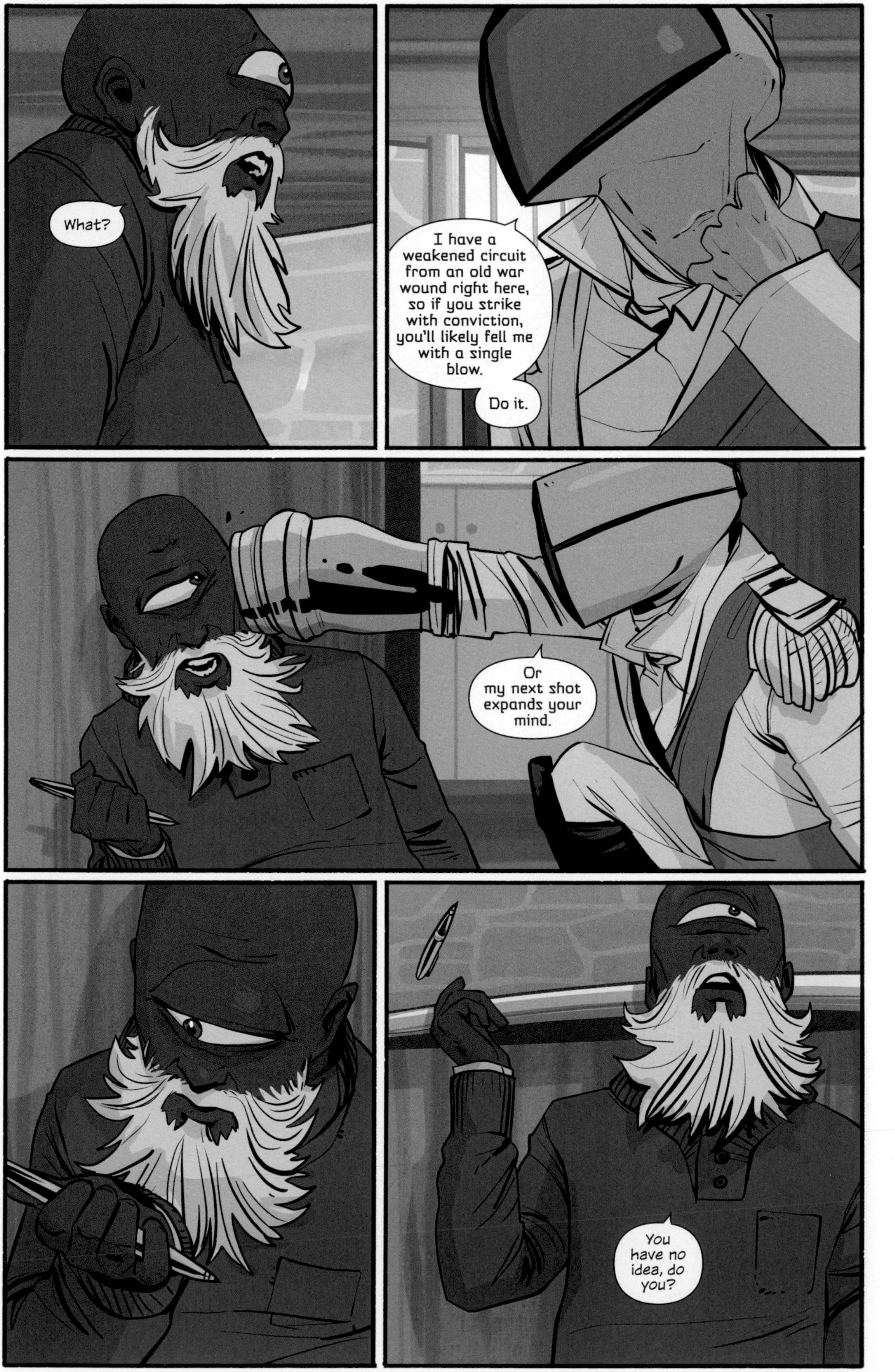
What?
I have a weakened circuit from an old war wound right here, so if you strike with conviction, you'll likely fell me with a single blow.
Do it.
Or my next shot expands your mind.
You have no idea, do you?

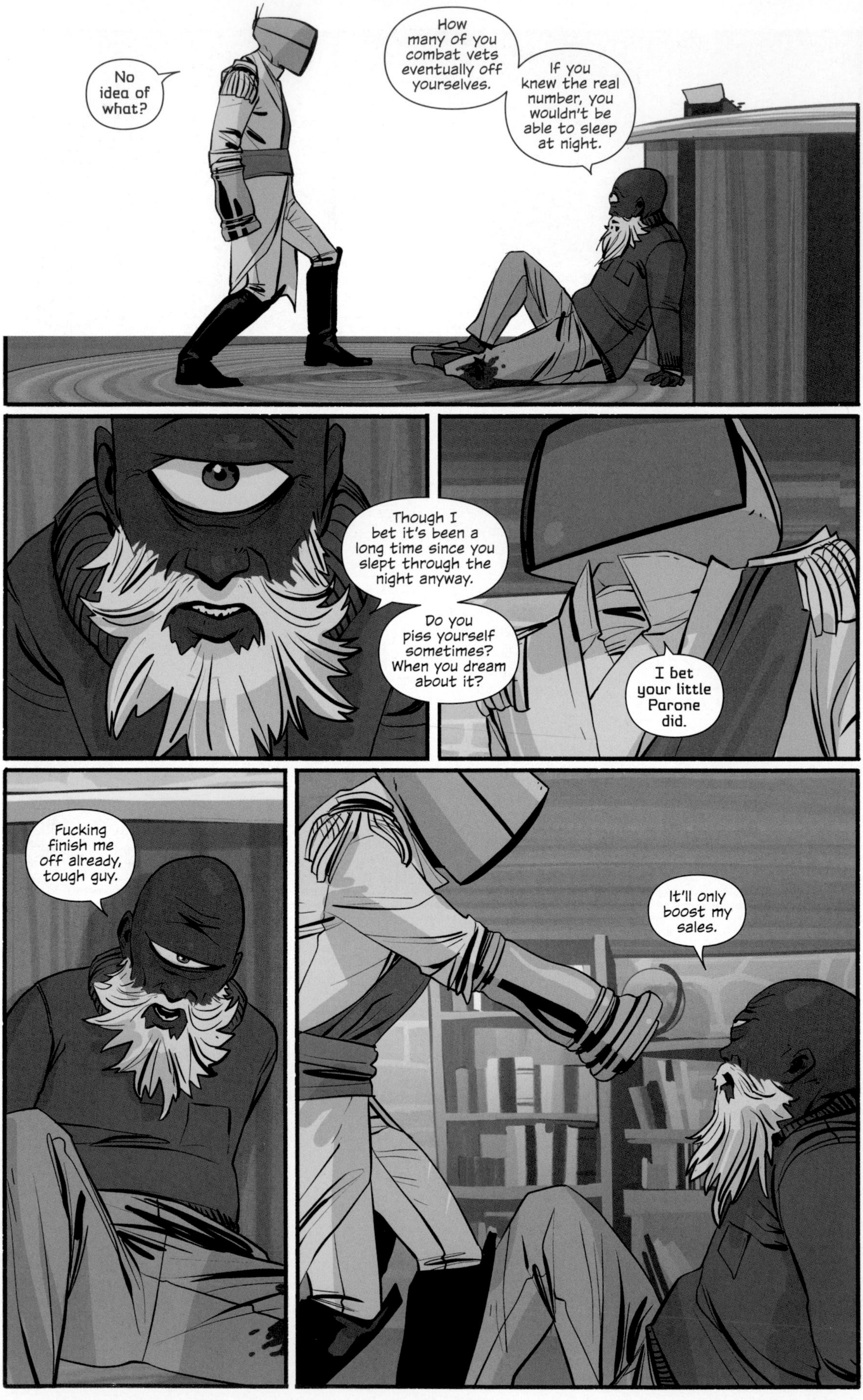
No idea of what?
How many of you combat vets eventually off yourselves.
If you knew the real number, you wouldn't be able to sleep at night.
Though I bet it's been a long time since you slept through the night anyway.
Do you piss yourself sometimes? When you dream about it?
I bet your little Parone did.
Fucking finish me off already, tough guy.
It'll only boost my sales.

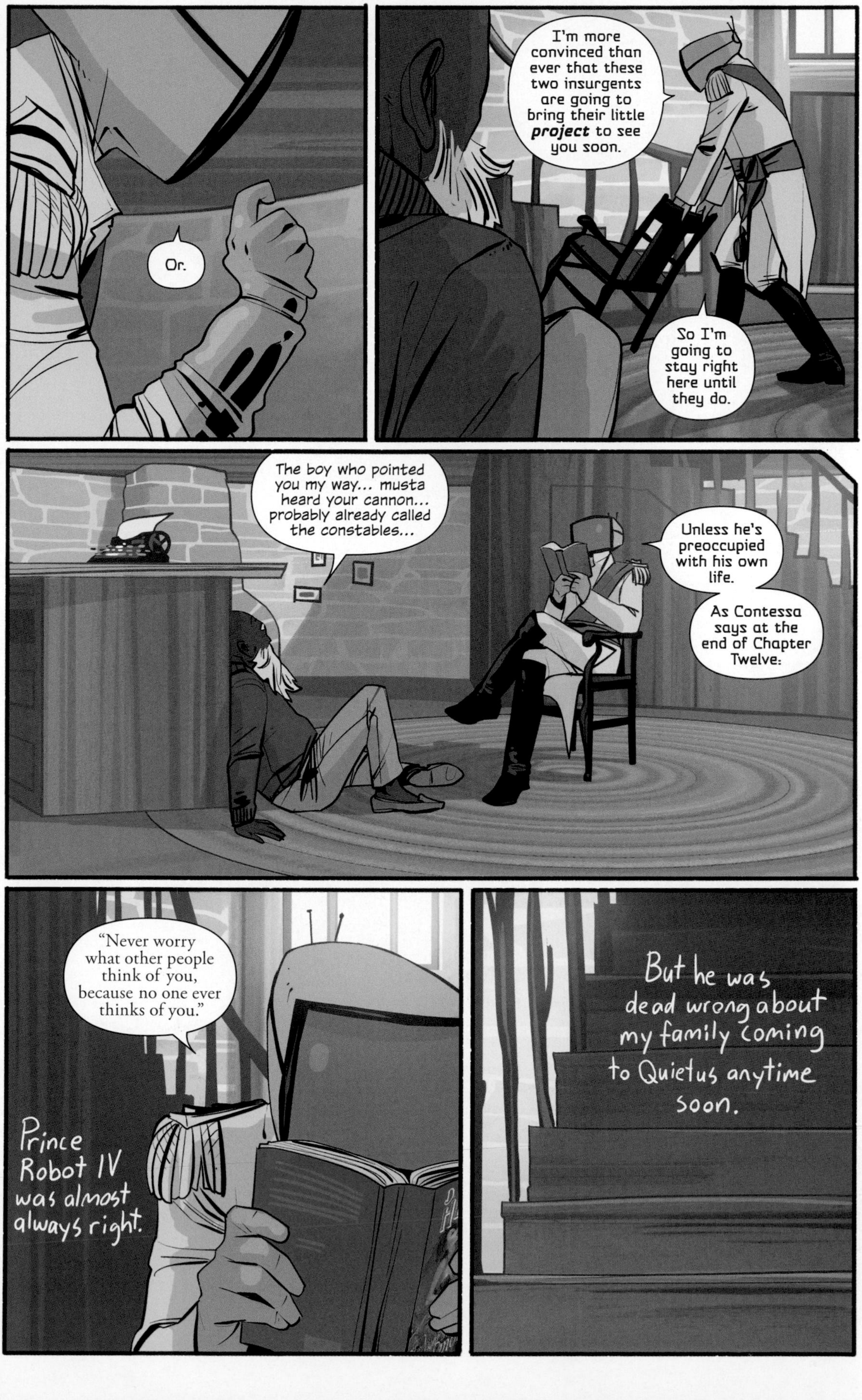
Or.
I'm more convinced than ever that these two insurgents are going to bring their little ***project*** to see you soon.
So I'm going to stay right here until they do.
The boy who pointed you my way... musta heard your cannon... probably already called the constables...
Unless he's preoccupied with his own life.
As Contessa says at the end of Chapter Twelve:
"Never worry what other people think of you, because no one ever thinks of you."
Prince Robot IV was almost always right.
But he was dead wrong about my family coming to Quietus anytime soon.

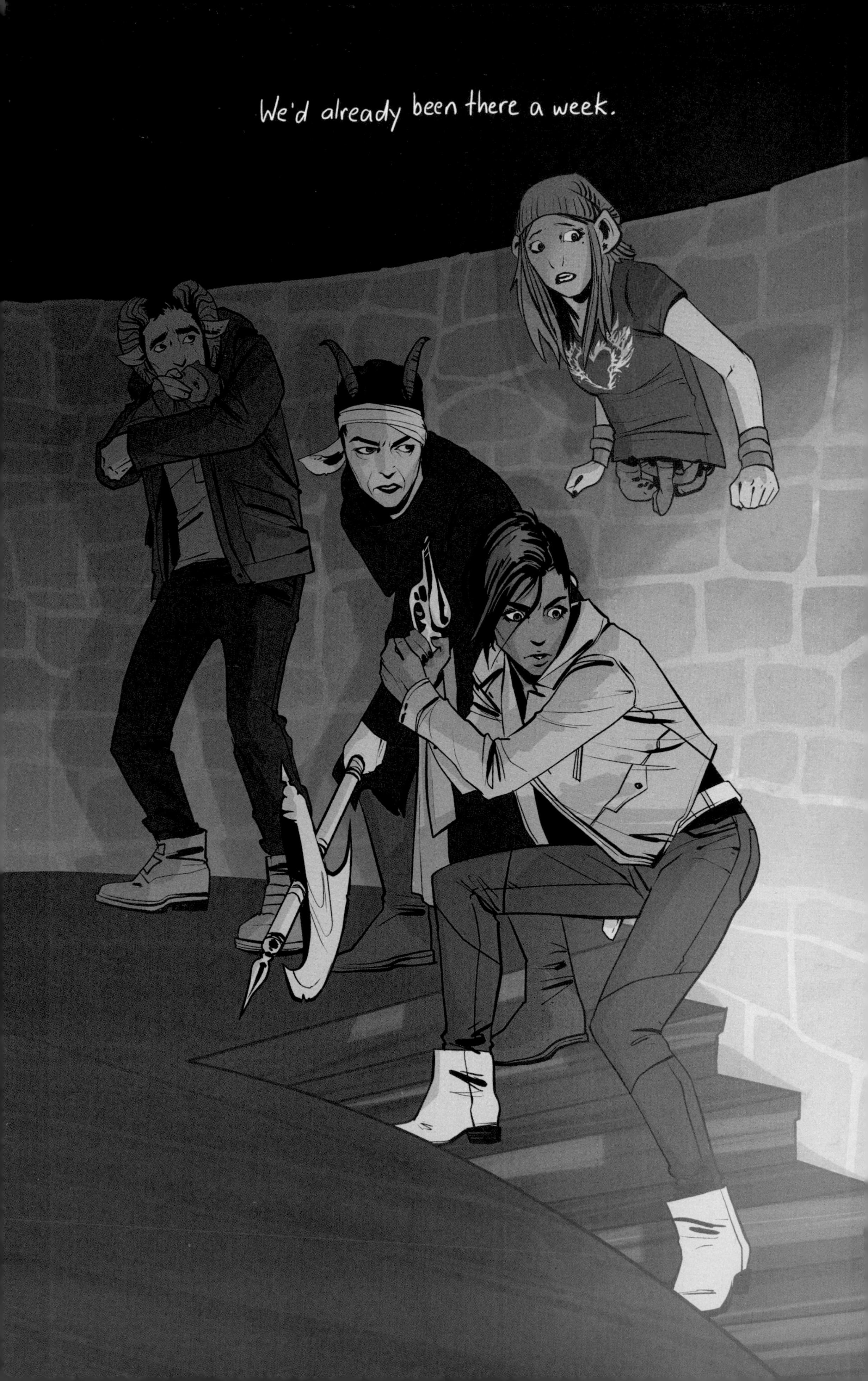
We'd already been there a week.

to be continued

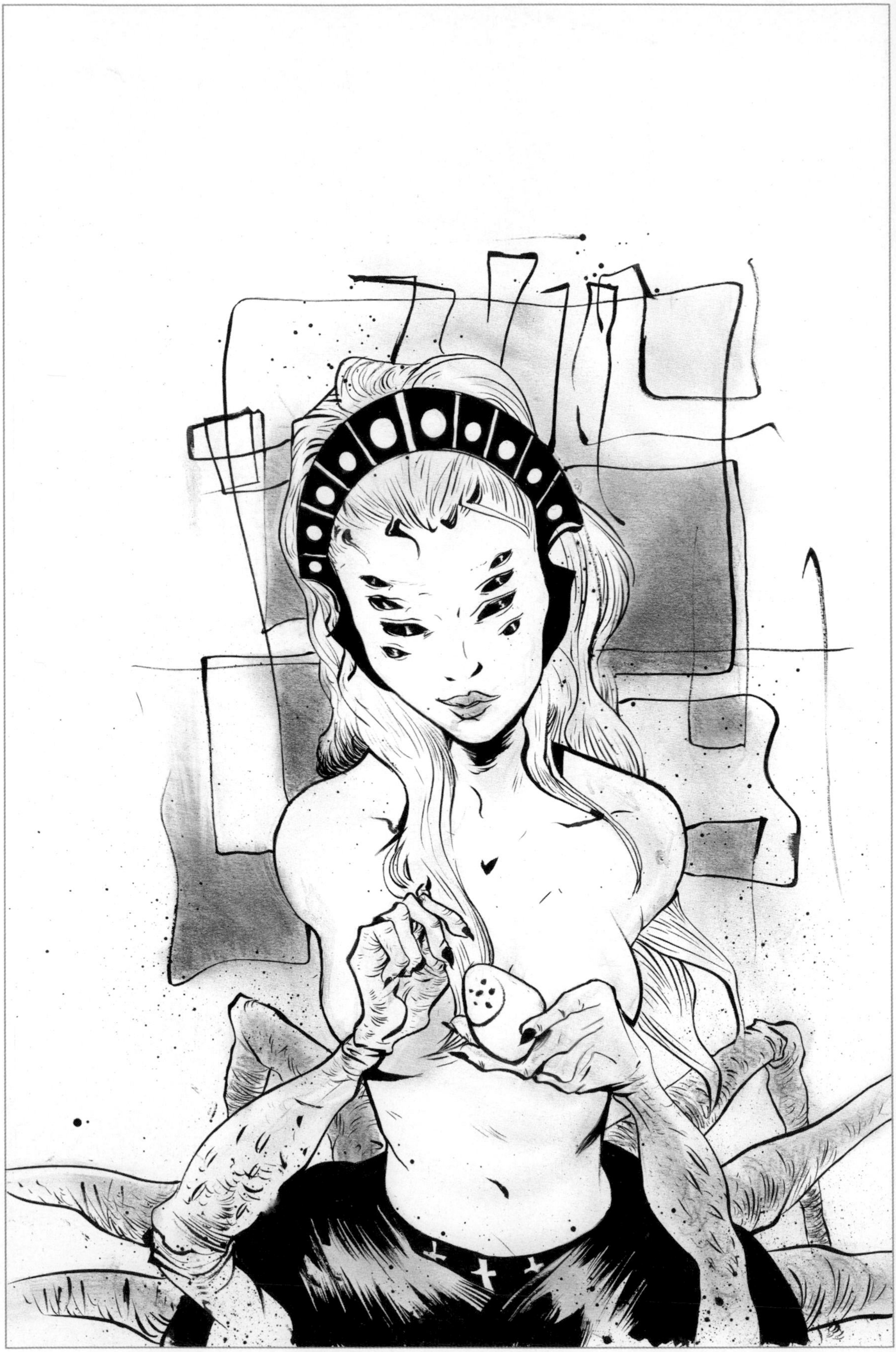

Chapter Seven Ghost Variant art by Paul Pope.

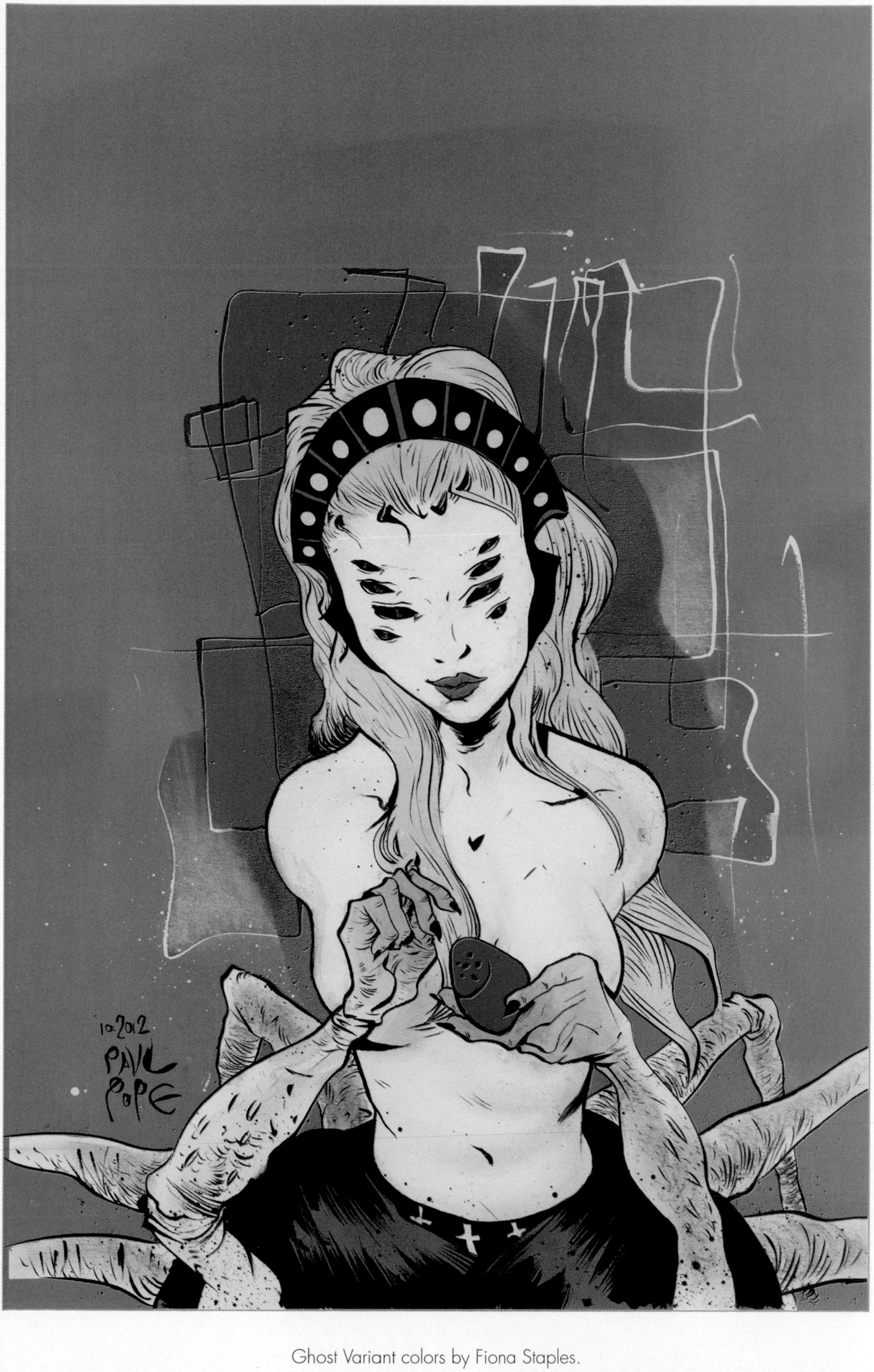
10-2012
PAUL POPE

Ghost Variant colors by Fiona Staples.

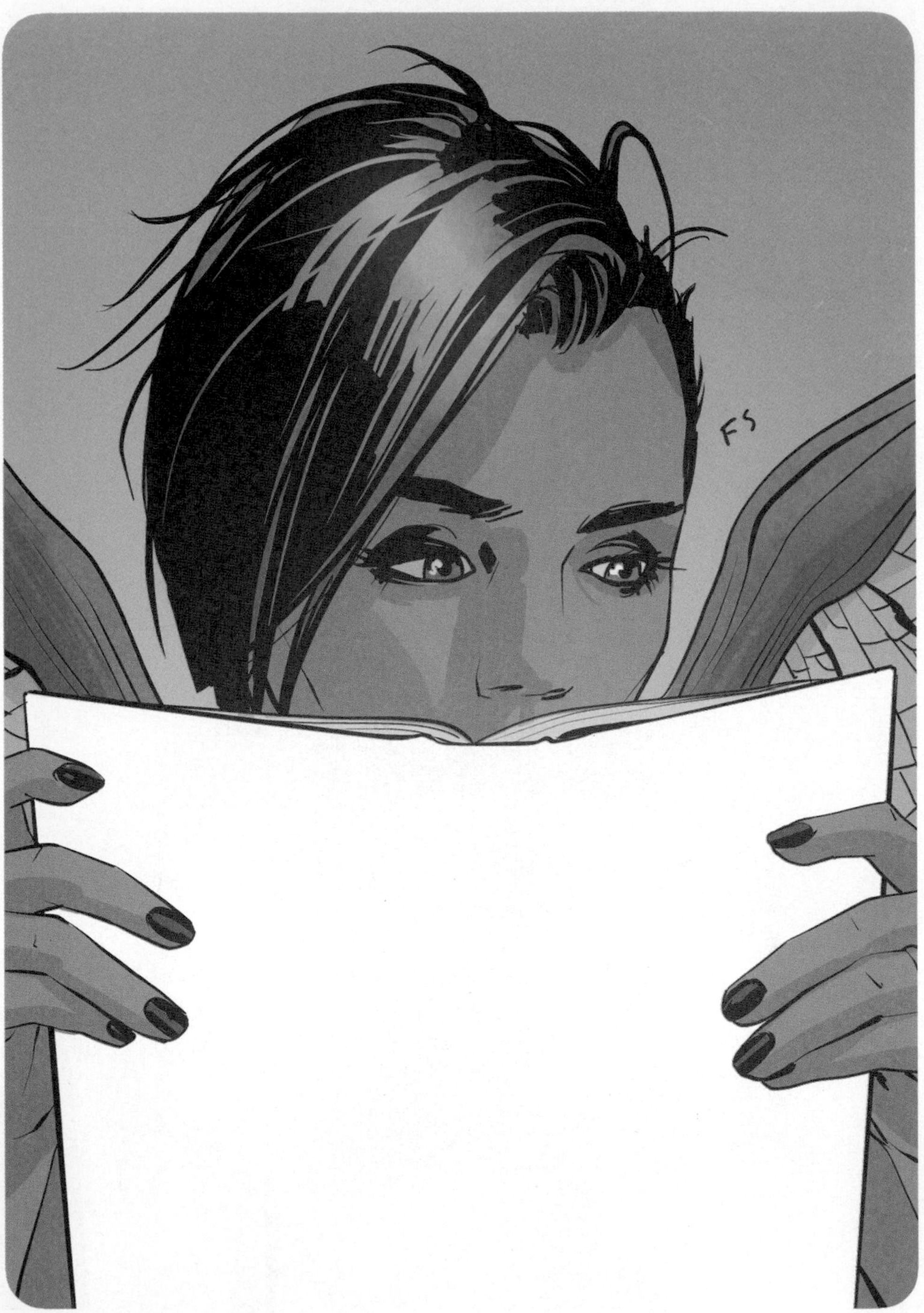

Exclusive Volume One bookplate for New York Comic Con 2012.

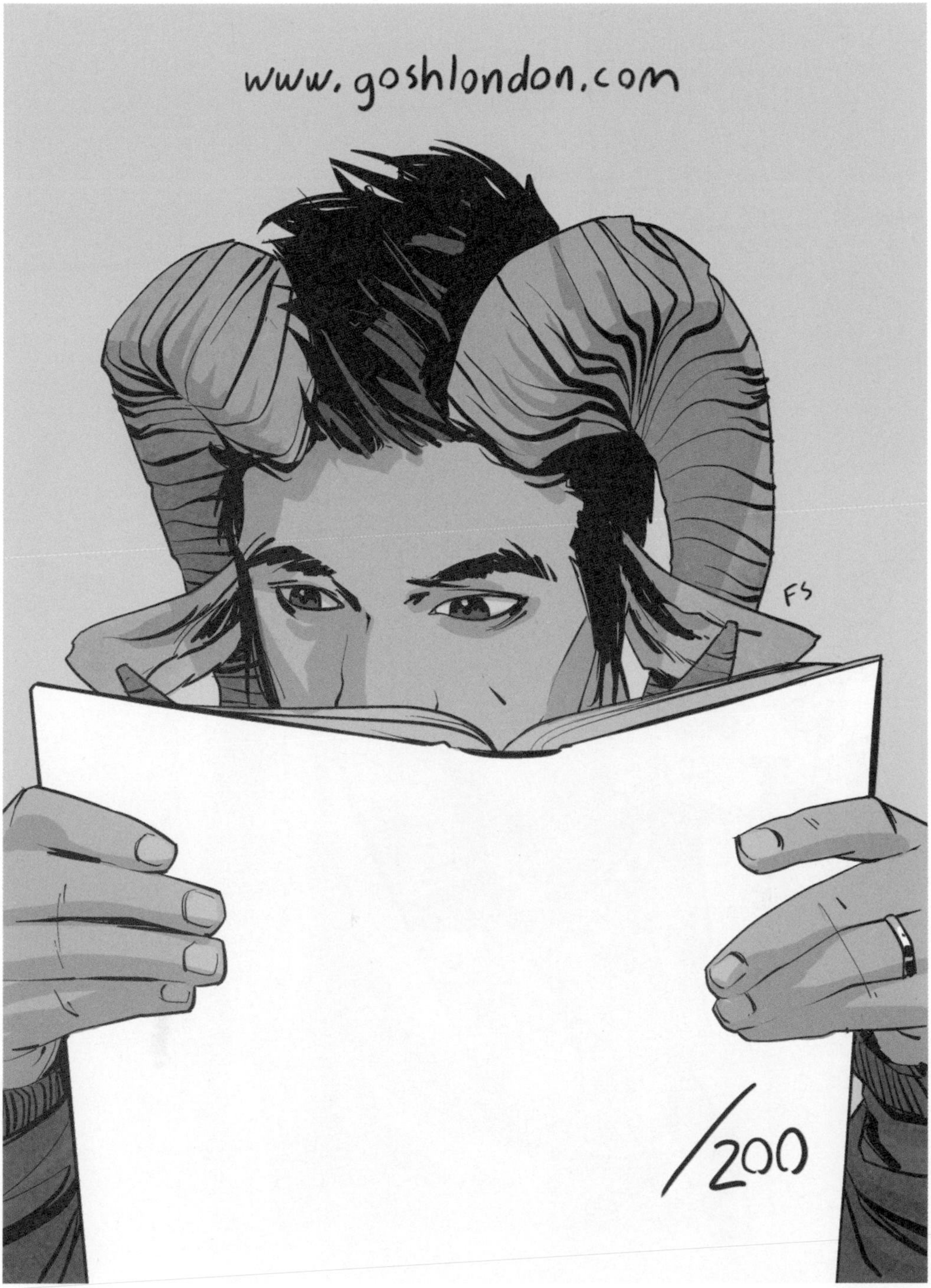
www.goshlondon.com
FS
/200

Limited edition Volume One bookplate for London store GOSH!

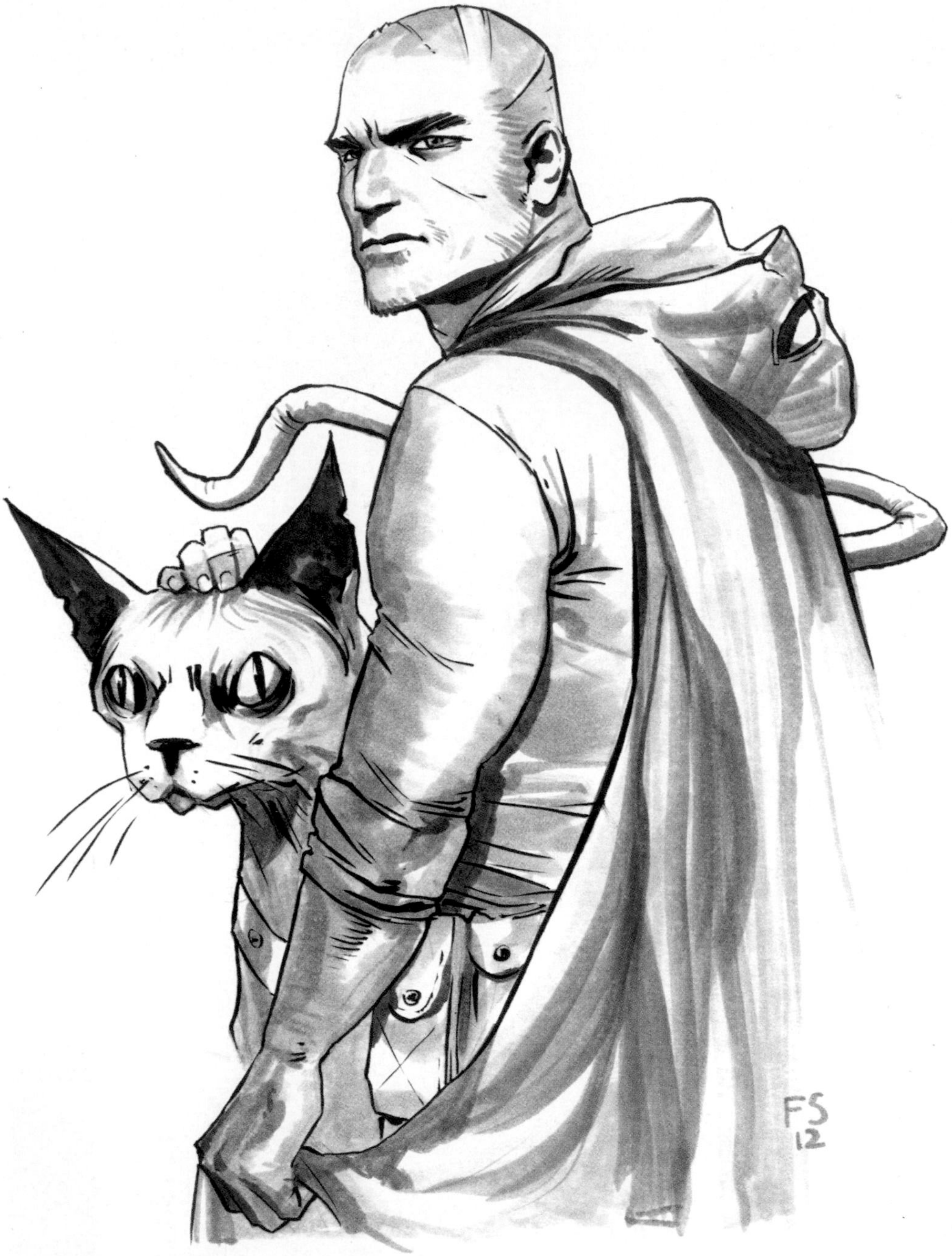
FS
12

The Will and Lying Cat marker sketch.